JACK PROBYN

STANDSTILL

VINCI
BOOKS

Vinci Books

vinci-books.com

Published by Vinci Books Ltd in 2026

1

Copyright © Jack Probyn 2018

A CIP catalogue record for this book is available from the British Library.

Paperback ISBN: 9781036705503

The EU GPSR authorised representative is Logos Europe, 9 rue Nicolas Poussion, 17000 La Rochelle, France
contact@logoseurope.eu

By Jack Probyn

DC Jake Tanner Terrorism Thriller Series

Standstill

Floor 68

DC Jake Tanner Crime Thrillers

Toe the Line

Walk the Line

Under the Line

Cross the Line

Over the Line

Past the Line

For Mum, Dad, and Alicia.

Prologue

FACTORY

July 31, 23:50

Homemade bombs are easy to make.

All it takes is some ammonium nitrate and hydrogen peroxide. Both can be found in household items such as haircare products and fertiliser. Mix the ingredients together below ten degrees to form crystals, then combine with water, flour, and an initiator, and you've got yourself a device capable of killing dozens and injuring countless more. On the face of it, it's simple. But both substances are incredibly volatile and must be handled with extreme care. It had taken Moshat and his brother months to learn the basics, but, for Moshat, homemade bombs wouldn't do. Killing dozens wasn't enough. For their operation, they would need professional, large-scale stuff. And they had the training to acquire it.

Moshat stood beside the desk and leafed through the files in the ring binder, counting off the seconds until it was time to begin, when his colleague entered the room. 'Come on, mate. Shift's over. You coming?' Adam said.

Moshat hesitated. 'I'm just finishing up a few more things.' The light above him flickered, making the shadow he cast over the documents he held in his hands more ominous. It was important to make it look like he was busy. 'You go. I'll catch you up or see you tomorrow. I don't know how long I'll be.'

'You sure?'

Moshat nodded, keeping his gaze fixed on the papers in front of him. 'It's fine. Just go home, your missus will be getting worried. She might think you're cheating on her.'

Adam chuckled, his oversized belly and sagging jowls wobbling with each laugh. 'Chance would be a fine thing.' He turned to leave the room. 'See you tomorrow, then. Have a good one.'

Moshat grunted as a way of response. *Finally.* He let a deep sigh of exultation. *Fucking finally.*

Now he could begin.

As soon as he heard the factory shutter door close, way off in the distance, he placed his pen on the table. It was exactly parallel to the three other pens, two pencils, a small rubber and a shatterproof ruler. After a quick readjustment of the ruler, he was ready to go. Everything needed to be perfectly aligned, perfectly in order, and perfectly well-hidden.

Moshat glanced over at the red clock hanging on the wall and then at the digital clock on his desk. 23:50. Ten minutes to go. He breathed out and relaxed, allowing the tension in his back and shoulders to ease. As he arched closer to the wall, the knots in his muscles loosened. *That idiot Gardner*, he thought, shaking his head. It had been a close call; he didn't think he would shake Adam away in time, like a piece of discarded chewing gum on his shoe. It was imperative that there were no delays. Delays were costly and could lead to further mistakes — or worse, they could lead to nothing happening at all. And so far, Adam Gardner had posed the biggest threat to the operation.

Moshat sat down on his chair. The wave of pain deep in his back returned with a vengeance. The injury hadn't been kind to him. It had changed the course of his career, meant his dream was ruined, and nearly left him paralysed and in a wheelchair for the rest of his life. The discomfort and hurt was a constant reminder of those responsible and how they now lifted trophies in the youth team for West Ham with promising careers ahead of them. Tomorrow he would ignore the pain, give in to it, sacrifice himself so he could see the operation through to the end and have enough painkillers in his system to knock out a horse. He would not let any signs of weakness ruin the worst terror attack London had ever seen, the attack which he had worked so hard to prepare for.

Moshat found himself transfixed by the second hand on the clock making its long and arduous journey around the face. He let out a sigh. It was no use. He needed to focus on something else.

He jumped to his feet, wincing as a bolt of pain pierced through his entire body, and shuffled over to the office window with his hand pressed against his lower back. Moshat rested his elbows on the ledge and rested his forehead against the glass. It was cold to the touch. Dim lights illuminated the factory floor below. Stretching into the distance as far as he could make out in the gloom, were train carriages — like giant slugs all lined up in a row. Each one looked powerful, yet tranquil, and most importantly, uninhabited. To many, the stillness of the factory at this time of night would have been enough to make their hair stand on end. Not him, though; in the two years he had been working in the factory, he had grown accustomed to the eerie silence during the nights often spent on his own there, and he had begun to appreciate what magnificent feats of engineering the trains were.

Moshat marvelled in their magnificence. They had the ability to transport thousands of passengers every day. They had the power to travel at vast speeds while keeping everyone aboard cocooned in a bubble of relative calm. They even had the ability to come to an immediate halt or derail at any moment and invoke the primal fear of survival in their passengers.

As he gazed at the trains below, an odd emotion welled up in him. Like an alligator's eyes breaking the still surface of the water, it had risen from the depths of his soul and then dipped back down. Was it doubt? He didn't know. Was he nervous? Was he afraid? Was he regretting the path he was about to take? Either way, it didn't matter; he couldn't let it matter. He and his brother had invested too much of their time and life, injected copious amounts of hatred and animosity into what was going to happen in the next twelve hours. It was too late to get cold feet and back out now.

Their lives would change forever. And everything needed to be perfect for it.

The phone in Moshat's pocket vibrated. He dragged it out, unlocked it, opened his messages, and read the most recent one.

'Adil,' he whispered to himself after reading the text, as if to not disturb the trains while they rested. He checked the time. 23:55.

He pocketed the phone, made his way down the stairs and headed towards the factory's exit. He approached the shutters and pressed a large green button on the control panel next to them. With a loud groan, the cogs and gears in the mechanism above him engaged, lifting the door and letting a torrent of cold air flood in over his feet.

Before him, silhouetted against the backdrop of the artificial light in the car park beyond, stood Moshat's brother, his features barely discernible except for the wide smile he wore on his face. Adil stepped forward into the factory. He wore a woollen hooded jumper with a leather satchel that hung off one shoulder and stretched across his body. His eyes and forehead were concealed by the low hanging hood. There was a commanding presence about Adil. Moshat's brother wasn't the biggest man, nor the most intimidating. Instead, there was something else about him: he had the aura of someone with the brains and skills that had the power to bring a country to its knees.

'You read your text messages, then?' Adil asked, pulling the hood from his face. His large, black, deep-set eyes seemed to absorb the light of the factory.

Moshat glared at him. 'You're early. Why are you early? You're not supposed to be early. You know I don't like when you're early. We have set times for a reason.'

'The sooner we begin, the sooner we can finish,' Adil said.

'What if Gardner or someone else was still here? What if you were seen? We cannot afford mistakes. Not this late in the stage. We have less than twelve hours until our operation begins. Can you imagine what would have happened if you were caught?' Moshat said.

'Relax, Moshat. Don't you trust me? I made sure you were all alone before I made myself visible.' Adil smiled and slapped Moshat on the shoulder. 'Now, stop complaining and let's get to work.'

The two of them moved over to a small workbench next to the stairs. It was littered with the day's rubbish of wrenches, dozens of screws and a hammer. Adil removed his bag and slammed it down amongst the carnage.

'What are you doing?' Moshat asked, rushing over. 'Do not make more of a mess than there already is, please. They'll know if it's been tampered with. I don't want your fingerprints over everything.'

Adil continued, heedless of Moshat's protestations, and picked up the wrench. He bounced it in his hands, gauging the density and weight of the tool, and said, 'What are we waiting for?'

Moshat nodded and started towards the office. In the middle of the room was Moshat's desk, neatly laden with stationary and paperwork. Moshat sat in his chair, and Adil grabbed one from the neighbouring desk and sat opposite him, placing his bag on the wooden surface.

Adil appeared to observe the room, casting his gaze around and taking in its neatness and ordinariness before he opened his bag and removed a wad of paperwork. Post-Its and scribbles decorated the pages. 'I have brought all of the plans and documents with me.'

'We won't need them. I have them all committed to memory,' Moshat said.

'Did you learn nothing in your training? Prepare, prepare, prepare.'

Yes, Moshat thought. *That old credo. The one I heard a thousand times while I sat in the mud, aiming down the sights of a sniper rifle, rain lashing at my face.* Moshat dipped his head. The two brothers laid the documents along the table in a row and reviewed them yet again for the next five minutes. They made sure there were no mistakes, no stones left unturned, no possibility that anything could go wrong. Once they had finished, Moshat suggested they go downstairs to the car and remove the contents from the boot.

They both started out of the office and left the factory through a side door to avoid patrolling security. The air outside was warm. When they reached the car, Adil opened the boot. Inside were three black duffel bags with the zipper only three-quarters of the way done. The outline of the bags was jagged, as if they were packed full of bricks.

'I will take two,' Moshat said stoically. The pain in his back had disappeared, and he would not let his brother know he was in any discomfort.

'Be careful,' Adil said. 'We don't want anything to explode now, do we?'

As Moshat hoisted the bags onto his back, he winced. Ignoring the hurt, Moshat carried the bags to the factory, maintaining a steady but brisk pace. If one bag were to fall from his shoulder and crash to the ground, he, his brother, and everything else within the factory, would be obliterated. Moshat entered the building, beads of sweat dribbling down his forehead and into his eyes in the summer heat. With a wipe to his eyes of the back of his sleeve, he strolled through a myriad of corridors, and placed the bags on the concrete ground.

As Adil joined Moshat by his side, he turned to his brother and said, 'You ready?'

Chapter One

EMAIL

July 31, 17:14

Detective Constable Jake Tanner burst out of New Scotland Yard into the busy streets of London feeling a mixture of apprehension and excitement. He was hot and a thin film of sweat, like a coat of dust resting upon a bookshelf, coated his forehead. The suit on his back stuck to his skin, and he felt damp every time he swayed his arms. He should have used the Yard's showers in the gym, but then he would have to explain to his wife, Elizabeth, why he smelt so fresh. *Instead, I'll have to explain why I'm so hot and sweaty.* If she asked, he decided, he would blame his perspiration on the weather.

Jake made it five yards out of the door before he was accosted by someone behind him.

'Tanner!'

Jake turned on the spot.

'Luke. To what do I owe the pleasure?' Jake asked.

'You left this in the briefing room.'

DC Luke Matthews raised his arm brandishing Jake's ID card and handed it to him. Jake thanked him.

'Hey,' Luke said, 'before you go, I wanted to say good luck. You did well in there, and no matter who gets the promotion, no hard feelings, right?'

'No hard feelings,' Jake lied and turned away.

He had been gunning for the promotion to Detective Sergeant in Counter Terrorism Command for the past few weeks. An email had popped into his inbox explaining to him someone had put him forward and that he needed to respond within the day if he wanted it. That meant there was no time to consult Elizabeth, so he put his name forward and hoped for the best. He knew what she would say anyway: that the workload was too much for him and that he needed to consider it thoroughly before applying.

First, he underwent a series of mental and physical examinations. All of them had gone well. But he wasn't the best; DC Luke Matthews had bested him at everything so far, sitting there smugly as he was told his position. And today, Jake had just endured the most exciting afternoon of the year: the firearms training. It was the first in a series of more developed and robust daily firearms exercises. In a few days' time, he'd find out the results. *And then I'll have to break the news to Elizabeth*, Jake thought, trying not to get his aspirations up. He respected Luke, but he wanted nothing more than to get the promotion. Despite the increased workload, it was the increase in numbers in his bank account that was the greatest prospect of succeeding. Money was a constant struggle for Jake and Elizabeth and the kids, and this promotion was the best opportunity they would have at some financial stability.

Even if Elizabeth didn't realise it yet.

Jake strolled along the street towards his car. The sun burned high in the sky, showing no signs it was turning in for the day. Meanwhile, the busy sounds of the city reverberated through the buildings. Sirens, beeping car horns and the general hubbub of people in conversation filled the streets. He stopped by an unmarked BMW X5. For the past couple of years, he had had the privilege of cruising the streets of London in it.

He started the engine and pulled away. Rolling up to a set of traffic lights, he looked at the clock on the dashboard and smiled. It was 17:17, the earliest he had left the office in months. The drill officer had sent them home early, and Jake was straight out of the door; he had a family whom he missed and loved more than anything waiting for him.

On his way home, Jake pulled the 4x4 into the local supermarket and purchased milk, beer, orange juice, and four pizzas. He and his family lived in Croydon, in the south of London. They rented a tall, slim house that had recently been refurbished. The area was peaceful most of the time, with good schools and bus links for the children. The only problem was it was now too small for them all. Not to mention the drive into work every morning was long and monotonous.

Parking at the side of the road, Jake switched off the engine, exited and walked towards the front door, balancing the pizza boxes in the crook of his left arm, the shopping bag from his left thumb, and fumbling in his pocket for his door keys with the other. 'Girls? I'm home!' he yelled as he threw his shoes off next to a piece of skirting board. Using his heel, he closed the door behind him.

The living room door to his left burst open. Exploding

from within it were his two girls, Maisie and Ellie. Ellie, Jake's youngest daughter, was the first to reach him and she hugged his leg. Maisie followed behind, hugging the other.

'I've bought us pizza for dinner,' Jake said, lifting the cardboard boxes in the air. The two girls cheered in excitement.

'Walk us, Daddy! Walk us to the kitchen!' Ellie said, clinging herself round Jake's ankles like a koala, her innocent brown eyes looking up at Jake. He smiled.

'Not today, Darling. Daddy's back is hurting,' Jake said. The girls let out a collective groan and hung their heads low. 'Come on, go to the kitchen and put the dinner on. Maybe we can watch a film tonight as well.'

This seemed to perk the girls back up again, for their eyes glistened in the light and their faces reddened with excitement. They released their grips on Jake's legs. He handed the shopping bags to Ellie, the pizza boxes to Maisie, and ordered them both to the kitchen. They darted. Jake's gaze followed them as they went, and then his eyes stopped at the figure stood in the doorway, resting against the frame, arms folded.

'Thought we already had dinner prepared for tonight?' Elizabeth said. She spoke calmly and deeply, which Jake knew meant she was unimpressed.

'I know,' he said, advancing closer to her. 'But I wanted to treat us. Plus, I got to finish work early, so I thought, "why not?"'

Jake bent down to her level, kissed her on the lips and slid his hands round her tiny waist. She kissed him back.

'Hmm. How come you're home early?' Elizabeth asked, pushing him away.

'Charming. I'll go back if you want.'

'You know that's not what I meant. You're not usually here until eight.'

'Mamadou said we could slack off a few hours early. It was his birthday, and they wanted to go for some drinks,' Jake lied. He stared into her eyes, waiting for a response, hoping she would believe him.

'And you came straight home? Why didn't you stay?'

'I stayed for one, but then came home.'

'Christ, how early did you finish? Anyway, I'm glad you're home.' Elizabeth gave him another kiss and the two of them entered the kitchen. Recipe books and months-old receipts littered the island in the centre. The rest of the kitchen was also messy, an insight into their chaotic lives.

Jake told the girls to head upstairs and get dressed for bed while Elizabeth cooked the pizzas in the oven. Once the girls had returned, and the pizzas were crispy and bronzed, they sat around the family table in the adjoining room.

'How was school today, girls?'

'Boring. Miss Robertson was teaching us science, and it was rubbish,' Maisie said.

Insightful as ever, Jake thought. 'Do you not like science?'

'No, it's boring. I don't care about the things in my body and what they do.'

'You should, Maisie. It's good to know what happens inside your body. You'll understand that when you get older, and then you'll be able to live for a very long time.' He took a mouthful of pizza. 'What else happened? Were there any lessons you enjoyed?'

'Geography.'

'What's so good about geography?' Jake scoffed.

'I know!' Ellie shouted, her mouth sending morsels of cheese and pizza base to the table.

Maisie stopped eating her food and told her younger sister to shut up.

'Maisie Louise Tanner, do not talk to your sister like that, or you will go straight to bed without watching the film!' Elizabeth said, dropping her knife and fork on the plate.

Maisie cowered back into her seat.

After deeming it safe to continue his investigation, Jake continued. 'Ellie, you were saying?'

'Oscar's in her class and I saw them talking today,' Ellie said, calming down.

Maisie's face became red with embarrassment, highlighted more prominently by her brown hair.

'Who's Oscar, Maisie?' Jake asked.

'A boy in my class.'

'Is he a nice boy in your class?'

'Yes.'

'Do you sit next to him?'

'Sometimes.'

'Is he just a friend? Or is he a boyfriend?' Jake asked the girls, first looking at Ellie, then Maisie.

'We're not supposed to have boyfriends just yet,' Maisie said shyly.

'That's correct,' Jake said. 'And don't you two forget it.' Elizabeth rolled her eyes at him from across the table.

For the rest of the evening the family ate the pizza, decided on the film to watch, and sat in front of the television on the sofa, until it was time to send Ellie and Maisie to bed. The girls went to their rooms with no sign of incipient argument, leaving Jake and Elizabeth alone with one another. Elizabeth rested her head on Jake's chest, and his fingers weaved through her blonde hair as he stroked it.

'How was your day, honey?' Jake asked, ignoring what was on the television.

'All right. Took the girls to school. Came home. Did some chores around the house. That was about it.'

'No new clients today?' Jake asked.

'No,' Elizabeth said. 'It seems no one wants professional looking headshots anymore. They've all been taken.'

'I'm sure things will pick up soon. Once we've saved enough money to get your advertising going, you'll be busier than ever.'

Elizabeth was a freelance photographer, and had been ever since she graduated from University of Central London with a photography degree. Many of her classmates had gone into corporate jobs and found successful lives for themselves. But not Elizabeth; she had stuck to what she believed in and allowed her passion for art and creativity to hopefully one day manifest itself into a flourishing career. So far, she'd only had a few clients, and the revenue generated was barely enough to offset the expense of the job. Another reason Jake's promotion was so important.

'Your mum goes away tomorrow, doesn't she?' Jake asked, changing the subject.

Elizabeth nodded.

'Where's she flying from?'

'Heathrow. She's getting the train from somewhere in London.'

'What time's her flight?'

'Two o'clock, I think. Why?'

'Just asking.' Jake yawned. He looked at his watch, saw the time, and suggested they disappear to bed.

Elizabeth agreed and together they headed upstairs. A few minutes later, they were both under the duvet in the same position they had been on the sofa, resting gently in one another's arms.

Elizabeth stroked Jake's chest. 'Jake...?' she asked quietly.

'Yeah?'

She said nothing for a few moments. 'Never mind. It can wait for another night. I love you.'

They fell asleep together without knowing what the next day would bring.

The low light cast from the computer monitors filled the room. A cup of coffee rested against the right-hand screen. The sound of silence deafened Adil. He needed a distraction, something to accompany his thoughts. He rose out of his seat, meandered over to the record player that hugged the wall next to the kitchen, and picked out his favourite. Moments later he relaxed as the soft sounds of classical music danced around his ears.

For the past few hours, he had been alone. Moshat had left for work late, and since then Adil had been drafting up the email.

At first, he hadn't known whether to send it. Between both of them, they had decided on something, but it wasn't enough. It wasn't anything *he* wanted to say. It wasn't going to garner everyone in the world's attention and focus it on him. It wasn't going to make him infamous, create a legacy in his name. If he wanted that to happen, the email would need serious adjustments.

As Adil sat at his desk and read the words on the screen for the tenth time, he smiled. At last, he had done it. He leaned back in his chair and pasted the text into an encrypted email server. He typed in the email address he had obtained illegally weeks in advance and scheduled it for delivery at 07:00 tomorrow morning.

In just over twelve hours' time, DC Jake Tanner, the owner of that email address, and the rest of Counter Terrorism Command would experience their most difficult adversary and the worst terror attack their city had ever seen.

Adil had been insistent on that point.

Chapter Two

DEBRIEF

August 1, 05:00

The morning alarm clock buzzed next to Jake's head, jolting him from an otherwise peaceful sleep. He begrudged the fact he was awake early. Sleep deprivation always made his job harder. He needed to be alert all the time and pay constant attention to what he was doing.

Jake took another glance at the numbers on the clock. 05:00. Early. Too early. *Not even the birds are awake yet*, he thought as he rolled himself out of bed, showered, and readied himself for work. Despite his best efforts not to disturb Elizabeth from her sleep, he bumped into the wardrobe multiple times, causing her to stir and roll over to the other side.

Once dressed, he kissed her on the forehead before going downstairs for his first coffee of the day and leaving the house. It was a glorious morning. The sky was a sweet pink colour, streaked with white contrails left in the wake of overnight airplanes soaring through the air. He closed the house door behind him at precisely 06:00 and started the car to begin the hours journey into the centre of London. As usual, the roads and car park were empty.

He parked up and walked into New Scotland Yard, his second home, with his stomach rumbling and his eyes still heavy. His first destination was the canteen which was open but deserted. He grabbed his usual breakfast: a yoghurt, two pieces of toast, and an orange juice. He entered the lift just outside the canteen. Counter Terrorism Command, or SO15 as it was now called, was the amalgamation of the Anti-Terrorist Branch and Special Branch, and was on the fifteenth floor. Jake's stomach somersaulted as the lift vaulted skywards. On his way, he acknowledged the few other life forms who entered the small capsule with a cursory nod.

Jake pushed open the door into CTC. A row of computer monitors faced him, and the hum of their fans was his only company while he ate his breakfast. At the head of the room were a series of large television screens, surrounded by an area of carpet that looked as though someone had eaten Rainbow Drops and vomited on it. On the televisions, the local news channels scrolled along the bottom. Jake paid little attention to them. Ever since his promotion into SO15 two years ago, his hours had doubled, and his sleep halved. In his previous life, he had been a top homicide detective in the Criminal Investigation Department, but his performance in the Haversham kidnapping case changed everything for him. He was given a new opportunity, a new role, and a new sense of fulfilment. And he hadn't looked back. Targeting and defeating terrorists on the streets of London was what he wanted to do more than anything, especially because it meant he could protect those he loved most.

'Good morning, Detective Dick!' a voice called from behind him. The door slammed against the wall. Jake looked down at his breakfast, struggling to keep a smile at bay.

'Morning, Tyler,' Jake said, keeping his head down. He took another bite of his toast and checked his watch. 'You're early, shouldn't you still be in bed? Whether it be your own, someone else's, or the hospital's?'

Tyler was Jake's partner. They had sat next to one another when Jake first joined the department. Tyler had an extra years' experience over Jake, and Tyler didn't mind reminding him of the fact. On their first week together, they had formed a bond surprisingly fast. Tyler's sense of humour combined with Jake's, and they shared banter with one another to no end. They were inseparable, and sometimes they would go to the pub on a Friday night, or whenever there was football on, and spend the evening talking, discussing the job, marriage, relationships, life.

'Not today. That's saved for the weekend. Work hard in the week, and play even harder at the weekend,' Tyler said, slapping Jake on the back. He set his bag on his desk next to Jake's.

'You sure you didn't get lucky? You're in a good mood this early... and you were last Wednesday, too.'

'They don't call it a hump day for nothing, Tanner,' Tyler said. He shot Jake a wink, and leaned back in his chair, resting his feet on the table. Tyler's freckled skin made him look younger than he was. Jake envied him for it; only a few years separated them, yet Tyler looked as if he were in his early twenties, a commodity most men dreamt of.

'It is a truth universally acknowledged that Wednesdays are the days of Satan,' Jake said. His computer system booted, and an image of his family appeared. Every day, it was a constant reminder of why he worked and what he had to live for.

'Don't start with that literature bullshit on me, Jake,' Tyler said, his smart shoes glistening in the fluorescent light.

'What are you talking about?'

'You know, the ones you read at university or something.'

Jake chuckled. His friend's ignorance baffled him. 'Wrong degree, Ty. I studied psychology, remember?'

'Oh, yes. I forgot you can read peoples' minds.' Tyler removed his feet from the table and leaned closer to Jake's face, with his index fingers pressed against his temples.

Jake smiled. 'Give me half an hour and I'll have you confessing all your deepest, darkest secrets.'

'If I told you those, you'd have nightmares.'

'On second thoughts, I'll pass.'

Jake inched himself closer to his desk and opened his emails. To his surprise, there was only one there, hanging at the top. Before he could read it, Tyler spoke again.

'So where were you yesterday then? I didn't see you for the entire afternoon.'

Shit, Jake thought. He had been dreading this moment. Tyler didn't know Jake was opting for a promotion, and he couldn't bear to tell him either. His partner would be upset and hurt. Every other time Jake had needed to disappear for one of his examinations, he had always got away with it; Tyler neither realised nor appeared to care. But now he did, and Jake didn't know what to tell his friend.

'Dentist,' Jake murmured, hoping that if he gave monosyllabic answers, it would end the interrogation.

'I see. Elizabeth been kicking your teeth in for being shit in the sack?'

Jake exhaled deeply, relieved Tyler had moved the

conversation onto the one thing he was obsessed with: Elizabeth.

'Not quite. If she hated it that much, she would have left a long time ago.'

'Well if she ever gets bored with you, send her to me. I'll be able to treat her right.'

'She doesn't go for boys with small toys,' Jake said and laughed, his voice carrying throughout the whole office.

'Fuck you.'

Jake smiled. His and Elizabeth's marriage always seemed to perplex Tyler. In Tyler's eyes, Elizabeth was a beautiful, stunning blonde who should have had a successful catwalk career, and Jake was a police detective with a receding hairline who had let himself go. The two didn't add up, and he didn't mind reminding Jake of the fact almost every day.

As the minutes rolled by, more bodies filtered into the office. The smell of cheap coffee wafted through the air, and the frantic noise of keyboards tapping drowned out all conversation.

Jake turned his attention back to his computer. He clicked on the email. He paid no attention to the email's title and got as far as the first line before the sound of a door slamming against a brick wall distracted him. Silence fell on the office.

'All right, team!' a deep voice bellowed. Jake spun round on his chair and saw it was his boss, Detective Chief Superintendent Mamadou Kuhoba. 'Debrief room, two minutes. Be there or you're all fired.'

'Wonder what mood he's in today,' Tyler said as the two of them rose to their feet, grabbed a handful of documents and a notepad each, and started towards the debrief room. 'Adolf Hitler tyrant or Josef Stalin tyrant?'

'I think it's more Donald Trump,' Jake said.

Jake and Tyler entered. Light flooded the room through seven floor-to-ceiling windows, and twenty or so chairs surrounded a large, oval table in the middle. At the head of the room was a large flat screen television. Seated in front of it was Mamadou, his wide shoulders and large head dwarfing the surrounding table. A plastic cup of coffee and a pile of paper and a ring binder, all covered in tiny rings of brown and orange coffee stains, were atop the surface. Despite being meticulously punctual, Mamadou was an organisational mess.

'Morning, Mam,' Jake said, taking a seat at the chairs nearest to the entrance. He and Tyler were first to enter.

'Sit down and shut up, Tanner.'

Jake did as he was told and waited for his other colleagues to filter in, his mind racing with justifications for Mamadou's mood. It wasn't unusual for Mamadou to act like an arsehole in the mornings, especially during their daily debrief, but Jake had never been ordered to sit down and shut up in the same sentence.

Less than a minute later, the rest of Counter Terrorism Command entered and found themselves a seat. As soon as the door shut, Mamadou jumped to his feet and stood in front of the television.

'Morning, team,' he began. 'You know the drill. Update me on everything that's going on. I want none of you sat on your arse doing nothing all week. There's always something to do, and if you're not doing it, you and I'll be having words.'

Mamadou stared at Jake as he spoke, putting him on edge. His boss's eyes seemed to bore into the cells of his skin.

'Edwards!' Mamadou continued, turning to the woman on his left. 'You can begin today.'

A small woman spoke. Her blazer was wrapped tightly around the upper half of her body, and her voice was nasally. She updated the room on the ongoing plan to thwart a potential terrorist plot in south London.

'A raid was carried out in the early hours of this morning, and there were three arrests,' DC Edwards finished.

'All confirmed perps?' Mamadou asked.

'Yes, sir.'

'Good.'

Mamadou continued around the room, prompting the next person to disclose any updates they had. When the time came for Jake to speak, he was tight-lipped. He had nothing to share. He had just closed a case and now he was going through the paperwork. Not to mention, Mamadou knew the *real* reason his workload was sparse — his interviews and tests for the promotion — so why was he trying to humiliate Jake in front of his colleagues?

The debriefing had finished by 09:25. As soon as Mamadou gave a wave of his hand, everyone in the room stepped out of their seats and on their feet.

'Not so fast Tanner, Stuart,' Mamadou barked, clearing his throat.

Fuck sake, Jake thought. *What is it this time?*

'Sit back down please, gentlemen.'

Tyler and Jake did as instructed. Mamadou stepped towards them and sat on the table.

'What is it, boss?' Tyler asked confidently. The way he spoke was an act, a façade, and Mamadou saw straight through it.

'Your attitude, Stuart. That's what.' Mamadou pointed his chubby fingers at Tyler. 'Now, I've been having a few discussions with the CID, and they're a little understaffed at the moment, and since you two are surplus to fucking requirements, I've offered your services to them.'

Tyler moaned, leaned forward in his chair, and instantly sat back after he saw the fiery stare Mamadou gave him. Jake didn't like this. He didn't like it one bit, but if he was going to stand any chance of getting the promotion, he needed to prove he was willing and competent enough to work well within the different departments of the Metropolitan Police.

'What's the case, boss?' Jake asked.

'The Emery kidnapping case.'

Jake had heard of it. The entire office had. A teenage girl and her boyfriend had been abducted in the afternoon and had been missing for four days. The kidnapper had filmed themselves and post a live stream of them raping the girl. The nation was shocked at what they saw, and the feed was immediately cut off by internet providers and search engines. Since then the entire country was out looking for them, but still they had found nothing. The Senior Investigating Officer, DCI Michaels, had made an arse out of himself on national television by explaining to the public a vital piece of evidence had been lost in transit from the crime scene to the laboratory. It was apparently now up to Jake and Tyler from CTC to save their jobs.

'Should be easy for you,' Mamadou said, smiling sarcastically. 'You've had a case like this before.'

It was true, Jake had experienced something similar. The case before he joined CTC. A barrister and their family had been brutally murdered in their own home, and their eldest daughter had been kidnapped. But with no murder weapon nor suspects, Jake had to use all of his instincts and determination to save the girl. In the end, he did, but it had almost cost him his life.

'What do we have to do?' Jake asked.

'Get down to CID and speak to your old boss, Darryl — he'll instruct you further.'

'Is that everything?'

'What do you mean, Tanner?'

'That was all you wanted to hold us back for? There's nothing else?'

Mamadou's eyebrows raised. 'What do you want me to tell you, Tanner? That there are budget cuts bigger than the department has ever seen before coming our way? That last night my cat ran away on my birthday? That my mother has cancer and has only a few weeks to live, if that?'

Jake said nothing. Tyler remained silent next to him, his mouth agape. Neither of them knew what to say. For a moment, Jake was hoping Mamadou would tell them he was joking, that none of what he had said was true. But when that moment didn't come, Jake knew something serious in Mamadou's personal life was taking place.

'I'm so sorry, boss,' Jake said, keeping his eyes fixed on Mamadou, who now hung his head low and looked to the ground. The three of them had been close friends ever since Jake joined CTC, but Jake had never seen his boss and friend in the position he was in now. 'If there's anything we can do, just say the word.'

'You got a cure for cancer?'

Jake didn't respond.

'Then no, you can't fucking do anything.' Mamadou looked out of the window, as if searching for answers. 'Jesus, I'm sorry, guys. I don't mean to be like this. It's just...'

Mamadou trailed off, unable to continue and ran his fingers through his grey hair and then brought them down to his face. Jake understood. Mamadou didn't need to say anything more. He had told them enough.

'Now,' he said, making eye contact with them, 'get your dicks out of your hands and get down to CID before I have to fire you or before you have to do what you're paid to. Whichever comes sooner.'

Just like that, Mamadou was back to his usual brutish self. But Jake knew deep down the man was hurting and in a lot of pain and emotionally unstable. Jake nodded to Mamadou, turned to face Tyler, and gesticulated for them both to leave. Tyler was first out the room, closely followed by Jake. They walked onto the lift at the end of the hallway, both completely unaware that the time to do their job would come sooner than expected.

Chapter Three

KIDS WILL BE KIDS

August 1, 10:10

It was the start of a perfect day.

The air was humid and the light bright as Moshat descended the small slope into Paddington Station. Men and women dressed in suits running late for the working day rushed past him, bumping into his shoulders without apologising. He ignored it; there were bigger things at hand, and little time to waste. It didn't stop him feeling contempt for them all, though. Who did they think they were? Why did they think they were so much better than everyone else? He didn't know, but it was one of the many reasons today *needed* to happen. He and his brother were working towards a better cause. A simpler, more just society. Soon everyone would realise the reasons.

Inside the station, Moshat found himself a seat in front of the large board that displayed the next five trains due to depart. The incandescent orange light hurt his tired eyes. Nevertheless, he gazed up at the board, observing the station names, the destinations, the departure times, just as he had done many times before. At this time in the morning, there was nothing untoward.

As he sat there, he couldn't help his mind wander. Was everything in position? Had they forgotten anything? Did they leave anything behind? Of course not. It was silly to think otherwise; he knew that. Their operation had been weeks — months — in the planning, and they had ensured every angle and eventuality was covered. It was in both his and his brother's nature to meticulously check the minutest of details. It was the way they were trained, first when they were seventeen and their carer had jetted them off to the middle of a rainforest in South America and a second time, almost a year ago, to the same destination. It had felt weird returning after nine years apart, and there had been so many new faces, so many different and exciting procedures and plots, but the welcome they had received was enough to inspire them to succeed.

As Moshat observed the train schedule, his head itched as the sweat from his scalp mixed with his woollen hat. He scratched his skull through the material, making sure his head remained hidden. A family of four, laden with suitcases and stress, seated themselves next to him. Moshat ignored them. He was good at pretending most of the population did not exist, but there was something about this family that caught his attention. Dangling from the mother's arms was a baby with big, glistening blue eyes, so bright they looked as if they carried the hope of the world in them. The baby wore a small denim jacket. The infant let out a little giggle as they reached out to touch Moshat's face.

'Sorry,' the baby's mother said, readjusting the child into a more comfortable position.

'It's OK,' Moshat said, smiling. He observed the father

of the family chasing a toddler no taller than Moshat's kneecap around the chairs. 'Must be a handful.'

'Tell me about it. It's our first holiday with the little one, and the four-year-old is the one playing up.' The mother laughed, and Moshat felt compelled to join in.

As Moshat smiled at the woman, he felt his soft woollen hat come off his head. Instincts took over and his muscles became taut. Turning he saw his beloved hat, the one his mother had given him the day she died, clutched in the pre-schooler's grip.

'Oh,' the father said, removing the hat from the girl's grasp and handing it back to Moshat. 'Sorry about that.'

Moshat wasn't impressed, although he willed himself to remain calm. He wore the hat for a reason, and he didn't like when it was removed. Especially in public. 'It's all right. Kids will be kids.'

With that, the father hefted the child into his arms and sat down next to his wife.

'Are you going anywhere nice?' she asked, as a way of mending invisible barriers.

'Nowhere in particular,' Moshat replied. 'You?'

'Greece.'

'Nice.'

'Yeah. Our flight's due to leave in a few hours, but our train's delayed. Good thing we got here early, eh?'

'Yeah,' Moshat replied, deadpan. His mood had seriously dropped.

Just as the woman was about to continue speaking to him, her husband said their train had arrived. She apologised to Moshat again for her child's misbehaviour, wished him a nice day, and departed. Moshat watched the family leave, feeling the pain in his shoulders and biceps induced from the family dissipate.

He returned his focus to the board. Only two trains were delayed, but the one he was after remained on time. Of course, it was on time. It had been on time for the past few days he had sat there and observed it before he left for work in the afternoons. The Heathrow Express was seldom late — and it shouldn't be because he worked on them for a living — but whenever it was, it always made up the time it had lost.

He had seen the same trains day in, day out, for the past two weeks. They were like dear friends to him now. He knew the train timetable forwards and backwards: the number of stops, the names of the stops, the times of departure and arrival, and in most cases, the numbers of carriages. He knew the numbers of the carriages for the train he would be on. It was his job to know, his role in manufacturing the devastation that was about to unfold.

Moshat reached into his bag and pulled out a note-book. It was frayed at the corners, and scraps of paper hung over the edges, as if trying to escape. Despite his insatiable need to make sure everything was immaculate and neat and tidy, he had allowed himself this one example of chaos. Here, in his tiny notebook, he could make as much madness as he wanted without having to feel a morsel of guilt.

He opened it to the most recent page somewhere towards the end of the book. A small table was scribbled in the centre of the page. Numbers littered the lines, and each corresponded to the time a train was due to arrive, when it did, and when it left, with a rough estimate of the number of people who boarded. The word Heathrow was written in capital letters at the top of the page and underlined multiple times, the way an organised murderer scratches out the name of their next victim with a knife.

On the page, Moshat scribbled more numbers and pocketed the notebook in his coat's breast pocket.

It was going to be the perfect day.

One down, three to go, he thought to himself as he reclined into the bench and observed the passers-by.

The 10:25 train had just departed from Paddington to Heathrow on the Heathrow Express.

He had just over an hour before he could begin.

Chapter Four

STRANGER

August 1, 10:15

New Scotland Yard never ceased to amaze Jake. It was like a labyrinth of corridors, offices, floor-to-ceiling windows, and departments. No matter where he went nor how long he had been there, he always discovered something new. The same applied now.

He and Tyler had taken a detour through the canteen first so Tyler could pick up a cup of coffee before they headed to the Missing Persons Unit on the seventh floor. The department was a smaller branch within CID. They started up a flight of stairs on the east side of the building that looked out upon the River Thames and the London Eye, leading to the MPU.

Jake stepped out onto the office floor, feeling a wave of nostalgia wash over him. Most of his career had been at CID, and as he scanned the room in search of familiar faces, he recognised none. *Where's Ashley?* She had been his partner on the case that had led to his tenure with Counter Terrorism Command.

The atmosphere on the seventh floor buzzed. The MPU office was much larger than CTC, with almost double the number of desks and computer monitors. Every one of them was being manned. Budget cuts in recent years had meant the Metropolitan Police needed a permanent change in residence, and a considerable downsize in numbers of personnel. Despite there only being six-hundred staff in the building, Jake saw someone new almost every day. It was like he was in school again — the ever-changing faces of children coming and going as they grew up. Officials and detectives stood on their feet pooling together in a group at the far-left corner of the room.

'What's going on here, then?' Tyler asked.

Before Jake could respond, they had their answer. DCI Michaels, the one whom Jake had seen on the news last night before he left for home, stood at the centre of the crowd, smiling and waving. A round of applause ensued from his colleagues, and he bowed his head a little.

'Seems like maybe we got here just in time,' Jake said, keeping his eyes focused on DCI Michaels and tilting his head in Tyler's direction. He kept his voice low.

'Or maybe he knew we were coming and couldn't bear to see us solve the case before him, so he finally pulled his finger out of his arse.'

Jake laughed. The two of them headed towards the crowd, preparing themselves to join in with the celebrations. As they walked, Jake continued to search for his old partner. Along the left-hand side of the office was a series of cubicles, reserved for the more senior ranked staff. Exiting from one, with a cup of coffee and laptop in her hands, was

Ashley. She came out of nowhere and took Jake by surprise. He could barely avoid colliding with her.

'Watch it!' Ashley barked as a droplet of brown liquid soared in the air and landed on her sleeve. She spoke with as much venom and bite as she did all those years ago when they had worked together.

Jake said nothing. He was too taken aback. Instead he stared at her, his eyes beady and his breath stopped. It felt good to see her again; he wished it hadn't been under such embarrassing circumstances.

'Jake!' Ashley screamed after realising who Jake was. She put her laptop and what remained of her coffee on the floor, then clasped her arms around Jake's neck. 'It's so good to see you.'

'Likewise.'

'How have you been? How's fighting terrorists treating you?'

'It has its ups and downs.'

'You know, I'm not happy with you.' Ashley paused and looked at Tyler, smiled at him and then returned her attention to Jake before continuing. 'I thought I asked you to keep in touch? It's been two years and this is the first time I've seen you.'

'My apologies. I guess I've just been busy. What are you doing now? How come you're in MPU?' Jake said, trying to sidestep the conversation away from his poorly maintained communication skills.

'Well, after the Haversham case, they thought they could do with someone like me.'

'And now you've got your own office, too?'

Ashley nodded. 'It's not much, but Darryl promoted me to DI a few months ago, so I get this new luxury.'

'Congratulations. I'm happy for you,' Jake said.

'Speaking of the chief inspector, where is he? We need to speak to him about the Emery kidnapping.'

'Haven't you heard?' Ashley bent down to the ground and picked up her things.

Jake shook his head.

'Michaels closed the case this morning. That's what all this fucking commotion is about.' Ashley flicked a look of disdain towards the group of officials.

'You never were one for public gratification, were you?'

'I don't see the point in celebrating doing your job. Call me a cynic, but that's what I feel.'

Jake smiled. Ashley always made him laugh, even when they hadn't seen eye-to-eye at first. Next to him, Tyler's phone rang. He answered and gave monosyllabic responses.

'OK. We'll be right up,' Tyler finished. He called off and looked at Jake. 'That was the boss. He wants us upstairs straight away. Says the Emery case doesn't need solving anymore.'

'No shit,' Jake said. He turned to Ashley, gave her another hug, said goodbye, and sauntered to the lift.

Just as the doors were about to close, Jake heard shoes running along the carpet. Ashley's face appeared. Seconds before the two metal panels shut her out, she shouted, 'Don't be a stranger!'

The thought made Jake think. He would make more of an effort to keep in contact with her. He never knew when her expertise and knowledge would come in handy. Jake's stomach lurched again as the lift climbed the floors of the building. They both stood still, sharing that particularly awkward silence you always find in a lift with other people. But Jake could sense there was something different about this one. He could sense Tyler wanted to say something. And straight away, he knew what.

'Come on, out with it,' Jake said. He looked at his partner.

'Was there anything going on between you two? I saw the way you looked at her.'

'I'm happily married with a family. Don't be stupid.'

The doors opened with a robotic *bing*, and they strolled towards Mamadou's office. Jake knocked, and after they were told they could enter, sat down first. Tyler closed the door behind him and joined Jake. Mamadou's office was large — larger than Ashley's had been, yet smaller than the debrief room — and the inside was organised chaos. Shelves of books, folders, and year-old case reports hung on the right-hand side of the wall. A decrepit chair that had its back missing rested overturned in the far-left corner of the room. It was a mess, everyone knew, but it was Mamadou's mess, and Jake couldn't help but feel a moment of compassion for his boss. Jake ignored the lingering stench that reminded him of pets, as if it had been deeply stained into the carpets.

'Gentlemen,' Mamadou said. On his desk was a pain au chocolat.

'Boss,' Jake said, nodding.

'Seems the Emery case is resolved. So, your attendance is no longer required, which means with both of you not busy over the next few days, we will need to find something else to keep you occupied.'

'We have been busy. And Jake had the dentist yesterday, so he'll be even busier today,' Tyler said, defending his colleague. Jake felt ashamed at his lie and looked down at his lap, hoping neither of the other men in the room noticed.

Mamadou looked to Tyler, who was leaning back in his chair with his right leg placed over his left knee cap. 'Stuart

— you raise a good case, but it's not good enough, I'm afraid. I've got a meeting with the Assistant Commissioner in twenty minutes, I would like you to tell her I'll be a few minutes late.'

'What?' Tyler protested. He sat forward on his chair, placing his elbows on his knees.

'You heard me. Now, go.'

Experience had taught Tyler when and when not to argue with his boss, and now wasn't one of those times. Sighing, he lunged out of his chair, knocked it backwards, righted it again, and departed the room. Jake swallowed; if Tyler was on messenger duty, then what did that mean was in store for him?

Mamadou cleared his throat.

'He doesn't know about the promotion, does he?'

Jake remained silent.

'Why haven't you told him?'

Jake hesitated. 'I'm afraid he'll react badly. He'll see it as a betrayal.'

'He will find out, eventually. Best you tell himself before the pain of finding out on his own becomes too much.'

'Yes, Mam.' Jake admitted to himself he would wait and find the right time to tell Tyler. It had to be planned and prepared for, otherwise it would seem like he didn't care about his partner's feelings at all.

'How did it go yesterday?'

Jake then told Mamadou about the last hour and a half of his day. How he had almost aced the test, performed under adverse conditions, and how it was neck and neck between himself and DC Matthews.

'I've heard he's been just as good, if not better.'

'Have you heard anything else? Any tips, suggestions I can act upon?'

'You know I can't do that, Tanner. That would be a conflict of interest. Not to mention a few complaints would be raised as a result, and you know I'm not one to deal with that sort of thing well,' Mamadou said. They both smiled, Mamadou's humour appearing more genuine than Jake's, whose was mixed with apprehension.

'Come on, boss,' Jake pleaded. 'At least give me a number. Out of ten, how likely is it I'll get it?'

Mamadou hesitated. His mouth opened and closed, the words milliseconds away from being released from his lips. Just as Mamadou was about to say something — was it four? Or five? — the door behind them barged open. DC Matilda Edwards stumbled in, her momentum knocking her off balance.

'Sir,' she began, breathing heavily, as if she had just sprinted to the office. 'We've just received an email from an unknown source. You need to see this.'

She strolled over to Mamadou, the distance between her strides so small it made her look as though she were in fact running. She passed a tablet she was holding to Mamadou and allowed him to read. Jake inched closer to the edge of his seat, pulse rising.

'For too long, we have allowed the oppressor to remain in charge. We have allowed them to sit in their high seats of power, govern the country and watch the lower classes struggle to survive. We have listened to them, and we have believed them when they have promised change. Well, now, it is time for change. And very soon, London, the government behind all our misery and turmoil, you will see just exactly how that change will be manifested. The greatest terrorist attack this miserable city has ever seen is about to unfold.' Mamadou lowered the tablet to the table when he finished and gazed up at Matilda.

'Who sent this?'

'Comms are working on it at the moment, sir,' DC Edwards explained. 'It was sent early this morning, just before the debrief meeting. Everyone in command has got it. They were all Bcc'd into the email and received it five minutes ago. Comms have just informed me that the original email was sent to one person in the office directly.'

'Who?'

Saying nothing, Matilda turned to face Jake.

'Jake, sir.'

What? Jake thought. There must have been a mistake. Surely. If he had received an email from a potential terrorist alerting them of an imminent terror attack, he would know about it, wouldn't he? Rising out of his chair like a greyhound out of its stalls, Mamadou raced out of the office, across the floor, and stopped at Jake's desk. Jake and DC Edwards were moments behind.

'Mam, I know nothing about this,' Jake said. He looked at Mamadou; there was a fire in the man's eyes that only needed a minuscule amount of oxygen more to burn ferociously and engulf the entire office in a blaze of rage.

'I don't care, Tanner. Unlock your desktop now.'

Jake sat at his desk, typed in his password, and waited anxiously for the operating system to load. He could hear and feel Mamadou's heavy breathing on his back. The last application Jake was using opened. It was his email inbox. At the top was the email he had opened and was about to read moments before Mamadou burst into the office, demanding everyone in the team to the debrief room. Jake read the words in the email. As his eyes scanned lower down the document, he became horrified. Dozens of thoughts raced through his mind. The worst terror attack London has ever seen? What could that mean? Who had sent the email? Was it from someone they had been monitoring, or was it a hoax? And why had they sent it only to him first and then everyone else in the office later?

'You sure you've never seen this before, Tanner? Looks like you saw it and didn't think to do anything about it.'

Jake opened his mouth to speak, but was shut down by Mamadou's large palm.

'I don't want to hear it, Tanner. Not now. Matilda—'

'Yes, sir.'

'I want you to find out who sent this, where it came from, and whether it holds any merit. Check the intelligence reports from last night, see whether anyone under suspicion has been more active over the past few days. For now, I want to keep the Assistant Commissioner out of it — not until we have something more concrete.'

DC Edwards nodded, clutched her tablet to her chest, and disappeared around the corner behind a desk. Jake was just about to stand and ask Mamadou what he should do when Mamadou's phone rang in his pocket. The conversation lasted less than twenty seconds, and as soon as it had finished, Mamadou stormed off. Jake struggled to keep up.

'What about me, sir? What do you want me to do?'

'Nothing, Tanner. You've done enough.'

'What about you? Where are you going?' Jake asked, noticing his boss was on the way to the lift.

Walking rapidly as he spoke, Mamadou said, 'The hospital. My mother's just been rushed in. She's had a heart attack.'

Chapter Five

DEVICE

August 1, 11:00

The fan inside the computer droned, filling the tiny flat with a monotonous and repetitive hum that would have been enough to drive the sanest person mad. But not for Adil — the sound was soothing to him. It allowed him to think. The inside of his home was dark. The curtains and windows were shut and all signs of life shrouded. The way it should be. The outside world needed to remain where it was for the next six hours. No one, under any circumstances, was to enter the flat. Not that they would; he had never spoken a word to any of his neighbours, so he saw no immediate reason why anyone would need enter.

It was important he stayed off the grid. For now, and forever. His computer forensics degree, training, and time spent on the dark web had taught him that much. To show your face, they told him, was to admit defeat.

Even venturing out to the Heathrow Express warehouse last night in the dark to meet Moshat had been a risk. But a risk worth taking. For, in a few hours, he and his brother would be known across the world, their faces made available to every police division on the globe. And they would be infamous. But Adil wasn't worried. They had a plan — they had a plan for everything — and nothing would change that.

Adil walked over to the record player behind him and delicately placed a vinyl on top. One of his favourites: Debussy's *La Mer*. He had just made a coffee, and he needed something in the form of a distraction. Music was the perfect option. He glided across the floor as he moved from the kitchen.

He sat down at his desk and stared at three horizontal screens. White numbers and symbols rolled up the central panel, until they disappeared, and an image of a mountain loaded simultaneously on all three, stretching from left to right. With the click of a few shortcuts on his keyboard, the centre screen illuminated, filling the whole window of an image of a train, motionless on a platform's edge. He pressed his mouse and the screen changed to another platform. Many people queued up dressed in suits and formal wear, sentencing their souls to a life of banality while chasing the impossible dream of truly living.

Adil moved his mouse, and the image on the display moved with it. *Moshat* — there he was, waiting and taking notes in his book. For a moment Adil observed his brother through the lens of the security camera. It had been easy — child's play, really — hacking into the Paddington Station CCTV circuit. And the Victoria Station CCTV circuit. And the King's Cross CCTV circuit. There had been no major firewalls or fail-safes that had impeded him. It had been an afternoon's work, and once he was in, he was in. A clear indictment of the most watched country's security levels. If he could do it in less than five minutes flat, anyone could.

Adil leaned forward to take a sip from his coffee. A red light flashed on the other side of his desk and caught his eye. He picked up the device emitting the light and checked it over. It felt heavy in his hands. It felt powerful. It felt... *evil*. There was something so unsettling about the small black box. Something so unsettling about the fact that the technology inside it emitted a signal that engaged multiple, localised electromagnetic pulses when pressed.

The red light meant it had entered standby mode, and on the underneath was a button that activated it. It had been a creation of his own design, and he feared it would not work when he needed it most. He and his brother had tested it in the sanctity of night on cars driving along the motorway. As soon as he pressed the button, all the electrical components in the cars within a five-hundred-yard radius lost control. Some crashed. Some skidded to a halt. And some didn't even realise there had been an issue. The device had worked fine and now the whole operation rested on it. Adil pressed the button on the underside, reactivating the device, and placed it back on the table next to its compatriot, its partner in crime: the trigger.

He wanted so much to press the trigger, to initiate the electromagnetic pulses, but he couldn't. *Now's not the time,* he told himself. His mind drifted to thoughts of the future and when he could unleash its wrath. He couldn't wait.

'You're special, aren't you?' Adil said, speaking to the two remotes on the table. He held the trigger in his hand, inspecting the leather pattern he had applied himself. 'Complete remote stop-start of all communications, in and out, at the press of a button. You are magnificent.' He kissed the trigger and put it back down next to the other device.

It was just a shame no one would remember him for his brilliance and ingenuity. Instead, it would be his destruction that would leave his and his brother's names in the history books.

Until it was time for their plan to start, there wasn't much for Adil to do. He filled the time by watching television in complete silence; he preferred to watch the images flick across the screen. He turned on his television, and thanks to a simple computer chip placed in one of his neighbour's television boxes one day, after he had pretended to be a Sky engineer, he could watch exactly what they were.

Nobody in his block knew he was watching television.

Nobody knew he was about to terrorise the whole of London.

Nobody knew he was even alive.

The mobile phone in his pocket rang. He removed the large, vibrating Nokia 3310 and read the display. There was no caller ID. Moshat. He had spent months masking the number's address, encrypting everything inside the phone and installing software so it would remain completely anonymous to the authorities.

Adil answered the call without ceremony. 'How are things proceeding?'

'Perfect so far. The 10:55 train has just departed on time. A few members of the British Transport Police are patrolling the station, but none have entered any trains so far,' Moshat said. His voice was low, to conceal his conversation from those sitting close to him. Meanwhile, Adil cast a glance over his shoulder to check his brother on the computer monitor.

'Relax. There is nothing to worry about. Remember, you know what to do should a situation with the boys in blue occur. Believe in yourself,' Adil said, bringing his voice to the same pitch he used when he calmed Moshat as a child. That was how their relationship had always been. And that was the way it would always be.

'OK. Speak soon.'

Adil hung up and continued to watch the people's mouths move but produce no sound. In the background, Chopin's *Nocturne, Opera 9, no. 2* played. He eased back in his chair, closed his eyes and lifted his head to the ceiling, exhaling deeply. *This is the best vinyl you ever bought me, Moshat.* Allowing the elegant sounds of the stringed instruments to wash over him, Adil glided his hands through the air with grace.

As soon as the piano started, Adil mimed the action, the tendons in his hands flexing as he mimicked the musician's movements. Playing a classical instrument had once been a necessary requirement when he attended Cambridge University, and he had hated it with a deeper passion than he had ever despised anything in his life. But, after many years of reflection and consolidation, he had learned to trust it, learn from it, and gain inspiration from it. Adil understood the layers behind the music, like the layers of peoples' lives he couldn't ever possible know, yet still tried to decipher and manipulate.

Once the song had stopped, Adil became irritable. Time drifted. Bored, Adil jumped to his feet, strolled over to his desk, sat down and tapped the mouse. The time was 11:00, and the image on the computer screen switched to another station. It was London St. Pancras International, and the 11:01 a.m. train to London Luton Airport had just disembarked.

In less than an hours' time, Adil and his brother would begin their game.

Chapter Six

STORM

August 1, 11:28

Mamadou barged through the revolving doors of Royal London Hospital into the reception area. He was out of breath and his feet ached from the run between the car park and the building's entrance. As much as he hated to admit it, he wasn't as young and as fit as he used to be. Resigned to a desk for the rest of his career, he decided he would have to give up the cheap takeaway meals and coffee; neither one of them was good for his heart.

'Excuse me,' he said, panting to the receptionist dressed in the light NHS blue uniform. She looked up at him, her spectacles covering almost all of her face. 'DCS Kuhoba, Counter Terrorism Command of the London Met. My mother, Mrs. Gloria Kuhoba has just been admitted here. She's had a heart attack. Could you please tell me where to go?'

'Certainly,' the receptionist replied. She typed on the

keyboard, examined the computer screen in front of her and explained to Mamadou his mother was in ward 13E.

'Thank you,' Mamadou said, rushing towards the lift, keeping his ID in his hands as he ran.

Frantically, he pressed the lift button going up, as if it would summon the vehicle quicker. A few seconds later, the doors open and Mamadou dived in, the hydraulics of the pulleys bouncing under his weight.

'Come on. Come on,' Mamadou willed, pacing from side to side.

As soon as the doors opened on the general surgery ward, Mamadou burst from inside. Overwhelmed by the sheer size of the building, he ran up and down the wards, his pace and fears multiplying with each step.

'Hello?' he shouted, looking up and down the corridor. There was no one around, no one who could help him, no one who could wake him from this nightmare and console him and tell him it was all just a bad dream.

Eventually, as Mamadou sprinted further ahead, his head darting left and right, peering into the individual rooms, he spotted someone in uniform. He shouted at them and they strolled towards him.

'Can I help you, sir?'

'My mother,' Mamadou said, unable to continue. His voice came out as nothing but a raspy whistle, and his lungs screamed at him. After pausing for a moment to catch his breath, Mamadou explained the situation.

The nurse, a young man with long black hair and a skinny, wiry frame, led him down towards the end of the corridor and pointed him in the right direction. Mamadou obeyed his instructions and arrived at another, smaller reception area. For the third time, he explained the situation.

'Mrs. Kuhoba is in surgery at the moment, sir. I'm afraid you must take a seat in the waiting area until either the doctor or a nurse is available to give you more information,' the second receptionist whispered.

'No!' Mamadou shouted, his body becoming tense with rage. 'I demand to see my mother *now*. Failing that, I demand to speak to someone qualified enough to tell me what is going on.'

Mamadou's voice echoed up and down the halls. Other nurses, who were absent-mindedly carrying out their daily tasks, turned and looked at him. He didn't care what they thought of him; his mother's life was in danger and he would do everything he could to help her in any way possible.

'Sir, if you don't calm down, I'm going to call security.' The lady behind the counter grabbed for the phone and held it to her ear.

'Listen,' Mamadou said, aware the damage had been done. 'Please, don't call security. I'll calm down and sit somewhere. Can you tell someone I've arrived and need answers?'

'I'll do what I can.'

Mamadou thanked her and sat down in the waiting area. He removed his phone from his pocket. He had two missed calls and three text messages. All from Jake. Mamadou thumbed through them. Jake had been keeping him updated on the progress, and there was nothing to report so far. As much as Mamadou wanted to focus on work, he found himself distracted by the paralysing thoughts of his mother lying on the hospital bed, unconscious, her chest carved open.

In the top corner of the room, hanging from the wall, was an old-school box television. The news was running, and Mamadou grabbed for the television remote that lay underneath a pile of health and lifestyle magazines. He hated the blatant irony that was being shoved in his face and turned the volume up. If London came under attack, he would know about it at the same time the rest of the world did.

Counter Terrorism Command was in a state of mild chaos. In the minutes following Mamadou's departure, everybody in the office was either on their feet or rooted to their seats, typing frantically or speaking clearly and bluntly into the phone to another colleague somewhere else in the building. Jake stood on the outskirts of the furore, uncertain on how to proceed. The email had knocked his confidence.

Fortunately for Jake, his answer strolled past him in the form of Assistant Commissioner Dame Frances Walken, who oversaw the Special Operations division of the London Metropolitan Police Service, which also meant she was in charge of CTC. He had seen her wandering the building, frequently accompanied by her two deputies, Simon Ashdown and Susanna King, but he had never seen her in person until now. She was an elusive figure, always in meetings with other senior members of the force or in COBRA meetings with the country's most powerful politicians and institutional representatives.

Dame Frances Walken was an elderly woman. Her hair was streaked with bolts of grey that reflected light and reminded Jake of Storm from the *X-Men* series. Her exterior seemed to be phased by nothing, and when she walked, it was as if she glided along the floor, keeping her back straight and head forward. As she edged past Jake, he could have sworn he felt a cold breeze that sent the hairs on his arms on end. His perception of her had already been determined before she could speak.

A noise to his left distracted him. Tyler appeared from behind a door, his hair dishevelled and windswept.

'What are you doing?' Jake asked his partner.

'Trying to stop her.' Tyler nodded in Frances' direction.

'What happened?'

'She didn't want to be told Mamadou would be late. Then she had a look at her emails and stormed up here,' Tyler explained. He stood next to Jake and the two of them watched Frances bank at the head of the room and face everyone in the office.

'Oh, shit,' Jake whispered. 'I've got a bad feeling about this.'

Chapter Seven

DISRUPTION

August 1, 11:31

Operation time.

The 11:31 a.m. British Rail Class 387 train from London St. Pancras International was ready to depart to Luton Airport.

The 11:31 a.m. Gatwick Express train from London Victoria was ready to depart to Gatwick Airport.

Everything had gone according to plan, and as Adil watched the trains depart on his computer screens, a wry smile flickered on the sides of his mouth. He was focused and in the zone. Their months of hard work were about to pay off. *Just wait until the real fun begins*, he thought.

Adil loaded a software programme on his computer and typed in his password. The entire left screen changed from its usual desktop background to live footage on board the Gatwick Express, and the right screen changed to live footage of the Luton-bound train. In the middle of the three-headed display was a software he had developed on his own. It was a computer networking system that meant he could hack into any of the mobile telephone devices, tablets, laptops — and just about any other form of technological device — within the signal's radius.

Over the past few nights, he and Moshat had planted the signals in each of the train's carriages. Now that the software was active, he had the ability to capture and intercept text messages, Facebook notifications, incoming calls and alerts, all on a rolling newsfeed on his computer. All their personal and private information was at his fingertips.

As he stared at the centre screen, the display soon became swamped with eleven-digit mobile numbers and their most recent activity. He perused through some messages, but moments later, stopped. There was nothing of any interest, nothing juicy that would entertain him — just the occasional soppy message to loved ones who the passengers foolishly believed they would see soon.

Adil chuckled to himself. *Poor bastards, they have no idea.*

His attention was distracted by the live video footage on either screen. By now, the passengers had placed their luggage in the holding bays, settled themselves down on the chairs, and continued their daily consumption of social media in their own little bubbles. No one was talking. No one was making eye contact with one another or even attempting a conversation with the person next to them. No one was showing compassion for or interest in their fellow man. Instead, the passengers just sat there, politely ignoring one another as if they didn't exist.

The trains were busy, too, with some passengers standing, clinging to their luggage, or straddling it between their knees. That was even better. The more pedestrians on board, the greater the injury toll. The greater the amount of panic. The greater the tension and pressure. All of which made for a delightful operation.

Adil made a quick count. Two trains. Fourteen coaches in total. At least eighty passengers to a coach, equating to over one thousand passengers in all. And that wasn't including the Heathrow Express train that would depart in eight minutes' time. It would be a lot for Adil and his device to handle. But his training hadn't been in vain.

Five minutes into the journey time, Adil minimised the communications-intercepting programme and opened another application he had developed himself. With Moshat's help to take photographs of the driver's cabin in the dead of night, Adil had recreated the central control panel of the trains he oversaw. A series of nobs, dials, and an array of levers and pulleys filled the screen. From his desktop, he could manipulate and control whatever he wanted with the click of a button. The speed of the train. The safety of the train. The temperature of the train.

And the latter was his first priority.

He moved his mouse to the button labelled "AC+" and clicked it until the digit beneath read 30. With the additional summer heat beating down on the train, the compartments would soon feel like a sauna. And he knew all too well that the pressure and discomfort caused by intense heat — combined with being trapped in a confined space — was enough to create a riot. Adil was playing God with them all. The passengers would do exactly as he said if they wanted to survive. If there was one thing he had learned from months of observation, it was that people would do anything if they knew it meant their survival was on the line. Today, he would exploit that desire.

Five minutes later, the effects of the increased heat began to show. Women cooled themselves and their children with makeshift fans constructed from newspapers and magazines. Dark patches of sweat adorned men's backs, armpits, and collarbones. A small film of condensation crawled up the carriage windows.

Adil enjoyed himself.

The time rolled to 11:40. The Heathrow Express was leaving Paddington Station towards London Heathrow Airport, the busiest airport in Europe. And his brother would be on it. There was no need to check in on Moshat's status; he trusted his brother to supervise it all. If there were any problems, then Moshat would have alerted him by now.

No news is good news, Adil thought. Now the fun could *really* begin.

All three trains were mobile. All were functioning properly. All were under his control. *Almost*. As Adil sat there, he watched the number on the Gatwick Express's air conditioning display descend to nineteen. The driver had changed it back to its original setting.

Adil chuckled. 'Oh, no you don't,' he said, moving the setting back up to thirty.

Already, Adil had encountered the first problem associated with his software. Until the train was entirely under his control, he couldn't monitor the driver's actions in the cockpit. He understood the limitations, so he already had a countermeasure in place.

The time ticked over to 11:50. In ten minutes' time, each of the three trains would roll into their respective destinations.

But not today.

In the middle of the onboard dashboard, Adil found the lever and button he was searching for. One controlled the speed of the train, the other implemented the handbrake. Adil moved the mouse towards the lever and dragged it down. Instantly, the speedometer of the trains dropped from seventy to zero.

Everything happened so quickly. Within seconds, the giant machines had come to a complete standstill. Next, Adil pressed the button that triggered the handbrakes and located another that locked the carriage doors. Just like that, three separate trains, all bound to separate destinations, on the outskirts of London were in his control. Now nobody could get in or out.

Not unless they wanted to suffer a consequence.

Once satisfied everything had been accomplished, Adil looked at the screens on the left and right. Passengers picked themselves up off the floor, heaved other commuters from atop them, and righted suitcases that had flown off the bays and crashed down. Nobody could escape the brutality of such an emergency stop — Adil just hoped Moshat had found himself a secure space aboard the Heathrow Express and had strapped himself in as best he could, just like they had discussed.

'Come on people, hurry. We're on a deadline here,' Adil said, staring at the computer screen. By now, everybody was on their feet, brushing each other down before the magnitude of the situation kicked in. A few Good Samaritans attended to those with broken and bloodied noses.

He quickly glanced over at the middle screen and saw a spike in mobile activity. Everyone on board was trying to find out what happened or to contact loved ones.

'Nope, no you don't. Not just yet, I'm afraid. Only when your Helpless Saviour says so.' Adil had given himself the nickname after his training in South America. During times of crisis, people often looked to some form of God when they in were dire need, an impersonal deity who only worsened its worshippers' suffering as they kept hoping for divine intervention. He would be that unjust God for these passengers. Deities were far from being able to stop him.

Adil reached for the radio-transmitting device on his table. It felt even heavier in his hands now that the time had finally come to use it now it was burdened with the weight of thousands of lives. He held it high in the air, allowing what little light was left in the room to bounce off it. Now was the time. Now or never.

He pressed the button.

There was a moment of complete fear and paranoia. Had it worked? Had he made a mistake? Was the electro-magnetic pulse device working on this large a scale?

For a while, he didn't know; he couldn't be sure. But when he observed the mobile numbers and their most recent activity, he relaxed. Not a single message had been sent in the last ten seconds. Not a single call had been dialled since, despite the furious attempts of everyone on board.

Then panic erupted. Men, women, teenagers, adolescents, and the elderly — they all held their phones higher in the air, hoping it would bring back the signal. People rose to their feet and move towards the trains' exits. Adil watched on as the passengers attempted to escape. The doors were sealed shut, and there was nowhere for them to go.

Adil observed arguments breaking out. Hand gesticulations and body language showed the fragility of the passengers and their growing inability to cope in extreme circumstances.

Their lives were in Adil's hands now.

Chapter Eight

ALTERCATION

August 1, 11:41

'Open the fucking door!' screamed a young man. A river of red ran down from his nose to chin and plumed onto his white T-shirt in a flower of blood. The flow was heavy, and it muffled and distorted his speech.

'What do you think I'm doing? Tickling it to see if that'll open it?' said a large man beside him. He was trying to pry open the door with his fingertips. He wore khaki shorts and an Adidas jumper.

'Try harder!'

'You try it if you think you're fucking Houdini!'

Both men stopped what they were doing and squared up to one another. The smaller and wirier of the two stood no chance. The taller, wider man had a stern look on his face that suggested he had experienced few beatings in his time.

'Can you stop arguing, please?' a middle-aged woman interjected, coming between the two. Her two children, both boys, clung to her hips. She looked young, her appearance made even more youthful with a face full of make-up.

With obvious reluctance, both men looked at one another, nodded, and backed away.

'It's useless,' the taller man said. 'The doors are locked. We can't get out.'

'How about the windows? They must have emergency glass for these types of things?' a man dressed in a suit asked. He was young with vibrant hair, and his sky-blue shirt was tight around his chest and shoulders.

The tall man laughed. 'Yeah, because this *sort of thing* happens all the time.'

'Don't get sarcastic with me, mate,' the businessman said.

'Oh, yeah? And why not?'

Now these two squared up to one another. Millimetres separated them in height, and they pressed noses as they growled and yelled at one another.

'Just stop!' the pretty woman screamed. 'This isn't helping anything. Put your egos aside and let's discuss this. We've all got planes to be on and family members or partners we're going to see, and killing one another won't help that, will it?'

The voice of reason had spoken. Silence fell on the fourth carriage of the Gatwick Express. It was an eerie silence, filled with an unspoken and immovable dread.

'What do you propose we do, then?' the man in the suit asked her.

'Well, I...' She hesitated, cautious of the sudden amount of responsibility that was being placed on her. 'Perhaps we should try the windows.'

With that, the businessman called down to the passengers nearest the emergency glass.

'Try to smash it open with whatever you can,' he said.

No one volunteered for the challenge. Everyone looked to one another for answers, for someone to put themselves forward. No hero stepped up.

After a long moment, an elderly woman rose out of her seat and barked orders at those opposite and next to her to move aside.

'Miss, are you sure you should do that? Is it safe?' asked a teenager in the carriage.

'It's called an emergency glass for a reason. I think an old girl like me can open it.' She rose out of her chair, moving towards the window opposite her, opened the glass box holding the emergency hammer, and held the tool firmly in her hands.

The lady made a small grunt as the hammer collided with the window.

Nothing happened. No showering of glass. No crack in the window. She tried again and again before collapsing in defeat. There was no escape.

Everybody crowded round to see what little damage the hammer had done. The elderly lady leaned forward to inspect the impact. She gently ran her finger along the window. There were small indents where the hammer made contact, but nothing more. A slither of glass, about an inch in length tried to run away from the first impact zone but made it no further. She scanned the hammer in her hands and squeezed the head tighter. It felt flimsy, rubber-like.

'It's a con,' she said, turning around to face the other passengers. 'It's just as heavy as a real hammer, but the head is made of rubber. Someone must have swapped it.'

Before she could say anything else, harsh sounds rang through the intercom system overhead.

It was classical music. *Ride of the Valkyries.*

Daa-da-da-da-DAA-da, da-da-da-DAA-da, da-da-da-DAA-da, da-da-da-daaaaaaa.

As the music climaxed into the crescendo, it became louder and louder.

The passengers protected their ears, wincing as the deafening noise filled the carriage. They looked at one other, each filled with the idea that someone amongst them was playing a practical joke.

Once they had worked out where it was coming from, they cast their gaze towards the speakers — they vibrated with such ferocity. This person apparently liked their classical music loud, and so would they. Then the music stopped, and the sound of the Gatwick Express driver spurted out muffled words overhead.

'Remain calm everyone. Please, for your own safety do not leave the train in case we get moving or until you are told it is safe to do so. The train is immobile at the moment and we hope to resolve this shortly —'

'Yes, everybody. You should do as he says,' a mysterious voice interrupted the driver through the intercom system. 'Welcome aboard the train of pain and misery. This is your new conductor speaking, and I regret to inform you you are now trapped. You must stay put if you wish to survive. For the next six hours you will be under my control, and you will do everything and anything I tell you to. If any of you so much as think about escaping, you will die. If any of you so much as think about trying to communicate with the outside world — firstly, you won't be able to because I have blocked all communication transmissions, so all those pretty little phones and laptops you've spent hours working to pay for will no longer work — and secondly, you will die. The terms are that simple.'

The voice paused. Everyone else in the train remained silent.

'At the end of the six hours, I regret to inform you, you may die. Your lives are very much in the hands of one person today, ladies and gentlemen. And that person is a Metropolitan Police detective named Jake Tanner. If he is unsuccessful in his attempts to meet my demands and rescue you, you will die. And, if you're wondering how I plan to do that, please cast your eyes up to the ceiling of the cabin you're in. Yes, those red flashing lights I've just turned on are hundreds of cubic centimetres' worth of explosives, locked just out of reach. They're hard at work letting you know they're there and that they're not afraid to go boom at the end of those six hours. They cannot be disarmed, so if you try it, I will see it and enjoy watching you blow up.

'I know how much you'd all love nothing more than to let your loved ones know you're safe and in such a frightening situation, but I'm afraid that can't be allowed. The only communication coming to your mobiles for the foreseeable future — and I hope it is foreseeable for most of you — will be from me, your Helpless Saviour.

'You have six hours to stay put and await your rescue. Failure to comply with any of the aforementioned terms and conditions will result in a serious penalty. Goodbye.'

The man beyond the intercom system disappeared and once again, the Gatwick Express was filled with silence, now laced with an almost tangible air of fear and worry.

The speaker's last parting gift to the passengers was a message that rolled across the display boards within the carriages. It read: YOU HAVE 6.00.00 TO REMAIN SEATED OR YOUR LIVES WILL BE PUT TO AN END. THANKS FOR YOUR COOPERATION, followed by a smiley emoticon.

With each passing second, the countdown number on the board reduced.

They were trapped, all alone in the middle of nowhere, surrounded by explosives, with one man coming to rescue them.

Chapter Nine

NOTIFICATION

August 1, 12:00

'Attention, ladies and gentlemen,' Assistant Commissioner Frances Walken said softly. 'Please, gather round.'

Almost immediately, everyone in the office, including Jake and Tyler, huddled together at the head of the room, the tension in the air palpable. He knew over the next few minutes, he would be in the firing line unless he could prove himself somehow. He would have to explain why he was the first one to receive the email but the last one to know anything about it. And he might have to cover for Mamadou, too.

'We have a situation on our hands. It also seems your Detective Chief Superintendent, Mr. Kuhoba has disappeared, as he is nowhere to be seen, so it is up to you and the rest of the team to manage yourselves accordingly. Before we continue, does anyone know where DCS Kuhoba may be?'

The room fell silent as everyone looked at one another,

searching for answers. Jake swallowed hard. He could feel dozens of eyes boring into him from all angles, judging him for not saying anything. He and Frances locked eye contact for what felt like an eternity, until she pulled away and continued her stare around the rest of the team.

'Well, then,' Frances said. 'What I want every one of you to do is ascertain who emailed and where it came from.'

'We've been unable to do that so far, ma'am,' DC Edwards said. She was still holding the tablet.

'What do you mean?'

'The Comms team have tried to locate the IP address of the sender, but it was encrypted beyond anything they've ever encountered before.'

'Has the email been sent across to MI5 for them to have a look at? They might pull something out.' Frances walked from side to side. Whether it was intended to invoke fear and intimidation into everyone or not, Jake didn't know, but it was working. He could feel his palms becoming sweaty.

'I'll get right on it. I'll send it via JTAC,' DC Edwards said before nodding to the Assistant Commissioner and returning to her desk. JTAC was an acronym for the Joint Terrorism Analysis Centre based within MI5's headquarters in Thames House, and the analysts there processed all intelligence in and out of the country's multiple intelligence agencies.

'DC Edwards,' Frances called back to Matilda, 'when you email them, advise them to change the threat level to critical. It's imperative we prepare for the worst, regardless of whether it is a hoax.'

'It's not a hoax,' Jake said, his mouth speaking faster than his brain had time to communicate its thoughts. After realising he had spoken out of place, he looked around him; all eyes were on him.

'Excuse me?' Frances folded her arms. 'What did you say?'

'It's not a hoax. If it was, then I doubt the person or people responsible could encrypt their email so much that the intelligence experts aren't able to break into it.' Jake's body went cold. He didn't like the attention, and he didn't like the unadulterated internal judgements that were being shot his way by his colleagues. 'Similarly, the generic prankster isn't advanced enough to schedule an email to one person individually and Bcc everyone else into the same email, only for them to receive it later.'

Frances's eyebrows flickered. 'How do you know such a thing occurred?'

Oh, shit, Jake thought. He had dropped himself in it now. Hook, line, and sinker.

'I was the first to receive the email,' Jake admitted.

'And when did you receive it?'

'This morning. About seven-thirty a.m.,' Jake lied.

'And you didn't think to alert anyone? Your erroneous judgement may have cost this city, DC Tanner.' Jake flinched. Frances continued, 'That's right, I know who you are. Your application for the role of DS has been in my inbox for the past few weeks. I hear you did well yesterday at the firearms training, but your actions so far today are causing me to reconsider your progress.'

Jake remained silent. Frances had just dropped the bomb. She had told the entire CTC department he might one day be their senior. And what made this situation worse was now that Tyler knew, and he could feel his partner staring into him.

Frances held Jake in her sights for a beat longer. 'However, I believe you're right, Jake. Chances are this isn't a hoax, and that we have a large-scale operation on our hands. So, here's what's going to happen: I want every one of you at your desks, researching the news, liaising with the airports and train stations, and boat yards on the Thames. Alert everyone to the fact that an attack may be imminent. And if they see anything suspicious, I want the CCTV footage loaded onto the central display immediately. If what we've got in store will be anything like the events of 7/7, I want you all prepared to be working long, difficult hours upstairs on the top floor. It's an open plan for a reason, team.' When Frances clapped her hands and cleared her throat, the meeting was adjourned. Like a football team ready to resume play, everyone around Jake dispersed and returned to their desks.

It was a race against time. Someone needed to find something quick. Especially with the catastrophic events of the 7/7 Underground bombings still feeling painfully fresh all these years on, nobody wanted the same to happen again this time.

Jake sat down at his desk and searched the web for any updates on suspicious activity across the country. His thoughts were plagued by Tyler's silence and how he might be feeling. Would he want to speak to Jake? Or would he want to be left alone? He realised this wasn't primary school anymore, but the same rules applied, no matter the age difference.

After a few minutes of scrupulous internet browsing and searching, Jake had something. It was a breaking news article from the BBC news's homepage. After scanning through it, Jake learned that a train bound to London Luton Airport had come to a complete standstill in the middle of its journey. There had been no reported signalling or technical failures with neither the train nor the railway company. And to make matters worse, nobody seemed able to contact the driver.

Jake's instincts took over. He jumped out of his seat and looked over to Tyler.

'I think I've got something. You coming?'

Tyler looked up at him, his expression unimpressed. 'No. I can do it on my own, thanks.'

'Come on, Ty. Don't be like that. I'll explain it all to you at the end of the day, all right?'

This seemed to appease Tyler, for he lifted himself out of his chair, smiled at Jake and told him to get his arse moving. As the two of them strode over to Frances, who by now was speaking with her two deputies, Jake filled Tyler in on his hypothesis. They stopped by Frances and Jake tapped her on the shoulder.

'Ma'am,' Jake began, 'check this out. A train bound for Luton Airport has come to an immediate halt. Nobody can get in touch with the driver, either.'

Frances shrugged. 'Interesting,' she said, 'but trains stop all the time, Detective. It's one of the many problems with the British rail network.'

Unimpressed, Jake stood his ground. He was just about to open his mouth until Tyler furiously shook his shoulder. Jake shot him a foul look, as if to say, *What now?* In his hand, Tyler held his phone. A BBC news notification illuminated the screen. Jake read the breaking news.

'What about now?' he asked, turning to face Frances, pointing at Tyler's phone. 'The same thing has just happened to two more.'

Chapter Ten

BLACKMAIL

August 1, 12:05

Frances was dumbfounded. She didn't know how to react. Jake observed the minutiae of her face — her eyebrows, her pupils, her nostrils — hoping she would give him an inclination into her thoughts. But none came.

'I'm sorry, Detective,' she said, looking into Jake's eyes. He noticed hers were green, although in the light, they appeared grey. 'The scenarios are circumstantial. If you can provide me with concrete evidence to support your claim, then I will listen to you. Meanwhile, Susanna and Simon will be in charge. Once we know more, then we will act.'

Just like that, Jake's hypothesis was shot down. Protesting his case crossed his mind, but he quickly thought better of it.

He felt a small tug on his sleeve. It was Tyler.

'What?' Jake asked as the two of them headed back to their desks.

'Come with me. I've got an idea.' Tyler turned and wandered around the corner, leaving Jake to chase behind.

They headed along the west side of the building. Smaller offices from other departments were on Jake's left, and on his right was a vast expanse of open space. Down below, at the bottom of the building, was the reception area. It would only take a drunken stumble one night for someone to go over the edge and plummet towards death.

'Ty, where are we going?'

'If *she's* not willing to help us, we need to find someone who is,' Tyler said, maintaining his pace. 'I've got a friend somewhere in this bloody building who might help us out. The only problem is finding her.'

'Who are we looking for?' Jake asked.

'Jennifer. Jennifer Boulder.'

For the next two minutes, Jake and Tyler snaked their way through the fifteenth floor of New Scotland Yard, searching for Tyler's mysterious friend. Jake didn't want to think about how the two of them knew one another; in most cases, the only women Tyler knew were ones he had met at a bar in Soho or in Shoreditch or in some other part of the city where there was an unhealthy consumption of alcohol. And in all cases, they were usually young and naïve to think he would be the one to treat them right. It was the one thing Jake hated about Tyler.

'Hello, Jennifer,' Tyler said, tapping a red-haired woman on the shoulder. Jake didn't know whereabouts he was, but after a quick scan of his surroundings, he concluded he was in a communications department; the number of computers around was triple that of CTC.

It took Jennifer a moment to register that someone was touching her. She jumped in shock, double took, and slapped Tyler around the face. A few heads nearby half-turned in their direction to see what the commotion was, but soon lost interest.

'You've got some fucking nerve coming up here, Tyler. If my husband sees me with you... God help you.' Jennifer looked around cautiously.

'You mean he still doesn't know?' Tyler asked, a smug smile etching its way onto his face.

'Why would I ever tell him?'

'Because it's the decent thing to do.' Tyler rested his arm on her desk. It was the first time Jake had seen Tyler fan his feathers in such a way, and he found it mildly amusing. 'It's a shame he doesn't know, and it would be an even bigger shame if he found out.'

Jennifer's brow furrowed, unimpressed with Tyler's use of blackmail against her. 'What do you want?'

'Your expertise.'

'With what?'

'I need you to show me some CCTV footage, please. The Gatwick Express, Heathrow Express and a train bound for London Luton Airport have all stopped unexpectedly, and we need to see it. Can you do that for us?'

'Give me a second,' Jennifer said, hanging her head low. Arguing with Tyler wouldn't be worth the fight.

She turned to her screen and opened an application. The logo was a dull orange with the image of a camera on it. As she opened it up, hundreds of smaller moving images appeared on the screen. Jennifer moved so quickly, clicked so vigorously, that everything moved in a blur. Within seconds, she had gained access to a 360-degree angle view of the three trains sat motionless in the middle of the railway lines. Every image the cameras displayed were grainy and from a distance.

Jake leaned closer to the screen. 'Can you zoom in on the front of the carriages, please?'

Jennifer did so, and Jake inspected the image. The driver of each train was moving, well and conscious.

'Are you able to communicate with any of the drivers at all?' Jake asked, leaning down to her level. The joints in his knees creaked.

'I can try, but I'm not promising anything.'

For the next few moments, Jake observed the screen for as long as he could until his eyes hurt. It took Jennifer three separate applications and a few phone calls to find out her answer.

'No luck. There's nothing going through. The mobile phone towers in the local areas are showing it as a complete black spot. You'd think, given there are a few hundred people on each train, we'd have something back, but we're not getting anything. All technology on board that train seems to have disappeared.'

'Can you tell us anymore?'

'I wish I could. That's as far as I can go with explanations.'

Jake thanked her before he and Tyler left her. They started their journey back towards CTC, feeling optimistic that they now had concrete evidence to support Jake's claim. It wasn't until they were halfway there that a thought occurred to Jake. It paralysed him, sent a nauseating wave through his mind, and he needed to confirm it before he proceeded any further.

'Stop,' Jake whispered, unaware he had spoken.

'What?' Tyler said on the half turn.

They had come to a stop by the centre of the building, and Jake rested himself against the metal banisters that ran along the floor. He reached for his phone, opened the address book icon on his iPhone, scrolled down until he found the contact named 'M In-Law', and dialled. There was no ring tone — just a brief silence, followed closely by the answering machine. He hung his head low over the banister.

Jake checked his watch and hoped that his suspicions were wrong.

'What's the matter?' Tyler asked, inching closer to Jake's side.

'The trains,' Jake said. Fear and shock and guilt compounded into one overwhelming emotion. A lump grew in his throat. 'Elizabeth's mother, Martha. She goes away today. Flying from Heathrow. She got the train from Paddington.'

There was a moment's pause. Tyler's face contorted as he struggled to piece two and two together.

'You think this has got something to do with the flights or the airports?' Tyler asked, his confusion displayed in his intonation.

'Forget the airports, Tyler. It's the trains. The terrorists have gone after the trains, and Elizabeth's mum is on one.'

Chapter Eleven

BONSAI

July 25, 12:00

It was dark outside. Much darker than it should have been for the time of year. The sky had become overcast with clouds and rain lashed down on the windows, creating tiny rivers that descended the glass. Adil's flat was filled with an even more sinister feel than it already had. The bonsai tree on his window ledge showed signs of suffering in the heat. He had found it online, purchased it, and had it delivered to the flat opposite. No one lived there, and on the delivery instructions he had requested they leave it at his flat if there was no answer at the delivery address. It was the perfect crime; he was just the kind neighbour that nobody would think twice about. Ever since that day, he had treated it with the upmost care, attention, and love.

'Did you know there's a science to growing plants, little brother?' Adil said, hovering over the plant like a protective mother. Next to him was a telescope which he had also bought on the internet, although delivery for it had been trickier to negotiate; it had required fake IDs at the local parcel collection.

His brother put down the blueprints and faced him. 'What are you talking about, Adil?'

'One can learn a lot from the process of maintaining and nurturing a plant back to health.'

'How so?'

'First, it can take time. Lots of time. So much time, in fact, that should you not have patience in the first place, you will be at a much greater disadvantage than most,' Adil explained, keeping his focus on the bonsai tree.

Behind him, Moshat leaned back in the chair and stared at his older brother, obviously curious where this topic of conversation was going.

'Second,' Adil carried on. 'A plant can be manipulated. Right from the start of its life, any plant, even trees, can be manipulated and shifted into the position we want it to adopt. So long as there is leverage.' He turned to Moshat. 'Do you know what that means?'

'That you're going insane?' Moshat said, the sides of his mouth turning upwards.

Adil let out a deep chuckle. 'No. What it means is that, just like a plant, humans can be manipulated in the same way, too — in whichever way we want. Our psyches can be trained and conditioned to do things that are positively rein-forced. They can be told to fear for their lives. They can be told to beg as if on cue. And just like that, they can be exter-minated, with the press of a button or the pull of a trigger. Do you understand?'

Moshat hesitated. 'No... now stop with the riddles and tell me what this has to do with the operation.' Moshat was becoming restless with his brother's unnecessary questions. It was just under a week until the biggest operation of their lives would take place, and there were still a lot of loose ends that needed taking care of.

'Are you feeling nervous, Moshat? Are you experiencing any doubt?'

'About what? The operation?'

Adil nodded.

'No, brother. I am fired up beyond belief. But do not worry — even if a morsel of doubt so much as enters my mind, I will eradicate it with my desire for revenge.'

'No,' Adil said. 'Doubt is good. Fear is good. Uncertainty is even better. It helps keep us grounded. It helps us make sensible and rational decisions. In small quantities, you will be fine. But if you allow it to grow or consume you, then that is when you must consider our reasons for this mission. That is when you must think of the uprising that will follow, so that Mother and Father can live on, not only in our names, but in others', too.'

When they had been growing up, they lived in a council estate owned by the government. The tower reached twenty storeys high. Crime and corruption was rife on the streets and the underpasses that ran through the estate. Every time either of them went anywhere, it was with the other for protection. Their bond strengthened throughout the years; they went to school together, where Adil shone academically and Moshat excelled on the football field. Adil had been the brother who was bullied. Despite being the older of the two, he constantly relied on Moshat to save him from harm's way in the school corridors or on the playground at lunchtime or break.

One day, Adil agreed to stand up for himself to the person responsible for all the taunting and suffering at a park an evening after school. The bully had agreed, and the time was set. There was, however, one condition. Each of the parties could bring someone else with them. At first, the bully had scoffed and launched a verbal assault on Adil. But after some consideration, he agreed.

Adil elected Moshat to join him. And when they arrived at the park, word had spread around the school. Nearly half of the pupils in their respective years attended. It was the fight of the term. And they had won. Together, Adil and his brother had defeated the bullies. No longer would he have to wander along the corridors in fear of being attacked.

Those days were over.

And so, they triumphantly made their way home. They felt euphoric. They could feel the adrenaline surging through their veins.

That was until they returned to a giant ball of flames. Their home — the place they lived, where they slept and ate — was nothing more than a burning wreckage of memories and pain, filling the air with the smell of blackened plastic, wood, metal, and flesh. Fire engine sirens and flashing blue lights illuminated the scene. Great jets of water expelled from their hoses, but it was no use. Many of the inhabitants of the tower block had already perished by the time the emergency services had arrived, Moshat and Adil's mother and father included.

That night, they lost everything. But they never lost each other.

They were sent to a hostel where they were given clean clothes, shelter, and some food. The local community aided the survivors in any way they could, but for weeks and months thereafter, Adil and Moshat, and many others like them, waited for an explanation and an apology from the government. What had gone wrong? By all expert accounts, the fire had been preventable.

Why had a tower building that had been so secure for the past twenty years of its life engulfed in a flurry of flames? How had the safety inspections approved buildings full of faulty wiring and flammable cladding? How had the government failed to keep the building up to safety codes for the sake of all the lives sheltered there? How had contractors been allowed to cut corners and use banned materials for shoddy repairs?

The longer the survivors waited for answers, the more unlikely it was any would come. Only excuses came. The tower tenants were even blamed at one point. Something to do with faulty toasters and kettles. But no real answers were given. No responsibility taken, no apology provided. Not even any real support — they had been abandoned, it seemed. The longer the brothers waited for the justice that never came, the more their anger and resentment towards the government fermented.

From that point onwards, Moshat and Adil sought revenge. Their desires were then fuelled further and radicalised by a man, slim in stature and with a deep scar along his chin, who sheltered them in his home. After their introduction, everything changed.

Moshat and Adil prepared in their small flat with their new mentor. At first, it was the early stages of physical combat training, and then, as they grew older, stronger, and wiser, they were sent off to South American jungles for their first-ever training abroad. There they learnt everything they needed to. It wasn't until nine months ago, in November, after a nine-year hiatus, that they had returned to those camps and continued their training for one final time.

And now here they were, about to bring the government that had failed them, to its knees.

'I have been thinking, Adil. How are we going to make sure the British Transport Police do not interfere with the trains while they are stationary?' Moshat asked, inspecting the Heathrow Express's blueprints.

'I am glad you asked. I have the perfect idea.'

Chapter Twelve

ENTER

August 1, 12:08

Jake and Tyler sprinted across the office, the air-conditioned, sterile air filling their lungs. They came to an abrupt halt inches in front of Susanna and Simon, who were both pacing as they held mobile phones to their ears. Things were getting tenser with each passing minute.

'Where's Frances?' Jake asked, hoping either of them would answer.

Susanna was first to respond. She held a finger to Jake, paused, said something into the phone, and then looked at him. 'She's in her office.'

Jake thanked her, exhaled, and headed to the fifth floor. He had never been to the Assistant Commissioner's office before — in his mind, it had always been like going to the head teacher's office at school whenever he got in trouble — and he was feeling nervous. But more pertinently, he felt afraid, afraid of what would be in store if neither Frances nor anyone else did anything about the trains. How would he explain to Elizabeth that her mother had been taken hostage in a terrorist attack, and no action had been taken to save her?

Jake knocked on the door and let himself in before Frances had a chance to respond.

'What are you doing, Tanner?' Frances said, rising to her feet. The move appeared instinctive, a lightning reaction hardwired into her brain.

'We've got an update on the train situation,' Jake said. He then explained to Frances everything he and Tyler had asked Jennifer Boulder to do for them, and the unsatisfying outcome that came as a result.

As Jake spoke, Frances displayed no emotion. Her facial features remained like stone, unassuming, unrelenting in the way they made Jake feel. He wished he could get inside her head.

'I'm still not convinced, Tanner. And I do not appreciate you barging into my office like this. We have informed Heathrow, Gatwick, and Luton airports, and their respective forces have been multiplied. SFOs and AFOs have been deployed there — they're en route as we speak.'

SFOs were Specialist Firearms Officers, and AFOs were Authorised Firearms Officers. The former group featured individuals who had undergone a twelve-week training course and had experience on a firearms team; the latter group had people authorised to use a firearm and had completed a basic training exercise. In Jake's mind, neither SFOs nor AFOs would be of any use.

'You're wasting your time,' Jake said. He was getting angrier each time this woman undermined him. 'You're wasting *their* time. The destinations of the trains are irrelevant. It's what's on board you need to focus on. This is way beyond any technical fault. There is the potential for thousands of casualties on those trains. We need to treat this as critical. Please, Assistant Commissioner. You need to believe me on this. I will put my job and my promotion and everything else I have worked incredibly hard for over the past ten years on the line.'

Jake breathed heavily. He had just signed his life away. The life he had built for himself and his family was resting in the hands of some potential, unknown terrorists. Even if his suspicions were wrong and nobody within the force disciplined him afterwards, he wouldn't be able to return. Of course, he wouldn't. He would have been responsible for one of the biggest cock-ups in the Met's history. There was no way he could show his face there again.

There was a pause in the room. The question suspended in the air. Jake waited for Frances to answer. They didn't have time for dawdling. They needed to find answers, and quick. Each precious second wasted made Jake increasingly nervous. He checked his wrist. The time on his watch showed 12:10. The trains had been sat there for twenty minutes and nothing had been done.

Frances spoke.

'Come with me.'

Chapter Thirteen

CONTROL

August 1, 12:12

Frances exited her office and walked the short distance to the lift. She remained silent for the duration of the trip. It was the first time Jake had seen her move with such purpose. As soon as the doors opened, she marched to the head of Counter Terrorism Command and stood with her back against the television screens, the light casting a prolific silhouette of her. She clapped her hands. It wasn't a loud clap — in fact, Jake supposed either Ellie or Maisie could have produced a louder sound — but it was enough to garner everyone's attention.

Within seconds, everyone in Counter Terrorism Command had surrounded Jake, Tyler, Frances, Susanna, and Simon.

'Listen up, team,' Frances began, her voice deep and clear, an air of authority resounded. 'Detective Tanner has brought some new information to light, and we are treating the situation with the three trains as the suspected act of terrorism. I want our SFOs pulled away from their destinations and redirected to their new ones. This is of the highest priority.'

The way she spoke was so clinical, so well-rehearsed and so strategic. These were the big leagues and Jake couldn't help but think one day he'd like a taste of it.

'Familiarise yourselves with the procedures. We can't allow for any mistakes or delays in our processes.'

Before Frances could continue, Jake interrupted. He wanted to take charge. He wanted to prove himself. He wanted to make sure everything was in place so that his mother-in-law stood the best chance of being rescued.

'We need to find out who is aboard those trains. That means we need the ticket and purchase information for everyone who bought a ticket for these specific times, and anyone who may have bought one for an earlier departure. I would suggest a fifteen-minute boundary either side. You never know, someone may have been running late or early and caught these specific ones to throw us off the scent.' Jake was taking command, and he liked it. He felt invigorated, as if he had the entire attention of everybody in the room, and they would do as he said. No matter what.

'Get in contact with the banks, the train companies — anyone — and find out that information. Once we've got that, we need to match it with anyone known in either the PNC or any other databases we have available. Someone will also need to oversee setting up a new index on HOLMES where we can all dip into the information we need at any point. Now, we can't see inside because everything is steamed up, so we must engage no one until we have clear visuals. We do not know who, or how many people we are dealing with.'

The PNC was the Police National Computer, and it stored the names and data of anyone who had previously been convicted of a crime in Her Majesty's country. HOLMES was the acronym for Home Office Large Major Enquiry Systems, where the indexing of all major crimes was in one place to allow different departments easy access to relevant information. The HOLMES system also enabled investigators to notice patterns and inconsistencies with evidence. It would be helpful for Counter Terrorism Command to keep a record of everything there because, as much as he hated to admit it to himself, Jake believed there would be an incredibly large investigation on their hands.

The atmosphere in the room filled with a deafening silence. The hum from the overhead fans and the odd rustle of people shifting the weight of their body from one foot to the other was the only thing he could hear.

Frances cleared her throat behind him.

'Yes. Thank you for that, Detective,' she said, stepping to his side. 'I also want some of you to scour the CCTV footage of the train platforms at the three stations — Paddington, Victoria, and St. Pancras International. Develop profiles for everyone on board, learn their habits, pick out anomalies. The passengers on those trains could be stuck for a while. We don't know what, or if, there are any demands. So, we need to prepare for any eventuality.'

'Precisely,' Jake said, finding the words coming out uncontrollably. He was on a roll and he didn't care whose toes he stepped on. Mamadou's absence had given him an opportunity to excel. 'Which leads me to another point. We also don't know *what* is on board those trains. For all we know, there could be nothing. But there could also be dozens of kilograms' worth of explosives. Until we can determine what we are dealing with, we are under no circumstances to interfere with any of the trains — there may be unprecedented amounts of collateral damage. Remember your training, guys. And remember, we need to check off everything on the Rainbow List.'

The Rainbow List was the list of official counter terrorist tactical procedures. Each colour of the rainbow referred to different tactical options.

'Red,' Jake reeled off from memory; he had been studying it recently in his exams. 'Motorways. Monitor the motorways. Engage auto number plate recognition teams on the outskirts of the city. If any names flag up after our searches and they're making a dash for it out of the city, apprehend them. Also, have armed mobile vehicles on standby around the city, should they be needed.

'Orange — bomb squad. DC Park, I want members of the bomb squad situated no more than a mile down the tracks of each of the trains. If there are any suspect packages on the underside of the carriages, inform them and set them to work. We don't want our men and women out there to be spotted. Which also means — DC Park, you'll be in charge of railways. Speak with the British Transport Police and the rail networks. Get them to shut down the lines and platforms. Make sure no other trains go near or past our targets. Search the railway lines and platforms for any suspicious packages or something that looks out of place.

'Light blue — aviation. DC Driscoll, disengage the SFOs at the major London airports, and increase the presence of our ACPOs and any other personnel we have nearby. Presence is key here, team. We don't want to alert the city that there may be a terrorist attack, but we also don't want the terrorists to think we're complacent. We want to create a preventive deterrent. Our presence will be the greatest tool in our box for this, along with the public's eyes and ears.' Jake swallowed before continuing. He looked out upon the vacant, expressionless, and dumbfounded faces in front of him. 'Now, does anyone have any questions?'

Jake was met with absolute silence.

'Then get to it!'

At once, the crowd dispersed like a glass of water shattering onto the ground, some disappearing off into the distance and around the corner of a wall, while some sat down at their desks and typed on their keyboards. He allowed himself a smile. He had just done what he had seen Mamadou do multiple times before. What made him feel even better about himself was that he had inspired everyone to get down to it and work.

'Nicely done, Detective,' Frances said beside him. Her expression belied any emotion portrayed in her voice. 'I hope you haven't set a precedent. We can't have everyone around here thinking they can take charge.'

'How did I do? Did I miss anything out?' Jake asked, feeling a little like an excitable school child, desiring praise for a school project they had spent months completing.

'Not that I can think of. But I'm sure there will be something that pops up along the way. Until then, I want you and DC Stuart to —'

'We need a specialist,' Jake interrupted.

'Excuse me, Detective Tanner? You are becoming increasingly hysterical.'

'We need a train expert. Someone who knows the industry inside and out. Someone who can advise us on the best way to proceed. How we can go about regaining control of the trains and saving everyone on board. That kind of specialist will be vital to the operation over the next few hours.'

Frances returned Jake's eager, beaming eyes with a blunt, cold expression. She turned her head, looked behind Jake, and raised her eyebrows. Simon was there behind him, and with a nod he confirmed he would start on it. He would find someone suitable.

'They need to be here in five minutes. Find the best person you can,' Frances said. She turned her attention back to Jake. She looked between him and Tyler. Jake could sense something bad was about to happen. 'As for you two,' she began. Turning her back to Jake, she scanned the office before her, found who she was searching for and rushed over to them. A few seconds later she returned with a man by her side. Judging from the man's stature alone, Jake deduced he was ex-military. The man walked perfectly — his posture resembled that of a store mannequin. As the man's wide shoulders, rugged features, and muscly neck came closer into view, Jake knew who it was straightaway. DC Matthews — the very man he was pitting against in his run for promotion.

'Jake,' Frances said, as she stopped by his feet, 'Luke will stay with you wherever you and Tyler go. He'll be acting as an extra man, if you like. Understand?'

'What is this, fucking babysitting duty?' Tyler said dryly, stepping to Jake's side. His voice was filled with disdain. If there was one thing Tyler liked least of all, it was being told what to do by someone he neither knew nor liked.

'DC Matthews is supervising.'

'We don't need supervising. We've both been in this job long enough to know what we're doing,' Jake said quietly, avoiding Luke's amused grin.

'Are you sure, Detective? You've already shown a

complete lack of regard to following orders and protocols, so I am left with little choice. My word is final, and there is nothing you two can do about it.'

Theodor Rosenberg sat outside the coffee shop on the corner of Leicester Square. It was buzzing with the excitement and heat of summer in one of the greatest cities in the world. Bodies bounced in and out of the front doors, each customer holding a takeaway cup. Pedestrians and workers and tourists sauntered past him, in their own worlds, enjoying their lunch breaks at their own pace. It was hot outside, and the sky was an intense, almost incandescent blue. The smell of coffee, magnified by the heat, wafted through the entrance to the shop and into his nostrils as the waitress brought him his drink.

She placed it down in front of him and he thanked her. He was having a cappuccino, freshly made with a large marshmallow on top. He didn't remember ordering one with a marshmallow, but he admired the gesture. Opposite him was his daughter; they were here for their annual catch up. Neither of them celebrated Christmas or birthdays, so it was the only time they saw one another. Living in separate ends of the country had made it difficult for them to meet frequently. He hated how it was, but they had been doing it for so long, he scarcely believed he would like it any other way. Sometimes habits were best left as they were.

'So, how is work?' Theodor's daughter asked.

'I retired almost two years ago, Alison.' Theodor smiled at her as he took a sip of his drink.

Alison groaned. 'Come on. You know what I mean! You were never one to call your projects "hobbies", anyway.'

'Fair enough. I've been keeping in touch with some guys I used to work with. And I've been helping at the local station near my new house. It's not too far from a nearby factory and museum. Now and then I go in there just to make sure everything is factually correct,' Theodor explained.

'Heavens, Dad. You still can't keep away from the train yard?'

'Working with trains has been my entire life,' Theodor said, taking another sip from his cup. In the distance, sirens echoed.

'Tell me about it. You spent more time there than you did at home.'

'Come, now,' Theodor said, feeling hurt and upset by his daughter's remark. 'That's not fair. You know I spent all of that time working so I could provide for you and Mum.'

The sound of sirens grew louder.

Alison said nothing. She kept her gaze fixed on Theodor and took a sip of her latte. Next to them, two unmarked BMW X5s skidded to a halt. Out stepped two men in suits and two Police Constables, the sun bouncing off their fluorescent strips.

'Mr. Theodor Rosenberg?' one man said. His voice was deep, and he had a Kentish accent. Proper. Pronounced.

Theodor's eyes darted between the four men now towering over him. He swallowed hard, feeling the skin on his arms crawl and his heart palpitate.

He nodded slowly.

'My name is Deputy Assistant Commissioner Simon Ashdown of the Metropolitan Police. I need you to come with us. You're not under arrest. It's a matter of national security.'

It hadn't been ten minutes since he and his daughter

had sat down, and already their short time with one another had been brought to an abrupt end. Before the door closed on his face, removing the world from view, he gave one last look at Alison's shocked expression, wondering when, and if, he would be able to see her next.

Chapter Fourteen

CLASSIFIED

August 1, 12:24

The first thing Jake noticed about the man was his smell. It wasn't an overwhelming smell of aftershave or light deodorant. Instead, it was the pungent smell of body odour and general uncleanliness.

There was a particular person, and word, that came to Jake's mind when he met Theodor: homeless.

Jake was kind enough not to say anything, and, as they shook hands, he felt the old wrinkled skin and moving tendons crush under his. The man's skin and underneath of his fingernails was stained with the indelible colour of soot and dirt. Jake looked him up and down and noted what he was wearing. Theodor Rosenberg wore horn-rimmed glasses, and a fedora hat. He removed the hat, revealing a balding patch in the middle of his skull. A great, beige duffel coat covered up most of what he was wearing beneath, but Jake was just able to make out a checked shirt with blue chinos breaking free from the bottom. Hanging from his waist was a battered and worn satchel with the image of a train stitched onto the front. The colouring of the graphic had faded, and Jake could just make out it was the front carriage of a steam engine.

'Thanks for agreeing to meet us on such short notice,' Jake started. 'I'm Detective Constable Jake Tanner, and this is my colleague, DC Tyler Stuart.' Jake introduced Theodor to Frances and made a point of not introducing DC Matthews.

'Nice to meet you,' Theodor said, bowing his head to everyone in front of him. There was a slight nasally twinge to his voice. Jake couldn't put his finger on it, but there was something about the man that helped him relax. 'I'm judging by the escort I received here that you need my help. Your colleagues in the car weren't forthcoming with information.'

A smile flickered on Frances's face. 'Your concerns are understandable, sir. However, we do not have a lot of time.'

In fact, we might not have any time. None of us know how long we had to begin with, Jake thought.

Frances held her hand in the air and gesticulated towards the debriefing room. 'Shall we?'

Theodor nodded. Frances led the way and the two of them were accompanied by Tyler, Jake, Luke, Simon and Susanna. It was a full house. The only person they were missing now was Mamadou. Both Theodor and Frances took a seat while all the other senior officers stood. Jake rested his hands on the back of a chair.

'We have a potential terrorist hostage situation developing on the outskirts of the city,' Frances began. 'And we have called you in because you're considered the best in your field of expertise. Our colleagues found you to be the most renowned train enthusiast in the country. We need advice on the technicalities associated with the attack.'

'What are we dealing with?' Theodor asked. He sat in his chair with his back upright, and his fingers laced themselves over one another in his lap.

Frances explained the situation to Theodor, keeping out any of the classified information, which was little at the moment. In fact, Jake scarcely believed there was anything confidential about any of it. They didn't have any names of anyone on board; they didn't have any names of potential suspects; they didn't even know what kind of threat would be unleashed on the city over the next few hours.

'Excuse my French,' Theodor said after Frances had finished explaining herself, 'but it sounds like we're up shit creek.'

'Indeed.'

'But how exactly can I help?'

'We need to work out what's halting communication with the train,' Jake said, looking at Tyler, as if it were just those two against the rest of them. 'How is it possible that nobody can communicate with any of these trains?'

'It's not.'

'What do you mean?'

'In the forty-plus years I've been working with them, never have I experienced a situation like this. Sure, trains have broken down in the middle of their journey in the past, but we've always been able to contact them one way or another. There's always a backup system, like a radio or something they can use to communicate with someone back at mission control. What this is... this is something different. Something I've never seen,' Theodor said.

Jake considered this for a moment, his mind whirring with possibilities and questions.

'So, something else is happening. Something outside the driver's control?' Jake thought of one very daunting explanation for everything that was going on.

Theodor nodded.

Turning to Frances, Jake asked, 'Is it possible that whoever is behind this has set off some sort of electromagnetic pulse that's disarmed and disabled all Comms on those trains? It would explain the black hole around the mobile phone antennas. Does something like that exist?'

'It would have to be a very sophisticated piece of technology for it to only be affecting the immediate area surrounding those trains,' Frances said. 'The CCTV feed from the line cameras is still working.'

Frances pointed out of the office window behind her as if to illustrate her point. Through the panels, Jake and everyone else in the room saw the wall of screens at the head of the room. The top left quadrant of the wall was populated with three separate images of their targets.

'Do you know of anything that's capable of such a thing?' Jake asked again.

'Yes,' Frances said. 'It's classified.'

'I don't give a fuck if it's classified. If you don't want our help then all you have to do is say, because there's not a lot Tyler, I, or anyone else can do when we're being kept in the dark. So, you either tell us and we do this properly, or all those people on the train's blood is on your hands. What will it be?' Jake marched over to the woman. Simon and Luke stepped in as a barrier before Jake could get too close.

'Fine,' Frances began, rising out of her seat. 'But let's get one thing straight: do not address me like that ever again. As much as I need you on this case, I am still your superior. Understood?' Jake glowered at her, but he nodded.

'Well, then. There is such a device out there. It is a prototype, thought to have been the only one in existence.'

'What can it do?'

'It works similar to the way an EMP works, like you said,
but it's different, much more sophisticated. At the flick of a
button, there is a short burst of electromagnetic radiation
creating a large magnetic field which disrupts everything in
its radius. That means no communication, no movement,
nothing.'

'What's different about it?'

'The device is constantly emitting the radiation. So long
as the switch is engaged, there will be no communication in
or out of that radius. But it can be switched off, just like
that. Considering the time those trains have been stationed
there, the prototype I'm aware of would have expired by
now, but it hasn't. It's as if there's a permanent black out.
Whoever is controlling this thing is doing so remotely, which
means they must be disengaging the device at will, so they
can communicate with those inside the trains for only a
moment, and then re-engaging it as soon as they are done.'

'Jesus,' Jake said. The people behind this were leagues
ahead of them, more than six steps at a time, and Jake got
the feeling it would only get worse. 'And what about the
prototype? Where is it now?'

'I don't know. The last I heard it was back with the
Americans,' Frances said, lowering her voice and stepping
forward to the windows. 'I believed it was the only one in
existence, the only one that could ever and would ever exist.
I didn't expect there to be more functioning devices such as
this to be in the city of London. Now, Detective Tanner, if
you'll excuse me.' Frances walked away, obviously trying to
calm herself down as she went.

The gravity of the situation struck Jake like a match on

a box, his fears and anxieties bursting into flames. *Dear God.* Had he really yelled at the Assistant Commissioner moments ago? He looked around the office. Everybody was looking at one another, but he felt cocooned, as if all eyes were on him. Jake's heart rate increased. His breathing increased. His alertness increased. His hands became clammy, and he felt faint.

For the first time in a long time, as he realised the potential danger Elizabeth's mother and the hundreds of other passengers stranded were in, he felt a panic attack coming. He had experienced them repeatedly after he had been stranded on a mountain, alone and fearing for his life, during a university ski holiday. They had abated in the intervening years, and they had been less frequent in the past twenty months. His line of work was the biggest trigger, living life on the front line in the battle against terrorism. It was his duty to keep his city safe, and he wasn't going to let an anxiety attack hinder him.

'Are you OK, Detective Tanner?' Theo asked.

'What?' Jake asked, suddenly aware of where he was. 'What? Yeah, I'm fine.' The last thing he wanted was to admit he was incapable of doing his job. 'We need to save these people, get them off those trains before something happens to them.'

'There have been no demands made yet, so we have time,' Luke said, trying to engage in the discussion and defuse the tension.

Just then, the office outside the debrief room was filled with a sudden screeching sound, the noise of a thousand bells and alarms sounding all at once. Jake darted to the door, thrashed it open, and strode over to the top of the room, shielding his ears as he ran. After a few deafening seconds, the noise ceased. Nobody knew where the noise came from. Nobody knew what it meant. Jake looked from Tyler to Frances, then from Frances to Theodor.

What the fuck was that? Jake thought.

Without warning, the screens in front of him turned black. All images of the trains had disappeared. Jake stood rooted to the spot, staring at the wall of darkness. An image of a yellow smiley face appeared. It wore sunglasses and had a joint in its mouth, smoke ejecting from the tip. Dangling from the emoji's neck, was the international symbol for peace.

'What is going on?' Jake whispered to himself.

Then his phone rang in his pocket. He could feel the vibration against his chest. He fingered it out and looked at it. There was no recognisable number. No caller ID. *Who the fuck is this?*

'Hello?' he answered.

As soon as he spoke, the line went dead. He looked at his phone in disbelief and then at everyone else.

Almost as if it had been rehearsed a thousand times, all the phones in the office rang. The noise echoed throughout the room as the phones harmonised and synchronised into one loud ring tone.

'How the —?' began Frances. 'Nobody should be able to ring here unless they're internal. I demand to know what is going on!'

Then, just as quickly as it had begun, the ringing stopped. A moment of tense silence followed. As Jake stood there, holding his phone, the screen lit up and rang again. It was the same caller. He quieted everyone around him by gesticulating at them with his arms. The caller was still ringing. There was no doubt in Jake's mind who the person on the other end was. It was the person responsible. There was no way it could have been a coincidence. *Clever*, Jake thought. It was a matter of playing games. The person responsible wanted to let everyone in CTC know they were in charge and that they would be the one to speak first, to place their cards on the table first.

Make them think they've got you where they want you. It'll make that much sweeter when they slip up.

The phone went dead.

'What are you doing, Tanner?' Frances whispered loudly.

Jake mouthed the words, *They'll call back.*

Right on cue, the familiar UNKNOWN NUMBER appeared on his screen, and he answered.

For a while there was silence, and Jake listened intently, waiting for any signs of life on the other end. Waiting for them to make the first move. After thirty seconds, Jake could hear breathing in his ear.

'Good afternoon, Detective Tanner.'

Chapter Fifteen

OBSERVATION

August 1, 12:28

The inside of the Heathrow Express was hot and chaotic. Moshat's scalp itched and irritated underneath his hat. Debris from the emergency stop was everywhere, and nobody had bothered to clean it. He sat next to the window in a four-seat section of the train. A table rested in the middle between him and his fellow passengers. Beside him was a single mother nursing a screaming child; immediately opposite him was an elderly woman whom he recognised instantly. Moshat ignored the elderly gentleman beside her. There was no relation, therefore no need to worry.

Over thirty minutes had passed since the Heathrow Express had come to a complete standstill. The initial reaction had been one of anger and frustration; everyone on board was busy and had somewhere to get to. Passengers flew out of their seats and across the coach. Luggage had dislodged from their compartments and the contents scattered across the floor. The only damage he had suffered was a bruised rib and abdomen. He had planned to sit facing in the direction of travel and, with a constant eye on the time, had expected the sudden stop. But since Adil's introduction on the overhead communications system, anger turned to fear and frustration to paranoia inside the Heathrow Express.

Everything was going according to plan. Everything had happened as it should.

But now, as he sat there staring at the woman opposite, those around him grated on his nerves. Despite Adil's warnings, some people insisted upon checking their mobile phones for a signal, incessantly asking questions.

'Is anyone's phone working at all?' one asked. Moshat paid no attention to who spoke.

'No, we've just been told nothing works, you idiot,' a woman from the other side of the carriage responded, shutting the person down.

'I think it's a bluff,' said a defiant teenage girl in the chair opposite Moshat. 'Why don't we try to break out of here?'

'Does anyone have something we can break open the window with?' asked a man who dressed as though he were still stuck in the sixties with a turtle neck and a blazer.

They weren't listening. They weren't paying attention to Adil's rules. They were being stupid, and would each be responsible for everyone's death. There was only so much idiocy Moshat could tolerate before he snapped and revealed to them the weapon in his bag. They would have forced him to threaten everyone's safety. But Moshat knew that would not happen. He was in this for the long haul, and he would have to wait.

He hugged his backpack closer to his chest, feeling the

gun at the bottom pressed against him. It was hard and discernible, like an erection in a pair of jogging bottoms.

As he sat there, continuing to stare at the elderly woman, his mind wandered into its imagination. He thought of the ways he could harm her, maim her. But not too much; Moshat just wanted to hurt her, not kill her. At least, not yet. He wanted to make sure DC Jake Tanner's mother-in-law was in his safe, capable hands. Martha Clarke would be his leverage. Both he and Adil had planned this specifically. They had known she would be on this particular train, at this particular time on this particular day because they had fabricated the reason she was on board. A few months ago, Moshat and Adil had sent Martha Clarke a notification in the post, telling her she had won a prize trip abroad to the south of France, all expenses paid. They had even created their own website and branding using the funding they received from South America to make the entire thing look legitimate. And a few days later, Adil and Moshat received a response, confirming she would be interested. They had taken care of the rest and now here they were, sat opposite one another.

It's funny how the little coincidences make us feel, Moshat thought to himself. It was important he kept a close eye on her and everyone else around the cabin. He only wanted to use his gun as a last resort. If the passengers on board threatened the efficiency of his operation, then he would have no choice.

For now, though, he would sit and observe. He had six hours to kill. He tore his gaze from Martha, who was preoccupied with the condensation climbing higher and higher up the window, and instead observed the full range of human emotions playing out in front of him.

He and Adil had spent weeks analysing the reactions to

terror, fantasising about the way everyone inside would react. And now that the time was finally here, he would enjoy it.

There was denial.

There was defiance.

There was bravery.

There was fear.

There was anger.

There was hysterics.

And finally — and most importantly — there was excitement.

What surprised Moshat most was that there was no unity in the face of adversity.

It reminded Moshat of his parents, and how, after their horrific death, there had been no unity between the government and the community. There had been no government-provided aid in the form of shelter, compensation, food, or water. Instead, they had been reliant on the community coming together, assisting them. And it was important everyone else in the world knew that — knew that there was pain and suffering every day and nobody was concerned enough to do anything about it. Soon, their message would be heard, and their hurt and pain would be recompensed. Moshat pulled out his burn phone from his pocket and inspected the time. It was 12:28, and if everything had gone to plan, then it would be around about this time Adil made the call to the great Jake Tanner of the Metropolitan's Counter Terrorism Command.

Chapter Sixteen

GAMES

August 1, 12:30

'Who is this?' Jake asked into the phone, his skin crawling with fear.

'Good afternoon, Detective Tanner, and congratulations! It's your lucky day!' said the voice on the other line. The speaker used a device that masked their identity. What came out was a deep, robotic, and monotone voice, reminding Jake of something he had seen in a horror movie once. 'You've been hand-selected to take part in today's game. Lives depend on you.'

Jake was going to speak but then thought better of it.

The voice continued, 'All you have to do is follow the yellow brick road of riddles and clues I give you, and then you might just find yourself in with a chance of saving some lives today, Jake.' The voice paused, as if waiting for Jake to respond. Jake didn't want to give him the satisfaction; he didn't like where this was going. 'But beware, if you answer a question wrong or put a foot out of line, Willy Wonka and his band of merry Oompa Loompas will wait on the other side with explosives. And they won't be afraid to pull the trigger. So, what do you say, Jake? Feeling up to it?'

The voice had finished speaking and Jake stood perplexed, his mind trying to calculate and infer everything he had been told. Who was this? Why had they chosen him? And what the fuck was with all the children's references? He didn't know, but in his ear, he could still hear breathing, multiplying the shivers that ran across the surface of his skin.

'Who are you?' was all he could think to say.

'I, Detective Tanner, am Willy Wonka, Tyler Durden, and the Joker, all rolled into one big ball of fun! I'm the voice inside your head that keeps you awake at night. I am the one who watches you sleep next to your wife. I am the one who knows your next moves before you even do.' The person raised his voice. 'But who are you, Detective? Who is the *real* Jake Tanner? The man with the badge? Is he as good as he makes himself out to be on his detective sergeant application form? Can he be as loyal as he leads himself to believe if he can't even tell his wife the truth?'

What the fuck? Jake froze. Images of Elizabeth, Ellie, and Maisie flashed into his mind. How did they know about his application, and the fact he had kept it a secret from Elizabeth? The thought chilled him to his core.

'What have you done with them?' Jake asked, his voice weak, almost like a whisper. He swallowed and cleared his throat.

'Nothing. *Yet.*'

Jake lost his temper. His family had been threatened and the only thing he saw now was red. 'Why don't you cut the shit and tell me what it is you want, what that email meant and how you hacked into our computer systems?'

'You're a brazen soul, aren't you? What were the words DCI Hughes said in his unofficial report about you when he suggested you for aggrandisement? Oh, yes, now I remember: "DC Tanner is a shining talent in the police force, with balls of steel."'

This was serious. Employee reviews were always kept internal, without the contents ever going as far as the person for whom they were written. Sometimes, it was classified information.

'How did you get access to that?' Jake asked, holding his breath.

'I am a man of many abilities, Tanner. I know how to do things way beyond your wildest imagination.'

It's a vanity game, then, Jake thought, *proving yourself to be more superior than the rest of us. Proving yourself to be better than the government and everyone who works for it. Superiority complex, seeking revenge, or both?*

'What do you want?'

'I want you to accept the challenge, and then I'll tell you the next steps of the process.'

'What do I have to do?'

'You're supposed to do as you're told and find these things out for *yourself*. You must rely on your intuition and hope it leads you down the right path.'

Jake's temper had reached the end of its tether. 'Tell me what you've done to the trains? What will happen to those people? What are your demands?'

'Easy, boy. Easy. Don't get too ahead of yourself, otherwise you'll burn out too quickly. We'll be spending a lot of time together, and that's the last thing we want. But what I can tell you, Detective, is that on those trains there are exactly thirty kilograms of explosives each, and there is a timer counting down from six hours. There are five hours, fifteen minutes, and forty-six seconds remaining. Forty-five. Forty-four. Forty-three. At the end of the six hours, sixty of those kilograms will explode, sending everyone and everything into oblivion.'

Jake said nothing, his brain now suddenly couldn't communicate to his mouth a response. He removed the phone from his ear, looked out around him to Tyler, Simon, Frances, and then back to Tyler, swallowed, before returning the phone to his ear. 'I'll do it.'

Those three words hurt him to say. But not as much as what was about to come.

The voice on the other end exclaimed their joy and, in the background, Jake could hear classical music. Then, the same music blared from every computer station in the office. Confusion and expletives erupted from those around him, making it difficult for Jake to focus on the voice speaking into his ear.

'I'm so glad you agreed, Jake. I was hoping you would. You're their *only* hope. I knew you would be the best man for the job.'

How had they chosen him? How had they known he was the man for the job? Had they been monitoring him? Or was it all a bluff? Jake didn't know, but either way, he wouldn't risk waiting to find out. He needed to act.

'On one condition,' Jake said, feeling the muscles in his body tense with anger. The pinks of his knuckles whitened. 'Give me your word that no harm will come to any of those passengers.'

The voice chuckled. 'How naïve you are thinking you can save everyone. I regret to inform you that that is not how this will work.'

'How *is* this going to work?'

'If you and everyone else on your team follow my

instructions and do as I tell you. Order the firearms squad to stand down at each of the three locations. Nobody is allowed within a two-hundred metre distance. Failure to comply will result in the closest train going *boom*.' The voice on the other end paused. 'Also, one million British sterling pounds. Cash. Information about the drop will be disclosed later. For this you have less than four hours.'

Jake made a mental note of the terrorist's demands.

'Fine,' Jake said.

'Fantastic, Detective. Elizabeth and the girls will be so proud of you. Be at North Acton train station in thirty minutes. Come alone, or you will fail, and innocent people will be killed. Remember Jake, you have less than six hours until things go *boom*.'

The voice on the other end hung up. As soon as the line went dead, all the computer and television screens in the office switched back on. Jake stood there with his mouth agape and his lungs faltering. Within seconds of removing the phone from his ear, he was bombarded with questions from every angle. Tyler, Simon, Susanna, Frances, Matthews, Theodor — they all suffocated him with their presence. Jake was in shock. He didn't know what to do. Without warning, the room spun, his vision became blurry, and his head ached with a numbing sensation that reminded him of eating cold ice cream.

'Jake, are you all right, pal?' Tyler asked, placing his arms around Jake's shoulders.

'I need to go. North Acton. Clues. Decoy.'

'Will someone get him a motherfucking glass of water?' Tyler bellowed next to him. His friend's vernacular brought a small smile to his face.

A few seconds later, Simon returned with a plastic cup in his hand and passed it to Jake. Jake took a long sip and, once satisfied, snapped his consciousness back into action. As soon as he felt better, he explained to Frances and everyone else in the room everything the terrorist had just told him, delegating the tasks around the room.

'Why North Acton?' Simon asked.

'I don't know.'

'Do you think there may be a threat to the Underground?'

'I don't know,' Jake said. He turned to Frances. 'But you need to increase police presence there without causing mass panic. Speak to the London Underground Network Operations Centre. Inform them of what is happening, but whatever you do, do not get Transport for London to issue an amber code warning.'

Frances nodded in affirmation. She understood what she needed to do. Before he set off towards the exit, Jake ordered Susanna to organise a patrol to his house.

'He threatened my wife and kids. Make sure they're safe. Report back as soon as you know.' Jake turned to Frances. 'They want one million in cash in less than four hours. Exact location unknown.'

'Where the fuck are we going to get one million quid from?' Tyler asked, becoming hysterical.

'I don't care,' Jake said. 'I need to go. Tyler, leave that up to them. You're coming with me. We don't have much time.'

Deep down Jake knew he was wrong. They had no time. On a good day, North Acton train station was a forty-minute drive away. And with the height of summer bearing down on the streets, it was sure to be made fifty times harder.

If he were to stand any chance of getting there on time, he would have to leave now.

'Not so fast!' Frances said, her voice reverberating off the walls. 'You will need Detective Matthews with you.'

Jake rolled his eyes. 'With all due respect, I don't have time for this bullshit. Matthews is just another spare body, surplus to requirements. We don't know what's waiting down there for us, and I'd rather not risk his life as well as ours.'

A moment of compassion came over him. As much as he didn't like Matthews babysitting them, he was still a human being with good intentions. In stressful times such as this, Jake wanted to stay true to his beliefs.

'It's fine,' Luke said, straightening himself. 'I'll assemble an entourage for you. Meet me down at the car in two minutes.' With that, Matthews left the room, already dialling a number on his phone.

Just another day in the office. Saying nothing more, Jake advanced to the exit. He was halfway across the floor when he heard a voice from behind him.

'Detective Tanner!' It was Frances. She had just been on her Brent phone, a secure telephone that encrypted the data and voice messages of both users. Jake stopped on the half turn and faced the Assistant Commissioner.

'Yes, ma'am?'

'That was the Home Secretary. I've got a COBRA meeting in five minutes. I'll try to keep them off your back for as long as possible.'

COBRA was the government's crisis committee, where all the most influential politicians, military and intelligence agencies and any other governmental departments met to discuss matters of emergency. They were the country's top decision makers, and they met during the first hour and a half of an emergency. First devised during the 1970s, its meeting rooms were situated somewhere within Whitehall, hidden underground, with fast and easy admission to Downing Street and the Cabinet Office. The acronym stood for Cabinet Office Briefing Room A.

Jake said nothing. Neither of them needed to; he and Frances both shared an unspoken form of agreement. Instead, they nodded at one another.

Jake checked his watch and already three minutes had passed since his phone call with the Joker. Time was running out, and so were his chances of arriving on time. He signalled to Tyler and together they left the office.

By the time he reached the car, five minutes had gone.

He would have to break the law on many levels.

But it didn't matter.

He was the law.

Mamadou was the only person in the waiting room. He had just got off the phone with DC Jake Tanner. Jake had informed Mamadou of everything that had been going on.

'Jesus fucking Christ,' Mamadou said. 'This is not good at all. Keep on top of it, Jake. You're doing a good job.'

'Cheers, boss,' Jake said. The noise of a car door closing sounded in Mamadou's ear. 'How's your mum doing?'

'I don't know. Nobody will tell me anything. As soon as I know, I'll assess the situation before I decide what to do next.'

Before Mamadou could continue, a person dressed in blue scrubs rounded the corner and entered the waiting room. Mamadou told Jake he needed to go and hung up the phone.

'How is she?' Mamadou asked, rising to his feet.

The doctor stopped a foot in front of him. She was

small, wore her hair in a net, and held her hands in her pockets.

'Please, Mr. Kuhoba. Take a seat.'

Mamadou did as instructed. The worst situations ran through his head, plaguing his thoughts and his ability to think comprehensively.

'Your mother had a heart attack. It seems the cancer has spread to her chest, and her body is shutting down. She experienced a lot of internal bleeding and we operated on her to get that under control. We're running more tests on her now. She's unconscious and under observation.'

'How long?' Mamadou asked. He leaned forward, resting his elbows on his knees and his head in his hands. He fought hard to keep back the tears.

'You'll be able to see her in an —'

'No,' Mamadou interrupted. 'How long do you give her?'

The doctor hesitated before responding.

'A few hours, at most.'

Chapter Seventeen

LIGHTS

August 1, 12:37

The flat was stifling in the summer heat. Adil didn't so much mind the sun as he did the unbearable humidity that always came with it. Months' worth of training in the sweltering Bolivian jungle had solidified this disgust in him.

With a deep and heavy sigh, he went into the bathroom and opened the only window he deemed safe to open. There would be no prying eyes in there. Not even in one of the most watched cities in the world.

Almost straightaway, he could feel the cooler air rush in and surround his feet as it entered. The taste of the air, however, was acrid — a plethora of chemicals, emissions, and other dirty poisons that clung to the back of his throat and nostrils. Adil coughed. He had always hated the London air; it reminded him of why he loved being back at Cambridge University where the atmosphere was cleaner and the pace of life much more relaxed. There he could develop and nurture his skills in the safety of his flat in the centre of town.

Adil wandered back into the living room and changed the stereo. Beethoven's *Fifth* had been playing. Five clicks of the skip button later, he landed on one of his favourites: *Adagio for Strings.* Not the Tiesto remix, but the original. He couldn't tolerate the hippy dance remix bullshit the Dutch DJ had done to Samuel Barber's masterpiece. He hated how classical music could be so defaced and mutilated, treated as if it were some sort of art that would just come and go.

He sat back down at his desk, reached beneath him on the floor, and opened his laptop. It was a big industrial-sized laptop normally used by the military. It could withstand a ten-storey plummet. It had been given to him as a graduation gift after he had completed his training, and he had loved it, using it wherever he went. He was inseparable from his laptop, and he treated it as if it were the child he knew he would never have. What he loved most about it was that, from anywhere in the world, he could use it without his actions being traced. He was incognito — an invisible force to be reckoned with. He was the wind that destroyed homes and buildings during a storm. He was the freezing, bitter chill in the night that murdered the weak. He was the drop of rain that, when combined with billions of others, swept through villages in a devastating flood.

He was the new face of terrorism, and everyone in the world would bow down to him. And him alone.

Adil opened the laptop and typed his password in. Blue and yellow flashed up on the screen. A series of code filled the monitor as the system booted itself. After a few seconds, the home screen loaded. Once it had finished, Adil clicked on a small icon with his mouse and waited for the system to reinstall.

A search bar appeared. In it, he typed the address, Thames House, Millbank. The system knew where to go, and within a second, an image of a black BMW appeared. It was a five series, large and with tinted windows. Despite this, however, two men's faces were visible from the front. *Detective Tanner and Detective Stuart*, Adil smiled, checking his watch, *you had better hurry*.

Just as his thoughts finished, the car pulled away and, following closely behind, was an entourage of three BMW F800GTs and two Vauxhall Astra Estates. Adil knew from experience that the BMW bikes were quick. Very quick. *But not quick enough. Looks like we've got a party on our hands.*

As Adil watched on the screen, the bikes disbanded from the convoy at the back and moved to the front, acting as the spearhead that would part any traffic up ahead. He followed their every movement with a click of the button, jumping from CCTV camera to CCTV camera. He would monitor and manipulate their every move.

On the right-hand side of the screen, he launched a new software. This one contained a series of flashing green and red circles. The circles corresponded to traffic lights across central London's streets. As Adil watched the convoy barrel south down Victoria Embankment towards Big Ben and the Houses of Parliament, he changed the first traffic light from green to red, and smiled a wide, evil grin.

They were the pawns and he the chess master. It would take all of Jake's ability to arrive at North Acton on time; Adil had no intentions of making it easy for the detective. Now Adil's fun could really begin.

Chapter Eighteen

FORFEIT

August 1, 12:40

The motorbikes pulled ahead of Jake, their sirens and lights blaring. Following behind, Jake floored the accelerator, keeping the two Vauxhalls in his rear-view mirror. The sudden increase in acceleration propelled his body and head back into its seat, pinning him there. For a slight moment, he felt nauseous until the sensation passed seconds later, and then he was back to normal.

They were on their way.

The train of authority had departed.

With the Thames running beside them, Jake relied on the motorcycle driver's knowledge of London's roads. He had never been good with directions in central London. They had, however, somewhat improved over the past few years, but they were nowhere near the level they should have been for a man of his status and experience. Constant reliance upon a satnav would never get him far in his career.

It was one of his flaws and he accepted the fact. The situation reminded him of DC Ashley Rivers.

She had had the best knowledge of London's streets he had ever met. *The cabbie who got away*, Jake reminisced. His nostalgia, however, was cut short as he came to a sudden halt at the end of Victoria Embankment. The traffic lights had suddenly turned red. Jake slammed his fist on the steering wheel and waited for the oncoming lanes of traffic to slow down, before he pulled out at the Houses of Parliament and continued towards Birdcage Walk, the road that ran parallel to St. James's Park.

In front of them was a row of endless traffic. The lunchtime streets of central London were busy, and Jake knew, at this current rate, he wouldn't make it in time. They had come to a complete stop, and it would take a miracle for them to get to North Acton on time.

'Turn the satnav on,' Jake ordered Tyler next to him. 'We'll need a shortcut.'

Tyler activated the onboard navigation system and entered the destination. For the next few hundred metres, they struggled to persuade the cars in front to move out of the way, arriving at Buckingham Palace and the Victoria Memorial with some difficulty.

'How we doing for time?' Jake asked, tapping his fingers on the steering wheel.

Tyler checked his watch. 'Twenty minutes. And we're still six miles away.'

Jake remained silent, calculating in his mind the gravity — and incredulity — of what he was about to do. It was madness. But it was a necessary risk he needed to take. Given the opportunity, he would have stayed where he was. But he didn't have that luxury, and every second he spent sitting in the traffic was another life lost. When he thought of it that way, he overcame his fears and swallowed hard.

Slamming the gear stick into first, and glancing at the satnav one last time, Jake banked the kerb, spun the car around the Victoria Memorial and breached into the Buckingham Palace gardens, narrowly avoiding civilians and dog walkers. Seconds later, the convoy were right behind him, with the motorcyclists returning to the front. Screams and shouts surrounded them in all directions as they drove across the grass. Jake was suspended in a moment of shock and fear, an out-of-body experience. Was this really him? Was this really happening? Was he really doing this? His adrenaline spiked and, by the time they came to the end of the park, at the Piccadilly junction by Hyde Park, his palms were sweaty and were coming loose from the steering wheel.

As they neared the junction, the motorcycles showed no signs of slowing down. They sounded their horns, revved their engines and entered the intersection. Out of nowhere, a lorry clattered into the side of them at full speed. There was a deafening crash as the front of the truck collided with the bikes, crushing them under its immense weight. Shards of metal and other bits of debris flew in the air like cotton wool snow. The officers flung to the side of the road, tumbling to the ground like ragdolls. Screams ensued. Tyres screeched. Jake slammed the brakes, lunging himself and Tyler forward into the dashboard. His eyes were transfixed on the carnage in front of him. Two innocent men had risked their lives trying to protect and escort him. He couldn't break his eyes from their limp bodies surrounded in blood and glass.

He felt sick.

'Fuck,' he said. It came out as a whisper. He couldn't

loosen his grip from the steering wheel and place the gear into first.

'Jake! Jake! Come on — we've got to go!' Tyler shouted next to him, slamming his hand on the dashboard.

It took a few seconds for Jake to come round. He looked out at the crowd of people and cars in front of him, their piercing eyes judging him, blaming him for what happened. There was no way out ahead.

Except for a small opening around the corner. Jake saw his opportunity and took it. He put the car into first and drove off, leaving the officers, and wreckage, behind. Opposite him was a place he used to frequent when he was a child with his parents. He had even taken Ellie and Maisie there one Christmas at Winter Wonderland.

Hyde Park.

With a strange sense of déjà vu, Jake mounted the kerb and continued through the park. It was the shortest — and quickest — way through. Jake just hoped there wasn't a similar demise at the end. Tyler grabbed the radio from the dashboard and alerted the local police and emergency services to the incident they had just witnessed.

Jake tried to ignore Tyler as he cut through the blades of grass in the park. It was like driving through a video game. Pedestrians, joggers, dog walkers, even rule-breaking cyclists — they all veered out of the way, diving to the floor, protecting themselves from the one-tonne vehicle charging towards them.

'We're going to have to risk everything here mate, brace yourself,' Jake said, clocking up to fifty miles an hour.

Eventually, they came to the end of the park. Jake, breathing heavily and with his foot firmly lowered on the accelerator, kept his eyes focused on the road ahead. He ignored Kensington Palace on his left side as he sped past it.

Nearing Bayswater road, Jake kept the odometer at a steady fifty miles an hour. Up ahead, he could see the traffic was sparse and the number of pedestrians low. Given past experience, Jake knew he couldn't take anything for granted.

'Jake, Jake — what are you doing?' Tyler asked, putting one hand on the dashboard and the other on the armrest in the car. Jake continued on, heedless. 'Jake! Jaaaaaaakkeee!'

As they reached the pavement, Jake put his foot down to the floor and closed his eyes. It was better not to see what was coming. They both screamed as they crossed the junction and veered across two lanes of traffic before Jake eventually regained control of the car. Motorists slammed on their brakes and swerved, narrowly missing Jake's BMW. Now they were running along parallel to the Thames, heading straight for Shepherd's Bush. The road was busy, with cars screeching to a halt, trying to move out of harm's way.

One driver, however, in a Mercedes C Class, panicked and veered across the side of the oncoming lane into Jake's path. Just in time, Jake quickly swung the car around the Mercedes, run another red light, and carry on. Behind him he heard a loud crashing sound. He feared the worst and, after checking his rear-view mirror, learned that one of the Vauxhalls behind him had smashed into the Mercedes, spreading debris across the road.

Fuck! Jake thought. He had avoided collision twice now, and his mind turned towards superstition.

'How far?' he asked as they neared Shepherd's Bush.

'About three miles,' Tyler responded. 'And we've got fourteen minutes.'

'Shit.'

'Shit, indeed.'

The traffic thinned out the further they got from the centre of the city, but that didn't mean they were any more likely to arrive on time. Jake raced down Wood Lane, past the former BBC Television Broadcasting Centre and, just as they were about to turn left onto the A40, a cyclist pulled out in front. Jake swerved the car to the right, veered onto the lane of oncoming traffic, and brought the car to a semi-controlled stop.

Tyler peered his head out of the window to check on the cyclist, making sure they hadn't knocked them off onto the road. Just as his head turned back to confirm with Jake, they both lunged forward. Jake's head hit the steering wheel; Tyler's face collided with the window arch. Glass from the back and side windows shattered into the back seats, with a few shards landing in Jake's hair and lap. The airbag blew up in his face, knocking the wind from his body as if he had just been punched in the stomach by a heavyweight boxer.

It took a while before they regained their senses. Jake's head throbbed, and his nose hurt. As he tried to turn to Tyler, the tendons in his neck screamed in agony.

'Tyler — Tyler, you all right?' he asked eventually, tapping his friend on the shoulder.

Tyler came to and eased back into the leather seat. He looked round at Jake and smiled.

'Never felt better, mate,' Tyler said. There was a thin trickle of blood running from his forehead down the side of his face.

Jake looked behind him to see the bumper of the Vauxhall impaled on the back of his BMW. At a glance, he could see the police constable driving the car was in the same shape as Tyler.

Jake grabbed for the radio, switched it to the correct frequency, and asked if the driver was OK.

'Yes, I'm fine,' the constable replied. 'Now get a fucking move on.'

With his head throbbing and vision starry, Jake switched on the engine, put it into first and drove off. This time, he was much more conservative with his driving, making sure the nausea in his head dissipated before bringing the car back up to whatever speed he, and it, could manage.

With only a mile remaining, Jake eased his foot down on the accelerator. The A40 was much more forgiving than any of the other roads they had traversed so far. Fortunately, as they neared their destination and departed the A road, the number of red lights reduced. It was as if they were being controlled by someone, somewhere — looking out for them when they needed it the most.

Tyler sat next to Jake nursing his wound with his sleeve and rubbing his temples. He grabbed his phone from the foot well, dialled a number and said, 'Simon, we've had a collision just before the A40 on Wood Lane with another vehicle. One suspected casualty. Detective Tanner and I are still en route.' He hung up the phone before the Deputy Assistant Commissioner could ask too many questions.

Eventually, after spending what was the most luxurious two minutes of their entire journey on the A40, Jake turned off and followed the signs directing him towards North Acton train station.

The Underground train station they were looking for was a few hundred yards in ahead. Jake couldn't bring himself to look at the time. Whether they had milliseconds, seconds, minutes to spare — he couldn't bear to live with the shame of having failed.

He braked and bumped the kerb, opening the car door before it had time to stop. He and Tyler jumped out and ran to the station. Jake's head pounded with every step. What surprised him most was that there was a new-found pain reaching from the base of his right leg up to his hip, a product of the earlier collision. *It must have got trapped under the wheel*, he thought.

Despite the agony, he could still run. He tried to ignore the shooting pain that ran up and down his entire body, but his attempts were in vain.

Tyler reached the station before Jake, who was close behind. They both rested their hands on their knees and bent forward, catching their breath.

'Jesus,' was all Tyler could say between his breaths.

'What's the time?' Jake struggled to ask.

Tyler checked his watch, 'Fuck!'

'What?' Jake asked.

'My watch is cracked,' Tyler said. 'And... we're two minutes late.'

'Shit!' Jake said, falling to the floor heavily on his arse. The sudden jolt in his body sent more pain up and down his spine, but he didn't care, he had failed and now the blood of innocent people would be on his hands.

Tyler joined him on the floor. Before either of them said anything, Jake's phone rang in his pocket.

Unknown number.

Was it a lifeline? Or just an opportunity for Willy Wonka to gloat?

Jake answered it and waited for the other end of the line to begin.

'Well, well, well, Detective Tanner. You've had quite the journey, haven't you?'

'I'm here,' Jake replied, his mind too shocked to respond. He had experienced things in a half hour that few constables or detectives would go through their entire careers.

'Yes, I can see. You and your friend look cosy on the floor. But, you're late, and I asked you to come alone, Detective. You are in direct breach of our agreement, and as a result, there will be a punishment.'

'No! He's not with me, he's just leaving!' Jake said looking at Tyler, bulging his eyeballs and nodding his head for Tyler to leave. Tyler took the hint and ran back to the car. 'See, he's all gone.'

'Yes, I can see that, thank you, Detective Tanner. I've been watching you,' said the voice. 'It looked like you had fun out there on the streets. You didn't make it easy for me, you know, driving through those parks all the time.'

Jake said nothing. He would let the voice think he was the one in control. And Jake had to admit that he was. For now.

'Nevertheless,' the voice said after a pause, 'rules are rules. This is going to look great on the news tonight.'

There was a clicking of a switch on the phone.

'No! Wait!' Jake said, but it was pointless. The other line had hung up.

Jake shouted into the phone and put it to his ear, hoping for there to be a response. There was none. He swore loudly in the open and rose to his feet. People were looking his way and talking amongst themselves. He didn't care. He couldn't care. Not now.

He hobbled over to Tyler, who was waiting in the car and opened the door.

'What's wrong?' Tyler asked, looking at Jake's dejected and mortified expression. 'What are you doing here?'

'We've fucked it, Ty. I think he's just blown up one of the trains.'

Adil hung up the phone and threw it onto his desk. He gazed at the middle screen of his setup, saw Jake lying there on the ground, dejected and disappointed, and smiled. Hiding behind his computer screens was the microphone he had used to communicate with the passengers on board the trains simultaneously. Now he grabbed it and squeezed its handle. At the base of the microphone were four buttons. One designated for each train, plus another for all of them together. Adil pressed a button. The light underneath the 'Luton' label illuminated.

Readying the display on his screens, Adil flicked through the CCTV feeds, searching for the final carriage of the British Rail Class 387 train. Dozens of passengers were on their feet, fanning themselves down.

Adil cleared his throat.

'This is your Helpless Saviour speaking. Can I have the attention of the passengers in the twelfth carriage, please?' On the screen, most of the heads turned and look at one another, and then up to the ceiling. 'Great. Thank you. Unfortunately for you all, I have bad news. It seems the person whose duty it is — the person's salary your taxes go towards — cannot follow simple instructions, and his actions have resulted in a forfeit. You are the forfeit.'

As Adil spoke, he opened the top drawer on the left-hand side of his desk, removed a mobile phone, and hovered his finger over the speed dial button.

'You, and everyone else on this carriage, will have five seconds to evacuate onto the next available carriage as fast as you can. Anyone who is successful will have the luxury of survival.' Adil paused, gauging the reactions of everyone on board. When none came, he counted down.

'Five...'

Everyone rushed to their feet and squashed together as they all tried to filter out onto the next carriage.

'Four.'

His finger held down the speed dial.

'Three. Two.'

Adil stopped. The CCTV feed on the screen went black. The footage of the outside of the train displayed the level of destruction and carnage. The entire roof of the carriage exploded into a giant mushroom of orange. Fire rained down on the track nearby, as debris and bits of body somersaulted through the air.

Placing the phone back in the top drawer, Adil said, 'I did warn you.'

Chapter Nineteen

RIDDLE

August 1, 13:02

They both sat in silence. Tyler lit a cigarette outside the vehicle while Jake rested his head on the dashboard, repeatedly slamming his fists into the steering wheel which was in pieces after the airbag exploded through its centre in the collision.

'I thought you'd quit?' Jake said, as the smell of nicotine rose through his damaged sinuses.

'Suppose we've both got things we keep from one another.' Tyler shrugged. 'Shit happens.' He puffed a ball of smoke into the air and paced around the car.

Jake pulled out his phone and tried to ring Simon. His attempts were met with the operator telling him the number was unavailable. Jake whistled over to Tyler.

'Try to ring Frances or someone in the office, please? We need to update them.'

Tyler nodded and pulled out his phone. He put it to his ear and waited.

To Jake's immediate surprise, his partner spoke. 'Simon? It's Tyler. Hold on, let me put you on speaker.'

Tyler held the phone away from his ear placed it on the dashboard.

'Hello? Can someone answer me, please?' Simon sounded pissed off. Jake was glad he was halfway across the city from him; he had heard from others in the office that his temperament was almost as volatile as Mamadou's.

'Yes, guv'. We're here,' Jake said, although he wished he hadn't.

'What the *fuck* is going on, Tanner? We're just dealing with clearing up the mess you've made! And not to mention the phones and computers and everything else in this godforsaken office has gone bust.'

'What about the trains?' Jake asked, interrupting him. He didn't care if he annoyed anyone anymore, the damage had already been done. He needed to know the extent of the damage to the death toll.

'One X-ray has gone,' Simon explained. Jake felt his heart sink. 'X-ray' was the term used to identify a target.

'Which one?' Jake asked.

'The twelfth carriage of the Luton-bound train.'

Jake's ears perked up. 'Just the one carriage?'

'Yes. Number of casualties unconfirmed, and almost impossible to determine. The windows are still steamed up on the trains, so it's difficult to find out what is going on behind them. The guys sent down there are hanging well back, so none of them got injured in the explosion.'

Thank God, Jake thought. His head still throbbed from the accident, and it was worsened by the torrent of guilt inside his mind. He was responsible for the deaths of everyone onboard. And he could never forget that.

Jake could feel his heart beating faster and faster. Faster

and faster. Faster and faster. Another anxiety attack was coming.

'It's all my fault,' Jake said out loud accidentally.

There was a moment of silence on the phone. 'They gave you an impossible challenge, Tanner. There was nothing you could have done.' Simon's frustrations had dissipated, and he spoke with an unfamiliar compassion in his voice.

Jake said nothing and tried to control his breathing. Exercises he'd learned from when he was younger still helped him today. He went into his imagination and envisioned being on a sun bed, basking in the sun.

After a few deep breaths he was feeling back to normal.

'There are others who are dead,' Jake said, referring to the motorcyclists. 'Tyler will bring you up to speed. He'll be back on his way now, but I need to stay here and finish this off. There's still more for me to do.'

Jake hung up the phone before Simon protested. It was Jake's stubborn manner that overruled Tyler's persistent nagging, requesting him to allow him to stay. In the end, Tyler conceded defeat, jumped into the driver's seat, and ignited the engine.

'I want you to be in charge when you get back. Find out all you can about who is behind this. Don't let Matthews control you or the operation. Contact me if anything goes wrong — you've got my number.' Jake closed the door on Tyler. 'Oh, and Ty, make the most of Theodor. I asked him there for a reason. Whoever is behind this knows a thing or two about trains. See if he's worked with anyone suspicious in the past, or if he knows who, how, and when someone would have been able to alter them in such a way they could plant fucking explosives on them. That shit doesn't happen in one morning. Understood?'

'Christ, Jake. If you carry on this way, I'll have to accept the promotion for you on Frances's behalf.'

The statement made Jake smile, a glimmer of hope in an otherwise unending chasm of darkness. 'Just doing my job.'

Tyler nodded and shook Jake's hand. Neither of them needed to say anything further. They both knew what it meant.

It wasn't a *goodbye*.

It wasn't a *good luck*.

It was a *see you on the other side*.

Jake wandered into the station and reached the ticket barrier. Just as he stood next to a Transport for London employee, his phone rang.

'Hello, Detective Tanner. Did you enjoy the fireworks? No? OK, well let's find out your next clue, shall we? The one that leads you to eternal salvation and happiness.'

'Why? Why are you giving me another chance?' Jake asked, confused.

'Because I'm in a good mood. I didn't make it particularly easy for you, did I? So, I should let you off somewhat. Also, it's my big day, and if I'm being honest, I want you to experience it all with me, just so you can see how much time and effort I've put into this,' the voice said.

'I can tell you've put in a lot of work.'

'You flatter me, but it won't get you anywhere. Now, listen up. I'll say this once, and once only.' The man on the other end paused. 'I am borrowed and used, people walk all over me, and where four arrive, four more appear. Where am I in the West End of London? Go there and await further instructions. You have twenty minutes.'

'Wait! I didn't get all that. No!'

Jake shouted into the phone, but it was no use. The

tormentor on the other end had hung up. Jake looked around the station and its exit, wishing he had allowed Tyler to stay. But he hadn't. Jake was on his own, left to work out the riddle with no help.

Shit, he thought, trying to remember every part of the riddle. He panicked as his time was already running out and he didn't even know where to begin. Clearing the uncertainties and pain in his head, Jake broke the riddle down.

I am borrowed and used, the voice had said. Jake cursed aloud as he realised that could have been anything. His knowledge of London's history wasn't the most extensive on the planet, but he guessed that almost everything in London had been borrowed and used by someone or something at some point. This was pointless and too vague. He moved on to the next.

People walk all over me. This one was easier. Words sprung into his mind at random. Rugs. Carpet. Hearts. Roads. Other people's self-esteem. The latter seemed too left field for him, and he dismissed it. He considered the rest, and in the heart of London, roads seemed the most likely.

So, he was looking for a road in London. Where in London? *West London*, the voice had told him. Content with the path he was going, he moved on to the final, most complex clue.

He replayed it in his mind over and over until it became nothing. The meaning of the words had become null and void. Angered at himself, he sought help.

'Excuse me mate, bit of a weird question, but it's important,' he said, turning to the TfL guard who had been paying little attention what was going on inside the station. Jake flashed his ID card. 'I need your help with a riddle. Where's a street in west London where "four arrive, and four more appear"?'

The guard stood there a moment, looking at Jake's dishevelled appearance and carefully considering whether to answer. Jake could see a look of fear buried deep in his eyes. The fear of being attacked if he refused to answer. Eventually, the man answered.

'Ermm, the only place I could think of is that place by Oxford Circus... the massive crossing in the middle of the square.'

'What do you mean?' Jake asked.

'There's that X-crossing in the middle of Oxford Circus, going from corner to corner. It was put in a few years back,' the guard explained.

'Who came up with the idea?'

'I don't know, some Asian guy I think. It was first done in Japan, and then we sort of took the idea and made it seem like we were the ones who conceptualised it. Like we always do,' the guard grunted. Jake could feel the man coming out of his shell, becoming more comfortable talking to Jake.

Jake nodded to him and held up his finger telling him to wait. He limped over to the wall and looked at the large map of the London Underground. He found North Acton and ran his finger along the red line to Oxford Circus.

He smiled, told the guard he was a genius, shook his hand, and then ran down the stairs. A train pulled into the platform as he reached the final step. Jake jumped aboard just as the doors closed behind him.

He was in. He had done it in time.

He was going to Oxford Circus.

Chapter Twenty

KALEIDOSCOPE

August 1, 13:14

The Central Line was unbearable in the summer heat. With an average temperature of twenty-six degrees Celsius during the hottest time of the year, it was enough to make even the most physically fit human perspire. The pores on Jake's palms and face opened and sweat trickled down his face before leaping into the unknown from the bottom of his chin. He could feel the wet patches under his armpits increase in radius with every passing minute.

He wasn't a fan of public transport. At the beginning of his career he'd had to use the Underground profusely in his local borough, but now he had the luxury of driving to and from work — and anywhere else he needed — every day, he had become accustomed to it.

And now he was finding himself cramped next to a morbidly obese man wearing a too-small tracksuit and a school of Spanish students who seemed oblivious to everyone around them, speaking and talking loudly to one another. He could just about make out what some of them were saying — he had studied the language at college — but none of it distracted him from the real problem at hand. He wanted to disappear into his own mind and consider the situation in every little detail, like Sherlock Holmes's mind-palace. But the disruptive noise of happy travellers and boastful businessmen kept him from doing so.

He'd been on the Central Line for ten minutes and was just under halfway to Oxford Circus when his phone started playing music. Confused, he fumbled around for it in his pocket, hoping it would be good news. A message from Elizabeth, perhaps, telling him that today was just a dream and that his mother-in-law was safe at home with the kids. Or maybe a message from Frances or Tyler telling him that the explosion on the train hadn't happened. Or maybe a message from Mamadou telling him that his mother wasn't in hospital, and it had been some sick and twisted joke.

It was nothing of the sort.

Displayed front and centre on his lock screen, bright and garish, was the same image of the yellow emoji smoking a spliff he had seen in the office before he left. Underneath, "HA-HA" flashed intermittently.

What the - Jake thought as he tapped the home screen. Nothing happened. The music continued to play, and the image remained, until the operating system rebooted itself after a few seconds. The sudden fiasco made Jake feel vulnerable. Alone. Nervous. Like he was being watched. Like his every move was being monitored.

It frightened him that his phone — the one thing he used every day and relied upon so much, not just in his personal life, but also in his work — could be easily manipulated and hacked into.

Technological warfare was the new front line of terrorism.

And, without necessarily killing millions, it had the power to reduce humanity to its base level. Jake imagined it for a moment. A world without the internet: no internet banking, rendering the transactions he and everyone else had become accustomed to as useless; all communications lost, agriculture and the transport of goods fallen into disarray; businesses malfunctioning. The twenty-first century would struggle to keep up.

He stared at his phone for a few minutes, the smile image still in his mind. Then he heard the familiar sounds of his ring tone, bringing him back to reality. The obese man beside him shuffled in his seat and rubbed up against Jake's arm. Through his clothes, he felt the sweat transferring to his own skin.

Tyler was ringing him. Jake answered it quietly, relaxing as he held the phone to his ear.

'Tyler, what's wrong? Where are you?' Jake asked, assuming the worst.

'I'm in the car, on the way to the office. Why?' Tyler said.

'I just wondered. You're safe though, yeah?'

'Yeah, I've had to go the long way. The traffic is an absolute mess.'

'OK — but what's wrong? What's the latest?'

'I've just got off the phone with Susanna. She said they've identified a potential suspect. According to CCTV footage, he's turned up at Paddington Station early in the morning, sat down for a couple of hours, made a few squiggles in a notebook, and then fucked off — every day for the past few days. We don't know how far back he's been doing it,' Tyler explained.

Interesting, Jake thought. He stored the information away for later.

'Have they got a positive ID?' Jake asked.

'Not yet. They're working on it.'

'OK. Send me through an image of his face. I want to recognise him if I see him.'

'Yes, sir,' Tyler said. 'Also, Frances is still in COBRA. She should be out soon. I'm not sure how it's going in there, but as soon as I hear, I'll let you know what the latest course of action is.'

'Thank —' Suddenly, the phone cut out as Jake moved further underground. He looked down at the floor and swore under his breath, putting his head in his hands and leaning forward. The sudden change in movement reignited the pain in his leg.

Today would be more difficult than he imagined.

'You all right, boss?' asked the obese man next to him, a heavy stench of cheese on his breath.

Jake was taken aback by the stranger's concern. He sat back in his seat and looked at the man, who smiled endearingly at him.

'One of those days,' Jake mumbled, smiling back.

'Tell me about it.'

Jake closed his eyes and tried to empty his mind. The image of the smiley face and the thought of the carriage exploding with everybody inside flashed through his mind like a kaleidoscope of death and horror. The conversation he'd had with the person behind the attack played like a recording over a tannoy. Then, images of Elizabeth. Maisie. Ellie. The ones he loved the most. All on the train. There they were, behind the windows, clawing at the glass, screaming, calling his name, trying to break free. And there he was, standing outside, staring in, held back by some invisible force, unable to protect or save them.

He opened his eyes fast, making a little grunt.

He needed to get off this train. The automated speaker system told him Oxford Circus was the next destination. The past ten minutes had felt like thirty.

The doors opened, and he spilled out. He ascended the stairs and tapped his Oyster card on the ticket barrier. The station heaved with people. Tourists. Workers. Civil servants. The homeless. Students. Families.

Busy was an understatement.

But it was much worse outside the station.

A sea of bodies moved slowly, meandering at their own pace. Jake fought against the current to break out onto the road. The heavy flow of people eased up, and he gauged where he was. He sprinted across the pavement, ignoring the oncoming cars hurtling towards him. An Uber driver skidded to a halt a few inches away from his injured leg. Jake ignored the profanities sent his way and carried on into the middle of the junction between Oxford Street and Regent Street. As soon as the pelican crossing lights had changed, civilians swarmed Jake from all sides, sending him dirty looks as they passed him.

His phone rang. He knew who it was at once, but he still found it a welcoming distraction. He answered the phone and waited.

'Jubilant congratulations are in order, Detective! You've made it to your first clue. They all get easier from here. Trust me, they really do. I was proud of that one. Cryptic, wasn't it? What did you think?'

Jake said nothing; he allowed the last of the stream of people to pass him. 'Yeah. Yeah, it was all right.'

'Just all right? I'm offended, Jake. And we don't want to

offend Willy Wonka, do we? He always had a sadistic side, didn't he? Gene Wilder, Johnny Depp. They were always a bit... *weird*. Have you ever seen the films?'

'Yeah.'

'Which one did you prefer?'

'I, I really don't know. I don't care.' Jake's attention diverted to the change in traffic lights. Cars started towards him. He stood in the middle of the four-way junction, and there was nowhere for him to go.

'There's no need to be blunt. This is a fun adventure — for the both of us!'

'I am treating it as an adventure, one I hope ends with me saving every life there is still left to save,' Jake said.

'But that's what this exercise is about, Detective. By the end of this section, you will be able to save one whole train. The clues on this wild goose chase you are now about to go on will help you find out which train contains a decoy detonator, leaving all the passengers to walk off risk-free,' the voice explained.

Jake didn't know what to say. This was big news. There was still a massive ray of hope he could save at least everybody on one train.

'What do I have to do?'

'Well, first, I hope the ransom is being collected as we speak. You will be the one to deliver it to me, Tanner.'

'Where to?'

'Let's not get ahead of ourselves. You must sit tight and wait to find out. Instead, I have another riddle for you: I am a vegetable in disguise. I soar high in the air with the birds. What am I? You've got half an hour.'

Chapter Twenty-One

COBRA

August 1, 13:25

Easy, Jake thought, putting his phone into his pocket and breathing a deep sigh of relief. This one hadn't taken him too long. The only thing that remotely resembled some sort of vegetable high in the sky, was the St. Mary Axe, otherwise known as The Gherkin. It wasn't the most attractive name, nor was it the most attractive building. But it had been the most instantly recognisable of all skyscrapers in the London city skyline.

Proud of himself, he waited until the traffic had ceased rushing past him, blaring their horns, to start back towards the Underground. He made it as far as the foyer until he had to stop. A sudden concern crossed his mind. He didn't know how to get there. He needed help.

He called Tyler.

'Tyler, mate, can you talk?' Jake asked, standing by the ticket machines, narrowly avoiding a mum with a pushchair and two other children dangling from her side.

'Yeah, Jake. Always got time for you,' Tyler responded, his demeanour improved. 'What's up?'

'I'm at Oxford Circus, headed to the Gherkin. What's the best way to get there?'

'I don't know, Central Line to Liverpool Street? Or a cab. Why are you going there?'

'Because I'm on a fucking wild goose chase, Tyler. That's why,' Jake snapped. Cautious of his expletive language around the busy district, he quietened and asked, 'What's the latest?'

'Theo's been running the show since I got back. He says there's always a log that records all the adjustments made to a train every time it's brought in for repairs — it's the law or something like that, so we're trying to get our hands on that as soon as possible, and then we'll let you know.'

'Good.' Jake felt comfortable knowing Theodor was taking control. 'How's the ransom coming along?'

'The Bank of England are working on it as we speak. The Commissioner and the Chancellor of the country's money are pulling a few strings, so we can get it in time. We just need to know where and when to drop it off.'

'Hopefully, we'll know the location soon. I've just been informed I'll be the one delivering it, right after I've found out which one of these fucking trains isn't going to blow up,' Jake said, turning to face the ticket machine as if to conceal his conversation.

Jake thanked Tyler for the directions and the update. He said goodbye and hung up the phone. Jake checked his watch. The time was nearing 13:20, which meant there was less than four and a half hours until the explosives detonated. He hoped there was enough time to rescue everyone.

With time running out, Jake dashed through the ticket barrier. His leg was still bruised and damaged from his earlier collision, turning his run into a fast hobble. Jake rushed down the flight of steps, barging through the crowds, giving himself priority over everyone else, onto the platform where he waited for the next train.

He stood on the platform waiting for the train when some text messages came through on his phone.

NAUGHTY DETECTIVE, USING YOUR PHONE TO DO YOUR DETECTING.
NO PHONES ALLOWED.
THAT INCLUDES TEXT MESSAGES.
THIS IS YOUR FIRST WARNING. FAILURE TO COMPLY WILL RESULT IN THINGS GOING *BOOM*.
I'M WATCHING YOU.

Jake stood there for a few moments reading each message as it appeared, re-reading them in disbelief as he tried to solidify their meaning in his mind. *This guy is seriously fucking with me*, Jake thought. There was no opportunity to do anything. No room for manoeuvre. Jake was left alone, responsible for thousands of innocent lives.

He was a puppet in the terrorist's grand show.

Soon, he would have to change that.

The Cabinet Office Briefing Room A had been silent for the past minute. There had been intense discussion in bringing everyone up to speed regarding the current situation for the past forty-five minutes, and Frances hated every second. Even though it was part of her remit to be present, she would rather be at New Scotland Yard, working with her team and making sure the operational side of things was running as smooth as possible. To her, COBRA meetings always seemed like a waste of time. They were always spent discussing the best solutions with no one making any concrete decisions. Since she had left New Scotland Yard, both Susanna and Simon had been keeping her up-to-date with Jake's exploits around the city.

'Who is orchestrating this attack?' the Mayor of London had asked five minutes into the meeting.

'We don't know,' Frances replied.

'What do you mean you don't know? Have the intelligence agencies not been able to identify who is behind the attacks?'

Neither Frances nor Alan Brockhurst, the Director General of MI5, who sat next to her said anything. There was no admission of guilt.

'Our teams are working on it,' Alan said. 'There have been barriers in our way, but we will notify you as soon as something comes in.'

'You mean to say nobody we've been running surveillance on has been acting suspicious recently? Nobody from ISIL claiming the attacks?' The Mayor of London didn't mind reminding people of how difficult he could be.

'You'd like that, wouldn't you, Thomas? Someone to blame. Someone to use as a scapegoat. But unfortunately, with our current intel, this entire thing is suggesting it has been a domestic attack. It is too articulated, too calculated to be ISIL or another organisation.'

As soon as Frances had spoken, the Mayor of London remained silent and cowered back into his chair.

A moment of silence passed as Frances scanned the room, waiting for someone to launch another attack on her.

After a few tense seconds, it was the Prime Minister who spoke next.

'Do we know what their demands are?'

Frances nodded. 'One million pounds. Cash.'

Again, there was a wave of silence that engulfed the room. Everyone seemed taken aback. Everyone except the Prime Minister.

'What do you think we should do, Assistant Commissioner?' the Prime Minister asked.

'I think we should assemble it for them. Most of it, anyway.'

'We do not give in to terrorists, Assistant Commissioner. Or have you forgotten that fact?' Glen Strachan, from the Ministry of Defence, said. His words felt like a personal attack on Frances, and she retaliated with an even stronger bite.

'No, Glen. I'm well aware of our standing on that. But you didn't let me explain.' Frances paused for effect, casting her stern glare to everyone else in the room. 'So far, all we know is that there will be a ransom drop made soon. That means whoever is behind this will present themselves in public. After the initial drop, that's when we'll apprehend them. Jake will have led them directly to us.'

'There's no way we can get that amount money in such a short amount of time,' restated Phillip Brown, the Chancellor of the Exchequer.

The Prime Minister turned to face them. 'I don't care, Phillip. Find a way to make it possible. The Assistant Commissioner is right — we will, at the very least, make them believe we have given in to their demands. And then when the time comes, we will detain them.'

Frances nodded in the Prime Minister's direction. It was the first time in her experience a decision had been made so quickly. Phillip remained in his seat while everyone else in the room stared at them.

'Phillip,' the Prime Minister began. 'What are you waiting for? We don't have time for you to waste here. Get out and get to it.'

At once, the Chancellor of the Exchequer jumped from his seat and exited the room. It was unorthodox for someone to leave the room before the meeting had concluded, but everyone else knew these were extenuating circumstances and that rules would be broken.

The Prime Minister turned to face Frances as soon as the door shut. 'How do you propose we proceed in the meantime?'

'We allow DC Tanner to continue as the figurehead of this operation. He is the one in direct contact with whoever is behind this attack. He is the one responsible for saving the lives of those people on the trains,' Frances said.

'You mean to tell me that one man is responsible for the lives of thousands of innocent civilians? You've got to be joking. We can't approve of that. What sort of government would we look like if we left it all to one man?' the Home Secretary said. She was a small, overweight woman in her late thirties, with a bobbed haircut and horn-rimmed glasses that advanced her appearance by ten years.

'Excuse me, Home Secretary, but isn't that what we do every day? Isn't that part of our undercover agents' jobs, to infiltrate terrorist and drug networks so they can thwart potential attacks?' Frances tried to maintain her composure. The Home Secretary said nothing. Turning to the Prime Minister, Frances continued, 'DC Jake Tanner is a highly skilled and resourceful individual. It is imperative we do everything we can to ensure his safety.'

'And what of the safety of everyone else in London?

Your officer has destroyed half the city, already killing two Police Constables and causing thousands of pounds' worth of damage!' the Secretary of Defence, Peter Clarke, piped up. He was yet another added to the growing list of people ready to stand against Frances.

'The loss of the two constables was tragic, yes, and they will be decorated posthumously for their achievements. But there are much larger powers at play, Peter. Jake and his colleagues had no other alternative but to risk their own lives. They were given an insurmountable task, and they were inhibited by the person responsible.'

'And look what happened,' Peter Clarke continued. 'Even though they arrived at North Acton, the carriage exploded, and everyone left inside perished. That'll be on the news already, and soon there will be a public outcry to find out what is going on.'

'We need to keep the media out as much as possible. The less the public know while DC Tanner is undergoing his investigation, the better,' the Prime Minister said.

'Our officers are already on it,' Frances said bluntly. She wanted the tirade to be over.

'Your officer has already got the blood of too many people on his hands for us to sit back and allow him to continue.' Peter Clarke was getting on Frances's nerves, and she shot him a look that ensured he knew that.

Frances was fighting a losing battle here, and she knew it. She took a moment to glance around the room, at her colleagues, until eventually she stopped at the Prime Minister.

'You asked me what you thought I should do, and I'm telling you to listen.' Frances swallowed. 'We mustn't panic the people of London. Closing the Underground network will only further the panic, so we must keep some of it open.

My deputies have been informing me that Jake is on the Tube, heading east towards the outskirts of the city centre. It appears he is on some kind of hunt to find out which of the three trains contains decoy explosives.'

'What makes you think that's a good idea, Assistant Commissioner?' The Prime Minister said.

'I'm not sure. I've got a feeling that DC Tanner will be pushed further and further away from the city centre, only to be told he has to rush back in an allotted time. It would fit the general pattern of events we have already seen.'

Now it was time for the Transport Secretary to step to the podium and voice her opinion. 'It will be a mountainous task closing some of the Underground, Frances. Hundreds of thousands of passengers set foot through it every day. If we close it, it will only add to the traffic epidemic in London. It will be even more difficult when we don't know what's going to happen. And how might that complicate things for your DC Tanner?'

'Let me ask you this, Frances,' the Prime Minister said. 'What if we leave the Underground open and the terrorists behind this attack repeat the events of 7/7? Whose head will it be on, then?'

Frances swallowed before answering. 'Mine. I will accept full responsibility, but I am almost certain it is an unlikely possibility. What the terrorists have demonstrated is that they are methodical, prepared, and intelligent enough to hide in plain sight somewhere in the city. If they were preparing anything like 7/7, then they would have already done it.'

'You're just guessing now, Assistant Commissioner,' the Mayor of London shouted. 'You have no evidence to back up this theory.'

'You're correct, Ian. I don't. But what if you ignore

everything I have advised against and everything I have said comes true? Which one of *you* will accept the blame for that?' Frances scanned the faces of the governmental ministers around the table. None of them returned her gaze. None of them were willing to shoulder the blame, and with that, Frances rose out of her seat and exited the room, leaving the door open behind her. She hoped she had made her point.

Chapter Twenty-Two

SEEN

August 1, 13:40

Moshat relaxed. He was enjoying the paranoia and angst that spread throughout the carriage like a virus. It brought out the best and worst in humans. It made people trust no one other than themselves. It made them second-guess someone's movements, including their own. After all, who could trust a stranger? Let alone a stranger on a train. Nobody knows what's going on inside anyone's head.

The paranoid schizophrenic sat opposite you, she's there.

The hedge fund manager in a suit and tie who regularly accesses child pornography, he's there.

The teenage girl who's been raped and abused all her life, just waiting to lash out and release all her anger and frustration and hate onto the world, she's there.

The computer geek who's been bullied his entire life for not doing what others expected of him, he's only got a short way to go before he does something terrible.

The quirky gothic left-wing couple all over each other in broad daylight, who knows what they're up to.

The eco-friendly terrorist obsessed with overpopulation and any means necessary to stunt the growth of humanity, he's calculating right now how to exterminate half the world.

The Darwin mega-fan silently sat there picking you off in his head, one by one. Survival of the fittest, he's there working at full capacity.

The Jehovah Witnesses ready to shove religion down your throat, they're there.

The lawyer who has notorious affairs with clients and uses it as blackmail to get what he wants, he's there.

The bigot and racist who believes in white supremacy, there's a few of those, too.

The sex pervert who undresses every woman he sees in his head, no matter the age range, he's there.

How can you ever know what these people around you are like? People come out of their shell in cases of extreme pressure. Something in their brain snaps, the part that withheld that aspect about themselves, releasing it to the world. How long would it be before he snapped, revealing to everyone around him who he was?

A smile grew on his face. Inside the carriage, arguments ensued. While most passengers remained silent, other more provocative personalities flourished like a flower growing in the sun.

'My son has a physical disability! He can't stand for too long. He needs to sit down!' one man dressed in a polo shirt shouted.

'I don't give a fuck. I'm just as entitled to this seat as your son. Besides, he can sit on your lap, can't he?' another man said. A dense beard and moustache shielded most of his mouth from view.

Before their altercation could escalate into violence, a shrieking noise overhead distracted them, bringing the whole carriage to a silent standstill.

'Good afternoon, intrepid travellers, I trust you are keeping well?' Adil's voice on the tannoy began. 'I would like to remind you that any physical violence on board is not tolerated and will be treated as an act of war. This will lead to serious consequences, the likes of which you don't want to experience. Please see your phones for further details.'

Adil's voice died away and was replaced with the sound of classical music, as if it were 1940s Britain at the peak of wartime.

All at once, every phone on the train did something. Some made ringing tones, some vibrated, others lit up. Moshat stared at the screen over the shoulder of the single mum beside him. An image displayed the fiery wreckage of a train carriage. All that remained from the explosion were the wheels and chassis. Chairs and other unrecognisable bits of debris had been flung from the train out onto the track. Shock and horror grew on the faces of everyone around him. Eyes bulged as they realised what it meant.

'Oh, my God,' said one woman in the distance.

'Dear God, please don't let me die like that,' another cried.

These peoples' sudden acceptance of faith disgusted Moshat. *Hypocrites. Atheist their whole lives until they're about to die, then suddenly everyone's devout.*

Moshat grabbed for his phone, conscious of the fact he hadn't joined in with everyone else and leaned back into his seat, sinking so that his groin was in line with the edge of the table. It was imperative he kept his phone concealed from those around him.

He unlocked it and read the latest text message he had received.

HELLO, LITTLE BROTHER. STAY CALM. EVERY-THING IS UNDER CONTROL. RANSOM MONEY BEING COLLECTED. DETECTIVE EN ROUTE TO WILLY WONKA'S CHOCOLATE FACTORY. BE SAFE. A.

Reading his brother's message, Moshat smiled. It was larger and more obvious than the one the situation allowed. Without realising it, Martha had caught sight of his expression and glared at him. There was a steely, unimpressed, and knowing look in her eyes; it reminded Moshat of a teacher he once had at school.

Moshat panicked. He had messed up. He wasn't supposed to have raised any suspicion at all. He was supposed to be an invisible man who would slip off the train at the end of the day, having raised no suspicion, so he could disappear to another country with his brother. And, if on the off chance his identity was compromised, he would be the innocent bystander who rose from the depths of his insecurities at the last minute and used whatever leverage he could for his escape.

Moshat tried to play it off. Looking straight back down at his phone and then into his lap, like an ashamed child, he prayed that she hadn't noticed him, and it was her resting face that filled him with so much dread. A few seconds later he rose his head and strained his eyes to see her.

Fuck! She was still staring.

The panic and fear within him multiplied. They hadn't

planned for such an eventuality. They had not expected Moshat to give himself away so easily to Martha, their leverage over the ransom. Moshat remembered his brother's advice: breathe in through his nose, count to five, pause, exhale from the mouth, count to three, and then repeat. The process may have seemed stupid and outdated to him at first, but the longer he tried it, the more he felt the effects.

It didn't, however, stop him feeling disappointed and disgusted with himself; he had raised suspicion and from here onwards, every move he made had to be careful and calculated. The seed of doubt had been planted in Martha's mind. And it would only grow.

Moshat looked up, ignoring her watchful gaze and observed his fellow passengers. They rose to their feet, putting their phones to their ears, attempting to contact friends and relatives.

'What are you doing? Are you trying to get us all killed?' a woman in the distance called. 'You've seen the picture. You want that to happen to us?'

'The carriage on that train was the end one. We're in the middle carriage. It won't happen to us,' a teenager with jet-black eyes and matching hair replied.

'How thick can you be? There are explosives every-where on this train, including *this* carriage. Why would you ever think we're safe? We don't know what this person's motives are, so let's not piss them off.'

The teenager said nothing more and put his phone away. Everyone else did the same, except for one or two who wanted to defy the rest.

Stupid acts of bravery, Moshat thought, staring into the foggy window. Drops of condensation ran down the glass, joining other smaller drops and charging towards the bottom. Moshat dared a quick glance in the old woman's direction. She wasn't looking at him anymore. Either she'd become distracted or had forgotten her suspicions. He prayed it was the latter.

The window offered him an escape from his mistake. His obsession to make sure everything about today was perfect had backfired, and at that moment, he didn't know if he would ever forgive himself for it.

For weeks, they had prepared the perfect plan. It *was* a perfect plan. But now there was a crack. And cracks led to crevasses.

Moshat had made his first mistake.

Chapter Twenty-Three

NAMES

August 1, 13:55

Jake's heart raced as he struggled to make his way through the rush of oncoming people meandering around Liverpool Street Station. The Central Line from Oxford Circus had been delayed by ten minutes, meaning that a fifteen-minute journey was stretched into twenty-five. Whether it was just a typical signalling failure he had seen so much on the news about, or whether it was because Frances and Transport for London had begun their negotiations, Jake didn't know. But he was certain that the longer he stayed on the Underground, the more his erratic behaviour would rouse suspicion that something was awry. And he knew, as soon as there was a press conference by the Prime Minister or Commissioner of the Met, hysteria would follow, and the Underground would become catastrophically busy. It was imperative they kept public safety at the forefront of their operation, including those taken hostage on the trains.

The pain in Jake's leg worsened with every step, and his

headache blurred his vision. He knew he was dehydrated, and he needed a glass of water — something, anything — to make him feel better. But thanks to the delay, he couldn't afford pit stops. The run to The Gherkin from Liverpool Street would be hard enough in his unfit state. His injuries would only slow him down further.

As his phone regained signal, it buzzed. A notification telling him he had one missed text message from Tyler popped up on his screen. Jake opened it and observed the image Tyler had sent him. It was an image of a man wearing a woollen hat seated at Paddington Station. He wore a thin jumper and carried a bag. There was nothing untoward about the man in the image. To Jake, he seemed just like any other random stranger walking along the street. But he committed the image to memory. And then the image disappeared. He tried to refresh the inbox, but it wouldn't work, the image was gone. It must have been deleted somehow. Then he remembered the text messages he had received about using his phone, and he hoped this one hadn't sacrificed one of his lives.

Jake set off for The Gherkin. His pace came to a slow jog as he neared the skyscraper. Pedestrians stared at him as he ran past them. He could feel their judgemental glances boring into his skin with every distasteful look. He knew there was something disconcerting about seeing a grown man, dressed in shirt and trousers, with soot and blood and debris staining his face and hands, sprinting along the street as if running away from something. He'd have thought the same thing if it wasn't his duty to apprehend terrorists and criminals. Society had become so afraid and paranoid of anything suspicious, it tried its hardest to keep well away from it. That way it was better to protect individual interests rather than the safety of all.

The twenty-first century had been cruel to society. Terrorism was at an all-time high, with the threat level balancing on critical, creating a ravine in the way people behaved and treated one another. The status quo had been distorted.

Out of order came chaos. And it took just one distortion to provoke it.

It took Jake three minutes to reach the base of The Gherkin. He checked his watch. 13:58. He had arrived on time with only seconds to spare. Allowing himself a few moments respite, Jake bent his knees, crouched down to the ground, placed his finger tips on the concrete to steady himself, and breathed deeply. He was exhausted and every muscle in his body liable to hurt, did.

'Hurry up,' Jake said, between exasperated breaths, checking his phone. Growing restless, he paced the length of the doors to The Gherkin's reception desk.

A security guard, dressed in full-black suit, with an earpiece and cable wrapped around his neck, stood motionless outside. His thick arms and shoulders bulged from the constraints of his shirt. Jake could feel the man's eyes staring into him suspiciously.

'Excuse me, sir,' the man said, approaching Jake. 'Are you lost?'

'No, no. Just waiting for a call,' Jake explained, hoping that would end the conversation.

Before the security guard could continue, Jake's phone rang.

'Lucky timing,' the security man said.

That isn't luck, Jake thought, surveying the surrounding area. *He's watching me. He can see and follow my every move. He knows who I'm speaking to. He's playing with me. I just need to outsmart him.*

'Hello.'

'Detective, I'm glad you made it, and in super-speedy time, too. Although, you look a little out of shape. A little round at the edges if you don't mind my saying so.'

'I do, but I'll let you off.'

'Generous.'

'But what about you?'

'What about me?'

'Are you in good enough shape?'

'I don't think that's any of your concern.'

'I'll take that as a no.'

'If you wish,' the voice said. Jake's ploy to get him into talking about himself hadn't worked. 'I know what you were trying to do, Detective, and it won't work on me just yet.'

'Yet?' Jake asked.

'Correct, all will reveal itself in due time, my dear Tanner. All you have to do is be patient.'

'Patience is a virtue, after all.'

'Indeed, it is! Well done, Jake. You're learning.'

'Thank you...' Jake hesitated. 'Sorry, I don't have a name to go by.'

The voice on the other end chuckled. 'How about you call me by whichever name you want? That way you won't forget it.'

'I sincerely doubt I'll forget anything about today.'

'Nevertheless, I give you permission to call me whatever you want. Be as creative as you see fit.'

Jake smiled. No more being Mr Nice Guy. 'OK, Dick-shit, thanks for the compliment. Oh no, wait. Hang on, what about, Glorified Attention-Seeking Arsehole? How does that work?' Jake chuckled into the phone. 'No, wait. I've got it: how about Useless Scumbag Piece of Shit Who Still Lives with His Mum after His Father Left Him at an

Early Age? I think I like that one the best. Not the most amazing ring to it, but it's definitely, *definitely* memorable.'

No more following the rules. No more giving into every demand without retaliation. Jake knew he could have made the entire situation worse, but it was a risk he needed to take. Whoever was behind this was egotistical — he had observed that much — and Jake needed to bring them down a few steps, knock them off the high-horse they were riding on and give them a taste of their own medicine. Jake could feel adrenaline course through his veins as he waited for a response.

Silence. Complete silence. *Fuck you, too*, Jake thought, holding an imaginary finger up to the person on the other end.

'I am a stone's throw away from the river. Over the years many of my stones have fallen in and witnessed births, deaths and marriages. What am I? Ten minutes. Oh, and Jake — if you ever mention my mother and father in such a way again, I will make sure your mother-in-law — yes, that's right, she's on the Heathrow Express — will be mutilated and harmed to an unprecedented level. And there will be nothing you can do about it, so I suggest you treat me with a little more respect and do as you're fucking told.'

The other end hung up before Jake could respond.

Even if he wanted to, he wouldn't know what to say. Jake's worst imaginations had been confirmed. He hadn't wanted to admit it at first, but now he knew Martha was on the Heathrow Express, and now her life was in even more danger than before, he didn't have a choice. He needed to save her.

Jake mentally replayed what his tormentor had said. And then, slowly, it all clicked. At first, he had considered this to be a one-man job, but after what he'd just been told, he was certain there was another one. Another terrorist was inside the Heathrow Express, ready and waiting to assault Martha, to use her as leverage over Jake to get him to do what they wanted. But were there any others? Jake didn't think it likely. Right from the start he had been chosen to take part, he had been the one they had targeted with the email, then the phone call, and now this. It was too much of a coincidence. If he was right, then what did that make the terrorists? What was their relation? What was their modus operandi? He would have to get Tyler onto it straightaway.

'Excuse me, sir,' the security guard said, breaking Jake from his reverie. 'I'm going to have to ask you to leave these premises.'

The man advanced towards Jake, placed a firm hand round Jake's biceps, swallowing it whole, and ushered him onto the pavement.

'Wait, stop!' Jake said, bringing out his ID card. The man inspected it and let go as soon as he realised who — and what — he was handling.

'Forgive me, DC Tanner.'

'It's OK. But I might need your help.'

'With?'

Quickly coming up with a lie, Jake said, 'Basically, in preparation for my Stag-do, some guys in the office have hidden all my clothes in different locations around the city, giving me different clues to find it all. I've got ten minutes to find the next one, and if I don't get to it by then, it means I've got no clothes for the trip,' Jake paused. 'We fly *tonight*.'

The guard laughed, lightening the situation. 'What bastards. That's a funny idea, though. One of my mates is getting married soon now you mention it. I might get my mates to do the same thing.'

Please don't, Jake thought, *if my ordeal is anything to go by, he's going to have a shit time.*

Smiling, Jake said, 'Yeah, tell me about it. Now, I don't have a lot of time.' He rolled up his sleeve to display his watch as an additional incentive to hurry this man along.

'What clues have you got?'

'I'm a stone's throw from the river, and over the years my stones have seen births, deaths, and marriages... and there was something about the stones falling into the river,' Jake explained, using the best of his memory.

'So, we're looking for a stone building, that's close to the river,' the guard said, more so asking for the answer than giving one himself. *Not the brightest spark, are you?*

'But it's got to be an old building, right? And one that will still run if stones and pieces of it keep falling away?'

'Right...' the guard said.

'Never mind, mate,' Jake said, after realising he was wasting his time. 'I've worked it out. Got to go, cheers though.' And he ran down the street, heedless of whether or not he was going in the right direction. So long as it was near the River Thames, he had a remote chance of being on the right track.

As he ran he worked out the clues in more depth. Where was an old building along the River Thames, one very close to the riverbank? Where in this same building had there been births, deaths, and marriages?

What sort of establishment would last that long to see all those things?

And then he realised. It had been so easy when he put his mind to it.

The English Monarchy, that's who.

And where did the English Monarchy get married, born, and die? In the Tower of London.

It had been so beautifully simple that Jake kicked himself for not thinking of it sooner. Determined, and pushing aside the pain, he sprinted down the busy London streets towards the Tower of London, feeling his body scream at him with every hundred metres he ran.

When he arrived, he just hoped he wouldn't need to gain access to the Tower itself.

Chapter Twenty-Four

RING

August 1, 14:08

Fuelled by anger and adrenaline surging through his body, Jake sprinted to the Tower of London. His heart beat louder and harder than it had ever done before in his life. The determination to succeed was enough to deter any thought of failure.

He was on a mission, and he couldn't wait to get his hands on the motherfucker responsible for this.

He took five minutes to reach the Tower of London, after almost using up all his energy reserves to make it on time. He was out of breath and had to stand upright, with his hands behind his head and arms winged outwards to refill his lungs. Exhausted and fatigued, he felt his head swaying and his vision blurring. Bile rose from the depths of his stomach up to his throat; he swallowed hard to keep it down.

The surrounding area was sparsely populated. In the distance, near Tower Hill station, Jake saw a small stall. The

Union Jack colours of red, white and blue drowned the stall of any individuality. In his raspy, panting breath, Jake purchased a bottle of water, and within seconds, it was gone. He purchased another two and swallowed the first like liquid down a pipe. He would save the second for later. Assuming he didn't lose it.

The drastic physical exertion combined with mid-afternoon temperature caused him to sweat profusely. Beads of liquid salt ran down his face into his eyes and mouth. The stinging sensation was minor compared to the pain in his leg which worsened with every breath in his body.

There was only so much training and pain a man could take before he gave up.

But he wasn't going to be one of those men.

Jake strolled to a bench, sat on it, and waited for the next instructions. And waited. And waited.

Five minutes passed with him sitting impatiently on the wooden bench. His head darted left and right, observing everyone and anyone who walked past him, judging their every movement, profiling them inside his head. He had become paranoid, afraid, unable to trust anyone. Eventually, he grew restless and risked a call. Jake unlocked his phone and dialled Tyler's number, preparing himself to speak quickly and coherently, to minimise the time spent using it.

Tyler answered on the second ring.

'Tyler — I don't have much time. I'm not supposed to use my phone, and this is my second warning. Shut up and let me explain myself! I'm at the Tower of London. I don't know where I'm going next, but I need you to listen. Martha, my mother-in-law, is on one of the trains —'

'Do you know for sure now?' Tyler interrupted.

'Yes. The guy on the phone told me. He said if I insulted his mum and dad again he would make sure

Martha was harmed. Which means there's almost definitely someone on the Heathrow Express. They must be sat on a similar carriage to her, otherwise they wouldn't be able to attack her and use her as leverage.'

'Unless it's all a ploy.'

'No, I don't think so. He sounded majorly pissed off when I insulted his family, which makes me think whoever is in the train might be related to the person behind all the calls and computer hacks. I think the guy in the photograph you sent me has got something to do with it. Keep checking him out and see what comes up. Check family history, friends, relatives — anyone — and find a connection. Also, before I go, if Elizabeth calls, tell her I'm safe and that I will save her mother if it's the last thing I do.'

Jake hung up the phone as soon as he could. He just hoped that Tyler understood all of what he'd said. His pulse raced as he sat there, waiting and waiting. Panic and doubt kicked in. Had he made the right decision? Had he been overheard? What if there was a punishment for using his phone a second time?

His head felt light and dizzy. The cold water now running down his digestive system made little difference. This was going to be the worst panic attack yet. Unprecedented. He could feel the waves of hysteria and nausea come flooding in, ready to swallow him in the sea of panic and fear inside his brain.

Eventually, after practising some techniques he had used for the majority of his life, his heart rate slowed down, the pain in his mind subsided, and his vision cleared.

Jake tapped his feet on the floor and drank more fluids. All around him, he observed people staring down at their phones. Samsungs, iPhones, Nokias, Sonys, HTCs. Technology everywhere, consuming the planet and turning them into a generation of socially inept buffoons. Again, he thought of how much would go wrong in the world if it all just disappeared. As he observed passers-by, every phone within a twenty-foot radius rang simultaneously.

What are you planning now? Jake was afraid of what might come next.

Some looked down at their phones confused. Some ignored the call and continued on with what they were doing. All, except for one. Jake watched her stop to his left. A woman with her hair in a bun, dressed in a pencil skirt and beige overcoat, suddenly stood still. She was checking her watch with the other hand against an ear. She faced the opposite direction to Jake.

A few seconds later, she turned to him, gave him a querying look, and then span away.

Jake examined her intently. And then, as soon as she nodded her head and started towards Jake, that was when he knew this woman was now involved in his nightmare.

'Excuse me,' she said. Her voice was coarse and sniffly. It sounded like she had the remnants of a flu or an incipient cold. 'Is your name Jake?' she asked him.

'Yes...'

'There's someone on the phone for you. They called themselves Willy Wonka?'

Chapter Twenty-Five

DEMANDS

August 1, 14:14

Tyler got off the phone with Jake. He pocketed his mobile and wandered back into the debrief room where Theodor had been explaining his story. The atmosphere in the office was like a classroom. The old man was the teacher and everyone else in the room — Frances, Susanna, Simon, and Luke — were the young children sat around by his feet, craning their necks to listen and learn. Theodor was just finishing.

'My experience has taught me a lot of things,' he said. 'And in my time, I've never seen something as callous and immoral as this. It pains me to see something happening to our society. This country wasn't built on one person — it was built on the millions and millions of people over the centuries who have given their lives to get us to where we are now —'

'Mr. Rosenberg,' Frances interrupted. 'You're getting sidetracked again.'

'Heavens! Forgive me.' Theodor hesitated. 'I would almost bet my career on the fact you are looking for someone within the locomotive industry. There is no way someone without the know-how or the access to the buildings would have been able to place such machinations on the carriages. The factories don't close until the early hours of the morning, and they are guarded with CCTV and security patrols.'

It's the perfect plan, Tyler thought as he realised the efficiency of the people with whom they were dealing. He stepped forward, holding his phone in his hands and said, 'That's what Jake thinks.'

All eyes turned to him, as if he had just walked into class late and everyone was resenting him.

'How does Tanner know?' Frances said, rising to her feet.

Tyler then explained what Jake had told him. After he had finished, Frances spoke first.

'We're still looking for a positive ID on the suspect in the photograph. Nothing is coming back so far.'

'What about the logs that Theo mentioned earlier? The ones that record the adjustments made to a train?'

'Dead end,' Theo said. 'Whoever did this omitted that information. If you could backdate when these trains were modified to contain the explosives, then you would at least have a name.'

Frances started to the door. In an unspoken agreement between everyone else in the debrief room, they all followed her. She paced to the head of the main office space.

'Attention, all!' she cleared her throat. Turning behind her to face the screens, she saw an enlarged, densely pixelated image of the unidentified suspect staring back at her. 'I need the name and address of this person right now.

Contact the Heathrow and Gatwick Express manufacturers. Get them to send across a list of names and IDs for those who have worked late at night, those who have been responsible for the modification or repair of the locomotives in the last two weeks, or both. We don't know how long this operation has been in the making, but that's all we've got.'

Heads dipped back behind their computers and people typed away. Phones in the office rang. In the intervening hours between the initial news bulletin of the trains becoming stranded and it being a potential terror attack, New Scotland Yard and the team had been inundated with calls. Most callers were civilians ringing up to find out where their loved ones were or filing missing persons reports. Each report was logged into the system and would have to be followed up on over the course of the next few weeks. It was the officers' duty to complete every case. There was also a dedicated hotline for concerned citizens to report any suspicious packages or if they had any relevant information that would be of use to the investigation. So far, nothing concrete had come in.

Whoever they were dealing with made sure they left no trace.

Simon's phone rang behind Tyler. Simon answered it and disappeared. Then, just as Tyler was about to speak to Frances, an officer sprinted to the front of the room, his shoes heavy on the floor, and his breathing exasperated.

'Ma'am,' he said, holding a tablet in their hands. 'I've got something. I found the Heathrow Express employment files, and I think I've got a positive ID on the suspect.'

'Name?'

'A Mr. Moshat Hakim. Twenty-seven years old. Lives in Ealing.'

The bedraggled man then gave Frances the full, registered address. She paused a moment to consider what to do next. Tyler made a mental note of the name. Just as Frances was about to speak, Simon returned.

'Deputy,' she said, 'I need you to organise a raid at this location. There is no time to waste. Organise who you can. I want a live feed.'

'I'll get the warrant.' Simon nodded and left the room, already barking orders into the phone.

Turning to Frances and his colleague, Tyler asked, 'What else do we know about him?'

'I ran a check on the PNC under his name, but nothing came up.'

'What about the intelligence reports?' Tyler asked.

'Nothing, again.'

'Jesus Christ,' Tyler said. This was bad. Really bad. If the suspect's name didn't appear on any of the databases, then that meant the attack was from left field, unannounced yet heavily coordinated. Finding the suspects and catching them would be made ten times harder. It also meant that the terror threat to the UK was ever increasing, and that there was a real possibility anyone could terrorise the city without being caught. Whoever orchestrated this attack was an exception to the rule, which made Tyler even hungrier to catch them.

'I want you to find out everything. Address. Family. Relatives. Friends. Check his social media accounts, if he's got any. Gain access to his email addresses. At the moment, he is target number one.'

The man nodded fervently and returned to his desk.

Tyler turned to Theodor and said, 'Theo — where was the last place you worked? Which company was it?'

Theodor stepped forward and scratched the back of his head.

'Heathrow. I worked in the factory along the express route.'

'Did you ever meet Moshat Hakim? Is there a possibility you could have worked with him at some point?' Tyler asked.

Theodor considered this a moment as he wracked his brains. Despite his age, his memory was still in as good shape as it was when he was younger. But now, as he was placed under immense pressure, his mind faltered.

'I can't remember. But I can think of someone who might. Adam Gardner. He's an old colleague of mine. We still keep in touch. It's been a while, but the last I heard he was still at the company.'

'Do you have a contact number?'

'Yes. I'll see if I can arrange a meeting —'

'Theo,' Frances interrupted, 'make it a video call. As soon as you get through to him, let me speak to him.'

Theo nodded and disappeared into the debrief room. A few minutes later, Theo returned and informed them all that Adam would be available in half an hour and that they had arranged a video call.

Over the next couple of minutes, the intelligence filtered into New Scotland Yard. Tyler and the team had learned that Moshat Hakim had a degree in engineering and had worked at the Heathrow Express for the past two years. He had a clean record and a good credit rating. His emails returned nothing interesting; they, too, were clean. There was nothing untoward about Moshat Hakim, nothing that suggested to them he was a terrorist. It was a potential dead end.

Then, suddenly, the multitude of screens on the giant wall went black. The brightness in the room dimmed. It was amazing how much artificial light the tiny screens emanated. What had once been the face of their lead target, had now changed into the same yellow smiley face they had seen before. The words naughty detectives, no more technology for you flashed on and off the screen in a green cursive font. Below that was a countdown clock of how long they had left until the explosives detonated.

Everybody rose to their feet and stared down at their computers, all witnessing the same thing on their monitors.

'What the fuck is happening? How the hell have we let this happen again?' shouted Frances, pacing over to the wall.

'They don't want us to continue investigating Moshat Hakim, that much is clear,' Tyler said.

'Then what the bloody hell do we do now?' Frances asked.

There was a pause. Everyone there already knew the answer, but they were too afraid to voice it.

'There's nothing we can do.'

Frances, stern and abrupt, frantically paced around the room as she continued barking orders. Nothing on the computer monitors had changed except for the tiny count-down clock below the smiley. And she, along with everyone else, began to get worried.

Each second ticked away on the red display. It was a constant reminder that time was running out and that soon, everyone on those trains would die in a horrific explosion unless Jake could save them.

A few minutes into the computer blackout, ear-splitting static blasted through the speaker system in the room. Tyler dropped to the ground, covering his ears with his hands.

Without warning, *Ride of the Valkyries* played. It started quietly at first, only reaching its crescendo as everybody in the room rose to their feet and stared at the wall of screens at the front of the room again. The image disappeared and replaced with individual letters typing onto the screen, one at a time, as if they were watching someone type their thoughts into a word processor. Tyler watched as instructions were spelled out. They read:

STOP. YOU WON'T FIND WHAT YOU'RE LOOKING FOR. NOW IT'S TIME TO FIND WHAT I WANT. ONE MILLION IN CASH. HAND DELIVERED. COURTESY OF DC TYLER STUART. 16:00. HE COMES ALONE. NO DELAYS OR PASSENGERS DIE.

Why me? Tyler thought after he read the message. Was it because he and Jake were close friends? Or had he inadvertently said something about the person behind the attack without realising it, and thus had upset them? He considered both options likely.

He had a task to do, and he was ready for it. How hard could it be, collecting one million pounds and then handing it over to a deadly terrorist? He was feeling braver than he should have been.

'Ma'am,' Tyler said to Frances. She had finished reading and stared at him accusatorially, as if he were behind it somehow. 'What's the ETA for the ransom? When can I expect it to be ready for collection?'

Frances checked her watch. 'We've got little over an hour. These things take time. It's difficult collecting together that much money.'

'At least they didn't order it in gold,' Tyler said, finding himself smiling. 'I would have needed a truck.'

Frances scowled at him, unimpressed. Tyler ignored her and advanced towards the screen. He inspected the pixelated words.

'Why Trafalgar Square?' Tyler asked, thinking out loud. 'It's out in the open. There's got to be something more to it than that.' He thought hard, his mind buzzing with theories. At last, he had it. 'They've chosen it because it's near to them. They want to leave the sanctity of their own home for as short a time as possible and be able to slip back into their hole with no one realising they were there.'

'What are you suggesting?'

'Conduct a search on every known associate of Moshat Hakim. Find out where they live. See if they have a registered address near Trafalgar Square, somewhere they might slide away under our noses.' Tyler was getting into the swing of things. He was filling in for both Jake and Mamadou in their absence, and he was enjoying having so much power and authority. As he continued speaking, Susanna disappeared to answer another phone call. 'I'm going to need protection. Jake will need protection. We'll need increased officer presence on the streets and in and around Charing Cross station — both undercover and uniformed. We'll need sniper support positioned on the top of the roofs in the surrounding area. If they have a clean shot, then they take it. If not, at least we'll have an ID, and we can track their movements on the CCTV.'

Susanna returned as he finished speaking.

'DC Stuart, the ransom will be ready in ten minutes. You and DC Matthews are to collect it and bring it back here,' she said. It was the first time he had heard her speak so authoritatively. And he liked it. She was about the same age as him, and as far as he could tell, she was single. *Although she's probably more married to the job than to anything else.*

And, just like that, his power had been stripped away from him by his babysitter, DC Matthews. It had been settled. Everyone knew what they were doing — even if they didn't agree with it. And shortly, they would deal with their target face-to-face. Tyler shot Luke and Frances a look of contempt as they left the office. He and DC Matthews drove the journey to the Bank of England in complete silence.

Chapter Twenty-Six

DECEPTION

August 1, 14:20

Jake had never been in a hostage situation first-hand before. He had only ever seen and heard about them either on the television or in the office. That was all about to change now. Sure, he had seen training videos and read the handbooks on how to deal with situations like that. But never had he envisioned the boot being on the other foot. Never had he envisioned himself being the captor.

The tables had turned.

'This is your new friend for the next few hours,' Willy Wonka, as he insisted on being called, said into Jake's ear. 'She's gorgeous, isn't she? Look after her, Detective, because if anything happens to her, then your journey will end.'

Jake stared at the woman before him, his mind a blank canvas, open for his tormentor's words to scribble across it. The girl before him was pretty; her make-up was heavily done, but in a fashion that did not look comical. Her eyebrows had been drawn on and made her look as if she were frowning at everyone she encountered. On her arm, dangling in the nook of her elbow, was a Chanel Bag. She wore heeled shoes. She looked strong, and Jake guessed she was both strong and tough. There was an air about her that suggested no male would ever get on the wrong side of her without avoiding a swift kick to the genitals.

'Yeah,' Jake said quietly, turning away from her. 'She is.'

'God, your taste in women is bad. Although your wife is the exception to the rule.'

'Don't you dare bring her into this,' Jake said, grinding his teeth. The woman overheard and gave a surprised look to Jake.

'Or what, Detective? You'll send the big bad Batman to come and kill the Joker?'

'I'm your Batman, motherfucker, and I'm coming after you,' Jake hissed down the phone. The woman cast him a look. She was just as scared as he, but she didn't have the nerve to ask for her phone back. 'What do we need to do?'

'Firstly, you need to be punished for using up another of your lives. I saw you use your phone a few minutes ago, Tanner. You don't listen, do you? Oh, well. As a result, this will be your punishment: this lovely lady in front of you, Jake, will be your hostage. She is going to follow you everywhere until you have completed the ransom drop, and then you will give her to me. Just a precaution, I hope you understand, just to make sure nothing bad happens to myself. She will remain safe and unharmed — so long as I do.

'More details for the drop will follow, but you best hope that your man, Stuart, finds you alive and well...' the voice trailed off. Jake was too angry to say anything back. Instead, he just listened and calculated his next move. 'On another note, I'm delighted to inform you that you've nearly come to the end of your merry adventure. Just one more stage stands in the way of winning the golden jackpot at the end. So here is your final clue: I am east of west and west of east. I don't know where I live, for I have moved county. Where am I?'

That was it. Nothing more, nothing less. Jake cursed and held out the phone to the woman. He almost dropped it as she tried to take it from him.

I thought these were supposed to get easier? Jake thought. *This is complete bullshit.*

He rose to his feet. The girl had walked away after giving an awkward smile. He started after her. She walked at a fast pace; Jake assumed it was to get as far away from him as possible. But she was going nowhere except wherever he went.

He followed her, picking up the pace. 'Excuse me!' he called out. She carried on and pretended not to hear him. Breaking into a slight jog so he was walking alongside her, he grabbed her arm gently and held her back.

'What?' she asked, flexing her acrylic nails.

Jake let go of the woman's arm. 'Please, I need to speak to you in private. It's important.'

She walked off again. This girl was strong-willed, and Jake admired that. But he couldn't leave without her.

'Please. Look, I'm a detective,' Jake said, pulling out his ID card, 'and I need your help. Just let me explain.'

The woman snatched it from him, looked at it closely and then at him, as if she were a cashier in a supermarket and he an adolescent using a fake ID, and the contents in his shopping basket consisted entirely of alcohol. Convinced, she handed it back to him. Jake observed the surrounding area. To the far left of where they were standing was a small bench. It looked well-hidden from any security cameras nearby.

'Listen,' Jake said, pulling her over to it. He was conscious of the fact their every word and move were being closely observed. 'I'm sure you want nothing to do with me after that phone call, and I'm sure you have loads of questions, but let me explain, please? Deal?' The woman nodded. 'First, what's your name?'

'Lucy Sanderson.'

'Lucy, nice to meet you.' Jake introduced himself. After he had mentioned the word terrorism in his job title, he was expecting a reaction from Lucy, but when one didn't come, he continued, 'We have a situation on our hands, and unfortunately, you've now been dragged into this mess, too, which I apologise for, but I need your full cooperation.'

Lucy said nothing. Jake took this as approval for him to carry on. He spent the next few moments explaining everything he knew. He started from the beginning and left nothing out. Her expression remained the same as he told her, and he wondered if she was listening at all.

'So, you have to come along with me and deliver the ransom money. Understand?' Jake finished.

'Yes,' she replied.

'You're not one for many words, are you?' Jake said, laughing and trying to lighten the mood a little.

'What am I meant to say? That I'm really excited to be risking my life on a day when I've got a job to go back to, a home to go back to, a *life* to go back to? Is that what you want me to say, Detective?' she said. She had a temperament like Mamadou's, Jake realised, and he liked it. It could prove to be helpful.

'No, not exactly. I just want to prepare you for the worst. If everything goes to plan, then we'll be saving thousands of lives.' Jake tried to think of any way he could improve the situation, but there wasn't one.

'I understand. So, where are we going now?'

'We need to work it out.'

As he was talking to Lucy, he couldn't help but think of an alternative route out of this. The way he saw it, there were two options: the first was to follow every step he was ordered to comply with. The easy way, the long way, the safest way. The second option was to risk another phone call somewhere private, somewhere they wouldn't be overheard. But if they were discovered, Jake knew there would be consequences.

However, perhaps there was a third option.

Jake considered this for a while. Lucy stared at him, waiting for his direction.

'Follow me,' he said finally, starting towards the Tower of London.

'What are we doing?'

'Hiding,' Jake said. 'We need to do this quickly, so we don't raise suspicion. In the meantime, I need you to figure out where we're going next. Here's the clue.' Jake recited the clue he had been told.

They advanced down the stairs by Tower Hill station, raced across the road, and down the steps leading to the base of the tower. Around them, the atmosphere was buzzing with people. In the far distance, Jake could hear a group of break dancers busking on the streets. They had stereos and loud speaker systems blasting songs with heavy bass. A crowd was forming around them.

It was the perfect disguise.

By the time Jake and Lucy reached the growing crowd, there was a dense mass of fifty people surrounding the dancers. Here they could remain well-hidden. They pushed their way through the people, Jake flashing his ID card, Lucy not giving a care in the world as she barged through the crowd like she owned the place. They stopped halfway. Jake crouched down a few inches and Lucy followed. The problem with being a tall guy was that he was always noticeable in crowds. It made him a fantastic lighthouse signal at festivals or concerts, but not so much when it came to being stalked by a terrorist.

Jake peered up to the nearest person beside him. A thin man, standing five-foot-ten, wearing tracksuit bottoms and a hoodie over his head all the while exuding the scent of marijuana, looked down at him. The man wore sunglasses, and Jake knew he was being shot a dirty look from behind them.

Jake asked to borrow the man's phone. 'It's a police matter, and it is imperative I use it,' Jake finished, feeling intimidated by the man's stare.

'Wha's tha' mean?' the hooded guy responded.

'What does what mean?'

'Impera'ive.'

'Oh, it means... ermm.'

'It means it's more than important, life or death things depend on it,' Lucy said. Jake cast her a look that said *where did that come from so easily?* 'I'm a lawyer. I should know these things.'

Jake nodded and then looked back up at the man.

'Nah,' the man said, 'I don't wanna be givin' my phone to some fuckface pig.'

'Sir, I'm different to the police, I'm MI5, and if you don't give me your phone, I'm going to get you arrested,' Jake lied.

The man didn't react the way Jake had hoped. Instead of handing over his phone, the man lifted his long baggy shirt, revealing a small handgun wedged between his boxers and tracksuit trousers. Jake stared at it for a while longer than he meant to. He'd never had a weapon this close to his face. And he hoped he'd never have to. Acting on instincts alone, Jake reached for the man's crotch, snatched the weapon from his waistband, flipped the man round, grabbed his hands and floored him, locking him in a painful hold. It all happened so quick the man barely had any time to react. *Stupid idiot,* Jake thought, *thinking he could take on a police officer.*

The man wriggled beneath Jake's weight; Jake pressed down on him and twisted the man's arms.

'Don't react,' Jake hissed. 'This will be much better for you if you don't do anything stupid. All we ask is that we use your phone. Now, I'm not in a position to arrest you, so here's what's going to happen: I'll keep the gun, and you're going to let us use the mobile phone, and then once we've done that, you're going to go one way, and I'm going to go the other. How does that sound?'

Jake didn't have time to hang around and wait for an officer to come and arrest the young man. Nor could Jake take the man with him to the next location; he would be busted as soon as he stepped out of the crowd. It was better to leave it. One less gun on the streets was the positive he was taking from it, and it was even better that it was now in his possession.

The man considered this for a moment.

'Back pocket,' he grunted.

Jake reached behind the man's back and pulled out something that reminded him of a small brick. It was sturdy and firm in his hands. It was a Nokia.

A burner phone.

Judgements and prejudices aside, Jake took it as a blessing that he encountered upon someone who had this sort of phone in his pocket; it would be much safer and less risky to call New Scotland Yard with a phone that wasn't traceable.

Jake gave the man the thumbs up and dialled Tyler's number.

'Hello, Tyler speaking,' was Tyler's voice on the other end. It was like music to Jake's ears.

'Tyler — it's Jake. I'm using someone else's phone quickly. I'm hidden in a crowd and praying this doesn't get us in the shit.'

'Jesus, mate, you sure it's safe?'

'I don't know, that's what I'm hoping you'll be able to tell me. If anything else explodes, you tell me, OK?'

'I can't. I'm not in the office. DC Matthews and I are on the way to the bank to collect the ransom as we speak.'

'What? OK.' Jake's mind raced. There were so many questions he wanted to ask but he knew there wasn't time. He inhaled deeply. How could he possibly explain this hostage situation? 'Tyler, things are going to get worse...'

'Why?'

'I've got a woman with me called Lucy. She's going to be the one doing the drop at wherever the location is,' Jake said whispering. He was cautious not to speak too loudly.

'What the fuck, Jake? How have you got someone innocent involved?' Tyler asked.

'It just happened. I don't have time to explain, but I need to take her with me to the next destination, and then we go to the drop-off point. I don't know what happens from there on.' Jake looked at the girl. There was a look of fear in her eyes. He admired her for not running away there and then. If she didn't want to be involved, she would have gone already. 'But I'm going to make sure nothing happens to her,' Jake added for reassurance.

'Trafalgar Square,' Tyler said.

'What?'

'Trafalgar Square.'

'What about it?'

'That's where the drop-off is.'

'How do you know?'

'Our dear friend Mr. Willy Wonka informed us. Dead-line is four p.m.'

'Fuck,' Jake said, checking his watch. He had to find out his next destination, get there and then meet at Trafalgar Square in just over an hour. 'I don't have long.'

'Where have you got to go, boss?'

'East of west, west of east, I don't know where I live, for I have moved county,' Jake repeated.

'What the hell does that mean? Jesus, this guy's a wack job!'

'Tell me about it. Do you have any idea what it might mean?'

'Hang on. Give me a second.' Tyler paused, thinking.

'Upminster,' another voice said through the phone.

'Is that Luke?' Jake asked.

'Yeah. I'm riding shotgun. You're on speaker.'

'OK. You're sure it's Upminster?'

'Positive. My grandad used to complain about it. Said there was something to do with commuters and drivers being pissed Upminster changed county.'

'Thanks, Luke. I appreciate it.'

'Be mindful of the time when you come back, mate,' Tyler interjected. 'It could be busy.'

Jake hung up. He hadn't factored the late afternoon rush into the travel time. If he thought making his way round London on the Underground during the day was bad... he would soon be in for a shock. Despite being one of the longest running underground services, constant problems and breakdowns and failures caused inevitable delays and frustrations.

Jake was going to need another way to get around town.

Jake returned the man's phone and freed his arms. The thug looked at Jake condescendingly and intimidatingly. *I hope our paths never cross again. And I hope no one else crosses it either.* Nodding to Lucy, he turned around and headed out of the crowd and back to Tower Hill station. As they broke out of the flurry of people, they ran. It had to look like they'd just found out where to go, made a wrong turn and needed to go back on themselves.

Jake pulled ahead and was twenty yards in front of Lucy when he came to the stairs. He turned round and looked at her. She was slowed by her heels. Soon, Jake knew, they would become a hindrance for both of them. Frowning at him, she removed her heels and ran the rest of the journey bare foot. Her shoes bounced around in her hands.

Jake and Lucy entered Tower Hill station, ignored the sign post that advised passengers that there were major delays on the Underground, and jumped down the steps. A District Line train was already on the platform as they descended the stairs. Jake dived into the carriage moments before the doors closed, landing heavily on his shoulder. Lucy fell on top of him. Jake breathed a sigh of relief.

They were on board and headed in the right direction.

Chapter Twenty-Seven

PRESS

August 1, 14:42

Tyler collected the ransom money at the Bank of England. It was the first time he had been to visit the archaic building, and the first time he had ever been in a bank to collect one million pounds. A part of him wished it was for him. But then the other half of him remembered the money would go towards saving thousands of lives, and no amount of money could compare to that.

He and Luke entered the bank, flashed their ID, waited until someone of the right pay grade attended to them, and entered a secluded vault on the first floor. The person in charge — a man dressed in a suit — handed over the briefcase containing the money, and that was that. There were no pleasantries. No names exchanged. It was just a simple in-and-out job. Inconspicuous and tidy, just the way the government wanted it. As far as the British public was concerned, they didn't give in to terrorists' demands, so everything was kept well under the radar.

Tyler and Luke left the bank, placed the briefcase in the passenger footwell, and raced back to New Scotland Yard. The blue lights and sirens opened the way through for them, and in a matter of minutes, they had returned. He was grateful for the sparse traffic. It was nearing 14:50 — the sun burned furiously in the sky and if he had been forced to walk, Tyler was sure it would have looked like he was trying to enter a wet T-shirt competition.

When Tyler and Luke returned, Tyler slammed the briefcase on the large, oval desk in the debrief room, and allowed everyone to gawp at it. It was probably their first time seeing such an amount of money, too. Something they would have only seen in movies.

'Did you encounter any difficulties?' Simon asked Tyler.

'No,' Tyler said. The only difficulty he faced was being seen in public with Luke. His new supervisor's presence had been pointless and infuriated him.

'Good,' Simon said.

Just as he'd finished speaking, Frances's phone rang. She answered it and spoke quietly into the receiver. As soon as she'd hung up, she turned to face Tyler.

'A press conference has been arranged outside Number 10. You're coming with me.'

Tyler didn't know what to say. Why had she chosen him? What was he going to do that would warrant his being there? He was just a simple DC, miles behind the ranks of the Commissioner and Assistant Commissioner.

'Thanks, ma'am,' Tyler said. 'Who's running it?'

'Me.'

'What about the Commissioner? Or the PM?'

'They've delegated it to me. They're still both sat in COBRA. It would appear the PM's too shy to stand up in front of terrorists, despite her campaign promises.' There was a moment of awkward silence in the room. 'But hey, enough of politics. Let's get to it.'

'What do you need me for then?'

'I've only got ten minutes to prepare. And you're going to help me with what to say. We can do it on the way.'

A heavy weight of responsibility fell on Tyler's shoulders. He felt both excited and afraid. If he told Frances the wrong information, anything that was incorrect or inaccurate, he would be the one in the firing line. He swallowed hard and thought of what she could and could not disclose.

Discussing a terrorist attack on London with the public always threw up an onslaught of hurdles. How much could they share that would maintain the public's faith in security, while simultaneously telling them enough so as not to make them think they weren't being told the whole picture? It was a political and policing minefield.

Tyler, Susanna, and Frances hopped into Frances's unmarked Land Rover and drove the short distance to Number 10 Downing Street. It had been kitted out with bullet-proof glass, and the underside was reinforced to deter any potential IEDs on the side of the road. Advancements in the way terrorists achieved their aims had developed, and so the police needed to adapt, too, in how they defended themselves against the real and dangerous threats they faced every day.

Four minutes later they arrived. Tyler was the first to jump the distance between the seat of the car and the floor. He opened his passenger door directly onto Number 10. On the other side of the car, Downing Street representatives placed the plinth Frances would soon speak from onto the ground. Beyond that, spread across the width of the building, was a line of hungry television presenters, news reporters, and journalists.

It was all a little overwhelming for Tyler. Dozens of video recorders and microphones and cameras flashed in his face, blinding him. Soon, he knew, his face would be all over national television, even if it was only for a moment and in the background. It would be his biggest claim to fame. But as he stood in front of the house that had been occupied by some of the most important and powerful individuals in the country, he felt small and insignificant. It didn't, however, stop him from feeling immense pride.

'Tyler?' Susanna said. She had stopped in front of him, breaking him from his state of reflection.

'Coming,' he said, brushing his faux pas off with a smile.

He followed Frances and Susanna into the building. He made it as far as the floor mat before he was ushered back out again.

'There's no more time to prepare,' Frances said. 'We'll have to address the press now.'

Disappointed, Tyler obliged and stepped out of the way to allow Frances past. Her Land Rover had shot off into the distance, and now there was nothing in the way of Tyler and the cameras. This was it. There was no going back now.

Frances strolled towards the plinth, her back straight and shoulders pushed back. She cleared her throat before beginning. As soon as she opened her mouth, the entire road erupted in a single flash, blinding Tyler and burning the inside of his retina.

'At approximately eleven fifty a.m. this morning, three trains were forced to a complete standstill by an outside terror attack.' Frances spoke clearly and with a fiery passion in her voice. In the car journey, they decided to keep it short and sweet. Straight to the point. 'Since then, the individuals responsible have made their demands clear. And it is evident to us that we will not back down to them. We will not give in to fear, and we will not be deterred by anything that they throw at us. We are the Great British public and nothing that has ever come our way in the past has brought us to our knees. And nothing will start now.

'We are working tirelessly to make sure those stuck on board the trains are returned home to their loved ones, and that the individuals responsible for this attack are brought to justice. And we will find them. If anyone has any information or notices anything abnormal that can help with our investigations, please report it to the Anti-Terrorist Hotline. Similarly, if anyone has, or has ever had, interaction or communication or any other sort of affiliation with a Mr. Moshat Hakim, report it and we will work together. You will be heavily rewarded for your cooperation. Thank you.'

Frances turned her back on the voracious news reporters, ignoring their questions and taunts, and strolled over to Tyler and Susanna. She was calm, and Tyler could sense the passion ebb from her demeanour.

As she approached, Susanna answered her phone. The three of them entered Number 10 Downing Street, hidden from view of the video recorders and microphones. They were greeted by a wide set man dressed in a dark navy suit. Around his ear was a radio communications device. Next to him was the Home Secretary who Tyler recognised at once.

'Thank you for doing that, Assistant Commissioner,' the Home Secretary said. 'However, I'm afraid we're going to need you to stay here at COBRA. You'll be allowed direct contact with your deputies. There are going to be more difficult decisions ahead, and it is of paramount importance they are made collectively.'

'Fine,' Frances replied, her voice replete with disdain.

The Home Secretary smiled gracefully and stepped aside just as Susanna returned from her phone call.

'Ma'am,' Susanna said to Frances. 'Adam Gardner is on the line in the debrief room.'

'Thank you.' Frances turned to Tyler. 'All right, DC Stuart. I want you to gather as much intelligence as you can from Mr. Gardner. It's your responsibility to make sure he tells us everything we need to know.'

Tyler nodded in affirmation, unsure of how much more responsibility he could take. As he headed towards the Land Rover, he couldn't help but think how much he'd deserve a cold one with Jake at the end of all this.

Chapter Twenty-Eight

COLLEAGUE

August 1, 14:55

Adam Gardner's pixelated double chin filled up the majority of the flat screen television in the debrief room. He had been waiting for the past ten minutes and he now appeared impatient as Tyler and Susanna entered the room. Theodor was already waiting inside; he and Adam had been catching up.

Feeling optimistic with his new-found confidence, Tyler sat on the left-hand side of the table opposite Theodor. He glanced at Theo and acknowledged him with a nod. The view of the London Eye outside the window caught his eye for a moment.

'Mr. Gardner —' Tyler began.

'Adam. It's what everyone calls me.'

'Adam,' Tyler continued, already taking a dislike to the man. 'How are you today?'

'Fine, thanks. Is this going to take much longer? I've got a job to get back to.'

'And we've got a job to do here, so if you wouldn't mind…' Tyler hesitated, waiting for a reaction. 'We were wondering if we could ask you some questions regarding Moshat Hakim?'

'Sure.' Adam shifted the webcam on his laptop so that his face covered the lower half of the screen.

'Firstly, could you please confirm this is in fact Moshat Hakim?' Tyler called up an image of the silhouette in Paddington Station onto the screen.

'Yeah, mate. That's him,' Adam answered within a second.

'And when was the last time you saw him?'

'Last night. About midnight. I left a couple minutes before, and he was the last one in the factory. I haven't seen him since. He's not bothered to show up for work today.' Adam hesitated. 'Am I under arrest here or something?'

'No, Adam, you're not, but you are helping us out a great deal.' Tyler turned to Susanna at the back of the room and raised his eyebrow. Turning to face Adam, Tyler continued, 'How well do you know Mr. Hakim?'

'Not really. He's always quiet. Keeps to himself, you know. When we're in the canteen at work, he'd just sit on the edge of the conversation, listening in.'

'Does he have many friends at work?' Tyler asked, removing the image of Moshat and returning to the live feed of the debrief room so Adam could see them again.

Adam searched his memory for a response. Before answering, he coughed down the mic. 'In a word: no. I didn't see him with very many people while we were at work together, and we worked the same shifts. He and I shared an office, which is about as close as he ever got to someone.'

'Were you and he friends?'

'I wouldn't say we were. If I'm honest, I felt sorry for him. That's the only reason I ever spoke to him. He seemed like a nice guy, and I didn't want him to feel left out.'

How noble of you, Tyler thought.

'Did he ever talk to you about his family life? Wife? Kids? Boyfriend?'

'Fuck no,' Adam replied. 'He wasn't one of those gays. I know that for sure.'

Jesus. I know I'm not a saint, but this guy. Tyler's loathing towards the man was growing with every sentence.

'How do you figure that?'

'Because one time, I brought my wife to the company Christmas meal, and he spent the whole night staring at her. I confronted him about it the day after. Obviously, I was taking the piss, but then the little pussy got proper apologetic and kept telling me there was nothing to worry about.' Adam laughed, his cheeks and jowls bouncing around like jelly.

'Christ,' Tyler whispered under his breath. He shot Theodor a look that said, "Seriously, this guy is going to help us? *Him*?"

Theodor returned the look with an apologetic expression.

'OK,' Tyler continued. 'What about any family? Did he mention anything about that to you? A brother?'

Adam hesitated. He took an abnormally long time, and after a few seconds, Tyler repeated the question.

'I heard you the first time, mate. I'm thinking.'

Tyler was thankful there was a screen and several miles separating them. For Adam's sake.

'Mr. Gardner, might I remind you if you do not tell us the truth it will be taken as an obstruction of justice and you could face jail time. So please, tell us what we need to know, and then we can both be on our way.'

Adam scowled through the television, the excess skin on his forehead partially covered his eyes, making him look like a giant potato.

'He mentioned he had a brother, yeah. Now I think about it.'

Fucking finally, Tyler thought. Now they were getting somewhere.

'Did he ever mention a name to you?'

'Erm… he might have done once. But I never paid attention to it. Alan? Or Andy? Something like that. Something that began with A.'

'Great. Fantastic. Thank you.' Tyler made a mental note of the information. Meanwhile, Susanna wrote the entire discussion down on paper. 'You've been a great help. We'll let you go soon, but we've got just a few more questions to ask. What did you talk about at work?'

'What do you mean?' Adam asked.

'Well, if you know nothing about the man you've spent the past two years sat in an office with, then I want to know what you talked about?'

Adam scoffed. Tyler had pushed a button, and he knew it.

'Football.'

'Any particular reason?'

'I'm a Gunner, and he's a West Ham fan. Said he had been all his life. He even used to play for the youth squad, apparently. Says he quit because of some injury or some bullshit excuse like that.'

'Did you believe him?'

'About which bit? The injury?'

'No. The fact he played professional football.'

Adam shook his head.

'Is there anything else that you can think of that may help us? Anything that struck you as odd over the past few weeks? Acting strange or nervous or erratic around the office?' Tyler thought he should have done the psychology degree and not Jake.

'No, mate. If I think of something I'll let you know.'

Tyler thanked the man for his time and ended the call. His portly face disappeared from the screen altogether.

'Jesus,' Tyler said, turning to face Theodor. 'What a specimen. Either he's punching, or Moshat has got shit taste in women.'

'Tyler!' Susanna barked. 'Attention back to the room, please.'

Tyler did as he was told. 'What do you make of all that then? Seems strange, doesn't it? He went from being a professional footballer to an engineer. That's quite a jump to make. And if he's been in the job for two years, then maybe this whole thing has been in the pipeline for longer.'

If he were right, then how did they stay under the radar for so long? How had they organised the entire thing unnoticed? He didn't want to think about it; the thought made him afraid of what else might be to come, what else might be in the pipeline from other fanatics out there.

'I'll get someone to contact West Ham, see if they can provide any information. And at least we've got a confirmation on the brother. We just need to find a name,' Susanna said. She had obviously learned a thing or two from her years spent with Frances judging from the concise, pointed way she spoke. 'I'll pass it on to Frances at COBRA.'

Susanna rose out of her seat and left the debrief room. Theo and Tyler shared an awkward glance at one another.

'What now?' Theo asked.

'We let Jake know. Somehow. Until then, we wait.'

Tyler checked his watch. In less than an hours' time, he would be en route to Trafalgar Square, one million pounds in his hand. A desire to take it and run burned at the back of his mind.

Chapter Twenty-Nine

POOR BEHAVIOUR

August 1, 15:17

The District Line train pulled into Upminster station. Jake and Lucy spilled out of the doors and onto the platform. The train journey had given them ample opportunity to get to know one another.

Lucy was in her thirties though she didn't like to admit it. She had been engaged once, but her fiancée had ended the relationship seventy-two hours before their wedding day. He had been sleeping around. Jake was silenced and appalled when she told him. In the nine years he'd been married to Elizabeth, he had always failed to see a reason to cheat. There was just no humanity behind it. Elizabeth was the best thing to happen to him in his entire life, and he wasn't going to throw that away with one stupid mistake. Sadly, he knew there were men that would.

Law was a big passion of Lucy's. She had graduated with first-class honours in criminal law and had landed herself a job as a solicitor in a local firm in the city. After accepting the position, she had moved away from her rural house in the countryside and into London. She enjoyed her job, but it wasn't what she wanted to do in life. Her biggest passion was policing, and growing up, she had always wanted to be a police officer. So much so, in fact, that after school she had applied for her local constabulary. But when it came round to the interview process, she had bailed out due to fearing failure and had taken the legal route instead. She liked the idea of enforcing the law in a different way.

Another passion of hers was computer forensics, a topic she minored in at university. In her spare time, whenever she wasn't busy preparing legal cases, she was often contracted by certain companies to hack into their computer network or business websites. If she was successful, then she would expose weaknesses in the company's online defences and offer solutions to improve it. That had helped her earn extra pocket money.

Jake had opened up to Lucy on the journey, too. He had told her about his home and work life, and how his family were the best thing to happen to him. Speaking to Lucy so openly seemed bizarre to him, yet so comfortable. As if they'd known each other for years and caught each other in the street for a catch up. The precariousness and danger of their position encouraged instant bonding and familiarity.

Lucy and Jake walked to the edge of the train platform. It was busier than Jake had expected, which made him feel even more nervous than he already was. The more civilians there were, the more casualties Jake and the emergency services would have to deal with - and they were already at full stretch. He just hoped his risk with the mobile phone had gone under the radar.

'We'll wait here,' Jake told Lucy as they came to a stop.

'It's likely we're going to move again. We just don't know where.'

Lucy nodded and stood with her back against a nearby pillar and her arms folded. She had accidentally left her heels on the tube in haste. A train pulled into the other side of the platform and Jake watched as different lives departed and went their own way, oblivious to what was happening around the city. He envied them.

'Hey,' Lucy said, snapping her fingers in front of his face. She'd noticed his staring into nothingness. 'You OK?'

'What, me? Yeah, I'm fine. I just want this to be over.'

'It's almost over. You'll be all right,' she said. 'And so will everyone else on those trains.'

Jake managed a half-smile and turned to face the other platform. Moments later he heard Lucy's phone ring. He spun on the spot and watched her fumble in her bag for it. She pulled it out and handed it to Jake. It was an unknown number.

'What am I doing here? Are we done now?' Jake asked, cutting straight to the point.

'You best believe it Jakey boy, you're at the end of the journey. Congratulations!'

'What's the prize?'

'I've told you, you've the privilege of determining which train contains lots of passengers who aren't going to die today,' the voice explained.

'And how do I work that out? Anymore fucking stupid clues for me?' Jake asked. Commuters gave him funny looks as they walked past him and Lucy.

'You follow your train of thought, Jake. You're a clever boy, you should be able to work that out. I'd be disappointed if you made it this far and couldn't fit the final piece in the puzzle.'

'Where are you sending me next?' Jake asked, speeding the conversation along. Time was running out, and there was no time to play the games. It had already taken them thirty-five minutes to make it to Upminster

Willy Wonka paused. A few seconds later there was a soft chuckle. It started out quiet and grew to a loud, hearty laugh.

'What's so funny?' Jake asked, getting agitated.

'Do you think I'm stupid, Detective Tanner?'

'What do you mean?'

'I asked if you think I'm stupid, *Jake*?'

'No, I don't. Why?' Jake slowly became concerned for the safety of everyone in the station.

'Then let me ask, why do you treat me like it? Why do you think pulling that little stunt you did back there was OK? Because, Detective, let me tell you this. It isn't. You have continuously disobeyed my orders, and you show no sign of remorse nor show any sign of having learned from your mistakes. Your behaviour has been reminiscent of the very government that is crippling this country, Detective. And as the country's hero today — the United Kingdom's front runner in the war against terror — you and everyone else around you will be punished.' Jake held his breath; casting darting looks at those around him. By now, the platform had filled completely, with rows and rows of passengers waiting for the next approaching train. The voice in his ear continued, 'At the other end of the platform, tucked neatly inside a box full of cables, is a device that is going to blow in the next thirty seconds. If you survive, then get to Trafalgar Square for four p.m. Lucy delivers the ransom or more innocent people suffer. Good luck, motherfucker.'

Oh, dear God. Jesus, no.

Twenty-eight seconds and counting.

Acting on instincts alone, Jake turned on the spot and sprinted towards the other end of the platform. His physical training from years ago in the academy hadn't all been that bad an experience, but right now as he sprinted, the pain in his leg had returned, making him wince with every step. Even the adrenaline wasn't enough to numb the pain.

Running down the middle of the platform, barging through a wall of bodies, he covered good ground.

Twenty-seconds and counting.

At last, he made it to the end of the platform. The number of people near him was comparatively thin. *It won't stop the blast radius from hurting or killing dozens of people.*

Jake came to a stop. There it was. A tiny silver box, about the same size as a waste bin, with a yellow electrical symbol plastered on it. It looked out of place, almost as if someone had put it there on purpose — and Jake was almost sure someone had.

'Jake!' Lucy called from behind him.

He turned to face her, a look of shock and fear tainting her pretty face.

Fifteen seconds and counting.

Chapter Thirty

LIFE AND DEATH

August 1, 15:19

Fifteen seconds and counting.

Jake's breathing was rapid, his nerves were on end, and he shook uncontrollably. The sound and atmosphere of the surrounding station became muffled and silent, as if someone were placing large plugs in his ear canals.

Lucy charged towards him, but soon stopped after Jake extended his arm out at her. 'There's a bomb. Tell everyone to get back!'

Lucy gasped, turned, and screamed for everyone in the vicinity to evacuate. Knowing the human race, they wouldn't do anything unless they had a reason. Despite Lucy telling them there was a bomb, few people moved, their earphones buried deep within their ears.

Jake had the answer. It broke every protocol and rule there was. But it was the only way he was going to keep everyone on the platform from harm.

As quick as he could, he released the gun he had stolen

from the hooded man and fired it into the air. Two at the small padlock that dangled on the side of the box, and one in the air.

Sparks flew as the bullet collided with the metal casing. The lock blew off and landed on the floor. Screams and shouts erupted from behind him. The repetitive thuds of footsteps assured Jake everyone was moving where they needed to be.

The fuse box door opened.

Five seconds and counting.

In a small plastic container Jake could see the timer ticking down. Wires protruded from a small device which housed the explosives. One bullet hole nestled inches away from the device. He had been lucky not to shoot the explosives and kill himself.

Three seconds and counting.

There was no time to do anything. No time to do anything except for one thing.

Run!

Jake turned on the spot. The platform had been cleared fifty feet. Jake hoped it was a safe enough distance. Without thinking, he dived off the edge of the platform onto the track. There was no other option; he was too close to the explosives, and as soon as they detonated, he would be killed, either by the force of the explosion or the small bits of debris that rocketed into his back.

Jake landed hard on the metal tracks. All the weight of his body crushed his right shoulder. Pain shot through the whole of his arm and upper body.

It was too late to worry about any incoming trains.

Then there was the explosion.

The sound was deafening. Even down on the track, he could feel the searing heat singe the hairs on the backs of his legs through his trousers. As he lay down cowering, pieces of burning shrapnel rained down on him.

He remained there for a few seconds, silent, regaining his senses, allowing the ringing in his ears to reach an equilibrium. The pain in his shoulder was excruciating, and with a slight wiggle of his arm, he gauged nothing had been broken or dislocated; it was just severely bruised and damaged.

He lifted himself up with his left arm and got to his feet. As he stood tall, he looked ahead of him. The noise and disorientation of the explosion had disrupted all his senses. In front of him, fast approaching, was a twenty-tonne train coach, the red and blue of the London Underground's logo about to be the last thing he ever saw.

The train applied the brakes. They screeched and hissed as metal collided with metal, sending sparks flying off in all directions.

Ten metres separated him from his imminent death.

'Jake!' Lucy bellowed. 'Jake!' Her voice was as high-pitched as the ringing sensation in his ears. Jake was brought out of his trance and looked up at Lucy, who was standing four feet taller than him. Crouching down she extended her hand for him to grab.

He took hold with all his strength. His life depended on it. Their hands tightened around one another, and he felt her pull him up. He jumped and rolled over the side.

Just as he landed on the platform, the train narrowly missed his feet. It clipped the heel of his right foot.

He was on the platform. Safe and alive.

Jake rolled onto his back, out of breath, and in a state of shock. His chest heaved as he lay on the cold, hard pavement. He closed his eyes. A soft hand touched his face and shoulder.

Lucy had saved his life, and for that, he was forever grateful. He owed her a gratitude that he knew could never be repaid.

She lifted him to his feet and brushed him down. As he turned around, he relaxed. The devastation behind him was minimal. There were no dead bodies littering the floor — only shards of metal and pieces of cable.

'Are you OK?' Lucy asked. Jake nodded slowly. His head hurt but he wasn't going to let it stop him.

'Come on, we need to go.' Jake started towards the platform exit and grabbed hold of Lucy's arm.

The platform had cleared out. Jake and Lucy were the only ones left, save for the crowd of people bottlenecking by the exit, trying to escape. Jake's entire body ached, and he winced in pain every time his limbs moved. He needed to keep moving, needed to keep his mind off it, needed to head towards Trafalgar Square in time. The only problem was how soon they needed to get there. Jake checked his watch. It was 15:23, and Trafalgar Square was just over twenty miles away on the road. Jake wasn't hopeful.

The pain in his head and body was made worse by thinking of a potential solution that would enable them to get there on time.

Jake turned to Lucy. 'Any ideas?'

She shook her head, but as they breached into the open road, a thought occurred to him. It wasn't much, but it was enough to give them at least a fighting chance. Now all he had to do was action it.

Jake exited Upminster station's foyer and looked around for what he was searching for. The cars and cyclists and pedestrians zooming past him disorientated him. He felt like he was in a movie scene appearing as some human experiment on the run who was only just feeling the effects of the drugs he'd been given.

Then, to his right, fast approaching him, something caught his eye. He stepped into the middle of the street and a motorcycle came skidding to a halt. *Perfect*, Jake thought. *Just what the doctor ordered.* Lucy caught up to him and stood directly to his left.

The bike was a Suzuki GSX-R600, sleek and nimble, with a red exterior and racing body kit. The new design and engine enabled a faster launch start, and faster, smoother turns. It was exactly what Jake needed.

The only problem was acquiring it. Nobody in their right mind was going to give this machine up so easily.

'Excuse me, sir, I need the bike.' Jake cut to the chase by flashing his ID card.

The man on the bike lifted his visor to inspect it.

'What for?'

'I work for Counter Terrorism Command, and I need to get to Trafalgar Square in about half an hour. Your bike is the machine for the job. It's in safe hands. I've ridden before,' Jake explained.

'You'll never make that, mate. Do you know how far it is?'

'Yes. We don't have a lot of time, sir.'

The man stared at Jake through the small slit of his visor and then at Lucy. He looked down at the bike as if saying a final goodbye.

'Fine,' he said. 'But take down my details and give me yours so if you fuck it up, you get me a new one.'

Jake nodded, and Lucy stepped in to note the man's details on her phone. As the man removed his helmet and handed it to Jake, the detective caressed his hands along the motorbike's handlebars. It had been a while since he'd last been on one. *You never forget, do you? Just like riding a bike.*

'Do you have another helmet for my colleague?' Jake asked, hopeful.

The man shook his head. 'Sorry, no. It's just me.'

'That's fine.' Jake turned to Lucy. 'Here, you wear it.'

'No, I can't,' she said.

'I'm not arguing with you, Lucy. *Take it.*'

Jake observed the bike for a moment, reminiscing, while Lucy put on the helmet. He had been twenty-three when he'd last owned one. He used to pick Elizabeth up and take her down to the seafront for the weekend. He loved the way he felt her cling to him so tight, bringing their bodies closer to one another as he felt the raw power of his bike's engine surge between his legs. He had enjoyed the responsibility, too; she was the precious cargo and he the pilot.

Now the same was going to happen. Except this time with a different woman, under different circumstances.

Jake and Lucy assembled themselves comfortably on the bike. Jake pulled the throttle and felt the power of the engine roar beneath him. A rush of adrenaline made him feel much stronger, alert and focused.

Nodding to the owner, Jake pulled on the accelerator. Lucy grabbed him round the waist, and they were off.

Twenty miles in thirty-six minutes with no police siren or flashing blue lights — it was going to take a miracle for them to make it in time. But that was on the busy streets of London, and Jake had no intentions on sticking to the roads.

Mamadou had been on the phone with Tyler for the past fifteen minutes. There was a lot for him to be filled in on, and Tyler tried to cover everything. Partly because Mamadou asked him, and partly because he knew he would have been in the shit with Mamadou if he later realised there was something he left out. Tyler informed his boss of the positive ID of Moshat Hakim and how he was their number one suspect. That they were still yet to find an accomplice — a potential brother who was also part of the entire orchestration. As much as it pained Mamadou to hear he was missing out, unable to fulfil his duty as Detective Chief Superintendent, he relaxed after realising Tyler, Jake, and the entire CTC team had it somewhat under control.

'It appears I've trained you well,' Mamadou said, laughing out of the hospital window.

'It seems that way, doesn't it?' Tyler said in his ear. 'How's your mum doing?'

Mamadou turned away from the window to face his mother. She lay asleep in the bed.

'Not good. She got out of surgery twenty minutes ago. She's hooked up to machine after machine. The nurses and doctors have been checking up on her every five minutes, monitoring her condition. They said over the next few hours, her heart could go again, and then that might be it.'

Mamadou spoke softly, clearly. It was unsettling to hear himself speak in such a manner. It had been a long time since he last had, and he knew it always meant bad news was just around the corner. The last time he had spoken like this was when his wife left him. They had spent the entire evening discussing their marriage, but after she concluded she didn't love him anymore, she packed her things and left.

Twenty years of marriage gone in an instant, never to be salvaged again.

'Mam...' Tyler said, bringing Mamadou out of his cursed thoughts. 'I'm so sorry.'

'It's fine. There's nothing you or anyone can do,' Mamadou said. He cast his eyes away from his mother to the television. 'Hold on, Stuart. What's this?'

'What?' Tyler asked.

'Is that you I see on the television? Behind the Assistant Commissioner, in front of Number 10?'

Tyler chuckled. There was a hint of smugness in it.

'Yeah,' he said.

'Christ — whose dick did you have to suck to get that privilege?' Mamadou asked. He was grateful for being in the room alone with his mother, lest anyone hear him and report him. 'You're doing my job for me, mate.'

They both laughed loudly. Laughter was good. Laughter took his mind off everything. Laughter made him who he was.

'I'll be after Jake's promotion next,' Tyler said.

'You found out about it, then?'

'Frances sort of blurted it out in front of the entire office when they had a lover's tiff.' Tyler paused. 'How's he doing? You reckon he'll get it?'

'Without a doubt. You think he deserves it?'

'More so than anyone else I know, boss. He works his arse off every day, and he cherishes his family. He told me they're the only reason he does what he does — to make them safe in the world. I won't be the one to stand in the way of that. If he needs me to, I'll fight his case for him.' Tyler's voice went quiet, as if there was a lump in his throat.

'You're a good friend, Ty. A shit detective, but a good friend.'

'Fuck off,' Tyler replied.

Just as Mamadou was about to unleash another insult into his employee's ear, his mother's heart rate monitor on the machine next to her beeped. The numbers next to the flexing line increased; his mother was going into another cardiac arrest. Mamadou dropped his phone. It collided with the hard ground and the screen cracked at the point of impact.

Mamadou rushed to the bedside and pressed the nurse's button. Within seconds, two arrived accompanied by a doctor. They stood either side of the bed and attended to her. Mamadou watched on in horror as the numbers on the machine representing his mother's pulse decreased rapidly. This was it. In a matter of moments, he knew it would all be over. He didn't know whether to run or stay.

One intensely fearful, prolonged minute passed. The doctor performed CPR while a nurse held a bag to the dying woman's mouth and pressed it rhythmically, forcing gas into her lungs. Mamadou's skin crawled as he watched the life leave his mother's frail body.

Then the beeping sound stopped. It was replaced with a flat line and a single, stretched-out beep. The doctor turned to face his colleagues.

'Time of death, 15:22.'

Mamadou collapsed to the ground, his entire world caving in on him.

Chapter Thirty-One

UNDERGROUND

August 1, 15:37

The engine roared through Upminster station like a Formula One racing car speeding down a tunnel. The noise echoed and reverberated around the enclosure, reaching deep inside Jake's skull.

Commuters and tourists standing in the foyer jumped aside as Jake and Lucy sped past them. Without any second thoughts, Jake pulled hard on the accelerator and drove straight through the ticket barrier. Pieces of the bike's body kit flew into the air, hitting the marshal standing by the barrier that they had just destroyed.

They were through. The foyer led onto an eastbound platform.

Jake skidded the bike to a halt, placed one foot down on the floor for balance, and held both the brakes and accelerator. Applying more pressure on the throttle, the wheels span on the spot. Rubber expelled in the air and there was a hideous screeching noise that filled the station. Jake turned the handlebars and guided the bike with his stationary leg so he was headed in the right direction.

As soon as he released the brakes, the bike shot off towards the end of the platform. Pedestrians and passengers dived out of the way as the bike charged towards them. The edge of the platform raced at Jake, approaching faster than he had expected.

The motorcycle propelled over the edge, suspending them in a moment of disbelief. Was the bike going to crash on the tracks, ruining whatever slim chance they had of making it to Trafalgar Square on time? With a heavy crunch, the bike landed, the suspension absorbing the weight of them both on top.

Jake steadied the bike and turned to face Lucy.

'You ready?' he asked.

'I don't like where this is going, Jake,' she replied.

Neither do I, he thought, pulling hard on the accelerator. The noise of the powerful engine reverberated, buffeting Jake's ears in a cacophony of pain. Jake struggled to hear anything else other than the bike.

He moved cautiously at first, getting himself used to the rhythm of the bumps and knocks. The layered flooring of the wood panels set his stomach on edge. The suspension on the bike was good, but not that good. Once confident with the manoeuvrability of the bike, Jake floored it. They shot off into the darkness, leaving a small plume of gravel and dust behind them. The inside of the Underground tunnels was bizarre. They were abnormally large. He had always assumed they were much thinner and narrower, but one track was big enough to fill half his house.

The tunnel curved to the right unexpectedly. His headlights only illuminated a few metres ahead of him, and he couldn't find the full beam switch. He was reliant on his reaction times and Lucy directing him.

He rounded the corner, bringing his speed down to thirty, before seeing a red light up ahead. Every train on the District Line from Upminster back to Tower Hill had come to a halt. Nobody was moving in and out of their stations. *A bomb alert must have been issued. Thank God!* The only problem this caused was the vast amount of stationary trains on the tracks.

As they drove further and further away from Upminster, a clearer plan formulated in Jake's head.

The red-light signal was enough for him to accelerate hard and cruise at fifty miles per hour. As they passed Hornchurch station, things became easier. The underground tunnels ended, and they burst into the sunlight. The sudden change in light blinded him momentarily and he almost lost control of the bike.

Now there were miles of open railway track he could play with. He could open the tanks and blast through to central London. He felt exhilarated, and leaned forward, making himself more streamlined, feeling his teenage arrogance come flooding back in droves.

Nothing was going to stand in his way.

The bike roared, and they were up to sixty miles an hour within fifty metres. Jake kept his eyes focused on the route ahead and was alert for any obstacles in the middle of the track.

So far, so good.

For the next five miles, Jake cruised at sixty-five miles an hour. The platforms they passed were an indistinct mirage of blue, brown, and red, the people a blur. Jake was focused and blocked everything else out. Knowing Lucy was still hugging to him urged him on. She was the precious cargo that needed protecting. If anything happened to her, everything would fail.

Congestion increased as they approached West Ham station. The number of stationary Underground trains grew, forcing Jake to slow down. The late-afternoon lunch rush would soon kick in and was going to bring a whole host of problems for them. The platforms were packed full of people waiting.

An idea came to his head, and he stopped metres away from the edge of the West Ham platform. Ignoring the funny looks, he reached for his mobile phone. He had already used up his three lives; there was nothing more the terrorist could do to deter him.

'Lucy? Ring my boss, Frances, and ask her to light the way for us to Trafalgar Square,' Jake shouted at her over the sound of the engine.

'What?' she replied, removing her visor.

'Tell my boss to get the guys at the London Underground Control Centre to stop all eastbound trains on the District Line and send them back the way they came. We need a green light on the Underground to get to Trafalgar Square in time. They'll be able to stop any opposing trains that'll get in the way. You've got about two minutes until we reach the Underground and get cut off.' Jake revved the engine a few times and sped off, hoping Lucy had understood everything he had said. He was sure Frances had worked her influence on the members of the London Underground Control Centre already, but it wouldn't hurt either of them to double check.

In her haste, Lucy almost dropped the phone. She juggled her handbag and a phone, meanwhile trying to cling onto Jake. Jake slowed down to reduce wind noise and make it easier for Lucy to hear. Her breathing slowed, and

Jake could feel her core muscles tense. She let go of Jake and scrolled through his phone, found Frances's number, and called it.

'This is Lucy Sanderson,' she said into the speaker. 'I'm with Detective Tanner and I need you to listen. I don't have long, so shut up and pay attention. We are headed west on the District Line. We are on a motorbike on the underground tracks, en route to Trafalgar Square.' She then recited to Frances what Jake had ordered. 'Green light, watch us on the cameras, move trains, just do whatever you have to! Make sure it gets done!'

Jake felt her arms reach round him and he eased the accelerator down again. They soon picked up speed. Nerves and fear overpowered him as they breached into the underground network of tunnels. He hoped Frances knew what she was doing.

And that she could do it in time.

Chapter Thirty-Two

PRICELESS

August 1, 15:40

The riskiest part of their operation was always going to be the ransom drop. They had known that from the outset. It was the only real time Adil would be vulnerable, out in the open. It was the only time he would be at risk of being caught. For months, he and Moshat had planned for every eventuality. They had observed and studied Counter Terrorism Command's tactics in previous terror attacks on the city and had established the way the command would respond to their attack, so they could plan accordingly.

There is always a plan for every outcome, Adil. You just have to search hard for it, his mentor had told him during his training.

Adil switched off his laptop and grabbed the microphone from his desk, placing them in his bag before he left the security of his flat, heading into the bright, poisonous world outside. He was running late. That stupid smart-ass Detective Tanner had delayed him. Exploding things had been a last resort. He hadn't wanted to press the trigger, but

Jake Tanner had been pushing his luck and it had almost run out. But Adil was looking forward to seeing the man in the flesh. Did he look even better in real life? Was he as handsome as the pixelated photos on his computer hard drive would suggest?

As Adil descended the steps of his flat block in the centre of London, paranoia raced through his mind. Had he left the curtains closed? Was his stereo off? Had anyone seen him leaving? Had he left anything behind?

Things inside his head were taking a turn, and he didn't like it. The next part of the operation *was* going to be a piece of cake. He was going to make sure. He and Moshat had worked too long and too hard for this to be a fuck-up.

He wasn't going to let his training go to waste. He didn't want to let down his parents. And he didn't want Counter Terrorism Command to miss out on all the fun he had planned for them.

He didn't want to let the government win; there was a debt they still had to repay.

It had been a while since he last saw proper daylight, and he understood why he'd tried to stay away from it for as long as possible. It wasn't agoraphobia; he had been conditioned to think that being out in the open was a source of weakness, that his every move would be watched. *Trust no one*, they had told him. *Not even those closest to you.* And he had placed that advice higher than any others.

Adil stepped onto the pavement. His heart rate increased, and his eyes darted between everyone who walked past him. He was certain someone was watching him. Sticking close to the sides of the buildings and walking at a pace, he kept his head low and face protected by his arms, pretending to play with his hair or forehead - another technique he had learned during training. For years, terror groups in the Amazon rainforest had been recruiting candidates, working in the depths of the undergrowth, planning and building for a better, more equal future. This training programme wasn't for amateurs — this was for pros.

You didn't find them. They found you.

And when they found Adil and Moshat, he had been surprised. Their carer, the one who had taken them in after their parents had perished in the tower block fire, had been one of them. He had studied their movements for weeks and offered his hand in sheltering them, housing them, and, inevitably, training them. At school, Adil had excelled at anything to do with computers. His afternoons were spent in detention after he had been caught hacking into the school systems and altering attendance records to make it look like he had been at every class, when in fact he had been skiving with Moshat. After he and Moshat journeyed to South America the first time, Adil developed his computing skills at Cambridge University, where he received a scholarship. It had been a nice gesture, he admitted, but it would never replace the gaping hole his parents' deaths left in his life. The government could send as many scholarships as they wanted, but it would never negate the fact they had been responsible for the tragedy that unfolded that night.

Tragedy aside, it had been an exciting fourteen years, and now here he was, the mastermind behind the worst terror attack London had ever seen.

The thought made him feel proud.

But then the euphoria subsided, and the paranoia crept back in, and Adil became aware of his claustrophobic surroundings. The skyscrapers and tall flat buildings towered over him, confining him into a box of brick and steel. He knew the route by heart; he had studied it every day online and traced the steps in his head.

Adil tried to force the immense claustrophobia out of his mind and think of something positive. The first thought that came to mind was the look on Jake and Tyler's faces. He had seen them both on images on his screen when he stalked the CCTV in New Scotland Yard. He had examined their body movements, their gestures, and their interactions with one another. He had never seen them in the flesh and now was his opportunity. It would be a priceless moment, preserved forever in the frame of a CCTV still image.

Forever.

By that point, he would be long gone, preparing for the next task. He had started the war of technological terror, and it was going to change the world. Not even Jake Tanner was going to stand in the way of that.

Chapter Thirty-Three

CHAUFFEUR

August 1, 15:43

For the past ten minutes, Tyler had been inconsolable. Images of Mamadou in the hospital, cowering over his dead mother's body, appeared in his vivid imagination. Were there other possibilities? No. Mamadou had disappeared on the phone, and there was that beeping sound. As soon as Tyler heard that, he knew what it meant. He just wished he could be there to comfort Mamadou, even if it was the one thing he knew his boss would hate, but so long as he was there. *Presence is key in times of need*, his grandfather had once told him.

After the phone call, Tyler had rushed into the toilets, slammed the cubicle door behind him, and vomited. His mind was plagued with intense thoughts — thoughts he couldn't tame. Once his stomach lining had resurfaced, he sat on the toilet seat and hyperventilated. His cocky and stoic exterior was a front, a façade that he had maintained for so long he had adopted it as a real personality. But deep down, behind the bravado, was someone who was sensitive and emotional, who had seen what people were capable of behind the privacy of closed doors.

The bathroom door opened and slammed against the wall with such force, Tyler believed a tile had been dislodged.

'DC Stuart — are you in here?' It was Theo. The old man's endearing nature made Tyler smile.

Tyler hopped off the toilet basin and unlocked the door.

'Theo, buddy! You all right?' he asked.

'Yes. I was sent down to find you. It's a quarter to four. You've got fifteen minutes to the ransom delivery deadline, and everyone's asking for you.'

'Who's "everyone"?' Tyler washed his hands with soap and dried them using four times the amount of paper towels he needed.

'DC Matthews, sir.'

Tyler rolled his eyes. 'Don't know what he's playing at. He's having a laugh if he thinks he's coming with me. There's a reason he won't be getting a promotion soon.'

'Promotion?' Theodor asked, confused whether they were both discussing the same thing.

'Never mind, Theo. That's a story for another day.' Tyler slapped the elderly gentleman on the back, and the two of them left the bathroom.

As they re-entered the office, Luke accosted Tyler. Behind him stood Susanna.

'Where have you been? It's time to go. We need to deliver this ransom, or both of our arses are going to be in the shit,' DC Matthews yelled. He was inches away from Tyler's face.

'*Our* arses? I think you mean mine, Detective. I don't need you to babysit me anymore. You lost that privilege a while ago when Frances didn't ask you to join us to Downing Street.' Tyler smiled smugly. 'Hey, maybe I should have gone for the promotion instead.'

Luke scoffed. 'Like you'd have stood a chance. You can't even hold a gun properly, let alone fire one in the right direction.'

The petty remark made Tyler laugh. It was childish insolence at its best, but he didn't care. They were only words. And he just hoped Luke could take as good as he could give.

'Of course, I can, Luke.' Tyler put his hand inside his breast pocket, removed it, mimicked a gun using his thumb and forefinger, and as he "fired", stuck his middle finger up.

Luke's face dropped, and Tyler's gesture was met with concealed laughter from around them. Even the sides of Susanna's lips rose — something Tyler thought he would never see.

'A car is waiting for you downstairs,' she said. 'Jeremy is the driver's name. He'll drop you off but won't pick you up. You'll have to find your own way home.'

'Can't be that hard, can it? It's a straight road.'

Susanna smiled. Unfortunately, this time it was a different smile, filled with derision. 'You'd be surprised.'

'You're the boss.'

Smiling facetiously at Luke, Tyler collected the ransom and made his way downstairs. As he exited the building, he noticed an undercover BMW 3 series. It wasn't much, but it would do. Tyler approached the vehicle. Standing outside, resting against the front right wheel arch was a tall, skinny man, whose safety vest made him look top-heavy and as if he would fall over at the slightest increment in wind.

'DC Stuart?' the officer asked, extending his hand.

Tyler nodded and returned the gesture. Despite the

man's wrists being no thicker than a tube of wrapping paper, he had an almighty grip on him, and Tyler could feel his tendons crush under the officer's strength.

'I'm Constable Davey. I'll be the driver.'

With that, the two of them hopped into the vehicle and sped off towards Trafalgar Square, leaving nothing but dust and the smell of burnt rubber in their wake. Within three minutes of veering left and right of the traffic on both lanes, Tyler arrived. He jumped out of the car, briefcase in hand, and strolled to the National Gallery, the only thought occupying his mind was Mamadou leaning over his dead mother's body.

It would be a long six minutes.

Chapter Thirty-Four

BETRAYAL

August 1, 15:45

Things had deteriorated dramatically since Moshat last received word from his brother. Martha had increased her surveillance on him, and he became increasingly worried with every passing glance he made at her.

The atmosphere was tense. It was hot and stuffy, and everyone had removed their outermost clothing. Some men weren't wearing any tops at all. The women cooled themselves and their children with makeshift fans from newspapers and magazines. The lady sat next to him held one. Now and then, a cool breeze brushed his face. Everyone was trying their best to cool themselves down.

Everyone except him.

Moshat remained seated in his jeans and jumper, layers of sweat forming on his back and legs. His hat had absorbed all the sweat that formed on his scalp. But by now it became unbearably itchy. He fidgeted.

'Why don't you take your jumper off?' Martha asked, her voice stern and unfriendly. 'It's hot, and you must be sweating buckets underneath all that.'

Moshat looked at her and said nothing. All he gave her was a smile. He didn't know how to react in front of her. For a moment, he thought about pretending to be foreign, to use another accent or language that would mean he wouldn't have to converse with anyone. But then he realised he didn't know a different language. That had been one burden in his life. Adil could speak Cantonese and Latin — he had learnt them as a requirement at Cambridge. But Moshat — Moshat didn't know any, he'd never had the mental capacity to do so. He was a failure in most academic pursuits and had only been successful in his engineering degree because Adil had done all the assessments for him. If it hadn't been for Adil, the whole operation would have been non-existent. The only thing Moshat excelled at in his life was football.

And even that didn't work out.

Moshat contemplated this as he stared at Martha. An instant bout of depression rolled over him. His presence made no change to the outcome of the plan. He would have to change that.

It wasn't until she repeated herself that he came to.

'Sorry, what did you say? I was thinking of my family,' he said in the vague hope she would chew on that rather than repeat herself.

'Aren't we all, my dear?' she said. Relief enveloped him, and he relaxed a little. 'Any kids?'

'Yes. One,' he said. Martha stared at him expecting more information. 'A little girl.'

'How old?'

'Two,' Moshat replied, trying to keep the details to a minimum.

'Is she at home with her mother?' Martha asked, resting her elbows on the table. 'Sorry, I don't mean to pry, but I don't see a ring on your finger.'

Moshat looked at his wedding ring finger and involuntarily rubbed it. *She's good*, Moshat thought, feeling more confident in himself. *Just as good as Detective Tanner, if not better.*

'Yes, she's back home. I'm flying out to see her. It's her birthday this weekend. I got time off work to spend with them.'

'That's wonderful. She'll be excited to see her Daddy I'm sure.'

'What about you? Going anywhere nice?'

'Yes,' she said. 'I'm going to the States.'

Liar.

'Very nice. Is that to see family?'

'No. I'm just going as a treat to myself. I don't have any family.'

Liar.

'I'm Jason,' Moshat lied. 'Nice to meet you.'

'I'm Amanda.'

Liar.

Everything she had just told him had been a lie. Her real name was Martha Clarke, and she had a family. Lots. Her husband had recently died due to a long-term illness, and she had two children — Elizabeth Jane Tanner and Isobel Clarke — seven grandchildren, and two dogs. She was retired and lived in a flat in the centre of London after a highly successful career as Minister of State for Housing and Planning that lasted over two decades. It had been Moshat's job to know everything about her. He had stalked her for the past few weeks while Adil learned everything he could about her family history online.

Their conversation ended. Moshat looked up at the scrolling orange display at the centre of the train. It read: T-MINUS 02:16:43.

Now he was getting excited. Adil would be on the way to collect their one-million-pound ransom. All he had to do was collect it, return to the flat, and wait until Moshat came home victorious. It was that simple. All Moshat had to do was sit and wait.

He eased back into his seat and crossed his arms. His thoughts were distracted by his irritable head. He didn't want to remove his hat. His hair loss had been a constant source of embarrassment in his life, and he was only twenty-seven. He first lost his hair when he was in the Academy at West Ham's football club. The other players took it well, but he still felt self-conscious about it. So much so, in fact, that part of his share of the ransom money was going towards a hair transplant. He had a wish list of particular things only he would understand the full reasons behind.

As he sat there scratching his head, he contemplated the possibility of removing the knitted hat. But then there was a loud bang. Everyone ducked and tucked their heads into their laps. Moshat sank lower into his seat, so far that his head was at the same height as the window frame.

The noise came from the intercom system at the top of the carriage. *What an idiot*, Moshat thought.

'Good afternoon, Heathrow Express!' Adil said, this time in his real voice. There was no device masking his identity — he'd allowed them to hear what he really sounded like. Moshat struggled to accept this. It hadn't been a part of their plan. They'd been over it time and time again, but this wasn't in the script.

What's he doing? Moshat thought. *Things are going well, so perhaps he's getting cocky? The bastard. He's costing us this whole operation.*

'I bring good news. If I collect my ransom in the next ten minutes, you have a greater chance of surviving than you currently do. As I'm broadcasting this to you, I'm on the way to meet the great Detective Jake Tanner. You might be pleased to hear he won't be putting any bullets in my head today. Maybe some other time. I apologise if this disappoints you.'

Adil broke off for a moment. In the background, Moshat could hear car engines, sirens, and car horns. *He's walking to the drop and broadcasting this? Is he insane?* Moshat thought. His blood boiled, and his frustrations were becoming apparent. His brother was fucking up the whole thing by not sticking to the plan. It was there for a reason, and Adil's total disregard for the way things were progressing made Moshat despise his brother.

Moshat's felt useless being sat there, unable to change what his brother was doing. What if something happened to him? What if someone found out what he was doing? What if he was being tracked, monitored? What if he compromised them both?

'As I was saying, if all goes well, you may or may not live. I haven't decided yet. I've got too much choice to choose from. There are two other trains in similar positions to yours. One has already had its last carriage blown up, while the other is slowly suffocating in the heat. And as for you guys, you've been... well, a little boring. But you've also been compliant, and I respect that.

'You do, however, have a decision to make. Hidden

somewhere in the eighth carriage of your train, you will find a detonator. That little device can blow up one of the other trains. Crazy, isn't it, how the beauty of life can be taken away so easily at the flick of a button? The question is, will it be you or them that dies? If you're successful in finding the detonator and decide amongst yourselves that you want to press it, you will end the lives of hundreds, possibly thousands, of people. But if you do not decide by the time the countdown ends, it will be your lives endangered. It is your life or theirs. You have until the end of the countdown to decide. Goodbye.' Adil hung up the device and surrendered the train to a deafening silence.

Jesus fucking Christ, Moshat thought. *What a bastard. How could you?* Adil had gone behind his back and planted the detonator on the train elsewhere, deviating from the plan. Now he and everyone else on board had the power to blow up the passengers on a different train, granting them immunity. The original plan had been for them to destroy the Gatwick Express, leave the Luton-bound train alone, and allow him and all the other passengers on the Heathrow Express to go free, including Martha. So why was Adil now threatening Moshat's life at the end of the countdown? Was he really going to detonate the train at the end of the six hours? How could Adil have betrayed him like this?

Jesus fucking Christ, Moshat repeated multiple times. He, and everyone else around him, panicked. Sweat started down the side of his face.

Everyone in his carriage erupted out of their seats and rushed towards the eighth carriage. Moshat was in the fourth, in the middle of the train. Hundreds of other bodies stood in the way of him and the detonator. In less than ten seconds, a wall had formed, cramped up against one another like cattle wandering into a slaughterhouse. They were being penned in, and soon it became claustrophobic; Moshat could feel himself struggling for air. Hundreds of fears raced through his mind. He had to keep his backpack safe and his hat on. He had to locate the detonator before anyone else did. He had to make sure he didn't suffocate in the sweltering heat.

How could his brother do this to him?

Chapter Thirty-Five

THE FOUR PS

August 1, 15:50

As Jake and Lucy descended the slope into the underground network of trains and train tracks, they arrived at a green light.

Thank you, Assistant Commissioner. Frances had done as Lucy and Jake demanded. Now, all they needed was the rest of the District Line to be as empty as this.

The darkness encompassed them. All Jake had to go by were the signal lights dotted along the tunnel and the motorbike's headlamp. The temperature dropped, and Jake felt a chill run down his back through his suit. The cold was bitter and took him by surprise. There was a torrent of wind blasting in the opposite direction, causing turbulence on the bike.

Even at the high speeds they were travelling, he could feel the bike wobble. It could mean only one thing.

There was a train near.

And it was headed straight towards them.

The giant headlights dazed Jake. In the distance, it looked like a giant wall with lights advancing towards them at speed. The front window of the carriage showed the driver panic and slam on the brakes. Jake saw the man jump out of his seat and reach for a radio. Jake came skidding to a halt and the back end of the bike swerved to the left. The noise of the engine reverberated and amplified in the tunnel.

Jake signalled with his hands for the train to reverse. But the driver didn't budge. Instead he flailed around the control panels and steadied himself on his seat. Jake reached into his pocket and pulled out the gun. He fired into the ceiling of the tunnel. Small parts of rubble fell to the ground a few inches from his leg. The driver dived to the floor of the cabin and peered above the control panel. Only his forehead and eyes could be seen.

'Reverse the fucking train!' Lucy screamed behind Jake as she removed her helmet.

The train driver fumbled around the centre of the control panel. He dropped a mug of coffee rested on the top. A few seconds later, the driver stood alert and Jake could see him signalling with his thumb and forefinger pursed together, giving the OK signal. Slowly, the train moved further away from them, steadily going faster and faster. *Fucking finally*.

Lucy put her helmet back on and Jake turned the bike. They were picking up speed. Jake kept the bike close to the carriage of the train.

Now he was up close and personal with the driver, Jake noticed he was younger than he'd first thought. Inexperienced, as well, Jake guessed. He had dark brown hair and was probably in his early thirties. There was a look of horror in his eyes, and he didn't break his gaze from Jake's.

Something inside Jake was telling him this was all going to end badly. If Frances hadn't been able to evacuate the whole of the District Line for them, then there would be numerous trains heading their way. It would be the end of the line before they'd even begun.

Jake checked the speedometer on the bike. Seventeen miles an hour.

Things had to speed up. With one hand, pushing the air in the direction they were headed, Jake signalled for the train to move faster.

Eventually, the number of signals and lights became more frequent. They were nearing a station.

Whitechapel. Halfway.

Jake didn't have to be a genius to realise they were still a long way off and stood no chance of making it on time, but that wasn't going to stop him. An instinctive anger rose in him. An anger that was only awoken by severe provocation and determination. An idea popped into his head.

It was the most far-fetched thing he'd ever thought of in his life. There was no possibility it could work. But it *would* work. It *had* to. For the sake of everyone's lives on those trains. Not even video games could recreate what he had in mind.

The train neared the platform at speed. Jake signalled for the train to come to a sudden halt. By the time the train reached its end, and all momentum had been lost, it was halfway down the platform.

There was another train on the other line heading east. No way out that way.

It was time to go.

Jake took a deep breath and turned the bike towards the end of the platform on the right a few metres away and mounted it. There was a small barrier that prohibited Jake from passing. He revved the engine and charged through. The barrier lock smashed and swung away from them. The bike climbed the platform. Almost in an instant, every living soul on the platform dispersed, like a herd of wildebeest being chased by lions. As Jake neared the train, hordes of passengers exited up the stairs. A survival of the fittest instinct had kicked in. The upmost fear reduced them to this state and Jake felt guilty. He'd just risked all their lives.

And he didn't think it was going to stop there.

They came to the nearest train door on the left and boarded the train car. All but a few passengers remained. The train was his playground for the next few hundred yards, and he was going to need all the space he could get. He hoped his reactions were just as fast as they had been when he was younger.

He stopped the bike in the middle of the carriage, put his feet down and pulled Lucy closer to him. She squeezed him. Through his clothes, he could feel her nails digging into his chest.

Stop wasting time and go! No fear! Jake accelerated, feeling the back-wheel spin on the ground for what felt like an eternity before they eventually shot off. They raced down the train. The white interior, interspersed with yellow poles and blue seats, whizzed past.

Dodging round the poles in the middle of the train's doorways, it turned into a slalom. Ahead of him was a man stood facing away, tapping his feet. He wore a hoodie and appeared to be looking down at a phone in his hands. Jake had two seconds to gauge his distance and berth around the man. Slamming on the brakes, the smooth surface of the train caused the bike to skid slightly. With an outstretched hand, Jake pushed the man in the back just before he roared past him.

Story to tell the grandchildren, Jake thought as he brought the bike back up to a safe speed.

Jake and Lucy arrived at the end of the train. The final door leading back into the underground tunnel was their next obstruction.

Jake removed the weapon and handed it to Lucy. She took it with trembling hands.

'What?' she shouted through the helmet, holding the firearm in front of her. In doing so, she pointed it at Jake's head. He flinched and pushed it away, directing it at the carriage door. Lucy held the gun in front of her, steadied, and pulled the trigger. Glass shattered and fell to the floor. She missed by a long margin.

Her hand shook harder now. After breathing slowly, she tried again. This time she closed one eye, focused on the objective, licked her lips, and fired. The circular button sparked and exploded as the bullet shot through it. Then, after a few precious moments, the two doors split open and showed the dark void of the tunnel.

Lucy kept hold of the gun and clasped her arms around Jake's waist. He accelerated and jumped off the train onto the track. The landing was hard and unexpected. Despite it being a fall of three feet, the added weight of Lucy on his back crushed him further forward into the handlebars. His head collided with the speedometer.

Jake pointed the bike in the right direction and darted down the tunnel. They were clear to go full throttle. They had to. There was no other choice.

Jake opened the tanks and reached sixty miles an hour. He enjoyed the acceleration and felt the adrenaline coming back to him. Stations whizzed past. And so did stationary westbound trains.

Yes! Jake thought. Frances had done it, she'd stopped all

the trains and push them back, giving them the green light to get to the station they needed. *I'll buy you a beer at the end of this,* Jake thought. *Or whatever else you fancy.* Confidence oozed back into him.

A few minutes later, they arrived at Embankment.

Lucy tapped him on the shoulder, gesturing to him that he needed to stop. Jake trusted Lucy's knowledge and pulled up the slope leading onto the platform. He was surprised to see the platform so deserted. Nobody in the vicinity was stood on either side. *They must have told people to move away. Frances's orders.*

There was something eerie about an empty train station, something very wrong about it. That usually densely populated areas were now abandoned provoked an irrational fear in Jake. Even though his motorbike antics caused the desertion, he still felt freaked out. Snapping out of his thoughts, Jake hopped of the bike, helped Lucy down, and continued the rest of the journey with her on foot. As they climbed up the escalators, the number of people within the station increased.

Together they surged through the ticket barrier, oblivious to whoever they knocked over. They sprinted across the street towards Trafalgar Square. Police officers in high-visibility jackets patrolled the pavement, creating the preventive deterrent the Metropolitan Police sought so hard to ensure. It was their list of the Four Ps — prevent, pursue, protect and prepare — that eliminated the threat terrorism posed to their country's security.

Less than five minutes later, Jake and Lucy arrived at the foot of Nelson's Column.

It was deserted.

Chapter Thirty-Six

ALIAS

August 1, 15:53

The black taxi cab collided with Adil's hip. He was knocked to the ground. He dropped his microphone and bag. Everything went black for a moment, and there was a searing pain in his head. His temples felt like they were on fire. The lower half of his body hurt.

A crowd of people swarmed around him, like flies to a dead carcass. Adil rose to his feet, ignoring their molesting hands. *No,* he told himself. He would not show signs of weakness by accepting anyone's help. He would be fine by himself.

His body shook, and his pulse raced. Placing all his weight on his right hip, a searing pain shot all the way down his leg and back up again. He would not succumb to the pain.

Adil swayed a little as the rush of blood to his head dissipated. Everybody around him continued to touch him all over his back and shoulders, making his skin crawl. There was something about being touched that he just hated. It made him feel vulnerable.

Pushing their arms away, he bent down to pick up his microphone and bag on the floor, realising how insane he must look with such items on his person. Before he reached the ground, a hand stretched in front of his face. There was no wedding ring on the finger, and the owner's nails and skin were dirty with sweat and oil.

Adil glanced up the length of the arm and followed it to the owner. Before him stood an overweight middle-aged man with flaming red hair. His outfit suggested he was single for a reason, and he had been for some time. Maybe even his whole life. There was a worried expression plastered all over the portly man's face. His eyes bulged with fear, and he shook just as much as Adil. Somehow Adil didn't think it was for the same reason.

'Oh, my God. I am so sorry,' the taxi driver said. His voice was wheezy and adolescent. 'Are you OK?'

'Yes,' Adil responded, trying to push his way through the crowd. He didn't want to be there any longer than he needed to be. He was already delayed, and any debacle now would only delay him further.

The incident attracted attention. Civilians who were going about their day had stopped and stared at what was happening. They brought out their mobile phones to record the situation, perhaps hoping their videos of Adil's pain would go viral — Adil didn't know, but the situation was worsening by the second.

Adil checked his watch. He was running late. Trafalgar Square was still another seven minutes away. And now Detective Tanner had a small window of opportunity to make it on time. He just hoped that this minor incident hadn't allowed that to happen. He *prayed* that it hadn't happened. Otherwise, someone innocent would have to pay for it.

Adil's first choice: the fat bastard standing in front of him. He hadn't had the same level of physical combat as Moshat, but he had been trained in how to defend himself and disarm someone. He wouldn't be afraid to test it out if he was forced to.

Adil snatched the microphone and bag from the taxi driver and tried to barge his way through the crowd again.

'Stop there, mate,' said the taxi driver, holding Adil back. It was no use, Adil was going to deal with this one way or another. 'Where are you going so fast? Are you OK? Are you hurt? Do you need an ambulance?'

There were too many questions for Adil to deal with at once. He just wanted them to stop. He just wanted them to all go away. He could feel himself becoming more irate by the second. The adrenaline-induced trembling had now turned into an anger-induced rage.

'No. I'm fine.' Adil glared at the man, gritting his teeth, intimidating him into backing away.

Saying nothing more, the taxi driver stepped aside and allowed Adil to pass. There were mumblings and questions asked from those amongst the crowd. Paying them no attention, Adil hobbled away, ignoring the pain in his leg that had already subsided.

Before he could make it to the kerb, two police officers dressed in high-visibility jackets approached him. Adil recognised them at once. They were PCs, Police Constables. Their presence had been increased twofold since this morning; Adil had been observing the CCTV cameras around the city from his flat, and he had seen an unprecedented level of high-vis jackets floating around the streets.

Now there was nowhere for Adil to run. Nowhere for him to escape.

'What seems to be the problem here?' one of the officers asked. He was small, and his facial features were dark and unassuming in the bright light. Bad cop.

Before answering, Adil made a mental note of their radio transmissions strapped to their shoulders, the stun guns clipped to their hips and their hands placed in their breast pockets. Gauging his opponents had been one of the first lessons he learned during his training.

'Nothing,' Adil replied, with a bemused look on his face, hoping that it would defer them.

'He's lying, officers,' interrupted the taxi driver, barging in front of him. 'I accidentally knocked him down. He was crossing the road, and I didn't see him.'

'Is this true, sir?' the constable on the left asked Adil. He was the taller of the two, with wider shoulders and more accessible shins. Good cop.

Adil hesitated for a few moments, considering the situation, deciding upon the fastest way out of this mess.

'It's fine. I don't want to make a big fuss about it all,' Adil said as calmly as he could manage.

The tall officer raised an eyebrow and looked to the other standing beside him. They exchanged a glance.

'OK, sir, I'm just going to need to take some details,' Bad Cop began. Adil looked surprised and there was a clear look on his face of disgust. 'It's just protocol.'

'But why? I already told you I'm fine. I don't want to press charges or make a statement or anything. It was just a little accident!' Adil was becoming tenser by the moment. The muscles in his body were taut with stress and anger.

'There's no need to raise your voice, sir. Calm down. It's

just precautionary. Now all I need is your name and address. Do you have any ID on you?'

'I've got somewhere I need to be, and I need to be there in a hurry. So, if you don't mind, I'd like to go!'

The smaller officer stepped forward and said, 'I'll ask you again, sir, do you have any ID?'

'No, no I don't. I left it at home, which is where I'm going now. So, can I get going, please?' Stress swam inside his head, mixing his thoughts with his words.

'No, where is —' Bad Cop started. He was interrupted by the taxi driver extending his driver's licence in his face. He observed it and passed it to Good Cop who noted down the details. Looking at Adil, the smaller officer continued, 'Where is home?'

'Soho.'

'Soho?' Bad Cop repeated. Adil nodded and waited for him to continue. 'And you say you're on your way back home, correct?'

'Yes.'

'But Soho's that way. Why are you going further away if you're headed home?'

'Because I was going back to work to pick up my wallet.' Adil's frustrations were leading to mistakes. And mistakes were leading to delays.

'Where do you work?'

'About ten minutes away.'

'So, let me get this straight. You left work, realised you didn't have your wallet, and now you're on your way to pick it back up? And then after you've got that, you're going back home which is where your ID is located. You didn't have your ID in your wallet. Correct?'

Adil nodded.

'And you took ten minutes to realise you didn't have your wallet on you?'

Adil hesitated. 'Yes, I keep it in my bag, and when I reached in to get my phone, I realised it wasn't there.'

Both Good Cop and Bad Cop scribbled everything Adil said in their notebooks.

'Very well, sir,' the taller officer said. 'But we will still require an address. At least a work address.'

'Fine, but afterward can I go?'

'Yes.'

'I work as a radio host at a small radio company in Covent Garden. 123.98 FM. Look it up,' Adil said and waited. He hoped he had connived a convincing enough lie. He hoped the radio back story would explain the microphone in his hand. 'And Jake is my name. Jake Isaac Tanner.'

Eventually, after spending a few moments trying to spell Isaac, the officer had finished, and looked up at Adil. 'Thanks.' He put the notepad back in its pocket. 'I think we have everything we need. You may go.'

Adil looked around. He gave one final look to the taxi driver and the two police officers before leaving. He corrected his clothing as a matter of statement and walked off in silence.

As he disappeared down the road, he could feel eyes glaring at him. He didn't dare look back; he'd already given them enough reason to judge him as suspicious without needing to add another.

Keeping his head down, he turned the corner and dared a glance behind him, lest the police officers had followed him. There was no one there.

He was becoming paranoid.

He hated himself for playing his little stunt. *If you'd just left everything as it was, then this wouldn't have happened,* he thought. He didn't need to scare everyone on board the Heathrow Express into thinking they had the power to detonate another train. He didn't need to secretly place another detonator elsewhere on the train and hope that Moshat would find it. He didn't need to place that uncontrollable power in his brother's inexperienced hands.

There was nothing he could do about it now. The damage had been done.

Instead, Adil focused on the objective at hand and checked his watch.

He was one minute away.

And five minutes late.

Chapter Thirty-Seven

BELLIGERENCE

August 1, 15:55

For a few minutes, nothing happened. Everyone was stuck, pressed right up against another human in front. They were all eager to find the device that would end this misery, save themselves, and sacrifice hundreds of others.

Bizarrely, Moshat sympathised with them a little. These people faced a mammoth choice. It was their lives or someone else's. And his brother's actions had been distrustful. For the first time in a long time, Moshat knew what it felt like to be human. Ever since his successes, and ultimate failure, at the Academy of West Ham football club, he lost any notion of being human. Ever since he had started out, his life had always been football, football, football. And that was all he ever thought about. He would play on his own on the streets, kicking the ball up and down the wall of the estate, until another child would join him, and they would play until the sun had dipped below the horizon and the garish light from the street lamps faltered. He would stay late after training, just so he could get in extra practice. But then things had changed. He got scouted one day at one of his football matches, and he joined West Ham, where he soon learnt the value of hierarchy and structure within the team. It was highly competitive. Survival of the fittest. And even when Moshat would make friends with other players, he would crush them if the opportunity for him to surpass them came around. He would tackle them so horrendously that the resulting injuries ended their careers.

He was the reason some of those boys' careers never took off.

He was the reason some of those boys' dreams never came true.

He was the reason some of these people on the train would never live to see tomorrow.

He felt sympathy grow within him. *These people are inno-cent. They don't need to die,* he thought.

But neither did mother and father, another side of him replied. He was doing this for them, and he didn't want to let them down. He didn't want to let Adil down. He often wondered what his mother and father would think of him and Adil if they could see what they had become. They would see the light in their evil: the determination, the resilience, the ingenuity, the power to see the difference between right and wrong. Not the fact that they were killing hundreds — thousands — of people.

'How hard is it to find a small black thing, seriously?' someone said a few metres behind him. 'You're all fucking retards.'

That's why they must die. Human belligerence towards one another; not treating one another with compassion and respect. That was what the terror organisation he was recruited by stood for. And then there was that word. *Retard.*

He hated that word; it had been used as an insult against him and his brother so many times before in his childhood. The word was a manifestation of his hatred and rage, and it made him want to beat whoever used it into a coma. He had the training to do so. He had the skills to do so. He had the knowledge *and* power to do so. So why couldn't he use it?

The speaker's comments sparked an enlightened rage amongst the other passengers around him. The prolonged exposure to the increased heat and claustrophobic confines of the carriage had now meant that a single word could ignite someone's short fuse.

Moshat put his head down and tried to ignore them. He needed an excuse to push himself to the front. But there wasn't one. He needed to get it as much as the next person. They all wanted the power. They all wanted to be the one to pull the trigger, committing the most selfish act possible: choosing another's life over their own. And, he admitted to himself, he wanted that power, too. He wanted to be the one to kill everyone on board one of the other trains. He wanted the government to see that he and his brother are serious. If the detonator got into the hands of anyone else, their plan would be rendered useless, all impact of meaning thrown out the window. No, Moshat had to be the one to pull the trigger. For his mother. For his father.

There was little he could do. He was still a few carriages away. Except for something. A final resort.

The gun inside his rucksack. That could get him what he wanted. But it had serious implications. He stood there considering his options, blocking out all the hands and legs and penises and breasts pressed up against his body.

He looked down at his watch. Just over two hours

remained. *Shit, that's a long time. Can I defend myself for so long? Can I keep the situation under control?*

Moshat didn't know. He had to overcome the first obstacle: finding the detonator. And then he would have to worry about the consequences. He was outnumbered several hundred to one, and he needed to be in control. That was the most important part: Moshat required the *only* option where he was in control.

And he *was* going to find it.

Chapter Thirty-Eight

FURTHER INSTRUCTION

August 1, 16:02

The sun still shone high in the sky. Nelson's Column cast a magnificent, towering shadow over Jake and Lucy. Planes and birds soared in the air up above, creating streaks of white in the electric-blue canvas sky. Pigeons down by their feet fought one another over the final piece of a hotdog bun on the ground.

Jake and Lucy stood there in the eerily quiet square. They twisted and turned, scanning every possible angle in search of signs of life.

'What is going on?' Lucy asked, looking into Jake's eyes. 'Why's it so empty?'

Jake didn't know. But he didn't like it.

'Perhaps it's Frances,' Jake said, thinking out loud. Lucy looked at him confused and he explained who the Assistant Commissioner was. 'Maybe she's ordered the police to evacuate any tourist sites of pedestrians, for fear of a potential attack.'

'Or maybe they've evacuated the area because this is where the drop is going to be made,' Lucy said.

Jake agreed with her theory. He knew the protocol. He had read about it in one of the case files on the PNC one day when he was in the office and had been sidetracked from doing what he was supposed to. There had been a high-profile kidnapping — one child of one of the many billionaires who lived in the city had been taken — and the kidnapper had demanded a ransom for their safe return. The destination: Piccadilly Circus. Dozens of sniper officers had been at the top of high-rise buildings, zeroing in on the target, waiting for the kidnapped girl to be handed over safely to the parents. It ended with the girl being returned to her family, and the kidnapper being captured. Although now, Jake didn't think this ransom drop would have the same result.

Jake scanned the area, searching the building roofs around him. Small, black dots were interspersed across the buildings. The snipers were in position. 'Come on,' he said, advancing to the steps towards the National Gallery. 'We need to get to a vantage point, so we can see him when he arrives.'

Unless he's doing the same. The thought made Jake's skin crawl.

He grabbed Lucy's hand and pulled her behind him. They sprinted across the concrete pavement, past Nelson's Column, reached the bottom of steps and climbed them to the top. As they reached the vantage point, Jake found a bench to sit on. His body ached, and he needed respite. Lucy joined him, her hair messy and dishevelled.

'Are your feet all right?' Jake asked her.

She giggled. 'They're fine. They've been used to worse after nights out in London. They're strong stuff!'

Jake looked down at his watch. Three minutes had passed since their deadline.

Next to him, on his left, the sound of heavy footsteps on the pavement stirred his attention.

'Excuse me, sir, I was wondering if you could help me?'

Jake craned his stiff neck and saw Tyler standing in front of him.

'Tyler! Where have you been?' Jake asked, jumping to his feet, feeling elated to see his friend.

'Could ask you the same question. I've been waiting for ages. Think I've aged a few years. How do I look?' Tyler said, touching his forehead and cheeks for wrinkles. In his hand, he held the briefcase.

'As gorgeous as the day is young,' Jake replied, smiling. It had been a long while since he last smiled like that. At least, it felt like a long time.

'Fuck you,' Tyler replied, and they both laughed.

After the laughter died down, Tyler's gaze fell behind Jake's shoulder. Jake followed his partner's gaze and looked at Lucy.

'Sorry, I forgot. Where are my manners?' Jake said, turning back to Tyler. 'Ty — this is Lucy Sanderson, my hostage. Lucy — this is DC Tyler Stuart, my partner in crime and friend.'

'Nice to meet you Lucy Sanderson,' Tyler said, bowing down and kissing the back of her hand. 'I think we owe you a drink after all this is over. My shout.' He winked at her.

'I'd like that,' Lucy said, blushing. Her pupils dilated, and her cheeks coloured.

Jake rolled his eyes.

'Come on you two, stop flirting. We've got a job to do. What's the latest? I've seen we're well protected.'

Jake was referring to the snipers positioned in the rooftops above.

Tyler craned his neck. 'Yep, under my orders, would you believe it?'

'Moving on up in the world,' Jake said.

'They're there just in case things go pear-shaped. If the square gets busier, and a shot gets harder, then they'll stand down.'

Jake looked down at the briefcase in Tyler's hands. 'Is that what I think it is?'

'Yep. The ransom is here. One million.' Tyler lifted the briefcase in the air and passed it to Jake. 'I've received no word from Frances regarding anything else. But we've got a positive ID on the man in the picture I sent you.'

'And?'

'Moshat Hakim. Born and raised in London. Twenty-seven years old.'

'Anything else?'

'Intelligence reports state that his parents died in the tragic Detson Tower block fire.'

'Jesus Christ,' Jake said, the cogs in his brain turning. 'That's what this is about. That's what this whole thing is about! They're getting revenge.'

Jake took a moment to think. He had seen on the news the riots and fights that had ensued in the aftermath of the fire. The social injustice that had wreaked havoc on London's streets combined with the very raw events of the 7/7 bombings had put the country under immense strain. Shops and restaurants and buildings and leisure centres were looted and destroyed, each of the affected civilians trying to get some form of recompense.

Then he remembered. Moshat Hakim couldn't be orchestrating the entire thing on the train on his own.

'What about a brother? An accomplice? The one who keeps tormenting us, the one who's been giving me the riddles, the one who will be here momentarily? Did you find anything on him?'

Tyler remained silent and shook his head.

'Nothing. Nada. The guy doesn't exist. According to reports, and what the police and fire services could find, Moshat Hakim's brother perished in the fire. His name was Hasan.'

'Impossible,' Jake said. How could this be? Who was behind this? Jake had been absolutely certain it was a duo. Now he questioned everything he thought he knew.

'I'm sorry, Jake. We'll find him. I'm sure of it. He'll show himself soon, don't worry. Besides, have you worked out which train is the decoy?'

Shit. The one thing he was supposed to have completed had slipped his mind. All the adrenaline from the past half hour had clouded his ability to process any information.

'I'm working on that,' Jake said quietly.

'How?' Lucy snapped behind him.

'I... I don't know,' Jake admitted to himself. 'Give me a minute to work it out.'

Both Lucy and Tyler kept quiet while Jake thought hard. He had a one-in-three chance of being correct. It was too risky to leave up to guess work.

'What was the last thing the bloke said to you?' Tyler asked, growing restless.

'He told me to follow my train of thought'.

'Pun intended?'

'He thinks he's being clever,' Jake said.

There was a pause between all three of them as they pondered over the final piece of the puzzle.

'Hold on,' Jake said, the bulbs in his brain burning

vigorously. 'Hear me out, OK? I went from North Acton to Oxford Circus, Oxford Circus to Liverpool Street, Liverpool Street to Tower Hill, then Tower Hill to Upminster...'

'Which means?' Tyler asked.

'That's my train of thought,' Jake said. 'That's where I went. I think it might be an —'

'It's an anagram!' Lucy exclaimed, beaming with excitement.

'It's an ana-what?' Tyler asked, a look of bewilderment etched over his face.

Lucy rolled her eyes, fumbled through her bag where she found a pen and paper, and wrote the initials of all the underground train stations Jake visited in order. Jake called them out as she wrote.

NAOCLSTHU

Anagrams are always a perfect excuse to show off, Jake thought as he watched Tyler's mind try to piece it together. He'd been proud of himself for noticing it. Finally, he felt as if they were getting somewhere and he relaxed with the knowing at least one train full of lives would be saved.

Lucy finished writing them down.

'Do you know what an anagram is?' Jake asked.

'Yes, you dick, of course I know what it is. It's difficult reading them upside down, that's all,' Tyler responded.

'Good,' Jake said. 'Now rearrange them so they make a word.'

Lucy held the notepad out for Tyler and he observed it. It took him a while, however a few moments later he blurted out the answer.

'Luton! That's the decoy. Luton! Oh, you're an absolute genius!'

'Get back on the phone to the Yard and let them know they can immediately evacuate.'

Tyler nodded, removed his phone from his pocket and dialled, the call already ringing before it hit his ears. Lucy and Jake looked at one another, pleased with their efforts. Before either of them could say anything, Jake noticed there was a crowd thickening on the outskirts of the square surrounding Nelson's Column. Then his phone vibrated in his pocket.

DETECTIVE TANNER. I CAN SEE YOU. GET THE GIRL TO PUT THE BRIEFCASE ON THE STATUE ALONE AND UNARMED. TELL HER TO AWAIT FURTHER INSTRUCTION.

Jake read the message twice, three times, and then a fourth. Was this all Lucy had to do? Why now? Why in the open where she could be seen? None of it made sense, and not one part of him felt safe for Lucy's safety. There was something else going on here, and it ate Jake inside not knowing what.

Tentatively, Jake showed her the message. As she read it, she cast him an uneasy look. Her brow furrowed, and she swallowed hard, taking in the possibility that she could soon be in life-threatening danger.

'Give me the briefcase,' she said, exuding confidence. Jake could sense she was putting it on. He wouldn't have blamed her for admitting to being scared — he'd have been feeling the same. Who wouldn't?

As Jake passed the briefcase to Lucy, Tyler returned.

'Frances is on it. She's evacuating the train,' Tyler informed them.

Jake thanked his partner and turned to Lucy. Pulling his

phone from his blazer, Jake disabled the PIN lock, and handed it to her.

'Just in case,' he said. 'Call Tyler's mobile if anything happens. We'll answer it straight away and help as soon as we can.'

Lucy smiled. It was a brilliant smile, one that he hadn't seen from her today — and he'd seen a lot of her. But he couldn't negate from the fact — nor was she able to conceal it all that well — that she looked terrified. They embraced, Jake wished her good luck, and she walked off.

'No pressure,' she said before departing.

Jake and Tyler watched her descend the steps and grow smaller and smaller as she inched further and further away from them. By the time Lucy arrived at the base of the column, the crowd surrounding her had thickened at an alarming rate. Jake's eye became alert to everybody in the vicinity. *I don't like this*, he thought, *I don't like this at all. What's happening?*

He found out the answer straight away.

All of a sudden, music blared from around the square. Swedish House Mafia's dance song *Don't You Worry Child*.

At the instant the song began, a flash mob of at least sixty people dressed in casual and unassuming clothes appeared. They performed around the base of the column, concealing Lucy, concealing the briefcase, concealing Willy Wonka.

Jake and Tyler were blind.

Chapter Thirty-Nine

DECOY

August 1, 03:30

'All right, little brother. Is everything sorted?' Adil asked as Moshat descended the step ladders.

The inside of the factory was cold and dark, and they had just finished placing the explosives for the final carriage of the Heathrow Express. The factory seemed like it was Adil's second home, he had spent so much time there. But more importantly, it *was* Moshat's second home, which made it difficult for Adil to slip the detonators underneath Moshat's nose undetected. Moshat had been by his side throughout the entire process, like a small child cowering away beside their mother on the first day at school.

'We're all set, brother,' Moshat said, embracing Adil with his wide arms.

'Shall we make sure we've got everything as it should be? Triple check?'

'We wouldn't be doing our jobs if we didn't.' Moshat smiled.

Together, they jumped off the train and inspected the underside of the carriages. The small EMP devices capable of disrupting telecommunications were already placed against the steel chassis. There were four in total, spaced between every other carriage. Once they had done their checks on the outside of the train, they checked the inside.

When they reached the front carriage, Moshat climbed up a step ladder and peered his head through the upper compartments, inspecting the most recently laid explosives.

Now was Adil's chance. If he wanted his brother to prove himself, it was now or never. While Moshat was in the ceiling space, Adil ducked underneath a table to his right, reached into his bag and fished out the detonator with a note attached to it. Placing it on the underside, he used two thick pieces of Blu-Tack. *I hope this holds,* he thought. It was hardly industrial stuff, but it was all he had.

From the floor, Adil could hear Moshat descending the steps.

'Adil?'

'Coming.' Adil pulled himself out from the table and brushed himself off.

'What were you doing down there?'

'I thought I saw something. It's nothing. Don't worry about it.' Adil touched his brother's arm and gave it a squeeze. 'Come, let us go to the cockpit and then home. After tomorrow, we can rest like kings — we will bathe in glory and watch the uprising unfold.'

Moshat and Adil entered the cockpit. Adil got down on his hands and knees, grimacing at the hygiene levels of the floor, and pulled the control panel apart. It fell open like a dishwasher door and was ten times as heavy. Inside were hundreds of wires encompassed in a spider's web of copper and plastic. With a smile on his face, Adil began. This was the final component to his machine, and it required his complete concentration. If the chip inside the control panel didn't work, then they would lose control of the Heathrow Express. The Luton and Gatwick train's modifications had gone perfectly. For months, he had been researching the complexities of control panel configuration. Nothing about it had excited Adil, apart from the fact he knew that no one could remove his chip. It would be embedded so far into the system that only he could locate it. Adil found the wire he was looking for, inserted a connector into it, and installed a SIM card-sized chip inside.

Just like that, it was done. Within twelve hours, he would have entire control over the hundred-tonne machine. All the operations and functions would be his to play with.

'The final piece is in place. We are good to go.' Adil came out of his hole and onto the seat.

'And what about Trafalgar Square?'

'All booked and ready to go. They'll be there on the dot, at ten minutes past.' Adil put his feet on the centre console. He'd earned himself a break.

'Good...' Moshat said and trailed off. Adil noticed his brother wanted to say more but was afraid to.

'Everything OK, little brother?'

'Yes... it's just...'

'You nervous?'

'A little. I just keep thinking, "what if?"'

'Explain. Talk to me.'

'I don't know, what if everything goes wrong? What if the trains don't stop when you want them to? What if the doors open and everyone escapes? What if there's a fault with the explosives? What if this Tanner guy beats us to it? What if Martha compromises us? What if she becomes too big a threat for me to handle? I just...' Moshat spoke quickly. He looked out of the window into the factory floor.

It was clear to see his thoughts were leading him down a bad path. Adil had to placate him.

'Listen — none of that is going to happen. OK? You have my word. We have spent months and months working towards this. Every angle has been covered and there is no possibility it could go wrong, understand? There is nothing for you to worry about,' Adil said sympathetically. He didn't like to admit it, but there was a part of him that felt doubt, too. He had to stay strong for them both. 'And, if what you say about Martha comes true, you know what you must do. She is going to be our insurance package, but I have every faith that our little dog, Detective Tanner, will do everything we tell him to. If she must die, she must die. It'll only make things more unbearable for him. After all, it is what *she* deserves, isn't it?'

Moshat nodded and smiled. The two embraced and then exited the train.

As they jumped down from the step, Adil said, 'Moshat, before we go, there is something I must ask you.' Moshat's eyebrows raised. '*If* something goes wrong, can you do it? Can you bring yourself to take innocent lives?'

Moshat hesitated before answering. His voice was quiet and reserved, like a child who had just been punished.

'Yes, I can do it. I will do it for you, brother.'

'No. Do it for Mum and Dad, Moshat. Do it for everyone else who perished in that fire. They'll be watching over us tomorrow, and they'll be guiding you through,' Adil said. Tears formed in both their eyes, and they hugged for a considerable time.

When they released each other, Adil suggested they go

home and rest. Moshat agreed and together they left the warehouse, without any trace of them ever being there.

As Adil closed the doors behind him, he gave one last thought to the detonator device underneath the table.

Less than twelve hours later, it would still be there.

Chapter Forty

RED-HANDED

August 1, 16:06

For the past few minutes, Moshat had been staring into space, into the backs of peoples' heads, oblivious to the moving crowd advancing past him. In his head, he replayed the events of last night: how Adil had been acting strangely and had crawled on the floor without sufficient justification. It didn't seem like anything important then, something unrelated. But now, as he considered it further, he realised everybody on the train was headed in the wrong direction.

The detonator wasn't in the eighth carriage; it was at the front of the train, closer to Moshat and further away from everyone else. Adil hadn't betrayed him. Adil hadn't jeopardised the mission and his life. In fact, he had done the complete opposite: he had given Moshat a second chance, a chance to prove himself. The sudden weight of responsibility felt heavy on his shoulders.

You clever bastard, Moshat thought as he considered his brother's concealment of the detonator.

But there was one thing that confused him. *If the trains are still going to detonate at the end of the timer, then what is the need for this detonator? Unless...* Moshat didn't like where his thoughts led him. *Unless I'm the one in charge of carrying out the orders. I'm the one in charge of detonating the Gatwick Express. Their blood will be on* my *hands.*

Had this been part of Adil's master plan after all? He couldn't be sure.

What he knew was that he needed to get to the first carriage. And fast, before anyone else did.

Moshat turned around and fought through the sea of bodies.

As he entered the front of the train, he made a quick head count. There were ten or so people who remained. He supposed they had either given up all hope of surviving or couldn't make it through the enormous crowd whence he had just come. Either way, he was hoping for less. More people meant more eyes watching him. More eyes watching him meant more suspicion.

And suspicion was the one thing he could do without.

Walking towards the end of the coach, he imagined the table that appeared so vividly in his imagination moments ago. He stood before it, replaying the events of the early hours of the morning in his mind: Adil stumbling underneath, disappearing for some time and reappearing, wiping his hand clean of dirt.

Biting his lips and holding his breath, Moshat crouched down and crawled below. He let out a little gasp as his eyes fell on it. There it was, the black object that was the same size as his fist stuck to the bottom of the table.

He ripped it off and saw there was a yellow Post-It note on it. He read the message.

M, the detonator on your train does not exist. That was a decoy. The detonator in your hands is the real deal. I have entrusted you with the power to destroy the Gatwick train. If you feel you cannot do it before the deadline, the Gatwick Express will explode automatically. Your train will remain the same — it will not explode under any circumstances. However, at the end of the deadline, just as you are about to be set free, release the trigger, and send the Gatwick Express into oblivion. Just in case the explosives on board don't detonate. We have to prove we are a force to be reckoned with. What you hold in your hands is a flick switch — if you let go, it will detonate at once. Only do so if you are absolutely certain. The power is in your hands now, brother. Without you, I wouldn't have been able to make any of this possible. Be safe. Speak soon. A.

Moshat read it, and then read it again. And it finally made sense to him.

'What are you doing?' someone asked from behind him.

Moshat turned on the spot, bringing his arms behind him, concealing the detonator and note. His face dropped as he saw who had spoken.

There she stood, Martha Clarke, the woman who had been staring at him, observing him. The woman who hadn't trusted him ever since he smiled. The woman he was supposed to use as their insurance.

She had caught him red-handed. And he had nowhere to go. But now he knew what he needed to do.

Chapter Forty-One

FLASH

August 1, 16:08

'What the fuck is going on?' Jake shouted in disbelief as he watched the flash mob unfold in front of him.

It didn't take long for a crowd to form around the performers. By now, a few hundred bodies had surrounded them, amazed at the spectacle. There was no way the snipers could get a clean shot of the terrorist without taking out any innocent civilians. Lucy had disappeared amongst the wall of bodies. She was vulnerable now. If they were going to save her, then they needed to do something. And fast.

'Come on, let's go!' Jake yelled, darting down the flight of steps and towards the commotion.

Jake spearheaded the attack through the crowd, barging past women and men and children of all ages, devoid of any care as to the repercussions of his actions. Jake came to a stop in the open space that separated the performers from the crowd. He scanned the environment. There was no one there. He could no longer see Lucy nor the briefcase, and since he had never seen his tormentor before, he didn't know if the creep was nearby.

Shit! Jake advanced further forward, this time breaching into the space occupied by the flash mob. At this point the soundtrack had turned from house music to rock. The dancing performers were like an undercurrent of sea water, moving independently from everyone else, yet moving in sync with one another at the same time. It disorientated Jake, and despite the look of absolute chaos, he thought there was something methodical and serenely beautiful about what was happening.

But he had to keep his mind in the present. He needed to save Lucy.

Jake observed the grey stone covered in bird excrement and chewing gum that had been there for so long it had become integral to the statue's foundations. He searched for clues. There were none. Just like a speck of dust picked up by the passing wind, Lucy had disappeared. If he didn't find her in the next ten seconds, she would be gone for good, left in the hands of the man responsible for so much death and destruction.

Jake advanced deeper into the flash mob. Before he could reach the midpoint, the music stopped, and the performers dispersed into the crowd. They filtered off into multiple avenues in every direction, confusing him further. As soon as the show had begun, it had finished, and with it, his chances of rescuing Lucy. It had been an ingenious plan, he had to admit. The terrorist had been able to wander in, collect his winnings of one million pounds, and leave again. Unseen.

Jake chased after the dispersing flash mob heading towards the main road at the end of Trafalgar Square. If

Lucy was going to be anywhere, it would be there. Jake's eyes scanned the horizon. Less than a second later, they found Lucy, her shoeless feet giving her away. Standing beside her, his hands pressing hard into pressure points on Lucy's arms, was a man who had to be the terrorist, Willy Wonka, the one responsible for everything. In the man's hand was a small device. It looked like a grenade.

It was much worse.

With a hand raised in the air and a smile on his face, the terrorist clicked the top of the device. For a moment, nothing happened. Everything seemed to go still for Jake as he watched the button press down. It was at that moment Jake started after her. In one stride, he covered two metres. On his second, he tumbled to the floor.

Above him was the ear-shattering noise of an explosion. The shock and force of it knocked him flat. His hands stung with the pain of gravel and dirt breaking the surface of his skin. He looked up. The top of Nelson's Column had exploded and was ablaze, tiny fragments of burning concrete and rubble cascading down on everyone from one-hundred and seventy feet.

Screams of terror filled the air as people in the surrounding area fled for their lives. Some were rooted to the spot in horror while others barged past one another, as if there was some sort of epidemic that had plagued the city feral.

Jake felt adrenaline surging through his body. He looked up. Lucy had disappeared again. There was no time to find Tyler; Jake needed to act now, or he was going to risk losing her for a second time in as many seconds. Stumbling to regain his composure, Jake sprinted towards the spot where he had last seen Lucy, ignoring the pain in his hands and leg. Within seconds, Trafalgar Square was deserted. Sirens sounded and Police Constables and PCSOs in high-visibility jackets bombarded the scene. The emergency response had been immaculate. Jake just wished it hadn't all been a waste of time and resources.

Jake stopped by the roundabout in front of him, darted his head left and right, and began to panic. He couldn't see them anywhere.

'Jake!' Tyler shouted from behind him. Jake ignored his partner and continued to survey his surroundings. 'Where are they?'

He didn't know. He needed to think. Where could they be? Where would he go if he was a terrorist who had just acquired one million pounds, had a hostage hanging round his arms, and had just exploded one of London's greatest and most popular landmarks? *He would want total anonymity. Somewhere he could blend in. Somewhere he could just disappear and in five minutes' time resurface in a different part of the city.*

'The Underground,' Jake said. It made sense; his tormentor's obsession with the London Underground had occupied him all day. 'Charing Cross. They can't have got too far. They'll be walking at a pace, not running. Lucy doesn't have shoes, and she's got a temper on her — she'll be making it as difficult for him as possible.'

Jake and Tyler started towards Charing Cross underground station, which was situated two hundred yards from them. A torrent of people spewed into the station, like a river of water pouring into a drain. Just as Jake and Tyler were about to join the queue of people trying to enter, something to Jake's right caught his eye.

Lucy.

Her hair. Her coat. Her feet. He was sure of it. Unmistakable.

'Over there!' Jake yelled, pointing to two figures in the

distance. Jake pushed back and sprinted after her, heading along the Strand.

Fifty yards and four lanes of traffic separated them. Jake could feel the muscles in his legs scream in agony. It had been a few hours since he last ate or drank anything, and his body was feeling the effects. Fatigue was knocking on the door, and soon, it would break down his body's defences like a battering room on a castle keep.

Lucy and her kidnapper turned right into Charing Cross station, momentarily disappearing. Jake and Tyler raced faster to catch up. As they turned the same corner, she had disappeared. The entrance to the station was busy, and Lucy was masked amongst the oncoming crowd. Jake could feel his pulse racing in fear throughout his body. His temples throbbed.

'We've got to get them before they get on the Underground,' Jake shouted at Tyler as he headed towards the station.

Entering the foyer, Jake lost sight of Lucy. Like a meerkat, he craned his head and observed the dozens of moving faces splitting off into a network of directions. In front were two constables. One spoke to a woman, while the other stood aimlessly next to her. They were Jake's last opportunity.

'Excuse me, officer,' Jake said, brandishing his ID card. He was out of breath, his voice hoarse. 'A male — Caucasian, dark hair — and woman — blonde, brown coat — just came down here. Where did they go?'

The officer in front of Jake seemed perplexed, as if he had just seen a dead relative.

'You're Jake Isaac Tanner?' the officer asked. He was tall, and after he had finished speaking, the smaller one joined the other's side.

'Yes. Why?'

'It's just...' the taller officer couldn't finish. 'We questioned a guy twenty minutes ago. He got knocked over by a cabbie. Told us his name was Jake Isaac Tanner. Fits your description just now.'

Motherfucker, Jake thought, catching his breath.

'Which way did he go?'

Saying nothing, the smaller officer stepped to the side and pointed to Jake's right. 'Underground. I thought he looked familiar. He was hobbling — think his leg's still fucked up from when he got knocked over.'

'If you see him again, arrest him. He's a terrorist.'

Jake thanked the two officers before sprinting across the station floor. A smile grew on Jake's face. He was feeling fired up. That bastard had used his identity. But it wasn't all bad — Willy Wonka was now injured and struggling to escape.

With one arm grasping his leg, and the other clasped around the hilt of the gun concealed in his blazer, Jake followed Lucy and her captor deep into the heart of the Underground.

Chapter Forty-Two

DARKNESS

August 1, 16:11

Jake had been beneath sea level too many times today, and he hated everything associated with public transport. The days' events had caused an unprecedented amount of chaos on the Underground. The display boards were littered with delays, and backlogs of people queued up as far as the stairs. It was like moving through concrete.

After speaking to the two PCs at the entrance to Charing Cross station, Jake had caught sight of Lucy's hair and chased after her moments before she disappeared again. Lucy and the terrorist were heading towards the Northern Line, southbound.

Just as he descended the flight of stairs behind her, a train pulled in. By the time he made it halfway down the steps, Lucy and her captor were already on the platform, carving their way through a wall of bodies waiting for the next train. It seemed the entire Underground had come to a standstill.

Fighting his way down the stairs, Jake spotted Lucy again as the distance between them grew. The terrorist dragged her towards the other end of the platform. *Where are you going?* Jake asked himself, keeping his eyes locked on Lucy's back. Every now and then, she glanced back at him. Despair swam in her eyes.

As Lucy and her captor cut their way through the traffic like a boat in water, dozens of commuters were left infuriated and enraged. The tannoy system overhead spoke.

'The train now approaching platform two...'

Jake didn't listen to the rest; he set his eyes on catching them before they got on the train. For an instant, he glanced back and saw Tyler right behind him. He lost valuable seconds in that glance. Without realising it, the train had pulled in, and he was nearing the platform's halfway point.

The train came to an eventual halt and the passenger doors opened. Those at the front of the queue filtered into the remaining space on the train, while those at the back inched forward, marginally increasing their opportunity of boarding a train at a respectable time.

There was little room for manoeuvre. Unless you were a terrorist.

Somehow, Lucy and her captor had blended into the crowd, and up ahead, Jake could hear cries and shouts of displeasure and profanity coming from the final coach of the train. *Shit!* He had missed them. They had somehow pushed their way through and entered the train while he stood and watched in disbelief.

The buzzing noise that signalled the doors were closing sounded, and the train started to move.

He didn't know what came over him, but he could feel his mind convincing himself it was the right thing to do.

Fuck, it was the *only* thing to do.

He swivelled on the spot and faced the crowd. With his arms outstretched, like a snow plough, he shoved people out of his way so he could reach the platform's edge. Everyone in front stood as firm as they could, making sure he couldn't get through. *Arrogant wankers.* A woman next to him screamed as she almost tripped off the edge and clambered into the moving train.

Jake reached for her and held her back. She gave him a slap on the face and he stumbled backwards, a stinging sensation reddening his skin. It tingled as the blood rushed to the area where the woman's hand had hit it.

'Oh my, God. I'm so sorry,' he said, holding his arms out to her.

'Fucking idiot!' she hissed at him.

He ignored her comment and watched the train rolling past him. The final coach was coming up and through the window he could see Lucy. As her face moved past, he caught a look in her eyes. They were screaming for him to save her. He could see she was losing hope. Jake had always been too far behind. It was as if he were constantly taking one step forward, then two steps back.

The train disappeared into the darkness. The red lights on the back of the train were gleaming, almost laughing at him, mocking him. In an adrenaline-induced bout of excitement and pure idiocy, Jake dived off the platform and chased after the train on foot. He landed hard on the track and felt the pain shoot up and down his leg.

Pain is temporary, he told himself, steadying himself on the awkward rail track.

The passengers on the platform gasped and screamed at him as he sprinted after the train. Just before he disappeared into the abyss of the tunnel, he dared a glance at the passengers. Men and women all in suits and shirts were gazing down upon him. Some had their phones out and recorded what was happening.

Bloody phones! he thought. *It'll be all over social media tonight. Not to mention there's going to be a shit storm with the national and international press after this.*

There was a noise behind him. At first, Jake thought it was an oncoming train that, because of the delays, was only moments behind the other, and that he was about to be sandwiched between them. As he turned around, he realised he had been wrong. Yes, there was something coming towards him, but it wasn't a train.

It was Tyler.

'What are you doing?' Jake shouted, still maintaining his stride. 'Go back! Go back to the Overground and wait for a call. Lucy has my phone!'

The noise of his voice echoed throughout the tunnel and everyone around him heard, including the mobile phones recording him.

Tyler nodded and skidded to a halt. Jake turned round and ran into the darkness. Within a few steps, he was gone.

Chapter Forty-Three

QUESTIONS

August 1, 16:13

For thirty seconds, Moshat stood there, staring at Martha, her eyes reflecting the artificial light in the cabin, left eyebrow raised. There wasn't the slightest hint of fear on her face. *There should be*, Moshat thought. Which made him worry even more. If she wasn't afraid, then what did that mean? What had he shown on his exterior that meant he knew he was well out of his depth?

If there was one thing no amount of preparation could have armed him with, it was how to tackle other people's reactions. Nobody, not even him, knew what was going on in someone else's mind. As much as he liked to think he did, he didn't. And he was naïve to think anything but. He didn't know how this woman would react as soon as he pulled out the Glock 19 from his bag. He didn't know whether she would scream or run for her life. He didn't know if she would stay, remain calm, and try to talk to him. Either way, the outcome would be the same.

Standing there, Moshat realised there was a new-found vulnerability to this feeling of sympathy that plagued his mind like a terrible disease, spreading its way through his psyche with each thought that passed through it. Soon, the feeling would combine with doubt and fear, and then his actions would be catastrophic for everyone involved.

But for now, his mind was empty and barren. He froze to the spot. His subconscious screamed at him, lambasting him for not reacting the way he should have. He knew how he should have reacted: talked his way out of the situation, just like he had practised many times over before. But now the entire dynamic of the situation had changed. He had been given the power, but what would he do with it? Did he really want to kill these people? Yes. Did he really want to kill Martha? Yes. Even if they had done nothing to harm him? Yes. *My parents had done nothing to harm anyone, yet they were the ones who perished.*

Something in Moshat's brain switched. He cleared his thoughts and reverted to a plan of action he and Adil had discussed at some length. The ins and outs. The dos and don'ts. The kill or be killed.

Moshat continued to observe Martha's face. *Time to cash in on that insurance package.*

'Do you want to play a game, Martha?' he asked her, his expression plain and voice robotic.

Martha stood there taken aback, her face awash with surprise and fear.

'How do you know my real name?'

'I know everything about you, Martha. I know your husband died recently. I know you have two pets you treat as if they were your own children. I know you have two children, and a third you lost to a miscarriage. I know lots about you. I've *always* known.' Moshat hesitated for a moment. He was enjoying this. 'I bet you were glad about your trip to the south of France, weren't you? Bet it came as a surprise when you got that out of the blue.'

Martha's expression remained the same, yet there was something in her voice — a weakness, a faltering — that Moshat leapt on.

'Who are you?' Martha asked.

'The person responsible for all of this.' Moshat opened his arms up and looked around the cabin. He removed his bag and retrieved his gun. He had used the Glock 19 in Bolivia, and it felt like a part of his hand every time he held one. There was no faltering when his fingers caressed the trigger.

'Who's the other person? The one who keeps speaking to us over the intercom?'

'He's my brother.'

'Why are you two doing this?' Martha asked, ignoring the weapon.

'We have our reasons.'

'What are you getting out of it? What's your purpose in this entire thing? Since we've been stuck here, you've remained silent, hidden away behind your phone. Why are you suddenly deciding to take action?'

Martha was launching an attack on Moshat, and he didn't like it.

'I was sent to keep a watchful eye on you, Martha. After all, you're Jake Tanner's mother-in-law, aren't you?'

'Yes,' Martha said, her face deadpan. 'What's that got to do with anything?'

'Your son-in-law has been the one responsible for saving every single one of you, and if he didn't do as my brother and I asked, then I was ordered to kill you, to use you as insurance to get what we want. It seems your son-in-law has delivered on his promises. So, for now, your life is in good hands. But my brother has since changed the dynamic of our little operation, and all bets are off, as they say. Your life is no longer in your son-in-law's, or my brother's, hands, anymore — it's in mine.'

Silence.

'So, would you like to play that game I mentioned earlier, Martha?' Moshat twirled the gun in his hands.

Silence.

'I'll take your answer as a yes. I'm going to allow you to ask me three questions. Anything you want. But I must warn you, if you ask any more questions at the end, then I am going to shoot you. So, choose them wisely,' Moshat said. A smile grew on his face. Feeling powerful and in control, he disabled the safety on the gun. It was like a symphony orchestra playing in his ears, prickling the hairs on his skin all over his body. It had been a long time since he last held one and aimed it at someone. *It feels good to be back.*

Martha looked at him, saying nothing, giving nothing away in her appearance.

'Why do *you* want to kill me?' Martha asked.

One.

Moshat hesitated before answering, considering his response.

'Because I'm angry.'

'Why are you angry?'

Two.

'Because of the social injustice in the world, Martha.'

'What injustice?'

Three. Nothing left.

'All of it.'

'What?'

Zero.

'Oops,' Moshat said, raising the gun in the air. 'Time's up. Looks like you won't be going to the south of France after all. At least, not in this world, though perhaps in another — if you believe in that sort of thing.'

Martha made a slight noise as she started to speak, but it was too late. Moshat pulled the trigger, and the bullet travelled straight through her skull.

A crimson mist spattered the walls and glass doors. She collapsed to the floor and made a loud thud, her lifeless body nothing but a heap. Once the noise of the gunshot had finished travelling around the cabin and ringing in his ears, screams and shouts ensued.

Moshat smiled and stepped over to her body.

'I killed you, Martha, because I can. And because you were one of the shameless, thieving bastards who pre-approved the cladding and faulty wiring around my old home,' Moshat hissed.

He laid his Glock and the detonator down on the table and waited. Not once did his pulse or heartbeat rise.

Chapter Forty-Four

EVACUATION

August 1, 16:18

Mamadou burst into the office. The door slammed behind him. He was miserable and angry and lost, and he was still riding on the wave of disbelief. Soon grief would kick in, and then everyone else in the office would suffer.

He had left the hospital four minutes after his mother was pronounced dead. He had tried to be practical: it would do no good if he hung around moping for the rest of the day. So he came back to work. There was a terrorist attack in his city that needed attending to. That would keep him occupied. He didn't care what any of the nurses and doctors thought about him after he left so hastily; he had said his final goodbyes, giving his mother one last kiss on the forehead, and found his own way of dealing with the loss.

And there was nothing more that he wanted to do than catch the sick son-of-a-bitch responsible for the lives of everyone on board the British Rail Class 387 train bound for Luton. Mamadou was mad. Worse, he was angry. And somebody would pay for what had happened to his mother, even if it wasn't their fault.

All eyes turned to face Mamadou as he barged into the room. He scanned the faces staring at him. Neither Jake nor Tyler — not even Frances — were anywhere to be seen.

With no obvious sign of anyone in charge of the team back at New Scotland Yard, Mamadou cleared his throat.

'DCS Kuhoba,' Deputy Assistant Commissioner Simon Ashdown said, approaching Mamadou from his left. He had just come from the debrief room. Behind him was a balding elderly man whom Mamadou had never seen before. 'Where the fuck have you been?'

'Don't start with me, Ashdown. You'll regret it if you do.'

Simon strolled up to Mamadou, stopping inches from his face, and said, 'Is that a threat?'

'You bet.' Mamadou's voice was calm at the face of it, but behind, beneath the mirage of tranquillity, there was a blazing fire waiting to erupt.

'My office. Now.' Simon pointed to the stairwell Mamadou had just come from.

'I'm not going anywhere. There are bigger problems than your ego, *Deputy*.' Mamadou placed so much scorn and disdain in the final word that a little spittle came out of his mouth. 'Now, could someone please tell me what the fuck is going on? What's happened in the last hour?'

It had taken Mamadou just over sixty minutes to travel from Royal London Hospital back to New Scotland Yard. The journey had been made arduous by the influx of double-decker buses and taxis on the streets. The earlier cancellation of half the Underground was taking effect. Using his blue police lights the entire way made little difference, and it only added to Mamadou's frustrations. In that time, he had been out of the loop and was unaware of what had developed.

'Nelson's Column has exploded. The ransom has been delivered. We've lost sight of the target. And to make matters worse, he's got a hostage with him,' Simon explained.

'Jesus,' Mamadou said. 'How could this have happened? Was this all on your watch?'

Simon didn't respond. He looked sheepishly around the room, his eyes unable to withhold Mamadou's glare.

'Anything else?'

'Yes. The Luton train has been confirmed as the decoy.'

'Superb. And what are you doing about it?'

'Nothing yet.'

'Why not?'

'COBRA haven't given the go ahead.'

'How long have they known?'

Simon hesitated. 'About twenty minutes.'

Mamadou's tensions rose. *Typical fucking politicians*. He removed his phone from his pocket, found Frances's Brent phone in his address book, and dialled. The Assistant Commissioner answered on the first ring.

'Mamadou — where on earth have you been? Have you not realised our city is under attack? You've got some explaining to do.' There was the sound of a chair leg screeching against the floor as Frances stood on the outskirts of the meeting room. He ignored her remarks.

'Why hasn't the Luton train been evacuated yet? What are you guys waiting for?'

Frances didn't respond. The only noise Mamadou could hear was distinct chatter in the background.

'Engage the SFOs now,' he roared. 'Get the SAS involved. I don't care how you do it. The terrorist is out in the open. So far, he's been controlling this entire thing from behind his keyboard. There's no way for him to remotely detonate the train if he doesn't know what's happening to it. We've received the green light from DC Tanner. You've sat on this information for too long to not have done anything about it. Pull your fingers out of your arses and do something. If you don't get those people off that fucking train in the next five minutes, I'm authorising it myself.'

Mamadou hung up the phone. He didn't care how he spoke to anyone anymore. The illusion of power based on rank had long been lost on him; it was just an excuse for narcissism to run amok. He would deal with the consequences later.

Turning to face Simon, he continued his onslaught.

'Have we got a positive on the terrorist cell who collected the ransom? Is he a confirmed relative of Moshat Hakim?'

Simon shook his head. 'Not yet. Intelligence are working on it. They've got his face on CCTV, and they're scanning for any similarities in bone structure. We've not got a location on him yet, but we're triangulating DC Tanner's phone. It appears he gave it to the hostage before she was taken.'

In times of threats to national security, the intelligence services could request the phone numbers of individuals from their network providers. From there, they could monitor all activity on the mobile phone, including listening to inbound and outbound calls. It had been used for the past few years to catch criminals and terrorists. They could also use mobile phone towers to give a precise location of the mobile handset at any point. It was only a matter of time until the terrorist came to a stop. And that was when they would strike.

Sighing deeply, and unable to comprehend the Deputy

Assistant Commissioner's incompetence, Mamadou said, 'Why didn't the sniper squad take him out? Would have saved us a whole lot of aggro.'

Simon hesitated before responding. 'Well, there was a flash mob, and the snipers didn't have a clean shot.'

Mamadou's mouth fell open and his eyes widened. *Clever bastard*, he thought. Even though he was a terrorist, and Mamadou hated him for it, he had to commend their ingenuity.

'Have you rung the company that organised the mob? Found out when and who booked that particular one?' Mamadou asked, already fearing the answer would be no.

'Yes,' Simon replied. 'DC Staines is on it.'

At last. Someone doing their job. For the next few minutes, Mamadou wandered around the room, asking each member of his team what they were doing. If it wasn't beneficial to the case, they were assigned a different task.

Mamadou stopped by DC Staines's desk.

'What have you got for me, Rhys?'

Rhys Staines turned in his chair and gazed up at Mamadou. 'The name the flash mob was booked under was a Timothy Brown. We think it may be an alias.'

'Did you get an address?'

'Moshat Hakim's flat, but we already sent teams there. Nothing. Wiped clean.'

This was not good. They were chasing loose ends that led to the small flat in Middlesex. There was no way either terrorist would go back there anytime soon. That flat was a decoy.

Mamadou and everyone else in the team was chasing after them blind.

It was all down to Jake. Mamadou was grateful for the detective's intuition to give the hostage his phone before she was taken by the terrorist. Without it, they'd have little to no chance. It would have taken too long to track her own phone.

'Excuse me, boss?' Mamadou heard on his right.

It was DC Matthews, standing to with his arms by his sides. His forehead sparkled under the artificial light. Tyler had told him about everything that had taken place with Luke and Jake, and as he stood there looking at the detective, he decided he would give him the benefit of doubt.

'Luke,' Mamadou said, nodding.

'Is there anything I can do?'

'No. Not yet. There will be. Sit tight, and as soon as we have confirmation on a location, I'll need you,' Mamadou said. Luke's face beamed. 'In the meantime, I want you to attend to Mr. Rosenberg, make sure he's OK. I fear his services may not be over yet.'

Reluctantly, DC Matthews nodded and turned away from Mamadou. As he watched the detective disappear into a different corridor with Theodor, the phone in Mamadou's pocket rang. He didn't check the caller ID.

'DCS Kuhoba.'

'Mamadou?' Frances asked.

'Yes.'

'We've given the officers trackside the "go". Luton train evacuation will commence shortly.'

Mamadou rang off. He started off to his office, made it as far as the door before someone shouted something behind him.

'Mamadou!'

He swivelled on the spot.

'What?'

'I think we've got another location. We've been cross-checking the mobile phone numbers, address and bank card details with the passengers on the Heathrow Express — in particular Moshat Hakim. Recent CCTV footage has shown he frequents a block of flats in Southbank, near the London Eye. We're waiting on a precise location.'

'Good. Don't come back until you do. I want all known or potential terrorist hideouts documented and sent to me before anything else happens. I'll be the one to let Tanner know.'

Mamadou slammed the door, pressed his back against it, and looked to the ground, an image of his mother in her bed ingrained in his mind.

He slumped to the floor, tears rolling down his cheeks.

Chapter Forty-Five

ONE DOWN

August 1, 16:20

Silence fell upon the meeting room as the Prime Minister gave the all clear. Members of the cabinet office and the remaining staff in the room all watched the television. A live feed displayed the Luton train. A camera had been placed atop the SAS commanding officer's head so they could all watch and remain in constant contact. They were using the latest technology able to withstand the electromagnetic radiation coming from the trains. The cameras on their heads were the only pieces of technology that worked. Now and then the image would cut out and pixelate.

It had taken much persuading to encourage the Prime Minister to start the evacuation. But she had given in, especially since Mamadou raised the most important point: this was their only available time. The chances of remote detonation were slim, and the Director of Special Forces had also agreed.

It was decided the SAS men, and the SFOs positioned

on the outskirts of the train would use glass cutters and a series of controlled explosives to enter the trains. The glass cutters would cut a shape in the train's windows, giving the passengers another form of escape.

'All call-signs "go"!' a voice from the television shouted.

Frances watched the evacuation play out in front of her eyes. The officer approached the train, stuck a small package of Semtex inside the joining where the two doors met, retreated to a safe distance, and initiated the device. There was a small ball of flames that blew a hole in the front of the door. Even through the TV, Frances could sense the panic those on-site were feeling.

The officer rushed towards the doors and pried them apart. With the help of the passengers on the inside, the doors flung open. Like a ruptured swimming pool, the passengers poured out onto the tracks and sprinted to safety.

Once the initial coach had been cleared, and there had been no sign of any suspicious activity in the explosive devices overhead, the officer continued down the rest of the train, his breathing audible through the television as he sprinted. As he approached the second carriage, the explosives detonated but malfunctioned the door.

'Get the glass cutter!' he screamed.

A second later, a man dressed in black from head to toe arrived, machine in hand. He placed it on the window and sliced through the glass. Within moments, a hole had been popped out and placed on the floor. The two officers then helped the passengers disembark.

As the commanding officer moved further and further down the train, everyone within COBRA watched in silence, afraid that a single noise would disrupt the SAS troops at work.

In less than five minutes, the entire operation was complete. It was an unprecedented success. The passengers had been cleared to a safe enough distance and were led back to a secure location. Meanwhile, a bomb squad advanced towards the train, ready to spend the rest of their evening attempting to defuse any onboard explosives.

The angle of the camera changed as the commanding officer removed his helmet from his head and held the camera to his face.

'All clear. Passenger evac complete. No hostiles. Multiple passengers sustained head trauma and other injuries from when the train stopped hours ago. The extent of the damage unknown. Emergency response triaging and attending to them all.'

Then the screen went blank as the live feed cut. A round of applause erupted around the room. Frances kept her hands placed firmly on the desk. It was too premature to be celebrating anything just yet.

The Prime Minister was the first to speak after the clapping had stopped.

'One down, two to go.'

Chapter Forty-Six

OLD FRIEND

August 1, 16:21

The near-darkness engulfed Jake. It was a different sensation from when he had been on the motorbike. The lights weren't as bright, everything moved slowly, and now he could see the tunnel in its entirety, it frightened him. He was right at the heart of the underground web that weaved its way in and around central London. He wouldn't forget *this* too soon.

It was cold down here, too, with gusts of cold air punching him in the face every time an opposing train went past. As he ran, his feet stumbled over the loose gravel and rickety wooden planks, almost sending him tumbling to the floor. In front of him was the train, constantly out of reach. Twenty yards separated them. As the train rounded the corner, he was just able to glimpse Lucy, the sight of her face taunting him like a cat with a piece of string. When was the next stop? When were they going to get off? When would he get a break?

With every stride, he could feel his leg muscles becoming weaker. Fifteen yards separated them. The train reduced its speed, slowing down as it arrived at a red signal.

Finally.

He made one last push and sprinted to the back door before the train had a chance to get away from him again. He hefted the handle using all his body weight, but it wouldn't open.

The pistons of the brakes let out a horrible noise as the air pressure equalised, and the wheels rotated. The train was moving again. Except this time at a walking pace. *Perfect!* Jake thought. *Much more manageable*.

Jake jogged behind the carriage, climbed onto a small ledge underneath the door, and clung to a thin bar that ran along the lower edge of the driver's window. He fought to keep his footing secure; as the train jolted and moved over the tracks, it threw him off balance.

Once satisfied he was in position, and not going to fall, Jake raised the gun and smashed the butt onto the window. The glass shattered into a hundred pieces and tore some skin on Jake's hand and forearm.

He didn't care. The adrenaline masked the pain and fatigue.

Reaching in through the window, Jake pulled the lever and opened the door from the inside. He was in. *Finally*. He lay there catching his breath. *Now let's get this motherfucker*.

A few seconds later, the train slowed down. Behind the door, he could hear the driver calling the next station: Embankment. Jake swore out loud and rushed to the carriage door. It was locked. On the side panel was a small ID card reader, like the ones he had to use at the turnstiles at work. Two red lights flashed on the machine.

He slammed his fist on the door and screamed out in

rage. Anger consumed him. He had never been this angry before, and it was unfamiliar territory; he was afraid at what damage he could cause in this state.

Without realising what he was doing, relying solely on muscle memory, he withdrew his ID card from his pocket. It was a long shot, but it was all he had. Jake slid the card through the reader.

The door opened. He stood there in disbelief, amazed at how impossible and difficult it should have been. Someone somewhere was watching over him, he supposed. Perhaps Frances had taken more extreme precautions for his sake than he was aware of.

Jake spurred on, exited the driver's cabin, and carved his way through the onslaught of passengers trying to disembark the train. In the distance, Jake saw the same smile that had gone into his soul and changed something within him. The same smile that had made him see red everywhere he went. The same smile that had invoked within him a burning desire to catch the bastard and finish the day.

The man responsible. Willy Wonka. Tyler Durden. The Joker. Whatever the fuck he wanted to call himself. And Jake wanted to end him more than anything.

Then, just like that, the face disappeared again behind a wall of heads, hair, backpacks. Furious, Jake charged out of the train, his ID card still in his hands, and chased Lucy and her captor to a flight of stairs that led out of the station. As he ran, he noticed she was still carrying the briefcase. She was still a vital part of his getaway. Jake presumed she would be for a long time to come. A woman holding a large bag of shopping clobbered into Jake's hand.

Lucy and the terrorist charged out of Embankment station. The funnel of traffic going into the station overwhelmed the flow of people coming out. Fortunately, the open area at the station's mouth was sparsely populated. Jake used this to his advantage.

'Freeze!' Jake bellowed at the top of what was left of his voice as he breached the top of the stairs. He raised the gun in the air and aimed it at the back of the man's head. Thirty yards separated them. It wasn't close, by any means, but it also wasn't too far. Jake was a good enough shot to make it. But he wanted to give this arsehole one — and only one — chance to hand himself in.

With the speed and grace of someone who didn't have a care in the world, Jake's target turned around.

'Do not move a muscle. Let go of the girl and hold your hands in the air where I can see them!' Jake tried to shout. His voice was becoming increasingly raspy.

Screams and roars of panic erupted around him as soon as he lifted his gun to aim. Everyone around him disappeared, splitting off in every possible angle like rats on a sinking ship.

Except for one.

Jake felt a searing pain in the back of his skull, and his vision turned a large, velvet, sheet of white. Losing his balance and stumbling to the floor, Jake lost all sense of where, and who, he was. There was a horrible, metal clang on the ground that rang around Jake's ears. And around. And around. Through misty eyes, he noticed his gun had fallen to the pavement.

Slowly rising to his feet, Jake came to, realised where he was, and looked behind him at the source of the pain. A man, fists clenched, and hood pulled up, stood towering above him. His forearms were on show, displaying numerous tattoos depicting tigers and pyramids.

Jake recognised him instantly. It was the thug whose gun he was using. The one who had let him use his phone. The one Jake had allowed to get away at Tower Hill. *The fuck did you come from?*

Jake stumbled to his feet, grabbed the gun and pocketed it before punching the man in the face and knocking him to the ground. Jake pinned the man to the ground and looked around. Lucy and her captor had gone.

'What the fuck have you done?' Jake screamed in the man's face.

Lucy was gone. And there was no way of knowing which way they went.

All the progress he'd made was wasted.

Chapter Forty-Seven

HAPPY FAMILIES

August 1, 16:22

The beauty of instilling fear into everyone was that it meant Moshat could get what he wanted no questions asked. Nobody in that train wanted to die, and nobody wanted to stand in the way of the only person who had the power to kill them. They would do as instructed.

Moshat sat there with his hands crossed on the table, his fingers laced between one another. The gun was pointing straight ahead of him. Next to it in his other outstretched hand was the detonator; the shape and form of it was a little disproportionate, but Moshat had moved it in such a way that satisfied his compulsive habits.

Out of the chaos came order.

The entire first carriage of the Heathrow Express was almost empty. Empty except for Martha's corpse slumped to the floor with blood oozing around her head and a few passengers at the other end of the carriage. He was finally in control. Both the train and the people were his to manipulate. As he sat there, an idea popped into his head. He pulled out his phone, opened the camera, and took two photos of Martha. The first was a long-range shot; the second was close-range, focusing on the bullet in her head and her lifeless expression.

He would use those later.

Once the screams and cries of the mothers and children had died down, he smiled. The gun shot had caused panic beyond his own comprehension. Everyone who had been in the first carriage with him had clawed and punched their way through to the other carriages. Some had fainted. Some had been too overcome with horror and fear to do anything at all. Those were the ones who remained. They were his next subjects, and there was nothing any of them could do about it. There was nowhere for them to go.

Moshat came to the realisation it had all been part of his brother's big plan for him. The flick switch made it look he was a suicide bomber, ready and waiting to release the lever and explode the entire Heathrow Express into smithereens. That power commanded respect.

Moshat was untouchable, the repetitive nightmare that keeps you awake at night. And no matter how hard you tried to shake him, no matter how much counselling you had, he would *always* be there.

A few minutes of nothing dragged by.

Moshat turned his head to face the nearest person to him. A middle-aged man with a large forehead and a small chin wearing jeans and a T-shirt. Behind his leg was a tiny face, the face of a young boy.

Moshat smiled and held his hand out to the boy.

'Come here.'

The father hid the child behind his legs, hiding him from view. Before the child would be out of reach, Moshat moved his hand to the gun. A collective gasp sounded from the onlookers. The father of the child froze to the spot, keeping his grip on his child's arm tight. Moshat commended the father's bravery with a wicked smile.

'Come here,' Moshat said to the boy again, breaking the silence. Now he pointed the gun at the dad and, using the middle finger of his other hand, motioned for the boy to move closer, for his index finger was wrapped round the detonator.

'Never!' the dad shouted.

Moshat chuckled to himself, looking down at the table. *Stupid. So very stupid.*

For the time he sat there, he was calculating — calculating every next move he made and any potential reactions, or actions, that might follow.

'You have three seconds to allow the child to come here, or I will shoot *her.*' Moshat nodded in the direction of the man's right shoulder. A tall brunette, much taller than the man, stood next to him. She wore a loose scarf that flowed around her shoulders and a tight-fitting top. Moshat thought she looked pretty.

At once, the woman cowered behind the man's arms, immediately confirming Moshat's suspicions they were family.

Perfect, he thought. *The real catch-22.*

Moshat had chosen her for one specific reason. Her height. She was the perfect target: taller than everyone else, which meant that if he missed — although, he'd never missed a shot in his life — then he wouldn't risk hitting another, useless target, and reducing both the impact of the shot, and their impression of him. If they saw he had missed one shot, then who was to say he wouldn't miss another?

Unnecessary bloodshed had to be kept to a minimum. All Moshat needed was his leverage.

'One...'

The family grouped together and hid behind the father. To Moshat's surprise, no one stepped forward to protect them. They were all as selfish as the last.

'Two...'

Moshat's lips quivered as he tried to hold back another smile. He couldn't help himself. The man faced an impossible decision. Wife or son. Which one would he sacrifice? Watching the man decide in front of his eyes, Moshat felt elated. If he had been in the same situation, he knew the choice he'd make.

'Three...'

'OK! OK!' the man screamed. 'On one condition.' The father reached for the boy behind him and held him in front of his legs.

'What's that?' Moshat asked calmly.

'I come with him.' Tears descended the man and son's face.

'That's noble of you, but I can't allow that, I'm afraid.'

'Please?'

'You don't get to dictate what happens here. I'm the one in charge. If you do as I say, then maybe your little boy might live. Hand him here. Don't make me count again.'

The man's reaction went as Moshat suspected. He bent down to the boy's level, placed both hands on the boy's shoulders, and kissed him hard on the forehead. The man sobbed, and the boy called out innocently for his father — begged him, in fact — to not let him go through with this.

'I promise, Ryan. I promise that nothing will happen to you. Daddy won't let anything happen to you at all. I promise, OK? Just do as the man says and you *will* be OK. I promise,' he said, his eyes pouring tears.

Now the mother had joined them down by the floor, crying and holding her son in her arms. *Happy families. Happy fucking families*, Moshat thought in a sudden bout of rage. *At least you've got a fucking family.* His smile turned down, and he continued watching.

'One…'

The family didn't need to be told twice. The parents stood upright, said their final goodbyes, and walked the child forward. The man let go of the boy a few yards away from Moshat and allowed the boy to walk by himself. Moshat moved over one seat and opened his arms for the boy to sit down.

'Welcome. You're safe here,' Moshat said, putting his arm around the boy. 'I won't hurt you.'

right towards the London Eye. Lucy didn't like this. The further she got away from Jake, the more vulnerable she felt. But, she considered, the further they travelled by foot, the more vulnerable *he* was. He kept mumbling to himself. Imperceptible words left his mouth and floated to her ears. They weren't foreign. No, he was definitely English — she had been sure.

At first, she believed he was from a different country. Perhaps he was from somewhere in Eastern Europe. Or perhaps he was Scandinavian? His skin colour was pale, so it was unlikely that he was from anywhere else. But after he had told her to shut up and stay quiet, then she had known for certain he was British, his London accent too thick to be assimilated.

Her captor was an unattractive man she had decided. Small, with thick, messy, greasy hair that looked as if it was still wet. He wasn't skinny, but he wasn't muscular, either. He looked as if he had worked out when he was younger, and the muscle mass hung in place. He was, however, strong. As they raced across the Jubilee Gardens, zigzagging in and around knots of people lying around the grass, she felt her forearm crush under his hand. He could outweigh and out muscle her without a problem. She knew that. And the thought made her skin crawl.

They came to a stop near a large building, less than one hundred metres from the iconic Ferris wheel landmark. They entered and climbed the steps to the top floor. Her captor tightened his grip around her arm as he opened a door and then shoved her through the threshold. He closed the door behind him and threw his laptop to the sofa. Lucy's bag and the briefcase rolled along the floor as she stumbled face-first onto the carpet. It stank. The stench of chemicals stuck to her throat and made her cough and convulse.

'Sit!' he ordered, pointing to the chair in front of her. His breathing was heavy. He lunged towards the windows, pulling down the blind after a brief look at the city.

Lucy stayed where she was. She needed to stall for as long as possible.

'Sit down, Lucy! I don't want to have to hurt you,' the man said. Growing restless, and his nerves on edge, he strode over to her, picked her up and pushed her onto the chair, reached into a nearby drawer, and tied her hands together using an obscene amount of Sellotape. 'Are you going to say anything?'

Lucy looked at him in horror. His eyes were wide with adrenaline and fear, too — something she had experienced all too much of in the past few hours. She thought he looked more afraid than in control.

Lucy shook her head. 'I won't make a sound.'

Her captor placed the Sellotape on top of the drawer and flung the briefcase containing the one-million-pound ransom onto the floor. He returned to the window, peering into the sliver of light at the bottom of the blind.

Lucy watched him. She wriggled her hands. They hadn't been tied together tightly. With some time and endurance, she could break free and ring Tyler, Jake — anyone. And then they would save her.

'Are you not going to check that?' Lucy asked, nodding to the briefcase on the floor.

The man pulled away from the blinds. 'No.'

'Why not? What if it's not all in there? Have you never wanted to see what one million pounds looks like?'

The man chuckled. *Oh, no,* she thought. Laughter like that meant he was insane; she had watched too many crime programmes and witnessed too many police interrogations to realise that. But at least he was distracted. She wanted him to remain calm.

'What's your name?' Lucy asked.

'You can call me James. It's better than what the tabloids will call me tomorrow.'

'Why are you doing this, James? You won't get away with it.'

'Oh, but I will.' James moved across the room, reached for another chair and sat opposite her. 'Nobody knows I exist. And nobody will *ever* know I exist.'

James's breathing rate had dropped dramatically. Now all Lucy had to do was keep him talking, distract him, buy some time.

'Is that what you want? For nobody to know who you are after all the effort you've gone to?' Lucy asked. While she spoke, she writhed her fingers over one another, loosening the Sellotape's grip around her wrists.

James responded with a smile. He touched her leg and said, 'Do you know what, Lucy? You've given me a great idea.'

Lucy held her breath, frozen with fear. What did he mean? What was he going to do to her? She shifted on the chair. She felt Jake's phone against her hip; she had stuck it into the waistband of her pencil skirt after Jake had given it to her. It moved to the small of her back. If only she could reach it!

Saying nothing, James rose to his feet and moved his chair to the desk. He unlocked the computer and loaded up what looked to Lucy like a Microsoft Word document. As soon as it opened, he typed furiously.

'James?' she asked, her fears multiplying. 'James? What are you doing? What did I inspire you to do?'

James stopped what he was doing and turned to face her. Sirens rang outside.

'You told me I should make the world know who I am,' James said. He cracked a smile, revealing a set of perfect white teeth. 'So that's what I'm going to do. Once I'm done, I'll let you have a read through. And then I'll be on my way. But you won't be joining me. You won't be leaving this room ever again.'

Jake stopped when he was done, and turned to face her with a smile

"You tell me I should make the world know who I am," Jake said. "I'll make a little trouble on my way there, just to prove that this is who I'm going to be. Once I'm doing all this, my understanding and the elite, the envy, flat and top... telling me you won't be leading the main lives is a..."

Chapter Forty-Nine

LOCATION

August 1, 16:31

Jake checked his watch. An hour and a half remained. He was exhausted. Every part of his body screamed with fatigue, and his head ached with a severe pain that felt as though he had a tumour. *He's the real tumour,* Jake thought, his disgust turning towards the man responsible for everything.

Jake was on the Golden Jubilee Bridge, resting against a metal barrier that was just high enough to stop him from climbing over and jumping into the River Thames. He had lost all hope of finding Lucy and her captor outside Embankment. So he had waited for a nearby Police Constable to arrive and arrest the thug he had pinned under his body weight. They were patrolling the streets everywhere and the two officers he had seen in Charing Cross station only minutes beforehand arrived and carried the guy away to New Scotland Yard.

Jake leaned further over the bridge's barrier, this time

staring into the murky brown torrent flow beneath him, the overlapping and shimmering waters blending into a mirage that mesmerised him. He considered himself a failure, a spent officer in the entire Counter Terrorism Command.

Instead of making himself feel worse about the situation and sending his thoughts spiralling down into a cataclysm of despair, he thought rationally. All he needed was to contact Tyler, and they'd be able to work it out together. Two minds would be better than one. The only problem was: Jake didn't have a phone. He had given his to Lucy before she was taken hostage for the second time in a day.

With a plan in mind, Jake turned and strolled along the bridge. He stopped next to a drummer who was vigorously tapping away at a series of buckets and pots and pans. The noise reminded Jake of the gun pressed against his chest. He wasn't supposed to have it - it broke about a dozen laws and as many protocols - but he was grateful he had taken it from the thug in the first place. He felt more at ease with it in his possession. Cautiously, so as not to raise panic on the Golden Jubilee Bridge, Jake unloaded the weapon and counted how many bullets remained. Two. *One for each of the people responsible.*

Jake put the magazine away.

'Excuse me,' he asked a woman in a floral dress. She stopped and looked at him. 'May I borrow your phone please? I need to make a call.'

The woman eyed him up and down, a look of contempt stretched across her heavily made face. She looked as if she were in her late-forties but had tried with every effort to make herself look half that, possibly with additional help from some Botox. 'No. Get your own phone.'

'Please. Look, I'm a detective.' Jake fished the inside of his blazer pocket for his ID, but he found nothing there. It was gone. He frisked his pockets, but it was no use. He must have lost it on the underground after using his card to open that door. When that woman knocked into his hand. How could he have been so stupid? By the time he realised it was gone, so too was the woman. 'Fuck!'

Dejected and feeling as if the world was against him today, Jake continued along the bridge until he found a secluded spot where he could rest his back. After a few seconds, his senses withered. His head felt light again, and behind his ears ached, sending sharp splinters of pain swimming around his skull. The troops were readying for attack. To keep himself distracted, he asked a nearby family if he could use their phone. Mercifully, they agreed.

'Thank you,' Jake said, dialling the number and holding it to his ear. After a few rings, the other line answered.

'Hello?'

'Ty — it's Jake. Where are you?'

'Where you fucking left me! In Charing Cross station.'

'OK. I'm on the Golden Jubilee Bridge. I lost sight of them at Embankment. Time's running out, and I'm worried about Lucy. Has she rung you yet?'

'No.'

'OK. Come and meet me here. Now.'

'Yes, boss.'

Jake hung up the phone and passed it back to the father.

'Sounded serious,' he said jokingly.

Jake eased a little and found a smile etching its way onto his face. 'You could say that.'

'Do you want us to stay while you wait?'

It was the kindest gesture Jake had received all day, his faith in humanity restored.

'If you wouldn't mind. Do you have a drink of water or something, please?' Jake said without thinking. He desperately needed a drink. Anything that would restore some of his energy and vigour.

'Sure,' the man said. He turned to his wife, who passed along a bottle of water. 'We've got plenty. Don't worry about us.'

Jake thanked them. He then told them everything about what had been going on, keeping some information he shared to a minimum, lest he give away too much and offend the family. Not to mention, what he was doing was unprofessional. But he didn't care; he needed to clear his head. After having disposed of all his thoughts, he felt his morale lift. Jake felt secure in telling the family everything. In a way, they reminded him of his own, and his mind wandered to his girls. How, at the end of the day, he couldn't wait to embrace Elizabeth, Maisie, and Ellie, and never let them go.

But the thought of family concerned him. *Martha*. She was still on board the Heathrow Express. Her life was still in danger. Jake needed to rescue her.

While he waited for Tyler, Jake got to know his acquaintances better. They were a family who lived a few neighbourhoods away from him. The father, Alex Tough, was an IT consultant, and Karen, his wife, was a teacher. It scared him how alike they were. Yet, here he was, chasing terrorists around the streets of London.

He knew which life he'd prefer: his own. One less terrorist in the world was one less potential problem for Maisie and Ellie. They were his world, and he wouldn't let anyone take them away from him. Ever.

Alex Tough had offered Jake some food, and despite being ravenous, Jake declined. But Karen had insisted, and eventually Jake gave in, tucking into a small homemade ham and cheese sandwich. As he enjoyed the delicious-tasting food, the family's youngest, tiptoed over to him and tapped him on the leg.

'What's your name?' she asked, her voice filled with innocence.

Jake gave her a brilliant smile and said, 'Jake. What's yours?'

'My name's Ellen,' she said. The sun bounced off her bright blue eyes and illuminated her face. 'Do you want to see my teddy bear?' She showed him before he could respond, revealing it from behind her back.

'Wow,' he said in a childish tone. 'Is it a boy or girl teddy bear?'

'Doesn't have one,' Ellen said.

At first Jake was confused, but then he understood. He looked at the parents and raised his eyebrows.

'That's interesting,' he said to them.

'We've not taught them genders. Hopefully, later in life, they'll learn and appreciate the diversity of the world we live in,' Karen Tough said, stroking Ellen's hair.

'That's a brilliant idea. I wish I'd thought of the same. Mine are a little too old now, I think.'

'It's never too late,' Karen said. 'I'd be happy to give you advice if you wanted it?'

'Sounds like a great plan. Once this day's over, though,' Jake said, and they all laughed. 'That's a very cute teddy bear you have there, Ellen.'

'I know,' she said and quickly scuttled away. There was a pause as everyone watched her run to her brother who was two years her senior. He was busy showing no interest in the world, engrossed in a computer tablet.

'Is he always on that?' Jake asked, nodding at the tablet.

'Unfortunately, yes. We tried for a while to take it away, but it helps distract him. Ethan's got ADHD.'

'Sorry to hear.'

'That's all right, nothing to be sorry abc —' Alex started.

'Jake!' Tyler interrupted. His voice travelled far — he was just over fifty metres away. Tyler reached them and stopped, bent double to catch his breath. Sweat dripped down his forehead, creating massive black spots on the pavement.

'Give... me... a minute,' he said, in between breaths.

Jake slapped him on the back. 'We need to get you in the gym more often, mate.'

'Don't you fu —' Tyler paused as he looked up to see the children. Ellen was staring straight at him while holding her teddy. 'That would be a great idea.'

Jake laughed and sat Tyler down. 'What's the latest?'

'I've heard nothing yet. Let me check.' Tyler reached inside his pocket and retrieved his phone. 'Four missed calls, all from Mamadou... Oh, look, and a text message.'

Tyler opened the message and read through it, and then handed the phone to Jake.

STUART! CONFIRMED LOCATION. COUNTY HALL FLATS, BELVEDERE ROAD, TOP FLOOR, FLAT 605. PRONTO!

Jake looked up at Tyler. *Mamadou, and everyone else in CTC — you're all geniuses.*

'Where is it?' Jake asked.

Tyler nodded behind Jake's shoulder towards the London Eye.

'Just behind that. Right next to Waterloo Station.'

'Jesus,' Jake said. 'He's been under our noses all this time. He's got the perfect view of the Yard from over there.'

The thought harrowed him. The County Hall Flats were next to some of London's most famous landmarks: the London Eye, London Dungeons, and Sea Life Aquarium. The flats also posed a very good vantage point to New Scotland Yard and the Houses of Parliament. *The person behind this could have been watching my every move. Maybe that's why they chose me. Maybe that's why I've been elected to take part in this entire thing.*

'Jake!' Tyler shouted at him, breaking him from his reverie. 'We need to go!'

Saying nothing, Jake turned on the spot, waved goodbye to the Tough family, and sprinted across the bridge to the other side. His body had recuperated, and he was feeling fresh.

Seven minutes later, they arrived outside the flats, breathless and with the only gun they had containing two bullets.

God help us.

Chapter Fifty

MANIFESTO

August 1, 16:45

Lucy froze. Twenty minutes had passed since James last spoke, and his final words to her chilled her to the bone. He was going to kill her, and if she didn't act quickly, then the lives of everyone on board those trains would be at risk, too. She needed to act fast. But she couldn't. Fear grappled her to her chair. Her plans for the weekend popped into her head. How she was supposed to be spending the weekend with her niece, Kate. How her sister and brother-in-law were going away for the weekend to celebrate their anniversary, and they needed someone to take care of their eleven-year-old. How she wouldn't be able to see the smile on Kate's face when she picked her up in her arms and embraced her.

Lucy loved her niece. They would always spend time with one another when Lucy had time off work. They would go to the park, go shopping, or sit in front of the TV and binge on snacks and biscuits. Kate was like a younger sister to her, and she made Lucy realise that she wanted kids in life, but her biological clock was ticking. She was in her thirties, and what did she have to show for it? Sure, she had a law degree and worked at a top firm. But it wasn't what she wanted. It wasn't the career in policing she had craved for so many years. And what about a boyfriend? That had been a close call, too. There *had* been someone, but that was a few years ago, and she hadn't gone on a single date since. There were only so many times she could use her workload as an excuse. Her ex-fiancée had hurt her. She had lost confidence and for the three months after their break-up, nobody had known whether she was alive or hanging from the railing in her shower.

But that had been so long ago. It was time she changed her attitude and did something about it. Was finding someone so hard? There were no decent men anymore, she had continuously been told. Jake seemed like a gentleman, but he was married. Tyler, on the other hand, seemed just as much a gentleman as Jake. And he was good-looking, too. Yes, Tyler. After today was over, she would take him up on that offer of a drink.

The sound of James clapping his hands brought her back to the flat. She hadn't realised it, but in the time she had been thinking, she had freed her hands.

'Lucy,' James said. 'I'm finished. Do you want to read it?'

Lucy looked at him, confused. But then she remembered: he had been typing a manifesto, and he wanted her to read it. What would happen if she agreed? He would kill her after she had finished. What if she said no? *The result would be the same.*

Better to prolong the inevitable.

'Yes, please.' The words were hard for her to say. Her throat swelled, and tears formed in her eyes.

Smiling, James swivelled her chair to face the computer monitor. Lucy swore inside; her hands were no longer hidden out of sight. It would be impossible for her to reach for the phone now because he would undoubtedly see.

Biting her bottom lip and hoping that any moment now Jake would burst through the door and shoot James, Lucy read the Word document on the screen.

ATTENTION: THIS IS A CALL TO ARMS ON BEHALF OF ADIL HAKIM

On the day of 1st August 2017, the world over will realise the threat of terror is ever-present in our society. The threat can take on many forms and may be disguised right under our very noses.

For years, governments and diplomats have sought to defeat terror with terror, violence with violence. But it doesn't work. It only fuels the desire for revenge rooted in malevolence.

The root of terrorism is narcissism. Mainstream media has manipulated us into resenting one another. Where is our compassion for our fellow man? We have all been given one life on this earth, and we must treat one another with respect. Nobody has the right to take a life from one another. Nobody has the right to subject a 'lesser' person to ridicule and injustice. What if the shoe was on the other foot?

That is what today's demonstrations have been about. They have not been designed to incite violence, but to incite an uprising. The merciless killings of human beings were necessary to make certain the government and our fellow man realises what is at stake. No longer is the threat of terror only overseas. It is here, in the United Kingdom, lurking behind closed curtains, working towards a more just and fair society. The ones who have been born and bred here, the ones who have paid taxes all their adult lives. They have suffered for too long. Before we fix other country's problems, dear government, why do you not insist on solving those that take place within your own borders?

Attitudes towards terrorism, and our acceptance and appreciation of one another, need to change for the better.

It is time to make that change. No more shall we sit back and allow poverty to plague our country's streets. We are here, and you will hear us. If not, then we will make sure you do.

If you are reading this, stand up. It does not matter the colour of your skin, your societal class, the clothes you wear on your back — you have been born into these constructs. Nothing differs you from one another. Nothing more makes you worthy of success. Nothing. It is time for us all to accept our differences and mistakes and make amends for them.

Lucy stopped there. She couldn't continue any further. The words on the page harrowed her, and she stared at the screen in disbelief. But one thing stuck in her mind. Adil Hakim. That was his name.

James turned her on the chair.

'Beautiful isn't it?' Lucy didn't respond.

She fumbled for the phone and unlocked it, staring into space.

'I thought you'd react like that. I suppose it doesn't matter now.'

James turned, walked to a vinyl player, placed the nib onto a track, and wandered into the kitchen. Classical music filled the flat.

It was now or never.

Lucy yanked her hands free, found Tyler's name in the address book and pressed dial. She hid her hands behind her as James returned. In his hand, he held a gun. It was like the one she had seen Jake use. But a gun was a gun, and she knew it would take one shot to kill her.

James stopped in front of her, flicked the safety switch off, and aimed it at Lucy's head.

'Please, Adil! Please don't do this. Let's talk.'

Chapter Fifty-One

TRIGGER

August 1, 16:48

'What do we do now?' Tyler asked as Jake and he rounded the corner of a coffee shop, hiding out of sight of County Hall Flats.

The streets were busy. It was nearing the end of the working day, approaching rush hour, and a vast number of tourists continued to litter the pavements.

'I don't know.' Jake cast intermittent glances at cars and cyclists moving past them. He checked his breast pocket. 'We need to assess the situation. There's no time to wait for a firearms squad to raid the property first. It's just us. And we don't have a lot of time. Did you see a weapon on him? Anything he may use to hurt Lucy or ourselves?'

'No, I don't think so. But I don't think we should rule it out. A guy like that will have protection. He's smart enough to work that out.'

Jake paused a beat to think. Tyler's phone rang. He

fished it out of his pocket, looked at the screen, and showed Jake.

Jake's name popped up on the lock screen as the caller ID. Which meant Jake's phone was trying to ring Tyler's. Lucy was trying to contact them.

She's still alive.

'Thank God,' Jake said aloud. 'Answer it!'

Tyler unlocked the phone and put it on loudspeaker, hovering it beneath both their ears so they had equal opportunity at hearing.

Complete silence at first. Except for some muffled noises. Someone was talking in the background. Classical music played in the distance.

'What you're doing is wrong!' Lucy screamed through the phone. 'Please, Adil, don't do this. This is not part of your plan. I won't tell them anything, I swear.'

'My brother and I didn't discuss you ever coming into the equation. Plans change.'

Adil? Brother. Adil Hakim? Was this a third brother, or the same one who had died in the Tower Fire? Jake felt a wave of relief consume him. He had been right about the two terrorists' relationship. And now he had a name to go by, Jake was going to enjoy making this even more personal than it already was.

Jake and Tyler listened. Feet stomped across wooden floorboards and then there was a change in music.

Ride of the fucking Valkyries.

'I love this song. It always relaxes me,' Adil Hakim said. 'Thank you for your cooperation today, Lucy, you've been excellent.'

'They'll find you, you know, then you'll have nowhere to hide,' Lucy shouted.

'Nobody's ever found me in years. Nobody knows I even exist. They won't start now.'

'Oh, yeah? And what about if I scream for help?' Lucy produced an enormous high-pitched sound that reverberated through the speaker.

They both looked at one another. Jake had a judgement call to make: how long to leave it before he went up there and stood face-to-face with Adil Hakim, the man who had made his day a living hell.

Jake stopped breathing. He heard the unmistakable sound of the barrel of a gun being cocked. Lucy let out a slight whimper, and she began to plead for her life.

'Fuck. Come on.'

Tyler and Jake sprinted into the building. Tyler kept the phone in his hands as they jumped up the steps two at a time. Years of training and experience had taught them both that in emergency situations, using a lift was always a last resort. The stairs were much safer and offered a greater chance of success. As they charged up the steps, Jake's heart raced, and his adrenaline reached maximum. The blood in his body fuelled the certainty he had in his brain that he would end this all here. Now.

But he still needed answers. Lots of them.

Jake and Tyler arrived at the top floor. They opened the stairwell door and crept along the dark green carpet that ran the length of the corridor. Tyler ended the call with Lucy as they approached the sign on the wall that showed flat 605 was on their right. Both men edged towards Adil Hakim's flat. By now, the screams had stopped, but Jake's thirst for vengeance showed no signs of abating. The corridor was filled with a deafening silence.

Jake stopped outside flat 605, holding his breath, and crouching low. Trusting his instincts, Jake slid across the floor to the far side of the door. Tyler remained on the nearest side. Tyler opened his mouth to speak but was quickly silenced by Jake who held his finger against his lips. A few anxious moments passed. The sound of footsteps approached them, grew louder, and then stopped. The noise was followed by a slight tap on the door from the other side. Jake looked up and saw the tiny peephole. He prayed they were both out of sight.

Jake held his breath as he waited. He could feel his pulse moving the thin skin on his temple with every heartbeat. *Thud, thud. Thud, thud. Thud, thud.*

Finally, after what felt like an eternity, the noise of footsteps disappeared deeper into the room on the other side. Jake exhaled. His body released all the tension in his shoulders. He closed his eyes, controlled his breathing once more, and tightened his grip around the gun.

Then, just as Jake was about to stand, Tyler's phone rang. It was still on loud, the ring tone echoing around the cramped confines of the hallway.

'What the fuck is that?' Adil Hakim screamed from behind the door.

Tyler frantically tried to switch it off. But he took too long. Jake stretched across the width of the door and snatched the phone from Tyler. They tussled over it for a second before the noise of lead feet stopped. Adil was behind the door again. Doing what, Jake didn't know.

From a half-crouched position, Jake faced the door square-on, rose to his feet, and kicked the door. It swung open with so much force it knocked Adil to the floor.

Jake charged in, gun first, and screamed, 'Police, freeze!'

The first thing Jake noticed about the room was how black it was. He had seen prison cells that were brighter. But Jake was too fired up to care. His eyes fell on Adil. Jake kicked Adil's gun away and listened to it slide over to a nearby chest of drawers on the right-hand side of room.

There he was: Adil Hakim, the man who had been the puppet master of this whole operation. For the whole day Jake had been taunted, having only the sound of the man's voice to go by. Now they were face-to-face. And there was nowhere for him to go.

'Well, well, Detective Tanner. We meet at last.'

Jake fought every ounce of anger and desire within his body to pull the trigger.

Chapter Fifty-Two

COLLISION

August 1, 16:53

Mamadou and Luke were stuck at a set of traffic lights at the end of Victoria Embankment. Luke was driving, and Mamadou was riding shotgun. They had just got a confirmed location on the potential hideout for Moshat Hakim, and Mamadou had requested Luke join him. Luke felt confident; it was his time to shine and show his superiors — and inferiors — that he wasn't a spent force, that he was capable of carrying out everything the job demanded of him. He had a promotion on the line just as much as Jake.

And he was going to prove his worth. As he psyched himself up, his ego rose with it. There was no room to make mistakes. If he did, then he knew Mamadou would be the first person to come down on him.

'What are you waiting for, Matthews? We're only going over the fucking river!' Mamadou shouted. Just as he'd finished, the red light pigmented into amber. Luke hadn't been concentrating and swore at himself for already falling at the first hurdle.

It was only minor, but he had made his first mistake.

Slamming the car into first gear, Luke shot off across Westminster Bridge. As they passed the halfway point, the car's mobile phone system sounded. Luke pressed the answer button and Mamadou answered, giving Luke no chance to speak at all.

'DCS Kuhoba speaking,' Mamadou said.

'It's Simon. We've triangulated Tyler's phone, and he's in the same position as Jake's. They're at the suspect's location. We've been receiving calls from neighbours complaining they can hear screams coming from the flat. Officers and SFOs on approach.'

'Tell them to seal off the building. I want all exits covered.'

'Got it.'

Mamadou hung up the phone and turned to Luke.

'What's our ETA?'

'Seventeen-hundred hours.'

'What do you mean? It's only over the fucking river! Seventeen-hundred hours is not good enough, Matthews. We need to be there sooner, before something serious happens to my men.' Mamadou slammed a fist against the window.

They came to the end of the bridge. A red London bus braked in front of them. Luke didn't see it. He slammed on the brakes, propelling Mamadou and himself into the dashboard. The nose of the car collided with the rear of the double decker. The windscreen splintered into a thousand pieces. The bonnet crumpled into a ball of metal rubble. Luke coiled back into his seat, wincing as a blinding pain bounced around his skull. His neck ached, and his shoulder stung from where the seatbelt had dug in.

That was his second mistake.

Mamadou shook him violently.

'Luke?' he said. 'Luke?'

A few seconds later, Luke opened his eyes. His vision was bleary, as if he had just woken up, and a river of crimson red trickled down the left-hand side of his face.

'You OK?' Luke asked.

'I'm fine,' Mamadou replied. He tried to undo his belt buckle, but it wouldn't budge. 'Are you?'

Luke nodded slowly. He leaned across the centre console of the car and helped Mamadou with his belt. Two minutes had passed since they crashed, and by now, a crowd of pedestrians, bus passengers, and taxi drivers had swarmed their vehicle. Mamadou ignored them, pushed open the car door, stepped back as glass as fine as sand sprinkled onto the floor and moved round to Luke's side. Mamadou's hands grabbed Luke by the shoulder and armpit and heaved him out of the car. Together they hobbled to the side of the road where Mamadou assessed the situation.

'Are you able to continue?' Mamadou asked, inspecting Luke's flesh wounds.

'Yes. I'll be fine.'

'Good. Don't let me down again.' Mamadou slapped him on the shoulder and helped stabilise him. Luke watched Mamadou reach into his pocket and remove his phone.

'Simon — it's Mamadou. We've had an accident on Westminster Bridge. Send support. DC Matthews and I are on foot.'

Mamadou hung up the phone before the Deputy Assistant Commissioner could respond. Now Luke could see where Tyler and Jake inherited their bluntness.

Just as they hobbled towards County Hall Flats, an emergency response team comprising an ambulance, fire engine, and a police car arrived at the scene. Within seconds, the entire bridge had been sealed off, and Mamadou and Luke slipped off the side of the road unnoticed. They would be seriously delayed now they were both injured.

Luke just hoped they wouldn't arrive too late.

Chapter Fifty-Three

BOY

August 1, 16:54

The young boy's hair felt soft under Moshat's fingers, reminding him of his own when he was little. The boy looked like the surfer type. With long blond hair that covered his ears and stopped at the nape of his neck, Moshat envisioned the boy in the future, standing in front of cameras in exotic countries with a surfboard in his arm, getting paid handsomely to ride some waves. The boy had a unique future ahead of him.

Moshat felt envious.

But he couldn't allow his thoughts to wander too much. There was still lots to be done. An hour remained on the timer, and he had decisions to make. He had already sent the boy's mother and father down to the other end of the train, where he could interact with the child without the parents — or anyone else — interfering.

Nothing would happen to the little boy unless Moshat was provoked. The boy was precious, Moshat realised that.

He just needed everyone else to make sure they understood how precious *he* was. If they didn't, then that would end badly for everybody.

As soon as the parents were out of sight, the boy observed the dead body that lay next to him on the floor, his gaze fixated on the pool of blood around Martha's head.

Moshat tussled the boy's hair again, letting it run through his fingers.

'What's your name?' he asked.

The boy looked up at him. Moshat got lost in his childish, ephemeral blue eyes. 'Ryan.'

'That's a lovely name. You're not scared are you, Ryan?'

'No? Just sad.' The boy looked down into his lap.

'Why are you sad, Ryan?'

'Because I don't want Mummy and Daddy to die.' Tears formed in his eyes.

In a random spout of compassion, Moshat pulled the boy closer to his chest. 'It's OK, Ryan. I know how you feel. Let me tell you a little secret,' Moshat leaned closer to the little boy's face. 'You should never fear death itself. It is inevitable. It is something none of us can stop. We can prolong it, but we cannot remove all possibility of it happening. What you should fear instead is the *cause* of death.'

Ryan looked away from Moshat, and his eyes fell on the gun on the table. Moshat grabbed the weapon before the boy could.

'No, no. That's not for you. It's still a little warm from when I shot that lady on the floor there.'

The boy said nothing and slowly retracted his hand back to his lap.

'Why did you kill her?' Ryan asked, his voice innocent.

In a lot of ways, he reminded Moshat of himself when he was younger. Curious. Attentive. Brave.

'Because she did a bad thing a long time ago, Ryan. That's why.'

'Why did that mean she had to die?'

'Because she did a bad thing.'

'That didn't mean she had to die. People make mistakes all the time, and then they get caught for it, and then they go to prison.'

'Well, you see...' Moshat hesitated. 'This lady didn't go to prison. She did a very bad thing and didn't go to prison for it. She represented an injustice, and no one seemed to care about it.'

'What about you?' Ryan looked up into Moshat's eyes. Those deep, effervescent eyes. 'What will happen to you? You killed someone. Does that mean someone's going to kill you?'

Moshat smiled. 'Maybe one day, but not in the same way as this. You see, the difference between me and this lady is that we are fighting for different causes. You are too young to understand now, but you will when you're older.'

'Does that mean you won't kill any more people?'

Moshat stopped. He was stumped. He was receiving a lecture from a toddler, and he didn't know how to react.

'It's not that easy.'

'But if she was a bad person... Well, you killed the bad person. Why does that mean you can kill other people? Will that not make you an even badder person?'

Moshat ignored what Ryan had said. The young boy had confused him, planted a seed of doubt inside his mind, and it would only grow the more he allowed the boy to continue.

'Do you want me to tell you something else?' Moshat asked, moving the conversation along.

The boy kept quiet for a moment before letting curiosity get the better of him. 'OK,' he finally said.

'I used to be like you. I used to have parents who loved me very much, and then, one day, they disappeared just like yours have now. But I've saved you the horror of seeing your own parents die before you... for now,' Moshat said. As he finished the sentence, the boy looked into the crowd in the desperate hope of seeing his mother and father. 'Don't worry, little buddy. Nothing will happen to them if everything else goes to plan, OK? If everyone else just does as they're told, then you and your parents will be reunited, and you can live together happily for the rest of your lives. You see, I'm not a big, bad man after all, am I?'

Ryan didn't respond. Instead, he pointed to the detonator in Moshat's hand and asked, 'What's that?'

'This? This is a detonator — do you know what that is?'

The boy nodded slowly.

'Very good. But this is a special detonator. This one here means it will go off no matter what. As soon as I let go of the switch, everything will go *kaboom!*'

The boy's eyes bulged as he stared at the device for longer.

'Can I touch it?' Ryan asked.

'I'm afraid not, buddy. That would be too dangerous.' Moshat played with the boy's hair again. 'How about we go for a walk? Your legs must ache after sitting and standing for so long, like being in the cinema!'

Something was going on inside Moshat's head. He was growing to like the boy, and Moshat saw him as a companion rather than a means to an end. It was a day of firsts for them both, and Moshat felt himself connecting with the young man.

'OK,' Ryan replied. His entire demeanour had changed; he became increasingly reserved.

'Good boy,' Moshat said, as he motioned for the boy to move from his seat.

Moshat shuffled awkwardly along while keeping the gun and detonator in his hand. He leaned over, picked up his backpack using the nozzle of the gun, and swung it round his shoulder. It was risky, but something he'd practised many times when he was bored. Looking down at Ryan, he smiled with him, and nodded for the boy to lead the way. Cautiously, Ryan wandered forward, avoiding Martha's body on the floor. Moshat kept close behind him, with his Glock aimed at the boy's head.

Moshat trusted the boy not to do anything foolish; he just didn't trust anyone else in the coach.

The two of them moved forward through the second carriage of the train precariously. Moshat sensed Ryan pulling ahead, eager to find his mother and father. Moshat couldn't allow that.

'OK, everyone, here's what's going to happen. The boy and I are going to walk through and return to my previous seat,' Moshat explained. 'If anyone so much as attempts to touch the boy, I'll shoot him,' he gestured to Ryan as he spoke, 'in the head and then you. If anyone so much as attempts to touch me, I'll shoot him in the head and then you. If anyone so much as attempts anything other than what I tell them to, I'll shoot him in the head and then you. In my hands, I have the detonator to ignite all these explosives on board and send us into oblivion. I hope I've made myself clear. You won't be warned again.'

Without needing a second warning, everyone around

him dispersed. Some jumped up on seats and tables to move out of the way. Riddled and paralysed with fear, everyone parted so that Moshat and Ryan could make their way to the fourth carriage without a problem.

'Now,' Moshat said, this time making his voice louder and clearer. 'What I want the rest of you to do is filter back into the seats behind me. I don't care if they're not your original seats, and you'll care to feel the same way — because if I so much as hear an argument or anything about someone else being in someone's motherfucking seat, I'll shoot him first and then you. Once everyone has found their seat, we wait for the countdown to finish. Then you can all go on your way back to your lovely, useless, and pathetic lives. Now I hope everyone understands.' Moshat came to a halt. 'And, when the time comes for us all to depart, under no circumstances is anyone to alert the authorities, who are undoubtedly outside, about *me*. I'm sure you can all guess what might happen if someone wants to be that foolish. His life is very much in your hands, people. Nobody needs to be a hero today.'

As soon as he had finished speaking, a state of panic developed, and everyone who had been behind him darted into the empty carriages, eager to get as far away from him as possible.

Moshat walked deeper into the train. He smiled. It had been so easy. He was getting a taste of power. They had given in to his demands so easily. They had believed he would shoot the boy, no questions asked. The operation was ending and he could almost taste the fresh air outside, the freedom, and his share of one million pounds. All he had to do now was wait.

Good little dogs, Moshat thought as he entered his fourth carriage. On their way there, Moshat had realised Ryan's parents weren't anywhere to be seen. *Poor little boy. Whose parents are willing to run away from their child if they know it means saving their own lives? Mother and Father would never have done that. They would have made the ultimate sacrifice.*

Once he and Ryan were settled in, other passengers filtered into the surrounding seats. A young family, holding a baby in one hand and a bottle of milk in the other, sat opposite him and Ryan. The man of the family still looked like he was an adolescent, with his skin covered in acne and pockmark scars. Moshat tried to ignore them, and their screaming child, as much as possible.

All he had to do now was wait, and he would be free to leave. And Adil would be ready for him when he did.

He closed his eyes momentarily and grinned, as if he were taking a drag from a cigarette after years of abstinence.

Soon, brother. Soon.

Chapter Fifty-Four

ANSWERS

August 1, 16:55

Jake aimed the gun at Adil Hakim's head. Tyler bound the man's hands together using the roll of Sellotape he found on the desk, and then rushed over to the window to thrash the curtains open. Light flooded in, blinding Jake. It was a harsh adjustment, but a welcome one. Outside, the sound of a train rolling out of Waterloo station echoed around the flat. Tyler moved over to Lucy and helped her to her feet. She was relieved to see them; as soon as she was standing and had finished rubbing the circulation back into her hands, she embraced Tyler.

'Nice place you've got here,' Jake said as Tyler moved over to the record player and switched off the music.

Jake chanced a glance around the room. A sofa and television were placed to his left. On the windowsill was a bonsai tree and standing next to it was a telescope, aiming at, Jake presumed, New Scotland Yard and the Houses of Parliament. In the far-left corner of the room, near where Lucy had been tied up, was a desk with three computer monitors. The rest of the flat was plain and boring, except for one thing. The smell. He had been warned about the smell of homemade explosives, but he had never experienced it before in all his years of service. The air was dense with the nauseating stench of chemicals. Bleach. And lots of it.

'It serves well for my needs,' Adil replied. He shifted his body weight so that he rested on one elbow.

'Get up on your feet, Adil Hakim, and sit on the sofa.'

Adil remained where he was and laughed.

'You think knowing my name will intimidate me? Do you want me to congratulate you, Detective? Tell you that you did your job well?'

Jake's blood swarmed with fury. He knelt down, placing his knee next to Adil's shoulder, and pressed the small handgun against the bridge of his nose, directly in between where his eyebrows met. Adil's expression remained blank as the cold metal touched his skin. His grimace and teeth-bearing smile angered Jake.

It took all of his strength and willpower to keep the man alive and not pull the trigger. That was something they didn't teach him all too well in the services: how to not pull the trigger and unleash a bullet in someone's head, even if they deserved it.

Answers first, he thought, *I need answers first.*

Jake rose to his feet, grabbed Adil by his shirt, and threw him on the sofa. In a blind rage, Jake punched Adil in the face. It felt good, feeling the man's bones crush under the power of his fist. Blood gushed from Adil's nose and collected in his mouth.

Adil smiled, his teeth stained a crimson red.

'I didn't think police brutality was your sort of thing, Jake,' Adil said.

'There's a lot you don't know about me, Adil. And it'll stay that way. Because where you're going, you'll never see daylight again. Now tell me what we need to know.'

Adil hesitated before responding. 'Ask and you shall receive.'

Chapter Fifty-Five

REVELATION

August 1, 17:03

'So, where do we begin?' Jake asked as he tossed the gun in his hands, staring into the man's face.

'Wherever you want to, Detective Tanner.'

'Why did you choose me? Why have I been the one to deal with all of this shit you've thrown at me?'

'How did it make you feel when I told you I had chosen you? Proud? Important? Wanted? Sad? Tell me.'

'What are you playing at?'

'I'm asking you a question.' Adil smiled vehemently. As he spoke, bits of blood and saliva expelled from his mouth and ran down his chin.

'I'll be the one asking questions here — but thanks for your concern. So, I'll ask again. Why did you choose me?'

'Would you like me to tell you?'

'I'd love nothing more.'

'Very well. It was fate. It seemed our paths were already

335

determined to cross. While you were growing up with your fancy education, I was mourning the death of my parents.'

'The Detson Tower fire,' Jake interrupted, already afraid of where this was going. 'But what's that got to do with me?'

'You have a connection to it greater than you know. Your mother-in-law, Martha Clarke, a former member of the Ministry for Housing and Planning, was one of the bastards responsible for the tragedy. She was responsible for my mother and father's death, Tanner. And she was related to you, an officer from the Metropolitan Police Service, so it seemed the perfect fit. Besides, you and her were the easiest to track. For weeks, we did our research on you. Stalked you. Observed you. And our findings were alarming. Nobody in your family seemed to know anything about the callous decision Martha had made, and her name was wiped from public records about the fire.'

'But you found them, didn't you?'

'I don't have a computer-based degree for nothing, Jake. I know what I'm doing. I've been taught by some of the best in the world. At first, my brother and I thought we could just kill her in the privacy of her own home. But then we thought, what was the point? That would be boring. Too easy. Too little a challenge. So, we reconvened and plotted the worst terrorist attack this city has seen in years.'

'What about your other brother, Hasan?'

'Hasan never existed. He was me, a figment of my imagination. I changed the records to show I died and created a new identity for myself. You'll never be able to find anything on me — it's buried too deep. Same with Moshat.'

'You and your brother must have been close then, to go through everything together? The two of you must have worked hard.'

'No,' Adil spat. A ball of blood landed in his lap. 'The idea was a manifestation of my brilliant imagination. That little louse couldn't do anything on his own. He had to get me to do it all. I had to be the one to help him find the job at the factory. I had to be the one to conduct the research, prepare the bombs, create the EMP devices, the likes of which the world has never seen. I had to fabricate the lie that manipulated Martha into being on the train. It was all me. The only thing Moshat was good for was getting me inside the factory.'

'It appears he played just as vital a role as you.'

'No!' Adil snapped. Jake was getting him riled up, and he liked it. If he carried on, then he would get to the bottom of this entire thing before Mamadou arrived. 'My brother doesn't need to be on the Heathrow Express,' Adil continued. 'I only told him he was there to use Martha as an insurance package.'

Adil's words span around Jake's brain until they settled with a heavy thud, their meaning impacting him hard. If Moshat didn't need to be there, then what was his purpose? Why were both Moshat and Martha on the train at the same time?

And then Jake had his answer.

'You're going to kill them both,' he whispered as a statement, his mind racing. 'No matter what happens, the Heathrow Express will explode, killing everyone inside it, including my mother-in-law and your brother.'

Adil smiled. 'Bingo.'

Jake crumbled inside. He went cold. He didn't know what to think. He didn't know *how* to think. There were so many thoughts and questions and concerns racing around his head he couldn't grab at one and voice it.

'Why?' was all he could manage.

'Why what, Detective?'

'Why are you killing your own brother? After everything the two of you have been through.'

Adil remained silent for a moment, and dropped his chin to his chest, as if deep in thought. When he looked up, something within his expression changed. His eyes appeared more hollow, more evil. There was a fire burning within them, and it was ripping at the seams to break free.

'Because he's the one responsible, Jake. My superstar brother, Moshat. The one everybody had tipped for greatness. He was going to be a football superstar, or so everyone in his classes and academies told him. He was going to be an international phenomenon. He lapped it up in school, but then it all went to his head, and he got mixed up with shit. By the time we were eleven, he had already started smoking. Back at that age, it didn't affect his performance much, so nobody knew anything about it. Not even my parents.

'But I knew. I was the one who saw him outside the school puffing away on his little sticks of cancer. And when I tried to confront him about it, he dismissed it and told me to fuck off. The night our parents died, he had been smoking in his bedroom, dangling out of the windows by the curtains. And before we left the house together later on, he stubbed out his cigarette on the window sill. The embers of his cigarette ignited the curtain, Jake, the rest of the flat, and the rest of the building — and everyone inside it. I'm certain of it.

'And now he's got a detonator I've given him which will blow him up if he releases its trigger. *He* was the one responsible for my parents' deaths, and now he's going to get everything he deserves.'

Shit, Jake thought to himself. There were no words that could have expressed his emotions. But time was running out, and he needed to find out everything more that he could.

'If this was all about getting revenge on Moshat and Martha, then what was with the ransom? Why was it necessary?' Jake lowered the gun to a forty-five-degree angle.

'It was never about the money. The money was just a ploy. I convinced Moshat it was necessary, that we would be compensated for our loss. But it was about more than the money — way more. It was about standing up for ourselves, for the lower classes, making sure that people like you — the ones who think they're all scum — finally see them as *real people*. It's about giving everyone equal and fair opportunities. The way we were brushed to the outskirts of society — no one should be treated in such a way as that, especially when it's not our fault we can't receive the same benefits as everyone else. Everyone in this country should be given as much equal opportunity as the next man, woman, or child who walks through that door. And it was going to take an act of terror to make the government realise that.'

Jake was dumbfounded. Adil's goals were just, but his means of achieving them were twisted and evil. How could Adil not see the disparity in what he was saying?

'I'm not a terrorist, Jake. I didn't kill as many people as you may believe. If anything, I saved them. The front carriage of the Luton train? I gave everybody ten seconds to get out before it exploded. But it had to explode, you see, to make sure everyone believed I would do it. The explosion on the platform at Upminster? That was so far away from everyone, even if someone had been standing ten feet away from it, they would have survived. And the Nelson's

Column detonation — the explosives in that had been placed there days before and were placed so high up it would have only injured those nearest it.

'In all these examples, only a handful of people have died compared to how many it could have been. I never wanted to hurt many people, but I *had* to act, even if some people got hurt along the way. To make an impact — to make the government sit up and pay attention — I had to do it. All of this is in my manifesto. You can read it later. It's in your inbox now.'

Jake lowered his weapon. He felt ashamed at his mother-in-law's behaviour. In that moment, he felt compassion and sympathy towards Adil. A moment of impulse made him want to stand aside and allow the terrorist to run and escape. But he knew that wouldn't be possible. Adil Hakim had killed and incited acts of terror against the United Kingdom. And for that, he would go to prison for a very long time.

'How do we disarm the bombs?' Jake asked after a few moments of absolute silence had passed.

'You can't. My computers are encrypted, and any false attempts to get in will erase everything from the hard drive.' Adil wiped his nose and mouth with his shoulder.

'Tell us the passwords, and we will work something out for you.'

'You know I can't tell you that, Detective. So long as my brother lives, so will the blood on his hands.'

'I understand,' Jake said. 'But my mother-in-law is still aboard the Heathrow Express. And you know deep down she isn't really to blame for this tragedy: your brother is. So, tell us how we can disarm the bombs, and then we can make sure he is dealt with properly.'

Adil shook his head. 'It's no use. If he hasn't already blown up the train, he would have killed her.'

'You can't be sure,' Jake said, his voice a whisper.

Adil stared at him with an odd expression on his face. 'I'm sorry, Jake.'

Jake looked up behind Adil and saw Tyler and Lucy both staring at him, neither of them knowing what to say. What was he going to do? What was he going to say to Elizabeth? How was he going to tell her that her mother had been murdered in a terrorist attack? The thought made Jake sick.

Before he could think of the next words that would come out of his mouth, the front door burst open.

Mamadou and Luke stood there side by side, panting heavily, their faces dripping with blood, sweat and debris.

'What do we have here?' Mamadou asked as he entered through the door. Luke followed behind him, leaving the door open.

'Boss, thank God you're here. I've got some news,' Jake said and moved Mamadou to the right-hand side of the room. Luke joined them and bent down to pick up Adil's gun from the floor. 'We need to evacuate the Gatwick and Heathrow Express. Moshat Hakim has a detonator that will blow the Heathrow Express no matter the circumstance.'

Just as Mamadou was about to open his mouth, out of the corner of his eye, Jake saw Adil leap up off the sofa and sprint towards the open door. Jake froze as he watched Adil run.

But then there was a loud noise, like the sound of a car backfiring. It echoed around the room and burst Jake's eardrums. Jake watched a bullet enter Adil's back and explode out the front of his body, decorating the plain wall in the corridor with a fine spray of blood. Adil's body collapsed against the wall and skidded to the ground. Jake's eyes followed the path of the blood, too shocked to speak. A thin stream of smoke was still visible at the tip of the barrel in Luke's hands.

Then Jake stared back at Adil's body on the floor in horror and disbelief.

The only one who could disarm the bombs was dead.

Chapter Fifty-Six

HACK

August 1, 17:14

Chaos erupted in the room. Jake's breathing stopped. Lucy screamed. Mamadou ran his fingers through his thinning hair. Luke stood frozen, arm still lingering in the air.

'What the fuck have you done?' Jake screamed at Luke, pushing him on the shoulder and knocking him over the coffee table. 'You fucking idiot!'

Lucy sprinted across the floor and into the bathroom, where she vomited.

'Get out of here,' Mamadou barked at Luke. 'I don't want you near this crime scene. If anyone speaks to you, tell them you had to use lethal force because he lunged at you. Don't make this worse than it already is!'

When Luke didn't leave, Mamadou pushed him in the chest, forcing him to withdraw from the flat.

It took every part of Jake's willpower to refrain from chasing after his insolent colleague and kicking him down the stairs. Jake was enraged. He clenched his fists until his nails dug into the palms of his skin.

The toilet flushed, and a second later, Lucy appeared. Her eyes and cheeks were puffy. Tears ran down her face. *She's going to need a whole load of counselling after this*, Jake thought. *We all are.*

'Are you OK?' he asked, putting his arm over her shoulders, already aware that she wasn't. 'It's OK, all right? You'll be OK. Do you want someone to come and pick you up?'

Lucy shook her head, and Jake told her to wait in the kitchen where she wouldn't be able to see anything else that might distress her further. Guilt came rolling over him like a duvet and wrapped itself around his body as he watched her disappear behind the corner; she had seen too much, and it wasn't fair on her. It wasn't fair on any of them.

Getting his mind back on the case, Jake sat down at the desk and said, 'The fuck are we going to do now, boss?'

Mamadou turned to Jake, looked at him with his giant, grey eyes, and said, 'Honestly, Tanner, I have no fucking idea. Never in my thirty-plus years of service have I seen something so amateur and stupid as that. We're going to have to get the forensics team. Which means we have to leave everything as it is.'

'We can't do that boss. We need to gain access to the computers,' Jake said, looking at the three monitors in front of him.

'You heard what he said, Jake,' Tyler interrupted. 'If we get it wrong, then we risk permanently deleting everything inside.'

'There may be another way,' Jake said. The thought had occurred to him when Adil had first mentioned the firewall issue they would have to overcome if they wanted to gain access to his PC.

'What?'

'Lucy.' Jake nodded to the kitchen. 'She's studied computer forensics. She's also a solicitor, so she's aware of the implications.'

'We can't involve her in this,' Tyler said. 'We'd need a warrant.'

'We don't have time for a warrant!' Mamadou shouted.

'She's the only option we —'

'It's fine,' Lucy interrupted. She stood in the kitchen doorframe. 'I'll do it.'

'OK, fine. Fine,' Mamadou huffed, stepping forward. 'Tyler — I want you to ring CTC and get a forensics squad here ASAP. Lucy, I want you to... well, take a seat, and let's see what you can do.'

Tyler nodded in affirmation and swapped places with Lucy. Jake rose out of the seat and allowed Lucy to replace him. She moved the cursor and waited for the screen to wake up. As soon as the background image appeared, Jake asked, 'Is it possible?'

'It won't be easy, but I think I can. After he tied me up, I saw him type his password in. I just can't believe he's...' she looked outside the flat door and froze.

Jake bent down to her level and blocked Adil's dead body from view. 'Hey, listen. If you can't do this, then that's fine. We can find an alternative.'

Lucy swallowed hard, contemplated for a moment, and then stared into Jake's eyes.

'No. I've got this.'

Spinning round on the chair, Lucy typed frantically on the keyboard. Jake looked at his watch. It was 17:18. They had just under forty-five minutes to rescue everyone in time.

Jake rose to his feet.

'Sir, I need to explain something to you.' Jake pulled Mamadou over to the side of the room while Lucy continued to type into the computer. He told Mamadou of everything Adil had said. Jake explained that Moshat held a detonator in his hands, that the Gatwick Express train needed to be evacuated as soon as possible, and that Martha and the remaining Hakim brother were on the Heathrow Express.

'What do you need, Tanner?' Mamadou asked.

'An emergency helicopter. If Moshat Hakim has murdered my mother-in-law in cold blood, I want to be the one to lock him up.'

'OK, Tanner. I'll see what I can do.' Mamadou dialled a number, and within two rings, he spoke rapidly into the receiver.

Lucy called to him. He wandered over and stopped next to her. She had a beaming smile on her face.

'I managed to get in,' she said.

'Fantastic! Now what?'

Lucy held her finger up to him, clicked on a few software applications, tapped on the keyboard, and then turned to him.

'Check this out,' she said, showing him the CCTV footage of the trains from the outside.

Martha, Jake thought. If they could see outside, then maybe they could see inside as well.

'No, Jake. I can't. I've already tried,' Lucy said, answering his thoughts. 'There was no CCTV feed to hack into. I know you want to see if your mother-in-law's still there, but I can't.'

Jake hung his head low. 'Thank you for trying. At least

we'll be able to monitor the trains from the exterior. What else have you found?'

Lucy turned away and loaded another computer application. This one displayed the mobile numbers of everyone on board the three trains.

'Is that all?' Jake asked, growing impatient as time was running out for them.

'No,' Lucy snapped. 'Let me show you this one.' Lucy uploaded the final application, which displayed the interior of the train's control panels. 'From here, we can unlock the doors and free everyone inside.'

'We need Theo,' Tyler said, surprising Lucy and Jake. He had just finished his call with CTC. 'He knows what all those buttons and levers do. He can help. Good thing you got him to stick around, Jake!'

'We can't,' Jake said. 'It would be too obvious to Moshat Hakim while he's sat there waiting to escape. Everything about this has been meticulously planned; anything out of the ordinary would throw him off into a panic, and he might be tempted to use his detonator. We'll need to do it nearer the time, be more intelligent about it.'

'What are you proposing?' Tyler asked.

'I don't know. I still need to work it all out.' Jake blocked out the two of them, so he could focus.

Jake returned his attention to the computers. He asked Lucy to call up the software that contained all the mobile phone numbers on it, and after she had loaded it, Jake scanned the data. At the top of the list were the most recent text messages that had been sent to the mobile phones on board each of the trains. Jake scrolled through the list. On the thirtieth cell, Jake saw a different message to the ones that ran all the way along the screen. It was simple. It was genius. It was

Adil's way of communicating with his brother without raising suspicion. If Adil could only communicate with his brother whenever he contacted the rest of the passengers, then it meant Jake, Lucy and Tyler could follow the same pattern.

Jake explained his theory to the other two.

'I reckon it'll work,' Tyler said, observing the screen as if to validate Jake's point. 'We need to get the tone right before we send anything to anyone.'

'What are we going to tell the rest of the passengers?' Lucy asked, her voice fraught with concern.

'That they'll be rescued.'

Over the next few minutes, the three of them drafted a text message to send to Moshat Hakim. It read:

LITTLE BROTHER, MONEY HAS BEEN COLLECTED AND IS SAFE. HOPE YOU ARE TOO? TANNER AT GATWICK. BOMBS DEFUSED. ABORT DETONATOR. GET OUT AND RUN TO ME. EAST OF WEST, WEST OF EAST. BE SAFE. A.

Silence filled the room as the three of them read the message and considered its implications.

'Are you sure it could work? Isn't it highly risky?' Tyler asked.

'No, think about it: from what Adil told us, Moshat will do anything he tells him. If he wants that share of one million pounds, he will do what he's told. Not to mention, if Moshat does somehow evade us, we know where he's going —'

'Upminster!' Lucy exclaimed.

'Exactly.'

Mamadou's heavy footsteps on the floorboards alerted them to his return. 'Gatwick Express evac is underway, and the helicopter is outside in the Jubilee Gardens. Get down there quick — it won't hang around all day.'

Without saying anything, Jake and Tyler looked at one another, nodded, and then headed out of the flat. Just as they were about to exit, Jake stopped mid-step and turned to face his boss.

'Mamadou — contact Theo. He needs to help Lucy with the train's control panel. They will need to disarm the door locks, so we can get everyone out of there as calmly as possible. And Lucy — send the passengers whatever message you want. Just make sure it seems like something Adil Hakim would say. I trust in you.'

'Got it,' Mamadou said. 'Now get the fuck out of here!'

Jake nodded, feeling the adrenaline return to his bloodstream, and joined Tyler who was waiting for him at the end of the corridor.

'Let's get this motherfucker.'

Chapter Fifty-Seven

PARADOX

August 1, 17:27

In theory, it had been a good idea — and it certainly seemed like a good one in Jake's head — but when it came to leaping into the helicopter, Jake had immediate reservations.

Jake and Tyler burst from the building exit after descending the dizzying flights of stairs and raced across to the Jubilee Gardens situated across the road from the block, opposite the London Eye. The helicopter was positioned in the middle of the gardens. It was an EC135, equipped with thermal imaging and a 360-degree camera on the underside. A large door on the side of the helicopter slid open, and a National Police Air Service officer gestured for them to get in. Blades of grass and tree branches buffeted in the wind. Dust and bits of gravel blasted Jake and Tyler in the face and blinded them as they advanced to the copter.

'It's ruining my suit!' screamed Tyler, his voice barely audible over the deafening sound of the propellers.

Jake climbed into the fuselage and buckled himself in. Extra tight. It was his first time flying in a helicopter, and the nerves and adrenaline combined in a toxic mix throughout his body. Tyler jumped in behind him, the weight of his body shaking the aircraft. Jake swore out loud, and in the front, he could see the pilot smirking. The other officer — who Jake realised was the co-pilot — slammed the door shut before heading up to the cockpit to sit next to the pilot.

Tyler strapped himself in. They gave the thumbs up and set off. As the helicopter increased altitude, Jake's heightened senses reacted to the tiniest of wobbles caused by the change in wind direction. *Everything will be fine*, he told himself, closing his eyes, blocking out the world.

After a few minutes of being in the air, Jake hazarded a glance out of the window and saw the spectacular view of London from above. They were at a few thousand feet now, and everything below them looked minuscule. Buildings and skyscrapers looked like giant LEGO models, a child's playground with an ever-changing and ever-moving life of its own.

Without warning, the helicopter tilted forward and reduced altitude. Jake yelped and grabbed for Tyler's shoulder with one hand and tore at the fabric of his seat with the other.

'Relax!' Tyler shouted at him with a smile on his face, clearly enjoying Jake's total discomfort. 'We're just speeding up.'

Jake didn't care. To him it felt like they were plummeting towards the earth. He closed his eyes, hoping the panic would subside. His chest heaved, and his pulse raced. Before he could steady his breathing, he felt a cold, hard slap on his cheek. It felt like he'd been stung in the face by a leathered football in the winter. Four distinctive points throbbed on the side of his face. He opened his eyes in shock and caressed his cheek.

'Stop being a bitch!' Tyler shouted at him over the noise. 'I'll slap it out of you if I have to!'

Jake scowled at his friend and looked away. The tough love act had worked, and the discomfort in his cheek distracted him.

After a few cautious looks out of the window, he felt confident enough to sustain his view, and he watched as they left the metropolis and entered the rural side of west London. As they flew alongside the M4, Jake watched the cars zoom past in slow motion. It was a paradox that had intrigued him, like watching planes fly in the air slowly.

'How much further?' Jake asked.

'We're here,' Tyler said, pointing down to the stationary Heathrow Express beneath them.

Jake gazed out upon it, feeling his skin prickle. The train looked eerie, sat there on its own with nothing surrounding it, like something abandoned and barren after the Cold War.

On Jake's orders, the pilot landed a hundred yards from the train along the tracks. Eventually, after what seemed like they were using all the remaining time they had left, the blades came to a halt and the door opened. Jake darted out and Tyler followed after him. He felt the familiar texture of rocks and train tracks under his feet.

In the distance were the armed officers Frances had sent earlier, waiting for him, watching as he came running over.

'Fellas,' Jake said slowing down his pace. As he stopped, he kicked up dust and fine gravel over their shoes. 'You all know what we're doing?'

'Yes, sir, we've had word from Mamadou and CTC —

we're well acquainted with the plan,' said one of them. He was a stocky character and spoke with a confidence and authority that only came with the accolade of being a leader.

'Good. There's no time to waste. Let's go!' Jake made his way to the coach doors.

Hundreds of thoughts spun through his mind. *Where was Moshat? Where was Martha? Were they still alive? How long did they have left? What if Moshat saw them — would he detonate early?*

Now was the only time to find out.

Chapter Fifty-Eight

SEND

August 1, 17:32

A few minutes had passed since Jake and Tyler left Lucy with the Herculean task of controlling the computer screens in front of her. She was now on the phone to Theodor Rosenberg, a man she'd never met before, but felt as if she had known for a long time. In a way, he reminded her of her dad: endearing in every way. In the short time they'd been speaking with one another, Theodor had introduced himself as a train expert and explained his credentials. After he had told Lucy that, she felt much more relaxed.

While she sat there staring into the computer screens, waiting for the green light to send the messages when the time was right, she watched the CCTV feed of the Specialist Firearms Officers advancing towards the Gatwick Express and evacuating the train. The entire process was accomplished in less than five minutes. The officers had placed small charges on the doors and detonated them, producing a controlled explosion that allowed the passengers to flood out of the carriages like water leaking through a cracked bucket.

After the mission had been deemed a success, she clicked through to the other CCTV feed focusing on the Heathrow Express. Using her intuition, she scanned the images looking for Moshat. Mamadou had shown her an image of him when she had asked for it. She had told him it would be important if she could find where he was sat so they could relay the information back to the squad on the ground. A few seconds later, she found the still image of Moshat sat in the corner of the fourth carriage on the train. Lucy felt an inexplicable rage rise within her as she watched him sitting there, staring out of the window as if there wasn't anything wrong in the world. *What's that next to him?* she asked herself. Realising, she zoomed in and saw a little boy locked in his grasp. *Dear God.*

'You ready to send the text messages first?' Mamadou asked, bringing her attention back to the flat.

'Yeah, I think so.' She looked back to the computer as if for reassurance.

'Don't be nervous, OK?' he told her. She was warming to Mamadou. She thought his brutish, aggressive nature was just a front and that deep down, somewhere, he *was* sweet and innocent.

'I'll try.'

Mamadou smiled at her.

'We're ready to go when you are, Lucy. Send the messages.'

Lucy nodded to Mamadou and swung round on the chair. She proofread the messages she had drafted in Jake's absence, making absolutely certain they reflected the words and syntax similar to Adil Hakim's previous messages. *That poor man*, she thought. Adil's story had horrified her. And it made her feel sorry for his death. Her feelings towards Moshat, however, were in complete juxtaposition. He deserved to die more so than Adil. But she didn't want anyone else to come to the same end.

Lucy hit send.

As she watched the messages disappear into the atmosphere and into space, she focused on the CCTV footage, paying particular attention to Moshat's reaction. She had staggered the messages so that Moshat received his first, and then everyone else on board received theirs afterwards, making it seem like the younger brother had been put beforehand.

Lucy watched Moshat reach into his pocket and place his gun on the table in front of him. Lucy noticed the man sat opposite Moshat and silently willed him on to act, to take the gun from him and shoot him in the head, but it would have been a very foolish move. The other passengers appeared to get their messages now.

As Moshat read the text, his expression changed. His brow furrowed, and he leaned forward, resting his elbows on the table and concealing the gun. Lucy could tell something was wrong, but not what exactly. Had he believed it? Had he been surprised by his new instructions? Or was he just going to blow the whole thing up anyway? Lucy didn't like to think about it, but before she could worry further, she heard a voice calling her name.

It was Theodor on loudspeaker.

'Theo! Oh, my God, you almost gave me a heart attack!'

'Relax, Lucy. It's fine, you've got this,' Theo said, his attempt to boost Lucy's morale was valiant but ineffective. She gave him credit for trying. 'Have you got visuals of the Heathrow Express?'

'Yes,' she said. 'I can see inside and out.'

'What's happening?'

'Nothing,' she lied.

'What about Martha, Detective Tanner's mother-in-law? She is supposed to be on the Heathrow Express.'

Lucy hesitated before responding. A lump in her throat swelled. 'She's dead, Theodor. She's dead. I'm sorry, but I needed to tell someone.'

Earlier, while Jake and Mamadou had been discussing something in the corner of the room, Lucy had managed to tap into the onboard CCTV. The first image that had popped up on the screen was Martha's dead body resting on the floor. No attempt had been made to cover her with a coat or a jumper of anything. It made her feel sick.

'I didn't know whether to tell him. I didn't know how he'd react,' she said, the lump in her throat growing.

'You did the right thing, Lucy. It would have made him angry and clouded his judgement. It is up to you, now, whether you want to tell him after this is all over, or let it remain between the two of us,' Theo said. When Lucy didn't respond, he continued, 'Has the control panel loaded in front of you?'

She opened the window on the main screen. 'Everything's there.'

'Good. Now, let's do a little test run, just to make sure you know what you're doing. And if you have questions or run into any issues now, it's better we resolve them before we do the real thing. Understood?'

'Understood.'

'Great. I want you to locate the circular dial on the left-hand side of the panel, with the small drawing of a fan on it — you know, like in cars. Now, once you've found that, I want you to lower it back down to the lowest it will go.'

Lucy located the control with ease and did as requested. She gave him the notification she was finished and that the onboard temperature had been turned down.

'What next?' she asked.

'Now we need to unlock the doors, so they can be opened when pressed. But don't worry — it will only disable the lock, it won't actually open them.'

Theo guided Lucy to a small, circular button on the bottom left-hand quadrant of the screen that had a diagram of a door underneath it. Lucy pressed the button and felt her heart skip a beat as she did so. She had been fearing this part of the process the most; if the doors automatically opened after she had pressed the button, then Moshat would know something was amiss. And then he would blow the train for sure.

'It's done,' she said.

'Excellent. Good job, Lucy. You've done yourself proud.'

Theodor's words helped, and Lucy thanked him just as Mamadou came up beside her. He touched her on the shoulder and said, 'Thanks for everything you've done, Lucy, but it's time to go. There's a police vehicle ready and waiting to take you back to New Scotland Yard where you will be interviewed. Don't worry, you've done nothing wrong. It's just protocol stuff. I'll take you to the car now.'

'What about you? What about Jake? What about Tyler?'

'I'm going over there now. There's another helicopter waiting for me. We'll update you as soon as we know something. I'm sure Theodor or someone else back at the office will be happy to accommodate you.'

Mamadou smiled, helped her out of the chair and out of the building. She grimaced as she stepped over Adil's lifeless body slumped against the wall and felt a load of bile rise from her stomach to her throat. She swallowed it down, but the images in her mind would remain forever. As she left the building and climbed into the police car, she couldn't help but think how much she had enjoyed it all, and that she was such an idiot for ever refusing to follow through on her policing goals.

Chapter Fifty-Nine

PLAYTIME

August 1, 17:44

The noise of the helicopter overhead grew louder and louder, causing a stir amongst those inside the Heathrow Express. The children were first to look, followed by their parents, and then by the ones who had lost all hope. The condensation around the windows had crawled back to the lower window seal, and the air around him was getting colder by the minute. Had Adil accidentally reduced the temperature on his console? Or was he getting cold with excitement?

As the sun lowered, and the sky became a darker shade of teal, Moshat fancied himself an easy getaway. Adil had texted him the new location, but Moshat wasn't sure why it had changed. Adil had said Detective Jake Tanner was onto him, but how could that be? Everything else was so perfectly organised that it was nearly impossible. *Unless we severely underestimated him.*

Sure, it was possible, but it was also unlikely.

Nevertheless, he trusted his brother — he had been the eyes and ears of the entire operation — and he wasn't going to question his brother's integrity. Adil was the boss. Adil had the intel, and Moshat would follow his orders. No questions asked.

The helicopter disappeared into the distance, and as Moshat watched it land, he saw two beacons of light illuminating the track in front of him. Soon they would be free, and he could descend into the shadows alongside his brother. Like they were supposed to. Like they had planned.

He couldn't wait.

Inside the carriage, children clambered up against the windows, trying to get a better look outside. Ryan, nestled under his arm, fidgeted and became intolerable; he was just a kid, like all the others inside who wanted to glimpse the spectacle outside.

'You want to look?' Moshat asked him.

The little boy nodded and looked into Moshat's eyes. Moshat usually hated children, but their innocence had always captivated him somehow. He'd never killed a child and hoped he'd never have to. They were the future, and he hoped they'd follow in similar footsteps to himself. *Like mini terrorists*. The thought amused him.

'OK,' Moshat replied, putting the gun into his lap, keeping his rucksack in between his legs. He lifted the boy and stood him on the table.

Ryan plastered both his hands on the glass, leaving tiny fingerprints. They were as discernible and thick as the stars in a clear night sky. *A forensic scientist's wet dream.*

It didn't matter if he himself left any prints lying around the place. Of course, he knew there would be, but there would be nothing connecting them to him. The only reason he existed was to land himself the job at the factory that made all this possible. *It's crazy what you can fake to get yourself a job. Be someone you're not. So long as you've got the intellect to do it.*

Ryan jumped down from the table and re-joined Moshat on the seat after the helicopter's blades switched off. Moshat checked his watch. Fifteen minutes to go. But before he could continue, he needed to clarify a few things amongst his fellow passengers. And he needed to do it before they were all evacuated from this train.

'OK, everyone,' he said, rising to his feet. 'I'd like to remind you all that you're not to say a single word to anyone on the outside about myself and the little diddly device I have in my hands, because if you do, we all go *boom*.'

The family sat opposite him gave him a curt nod and then huddled closer to one another.

'I'm going to put my gun away now, but nobody needs to get any funny ideas and come tackling me to the ground, because it will end badly. Nobody wants that sort of blood on their hands, do they? Because *you* would be the one to blame, *you* would be the one who would cause all those deaths. Not me. Remember that.' Moshat placed his gun in his waistband and waved the detonator in his air, validating the immensity of his claims.

'All right, little man,' Moshat said, turning to Ryan. They'd been sat together for a long while, and Moshat could sense the young boy was trusting him. And he was beginning to trust the little boy. 'I'm not sticking around to help you find your mum and dad, OK? So, I'm sure these lovely people opposite us will do that for me, won't they?' He pointed to the family opposite. They nodded.

Moshat tussled the boy's hair involuntarily. It felt natural, instinctive. Like he was an older brother. He didn't know what came over him, and he didn't like it. He'd shown multiple signs of compassion and weakness. If his mentor

— or worse, his brother — had been there to witness it, his head would be halfway down the toilet now as punishment. *Never again in my life will I show compassion or mercy*, Moshat promised to himself.

A sound outside distracted Moshat from his trance. He recognised the voice at once. He would know it from anywhere. It was DC Jake Tanner. He had heard the detective's voice many times during their observation and preparation stage whenever the detective was speaking to his wife or discussing something at work with his colleagues. It was a sweet symphony in his ears. It was a sort of memento; both he and Adil had outplayed him at every stage. It was only a matter of time until Moshat outwitted him again and slipped away in the darkness.

'May I have your attention, please? This is Detective Jake Tanner of the Metropolitan Police. We are here to rescue and escort you to safety. Please listen carefully and follow my instructions.' Jake's voice outside was clear and concise.

Moshat smiled.

It was playtime.

Chapter Sixty

THE HUNT

August 1, 17:44

Fifteen minutes until detonation, and there were still several hundred passengers that required evacuating. The only problem was getting them all out in time and escorted to a safe enough distance, but first, Jake had to let them know what was going on. Had to let them know they were all about to be rescued. Had to let Moshat think Jake was an incompetent police detective who knew nothing about his presence on board.

But when the time came, Jake would spring the surprise and strike. He would make sure of that.

One of the PCs who had been sent to attend the scene by Deputy Assistant Commissioner Simon Ashdown carried a megaphone on him. He was prepared, he told Jake. Jake thanked the officer, commended him for his smart thinking, and took the speaker from him.

Pursing his lips as he held the megaphone close to his mouth, overcome with a fresh bout of exhaustion, Jake addressed the passengers. He informed them that soon the doors would open and that they would need to follow the avenue of police officers who had been organised in a line on either side of the train. The officers would funnel the passengers to the front carriage, even those at the other end, a few hundred metres away. It had been a contingency plan: if they offered Moshat two directions of escape, it would increase their chances of letting him slip through the net.

And that was something none of them could allow.

After having finished explaining the procedure to everyone on board, Jake returned the megaphone to the officer and looked up and down the train. All set. Everyone was in position. Now all Jake needed was a utensil or tool that would allow him to open the carriage doors.

'What about Lucy?' Tyler asked. 'She should have opened the doors remotely.'

'If she hasn't, I want to be prepared.'

Just as Jake finished speaking, a man dressed in a navy woollen jumper approached him. The National Rail logo on his chest was imprinted in a fluorescent white that shone in the setting sun.

'I've got something you can use.' The National Rail employee fished into a Stanley bag and produced a hammer and handed it to Jake.

It was a little unorthodox, but Jake obliged. If that was the only thing they could use, then so be it.

'What's your name?' Jake asked, bouncing the hammer in his hands. It was heavier than the one he had at home.

'Oliver, sir.'

'Well, Oliver. I hope you're ready to help me bust open these doors.' Jake hesitated. 'Have you got anything else in there?'

Oliver searched the contents of his bag. A few seconds later he produced a crowbar.

'That should do it,' Jake said. 'What's the best way to open them?'

Saying nothing, Oliver waltzed up to the nearest door, pointed to a section at about a third of the way up from the bottom, and smashed his crowbar into that exact spot. Pushing all his weight onto the crowbar, Oliver pried the door open. It gave way in a lacklustre motion, as if it were reluctant to move at all.

A flood of people rushed out of the carriage and sprinted to the safety point. Oliver, Jake and Tyler took a step back as they watched men, women, and children all sodden with sweat and fear disembark. Within seconds, the first carriage had emptied, and as Jake moved closer to inspect it, he saw something on the floor. A puddle of red. It glistened under the artificial light. Thick shoe prints decorated the puddle where others had disregarded the dead body. Jake stepped onto the carriage, and all his senses dismantled. He gasped when he saw Martha's lifeless body on the floor, the bullet hole in her head a pertinent reminder why he needed to find Moshat Hakim. And kill him.

'Jake!' Tyler shouted, grabbing him by the ankle. 'Jake what are you doing? We don't have time for this. We need to go.'

Fuelled by the devastation of his mother-in-law's death, Jake jumped down from the train and ordered a nearby SFO to carry Martha to a nearby ambulance. She was going to have a dignified passing. He would organise a funeral for her as soon as today was over.

In a state of shock, Jake said, 'Oliver, what are you

doing here? Get on the other side. Two streams of traffic are better than one.'

Oliver voiced his acknowledgement and disappeared behind the train. Turning to Tyler, just as he was about to advance the length of the train, Jake said, 'If he escapes, we're fucked. Find him at all costs. Use lethal force if you must. He's a threat to everyone.'

Tyler replied with a nod.

Time to get to work, Jake thought, bouncing the hammer in his hands, feeling an unprecedented strength and fury flow through his arms. The image of Martha had been stained in his retina. He couldn't wait to get his hands on Moshat Hakim.

Pushing on, Jake moved down the train to the next door, and the next opportunity to save as many people as was possible. With one clean swing of his arm, he brought the hammer down on the nearest door. He missed the sweet spot that Oliver had shown him, and the hammer head landed heavy on the door frame, making a dent in the metal. After a few pulls of the hammer, it came loose from where it had been wedged in, and Jake swung again.

Bingo.

The door sprung open as if it had been recoiled for so long, like a snake waiting to attack. Jake continued ahead, allowing the passengers behind him to flee, and the SFOs to do their job in escorting them to safety.

Moving to the next carriage, Jake repeated his swing, this time hoping his aim was better than the first attempt. It was, and the door opened. He was feeling good. He was getting the hang of it. But before he could get too carried away with himself, he saw the one thing he had been anticipating all day.

Moshat Hakim was sat on the fourth coach. He was still

wearing his hat, unmistakably identifying him as the murderer and terrorist he was looking for. The man who had mercilessly killed his mother-in-law. But what was that next to him? Did he have his arm around a child? Jake was sure of it. *Fuck. Now he's got leverage.*

Jake continued down the rest of the train until he arrived at the sixth carriage. He paid no attention to the flood of traffic erupting from the coaches behind him. There were still passengers that needed saving.

As Jake swung the hammer, it collided with the button and the door flew open. It was a miracle. Lucy had done it! She had disarmed all the locks on the doors, and now Jake could save precious moments as he ran down the remaining length of the train.

At the end of the Heathrow Express, Jake skidded to a halt, kicking up litter as he went, turned one-eighty, and sprinted back to the safety zone by the helicopter. Jake caught up with the fleeing passengers and ran alongside them, maintaining a slower pace so he could help any stragglers who fell behind. Their safety was his number one priority.

Just as Jake reached the outside of the third carriage, something on the ground caught his attention. A shape, camouflaged by the hundreds of legs and bodies that ran past it, lay cowering, shielding itself with its arms.

It was the young boy Jake had seen wrapped tightly under Moshat's arm.

He was hurt, holding his arm and crying into the gravel. Overcome by a paternal instinct, Jake dived into the crowd, formed a narrow divide in the people behind him, and carried the boy in his arms.

'Here!' a woman to his left screamed. 'Give him here!'

Jake came to a stop, bent down and placed the boy on the ground.

'Are you his parents?' Jake asked. The man of the family held the little boy, meanwhile the mum bounced a screaming baby against her chest.

'No,' the man said. 'That bastard terrorist gave him to us before sprinting off into the distance. His parents are somewhere in the crowd.' The man pointed in the direction of the helicopter.

'Go. Find them. Get him to safety. Speak to one of the officers, they'll be able to help.'

'But *he's* still there. *He's* still amongst everyone. And *he's* still got that detonator on his wrist,' the man said before turning away.

'I know. That's why I'm going to catch the son-of-a-bitch.'

Chapter Sixty-One

THE CHASE

August 1, 17:48

The rendezvous point was illuminated by a floodlight positioned at the front of the helicopter. Jake stood at the foot of the aircraft, casting his eye upon the crowd of four hundred evacuated, frightened passengers moving like coral on a seabed, swaying in the current. He quickly lost hope. There were too many people for him to locate Moshat, too many variables that meant he could get away.

There was only one option.

'I'm going in,' Jake told Tyler, pulling his gun from his pocket and keeping it down by his hip.

Tyler gave him a worrying nod and agreed to join. As they lost themselves amidst the sea of bodies, they split up, Tyler disappearing behind a large, overweight man, and Jake veering off to the right, near the outskirts of the crowd. *Where are you?* Jake asked himself.

Screams and gasps sounded from behind him. Jake swivelled and saw, in the distance, a Special Forces agent pulling someone down from the helicopter's platform. A man had tried to make a grand escape. Another officer appeared, and the two agents wrestled the man to the ground.

Just as Jake returned his attention to locating Moshat, a gun fired in the air.

Panic. Everybody within the vicinity dropped to their knees, cowering away from the bullet which Jake assumed had been offloaded because of the tussle between the officers and civilian.

Everyone ducked to the ground, except for one man.

Moshat Hakim.

For a second, Jake froze, unable to free his limbs from an invisible force holding him back. For an even longer second, he and Moshat stared at one another, a smile growing on the terrorist's face.

Jake glanced to his left. Tyler was stood thirty yards away looking back at him. They stood either side of Moshat in the middle of the crowd, a two-pronged attack ready to launch. There was only one way for Moshat to go.

As fast as a bullet propelled from a gun, Moshat turned, shoved a woman out of his way, and sprinted back towards the train.

'Split up!' Jake shouted to Tyler, raising his gun to a more threatening level.

As Jake trudged through the people, jumping over their limbs, he didn't like the feeling in his stomach that something terrible was imminent. Trying to ignore it as best he could, he breached the outskirts of the crowd, and was in an area of open space with Tyler to his left. Moshat pulled ahead; by now he was at the head of the train. In a few precious seconds' time he would be.

Fifty yards separated them. Jake saw Moshat reach into

his waistband and brandish his weapon, the setting sun's light casting an ominous shadow over it. Jake observed him. His face, stance, position, height, weight. Everything that would be necessary to take him on when, and if, the time came. Moshat disappeared down the left-hand side of the train, on Tyler's nearest side and out of Jake's field of vision.

For the next two hundred metres along the length of the train, Jake would be running blind, hoping he would meet Moshat at the end. Through the compartmentalised windows, Jake saw Moshat's figure sprinting inches ahead of him. Tyler was nowhere to be seen. Moshat was five years younger than Jake and had the advantage of youth and athleticism on his side.

Jake, on the other hand, had the hindrance of a poor fitness regime, and after the days' events, a body depleted of its energy reserves. He was running on empty.

Jake fell behind. Fast.

He needed to shake things up. Change the dynamics of the chase.

Sliding to the ground and twisting his knee, Jake clambered through the metre-wide gap that separate the end of the fourth carriage and front of the fifth. In the small, enclosed space, Jake became claustrophobic, but the surge in adrenaline through his body stamped out any onset of an anxiety attack; he was too pumped to care.

After jumping down on the gravel on the other side, Jake stumbled, regained himself and returned to the pursuit. There was ground to make up. Serious ground. Moshat was at least sixty yards ahead of him at this point, the end of the train just in sight.

It was time to alter the dynamic.

'Freeze!' Jake bellowed at the top of his voice, aiming

the gun at Moshat's rapidly disappearing back. His finger hovered over the trigger.

There was no response. Moshat continued at full pace heedless of Jake's threats. The distance between them had grown to seventy feet. Moshat's silhouette was getting smaller and smaller. Soon he would be out of Jake's reach. *Fuck*! Jake lowered the gun and continued after Moshat before all hope was lost.

He did, however, have one final option. Merely holding the weapon in the air and screaming a word wasn't enough to deter Moshat, he had learned that much. But what if he pulled the trigger instead, ending this entire day?

Moshat reached the end of the train, and just as he was about to veer right and disappear out of sight, Jake raised the gun again, aimed at Moshat's back, steadied himself, and fired.

Shards of glass blew out from the window nearest to Moshat's head and rained down on him. Moshat rounded the side of the train, stumbled to the ground and lifted himself to the feet. Jake continued his pursuit, gun raised. As he rounded the corner Moshat had just regained control of himself. Jake aimed the gun at the terrorist's head.

'Stop right there!' Jake shouted again. The ringing from the gun shot still echoed around his ears.

'I have, Detective. Do you see me running?' Moshat replied, his voice calm. His hat was no longer on his head. It had fallen off as he sprinted down the track, and now it rested on the railway line.

'Stay there and I won't shoot you.' Jake hated himself for having used his last remaining bullet, but it was a necessary risk to make.

'You wouldn't do that anyway, Detective. You're not a

trigger-happy police officer, unlike some of your coun-
terparts.'

'You know nothing about me!'

'Wrong, and you know I'm right, Jake. Stop lying to
yourself. You don't want to kill me, and you're going to let
me go.' Moshat stood there nonchalantly, his shoulders
back, his weight resting on one leg.

'Oh, believe me, little brother. I want to kill you, I can
assure you.' At the mention of "little brother", Jake saw a
small change in Moshat's expression.

'What are you talking about?' Moshat snapped.

'I don't need to kill you, because you're going to give
yourself up.'

'If you kill me, then everyone else dies, too, Detective.'
Moshat lifted his hand in the air. Jake recognised what it
was and looked horrified.

'You're bluffing.' Jake remembered what Adil Hakim
said about the detonator: it was going to blow the Heathrow
Express train as soon as Moshat lifted his finger from the
trigger.

'Am I?' Moshat said.

The sound of an incoming helicopter overhead
distracted them both.

'Oh, look! The cavalry has arrived.'

Jake stared into the floodlight above. The light blinded
him. As he returned his attention back to Moshat, the man
was already on the half turn, making his way into the wood-
land area at the side of the railway. Jake gave chase. He was
twenty yards away from the train when Tyler reappeared at
full speed on his right-hand side and rugby-tackled Moshat
to the ground, their bodies rolling on top of one another.

Moshat let out a yell as he landed hard on the ground.
Tyler made no noise as his body fell on top of Moshat's.

And then it happened. Everything Jake had worked hard to relinquish. Everything he had tried to stop, happened.

And it did so quickly.

The Heathrow Express exploded.

Jake felt an intense, searing heat, burning his right-hand side. Then came the deafening, ear-shattering noise. Closely followed by an invisible force that propelled him ten feet into the air. To his right, along the length of the train, a small squad of SFOs flew into the air. They had been moments away from joining Jake and Tyler and apprehending Moshat.

Jake collapsed to the ground, landing heavily on his left shoulder, dazed. The world span in a roulette wheel of green, orange, red, heat, and blue. His head rang with an unimaginable pain and he laid on the ground, unable to lift himself up.

Rolling onto his back, he allowed his lungs to inhale fully before hyperventilating. As he lay there, chunks of metal and other debris showered down on him in a fiery downpour. A large piece of metal landed inches away from his head.

Slowly, as he regained what little consciousness he had left, Jake rolled onto his front and lifted himself to his feet. The weight of his body was too much for him to control and he stumbled to the floor. Everything span.

Jake tried again, this time with better luck. Behind him was the burning wreckage of the Heathrow Express. Huge brilliant orange and yellow flames illuminated the surrounding area. What had once been a towering train was now missing its top half. The roof, seats and suitcases sprawled out across the ground. The sky was filled with a dense, desolate cloud of black.

'Jake! Jake!' a frantic voice shouted over to him as he

gazed at the machine. Whose was it? Was it Tyler's? Mamadou's? He didn't know; all he could hear was the incessant ringing noise in his ears. 'Jake! Jake! Are you OK?'

Following the source of the noise, he saw Tyler with blood dripping down the side of his forehead.

'Yeah,' Jake trailed off, a sheet of white slowly creeping in his peripheral vision. 'I'm fine. Where... where is he?'

Tyler said nothing.

Pointed to the wall of trees.

Chapter Sixty-Two

THE FEAR

August 1, 17:51

Jake delved deeper into the undergrowth, ignoring Tyler's calls behind him. Everything hurt. Every part of his body lambasted him for putting itself under such physical strain. Both his shoulders sent sharp rods of agony splintering up and down his arms with every swing as he ran. The pain in his leg from earlier had resurfaced, and with it had come another: the opposite knee was badly bruised and torn now, too.

Nothing was going to stop him. Jake tightened his grip around the hilt of his empty gun. He willed his mind to focus on one thing. Moshat.

Advancing through the small forest, Jake followed the trail of flattened grass and small droplets of blood on the floor. Tyler had finally caught up with him, but even together they were alone and defenceless.

'This is crazy,' Tyler said, almost tripping over a jutted tree root. 'We'll never find him.'

'We will.' Jake scanned the tree line for any signs of life ahead.

'We've got nothing to stop him with.'

'Go back. Grab a gun. Get Mamadou. Get support. I'll stall him,' Jake said, the pain bouncing around his skull increasing with every step.

Tyler held Jake back by pulling his shoulder. 'Take this, you know what to do with it.' Tyler handed Jake his mobile phone, slapped him on the back, and ran off into the distance towards the burning light.

After he'd watched his friend disappear, Jake turned and pushed deeper into the undergrowth. At first, he moved slowly, keeping his eye on the path of blood, but when he noticed the frequency of the droplets reduce, he increased his speed. He needed to catch up with Moshat. And fast.

Where are you?

Behind him he could hear the sounds of sirens blaring. In front, he could hear the noise of an industrial estate; lorries, engines, and heavy machinery were all being operated somewhere in the area, he was certain.

Find him before he gets anywhere near that noise, for God's sake, Jake. Make sure he doesn't escape.

Soldiering on and keeping his empty handgun by his side, he came to an open space. It was circular and in the centre was a large mound of earth. Jake moved along the outskirts, and then towards the middle. He felt insecure, vulnerable, open to attack.

A clapping noise behind him caught his attention, and he swivelled on the spot, his delirium knocking him off balance slightly. It was a single clap. Then there was a loud bang, this time to his right. Jake turned on the spot again. *He's just toying with you. He's here.*

'Stop it!' Jake yelled twisting and jolting his head at

every angle as he kept rotating, heedless of how nauseous it made him. 'Stop and come out!'

Leaves and twigs crumpled as Moshat appeared from behind a tree and walked towards Jake, clapping his hands. In his right hand, he held a gun. He stopped in front of Jake, released the magazine, and removed all the bullets except for one.

Jake saw the same hideous smile on his face as he slammed the magazine shut.

'Congratulations, Detective, you've killed hundreds of innocent civilians.'

Jake chuckled to himself, coughed slightly, and bent down to his knees, keeping the gun in his hand. The mound spun. The trees spun. The gun in his hand spun. His breathing became sparse.

'Having another anxiety attack are we, Detective? Susceptible to those, aren't you? They must be a constant burden on your life. I hope my brother and I haven't induced many of them for you today?' Moshat walked closer to Jake, keeping his gun aimed at Jake's skull.

It was just at the right height, inches away from his reach.

Perfect, Jake thought. But if he was going to stand any chance of disarming his opponent, he would need to be quick.

With one swift roundabout swing of his right arm, Jake punched Moshat's wrist and sent the gun soaring through the air. Clenching his left hand into a fist, Jake jabbed Moshat in the stomach, watched his opponent bend double, and shoulder-barged him to the floor. Within seconds, Moshat was on the ground and the gun in Jake's grasp.

He let out a sigh of relief, for whenever he had practised

the move in training, it had always gone horribly wrong. But not this time.

This was real life, and there were no second chances.

'You're right,' Jake said, finding it hard not to smile. 'Panic attacks *were* a constant burden, but I think you and your brother have finally sorted that out for me. So I suppose I owe you my gratitude.'

Moshat said nothing. He was still clutching his stomach and trying to catch his breath. The noise of the sirens and helicopter engines had ceased. All that remained were the noises of the industrial estate nearby, which seemed to harmonise with the songs of the birds in the trees.

'I think you and I need to have a little chat, don't we? A catch up, if you will, so you can bring me up to speed on everything you and your big brother have been up to,' Jake said after Moshat made it clear he wasn't going to respond.

'I'm getting out of here alive, over there, and you're not going to stop me.' Moshat pointed in the direction of the site behind him.

'How do you figure?' Jake asked. 'I'm the one with the gun.'

Silence. Moshat was playing the hard game, and Jake knew it.

It was time to cause a stir.

'You know this is all over for you, don't you? There's no running. No hiding. We will find you.'

'Really? How?'

'Because we know where you're going. There's no one left for you. No one's going to be at Upminster when you meet Adil. Instead there will be a handful of police officers who would love nothing more than to see your arse get arrested.' Jake's body slowly regained its energy. Moshat cast a horrified look towards Jake. 'Oh, didn't you know? Adil is dead, Moshat. It's over.'

Moshat's face hardened. He was quiet for a few moments before whispering, 'How?'

'Shot in the head.'

'Who did it?'

'Is it important?'

'Where's his body now?' There was no emotion in his voice anymore.

'Last I checked, his pathetic, pointless body was laying halfway out the door of his flat, gunned down as he tried to make his escape.' Jake smiled. Antagonising Moshat was working.

'What was your plan?' Jake asked, 'I mean, what were you going to do afterward? Run away with the money and build a new, better life with your brother?'

'Something of the sort.'

'Was your life here really that bad you had to resort to terrorism?'

'Are you angry at me, Detective?'

Jake didn't respond, afraid of where his line of questioning was going.

'Are you angry that I murdered Martha?'

Jake didn't respond.

Moshat reached into his pocket, removed his phone and produced the image of Martha he had taken earlier. Jake felt cold.

'She had to die. She was the one who killed my parents. I couldn't let her get away with *that* so easily.'

'I think that's a story for another day.' Jake said, trying to remain calm and force the image from his mind. 'But let me ask you, what are *your* reasons for this, Moshat? Why have *you* sought revenge?'

Jake wanted to hear both brother's accounts, partly because he needed to stall for time and partly because he had been so affected by what Adil had said, so influenced by *Adil's* story, that now he desperately wanted to hear the other brother's. Only then would he decide who he trusted more.

Moshat considered Jake's question for a moment. He cleared his throat before beginning. 'Were you or anyone you hold dear to you bullied as a child? Have either Ellie or Maisie been bullied since starting school?' Jake shook his head. 'Adil was. And severely, too. To the extent he no longer wanted to attend school anymore. He was the more introverted of us two. Liked to keep to himself, sit with his games consoles. Me? I was a jock, one of the naughty kids who always got into trouble. I played for the school football team and had trials at different clubs. I was popular, but I soon lost my notoriety when I defended him against his bullies. It was us against the world — it always had been, and it always will be. We looked out for one another, just as Ellie and Maisie do. Being a sibling means having an unbreakable bond that no amount of trauma or exposure to the harsh realities of the world can break.

'But then our parents died. We were left homeless, with no help from the government responsible for it all. They did fuck all about it. They denied it was any of their fault and completely neglected to care or even house us afterwards. None of the government officials came forward and took responsibility, but that's what I'm doing today, Jake. I'm taking responsibility for those people I've killed, even if the government wasn't prepared to make that sacrifice all those years ago.'

'You personally? What about your brother? Does he not

get his name written in the history books? After all, he did all the work.'

'Shut up! He didn't do it all. I did. I was the one who... who...' Moshat trailed off.

'Exactly,' Jake said. 'You're a fraud and a cheat who can only get by on his brother's talents and not his own.'

Moshat tensed and lunged at Jake. Jake switched the safety off the gun and pointed it in Moshat's face, who paused an inch away from the barrel.

'You don't fear me, do you, Detective?'

Jake didn't respond. His breathing was loud through his nose.

'That's a surprise. You're an exception to the rule. Everyone respects me because they're afraid of me. But if you don't fear me, then what does that mean?' Moshat nodded at the gun in his face.

'It means I have no respect for you. And that I would love nothing more than to pull this trigger and end your life.'

Moshat stepped forward until the nose of the gun was pressed firmly against his forehead.

'Do it.'

Jake's index finger stroked the trigger and applied pressure.

Chapter Sixty-Three

RECRUITMENT

August 1, 17:55

The light emanating from the burning wreckage illuminated the sky, dwarfing the helicopter's floodlights. The intense heat warmed Tyler's muscles and singed the hairs on his arms as he ran past. Flames spat at him from different angles as he manoeuvred his way through the debris and badly injured firearms officers on the ground.

The acrid smoke that billowed in the air filled his lungs, causing him to cough and convulse as he came to a stop near the helicopter. He had to make a wide berth around the massive crowd. He stopped a few feet from Mamadou and gazed upon the carnage behind him. The train now looked like something out of a disaster movie, and on the other side of the tracks, fans of water burst from the fire engine's hoses, dousing the flames.

Mamadou grabbed Tyler's shoulder and pulled him to one side, out of earshot from everyone else. 'Tyler, what the fuck is happening?'

'Jake — Jake's in the woods alone with Moshat. I need to go back. *We* need to go back,' Tyler explained, panting, struggling to remove his eyes from the horrific beauty of the burning train.

'What do you mean he's in there alone? What's he doing?'

'Moshat escaped. Jake chased after him. He told me to get help.'

'What help do you need?'

'Guns. Men.'

Next to him was one of the SFOs Frances had deployed earlier in the day. In his hand, he held a SIG 5.56 carbine machine gun, fully customised with an extended magazine and aim-point sights. The weapon was elegant and deadly. And Tyler needed it. Rushing over to the SFO, Tyler requested the SIG, acquired it, and placed it firmly in the crook of his shoulder. Tyler was just about to set off when Mamadou joined his side, a Glock 17 in his hands.

A shadow joined alongside them, lurking behind the light.

'What the fuck is he doing here?' Tyler asked, realising it was DC Matthews who was now accompanying them.

'Three men is better than two, Stuart.'

And that was that. Mamadou had spoken. The three of them cocked their weapons, started down the track, past the train, and into the woods, giving the incoming emergency services and remaining AFOs free rein over the situation.

Tyler hoped his friend was still alive.

Chapter Sixty-Four

THE WOODS

August 1, 17:56

Jake's fingers hovered over the trigger.

'No,' he said. 'I won't do it. I think we should discuss you and your brother.' The mental clock inside his head was ticking. It had been five minutes since Jake last saw Tyler, and he hoped his partner would return soon; he was running out of conversation topics to stall Moshat.

'What would you like to know, Detective?'

'What was the last thing he said to you? What was the power he entrusted you with?'

Moshat hesitated before answering. His expression looked confused. 'He left me in charge of the detonator.'

'What did he tell you about the detonator?'

'That it would blow up the Gatwick Express.' Moshat's voice became quieter and quieter. He shuffled away from the barrel of Jake's gun.

'And look what happened. The Heathrow Express exploded instead.' Jake knew he'd uncovered a stone that would let out an entire world of doubt in Moshat's mind. 'He lied to you. He told you your initiator was designated for Gatwick, but it wasn't. Imagine if you had detonated while you were on board the Heathrow Express. You and everyone inside would have been incinerated. Why do you think he did it, Moshat? Why do you think he lied to you and persuaded you to kill yourself?'

'You're lying! It was a mix-up. It must have been. He wouldn't have done that.'

'It's true, Moshat, and you know it. But I want you to tell me *why* he did it. Why would your brother take such drastic measures?'

'Be quiet!' Moshat shouted, becoming visibly frustrated.

'I'll tell you why, Moshat. He betrayed you because he hated you. Martha was not the only one to blame for your parents' death. *You* were. You killed them. Your secret smoking habit killed them right before you left to defend Adil against those bullies on the night they died. Admit it to yourself. You and I both know, deep down, after many years of having repressed it, you've convinced yourself you were never to blame.'

'Shut up! Shut up! Shut up!'

Before Jake knew it, Moshat lunged at him again, covering the distance that separated them in a second. Jake's reactions were too slow. By the time his finger was half-pressed on the trigger, Moshat had swiped Jake's outstretched arm to the side, knocked the gun to the floor, and punched Jake in the chest. Moshat used the palm of his hand, and Jake could feel his ribcage crush under his immense force. Jake stumbled back and fell to the floor. As he hit the ground hard, his head whiplashed on a tree root and he screamed out in pain.

Jesus, fuck.

Through half-opened eyes he saw Moshat diving to grab the gun. He scrambled to his feet and tackled Moshat to the floor. It was too late. The gun was already concealed in Moshat's hands. Jake over cooked it and his body rolled to the floor.

In an instant, Moshat was on his feet. Still lying on the dry soil, Jake saw through blurred vision a piece of Moshat's T-shirt dangling low. He grabbed it and pulled it down hard, sending Moshat off balance. There was only a split window of opportunity where Jake would get out of this alive.

And he took it.

He swung a fist toward Moshat's midriff. But he missed. Moshat, poised and more alert than Jake, ducked and delivered a powerful left hook to the back of Jake's head, knocking him to the floor.

Before Jake could move again and ready himself for another spar, he heard the click of the gun, followed by complete silence. *It's over*, he thought. *I've failed.*

Moshat stood over Jake, legs either side of his body, with the gun aimed at his forehead.

'Please, don't do this,' Jake pleaded, the back of his head throbbing uncontrollably.

'Give me one good reason,' Moshat replied.

'I, I...' Jake couldn't think of anything to say. His mind raced too quickly to comprehend anything. 'I've got a family. They need me. You don't want to do this.'

'Too slow.'

Everything went still. Jake closed his eyes. In the distance, he heard voices calling. He wasn't sure if he was dead already and imagining things or if it was reality.

Then the voices became more distinct. And then there was silence.

A gunshot echoed throughout the woods.

Chapter Sixty-Five

WISH

August 1, 17:58

Jake opened his eyes. Frisked himself. Checked for any signs of thick blood on his clothes or a gaping hole in his body.

There was nothing.

Had he dreamt it all? Was he dead and now experiencing an augmented reality in the afterlife? Jake shifted his body weight to his elbow. Then, before he could regain any of his senses or his surroundings, a shadowy figure bolted past him. In a daze, Jake believed it to be Moshat.

He stumbled to his feet and followed the shadow, oblivious to what was around him. Disorientated, Jake staggered to the floor. He was losing ground behind Moshat, dropping from ten feet to fifteen, then to twenty. Thirty. Until he came to a halt, his legs and mind struggling to keep up.

Then he heard his name. 'Jake! Jake! Get back here!'

Bewildered and confused, he turned to face the noise. The world span. The pain in the back of his head blazed.

He touched his skull. His thick brown hair was now matted and congealed with blood.

Far away, Jake saw two figures. One laying on the floor, the other on their knees, attending the dormant figure.

'What?' he mumbled to himself.

Cautiously, Jake shifted towards the figures. Darkness had enveloped the woods, and his sense of what was up and down had disappeared. His foot caught on a tree root and landed him hard on his hands. He felt the skin tear away as they met with a thorny leaf stem. Breathing heavily, and feeling exhausted, he struggled to his feet.

'Jake! Hurry the fuck up!' the voice shouted to him again. He knew that voice; it was Mamadou's. But it sounded different. His voice was raspy and sounded as though there was something in the back of his throat. Jake had never heard Mamadou speak in such a way before. 'Get your fucking arse here now!'

Oh, God, he thought. He came to the sudden, and worrying, realisation it was indeed Mamadou who was screaming at him. Which could only mean one thing.

Something was wrong.

So very, very wrong.

Breaking into a limping run, Jake came to the small clearing he and Moshat had fought in moments ago. Mamadou's silhouette increased in size and clarity. There was a look of horror in his expression. Then Jake looked down to the ground.

Tyler lay there completely still.

Jake bent down by Tyler's side. 'Ty, Ty! Wake up, mate! What you playing at?'

There was no response. Jake moved his hand to Tyler's chest and felt a warm, wet patch seeping through the thin material of his shirt. Growing afraid of the devastating truth with every passing second and wanting to deny it ten times over, Jake looked at his own hand. It was red with Tyler's blood.

'Tyler! No, no, no — wake up! You can't die before the weekend, we had a deal. What about that drink tonight?' Jake shouted. He felt himself starting to cry.

'Jake, he's gone,' Mamadou said, touching him on the back.

'He... he can't be.' Tears rolled down Jake's cheeks faster than rain in a storm. He bent forward and rested his head on Tyler's bleeding chest.

'How?' Jake asked through sobs.

'DC Matthews arrived first, aimed his gun at Moshat but couldn't fire. He got his foot caught on a tree root and stumbled to the floor. The noise alerted Moshat, and he fired at the nearest thing. His bulled missed Matthews and caught Tyler right in the chest, and then he disappeared.'

Jake said nothing and kept his head on Tyler's chest. The truth had hurt him, and he was inconsolable for the next ten minutes. He didn't want to be there. He wanted the day to be done, and Luke and Moshat and Mamadou and everyone else to disappear. He just wanted to be alone with Tyler. To say goodbye.

A few minutes later, Jake was pulled out of his own grief by a set of footsteps.

'Gone.' It was Luke. He was panting heavily. 'Gone. Can't find him.'

In an instant, Jake leapt to his feet and charged at DC Matthews. He swung his fist at his face and made a good connection, feeling the man's jaw crumble under his knuckles. Luke fell to the ground and cried out in pain. Jake jumped on top of him and straddled both his legs.

'It's your fault he's dead! It should have been you

instead!' Jake shouted in his face, annunciating every word with a mouthful of saliva and blood.

Before he was about to release his fifth blow on Luke, Jake's hand was held back by Mamadou. He was pulled off and thrown to one side.

'Stop it! Now!' Mamadou shouted, lifting DC Matthews from the ground and brushing him down. 'Go and get help.'

Luke didn't need telling twice, and a few seconds later he sprinted off towards the Heathrow Express.

Jake lay there on his back, chest heaving, blood draining from his body, lights fading.

'You OK?' Mamadou asked him softly, crouching to his side.

Jake responded with silence. He didn't want to talk to anyone. He didn't want to see anyone. He didn't want to hear anyone. The only people that could make him feel better were either his family or Tyler, and none of them were there.

In the end, Jake got his wish as he lost consciousness and passed out next to Tyler's body.

Chapter Sixty-Six

HOSPITAL

August 2, 11:00

The constant beeping sound of the respiratory machine next to Jake's head woke him. As he opened his eyes, allowing the harsh artificial light in, he felt a tight, warm pressure around his left hand. Elizabeth.

'Daddy!' Jake turned his head to see both Ellie and Maisie perched on the other side of his bed. They both lunged at him and clung to his neck. He winced in pain, but it didn't matter. He was safe and so was his family. Nothing could ruin this moment.

'How are you feeling?' Elizabeth asked him.

'Sore.' Every bone in his body ached, and as he lifted himself higher in the bed, his muscles shook. He felt so weak. 'How long have I been out?'

'About fourteen hours. They brought you in just after you passed out, ran tests on you, and kept you under. Just to stabilise you.'

Jake nodded. There was something he wanted to ask,

something he wanted to get off his chest, something he wanted to make sure *was* just a dream, and not a brutal reality.

But he didn't have the courage.

'And...' he started, 'Tyler?'

'I'm sorry, Jake,' she said squeezing his hand tighter. 'The doctors said he was gone there and then. There was nothing anybody could do.'

Jake sat there in silence and looked round the hospital room. It was clean and sterile. A bag overloaded with Elizabeth and the girls' clothing was on the far-right side of the room. Jake looked at Ellie and Maisie.

'Are you OK, Daddy?' Maisie asked.

Putting on a brave face, Jake said, 'Of course I am. Nothing can hurt your Daddy.'

'I love you, Dad.'

'I love you, too. Both of you. Very much, OK?'

Elizabeth touched Jake's hand, distracting his attention away from the girls. Jake looked at her. Her expression was solemn, and her eyes fixated on the bedsheets. She couldn't look him in the eye. Jake feared the worst. His thoughts turned towards Martha. Did Elizabeth know? How was he going to tell her? How would he ever be able to explain what had happened to her? How would she forgive him? It had been his duty to protect and save her, and he had failed.

'Jake,' she said. 'I know.'

Jake wasn't sure what to say. 'How did you find out?'

'Mamadou told me. When you were brought in, he sat me down and explained what had happened. He didn't want you to tell me, said it would have been too difficult for you. They showed me to the body and asked me to ID her.'

Elizabeth trailed off. Her eyes watered and as she blinked, tears ran down her cheeks. Saying nothing, Jake pulled her to his chest, ignored the pain, and embraced her. They didn't say anything. They didn't need to. Sometimes silence was the best treatment.

A minute later, Jake pulled away and stared into her eyes.

'Liz, I'm so sorry.' He was inconsolable, and he could only imagine how she was feeling.

She touched his thigh. 'It's OK, Jake. We'll sort it out once you're recovered and out of here. I'm still processing it all.'

Ellie jumped off the chair next to him, ran behind Elizabeth, reached into another bag, and produced a book.

'Daddy, look at my colouring-in!' she said with so much excitement. Jake admired a child's innocence in situations like this. No matter the occasion, they always made him feel better and forget about all the problems in the world. At that moment, they were the world — they were *his* world — and that's all that mattered.

'Show me what you've been doing. Did you do it while Daddy was sleeping?'

'I did it in school!' Ellie opened the book. From it, she produced an image containing a series of trees and a deer in the middle.

'That's wonderful, Wellie. I'm proud of you. Did Mrs. Washington give you a gold star for it?'

'She certainly did, didn't she, Ellie?' Elizabeth said, stroking her daughter's hair.

'Yeah.'

'You've done a fantastic job,' Jake said and kissed her forehead. He looked over to Maisie and saw she was pouting. 'How was school, Maisie? Did you and your boyfriend have a good day?'

There was a look of horror on Maisie's face. 'I don't have a boyfriend!'

'It's OK. I know you do. But it's OK, I don't mind. Although I'd like to meet him some time, make sure he's good enough for my little baby girl,' Jake said, and together, he and Elizabeth laughed. Each breath pained him, but he continued regardless.

'I'm nearly ten! I'm not a baby girl anymore, Dad!'

'Yes, you are, and you always will be. Don't you ever forget it.' He kissed Maisie on the forehead. Then, feeling as though he were strong enough to withstand their squirms, he tickled the girls. They wriggled and writhed underneath his arms and he brought them to his chest and laughed again. The perfect moment of happiness and family, where he had almost forgotten everything that had happened over the last twenty-four hours, was diminished by a knock on the door.

Jake called for them to enter.

'Morning, buddy,' Mamadou said, walking through the door. 'Sorry to intrude like this, Elizabeth, but I was wondering if I could have a word with your husband, please?'

'Come on, you two,' Elizabeth said to the girls as she stood up and lifted Ellie into her arms. 'You'll be able to spend as much time with him as you want later, but Daddy's got to do some grown up stuff now.' As they left the room, Elizabeth said to Mamadou, 'He better not come back any worse than he is now, or you'll have me to contend with.'

'I promise,' Mamadou said, closing the door behind her.

Mamadou joined Jake's side, his expression making him look as if the previous day had aged him considerably.

'How you feeling?'

'Beat,' Jake said. 'You?'

'Yeah, I'm fine, mate. Just dealing with the shitstorm now.'

'What's everyone saying?'

'Oh, you know. The usual: we waited too long to do anything about it, worst terror attack since 7/7, all that sort of shit,' Mamadou said, smiling. 'Our worst nightmare isn't it? Although, they're painting you as some kind of hero. I don't know what they're smoking, but I want some of it!'

Jake couldn't help but laugh. There was something in that moment that made them seem like they were more than friends. They were family. The divide between employer and employee had gone, and it reminded him of Tyler.

'And what about Tyler?' Jake continued.

'What do you mean?'

'Tyler's the real hero, he died protecting me, if it hadn't been for... Matthews,' Jake said and felt himself tense up with anger at the mention of Luke's name.

'Don't worry about him — Frances is handling it. There'll be an enquiry into Adil Hakim's death. They'll argue whether the use of lethal force was reasonable, but we'll have to wait and see. I reckon he'll be out of the door in a few days.'

Jake paused. 'What happened after I passed out?'

'By the time you'd lost consciousness, the entire area had been evacuated. The stranded passengers that hadn't been injured either went back home or to the airport and prayed they got another flight. We sent out a search party for Moshat, but it was pointless. He was long gone by then. We think he hitched a lift by a lorry driver at one of the factories in the area. Anyway, after the search party came back empty-handed, emergency services brought you and Ty to hospital,' Mamadou explained.

'And what about the Gatwick Express? Any fatalities?'

'No. One person fell over the track while being evacuated. Ended up twisting her ankle. Nothing too serious. Several passengers had been injured earlier on in the day while aboard the trains, but I wouldn't think about it too much. You need to rest, but before you do, there's something else I need to discuss with you.' Mamadou reached into his blazer pocket and fished out a letter. 'Your recent promotion. The results are in. And there's another little surprise in there as well. I'll let you and Elizabeth discuss it through. Take your time in responding. HR knows about your situation.'

Jake took the letter from Mamadou. Saw the MI5 and Metropolitan Police crests on it and placed it on his lap. The letter felt heavy in his hands. Made heavier with the burden it would now place over Jake's shoulders. Mamadou climbed out of his seat.

'Oh, I almost forgot — there's someone else here to see you, too. And I need you to file a report as soon as you mentally can. You know, police stuff and all that. I'll put it off for as long as possible, but you know how it is.'

'Cheers, boss,' Jake said and watched Mamadou walk towards the door. 'Mam?' His boss turned round. 'Your mum?'

Mamadou's eyes teared up, and he shook his head. He couldn't speak.

'I'm so sorry. Let me know when the funeral is, please.'

Mamadou nodded and left. He was replaced by Lucy, who walked into the room with a beaming smile.

'You're awake!' she shouted. She looked weak and tired, which Jake assumed she was considering the catastrophic events she'd been privy to. 'How you doing, trooper?'

'Never better,' Jake said. 'How are you?'

'Knackered, but at least work gave me the next few days off to recover.'

'That's good,' Jake said. 'But, how are you?'

'I told you, I'm fine.'

'Yes, but what you've been through is terribly traumatic. You've seen things explode, got yourself kidnapped, almost died a few times, and you've seen someone else get shot. Those sorts of things mess with a person. You can't be the same afterwards. I wanted to make sure you were OK,' Jake said softly.

'I'll be all right.'

'And if there is something wrong, please come let me know.'

Lucy hesitated, pursed her lips, and looked to the ground as if she were about to say something.

'What is it?' Jake asked.

She looked up at him, stared into his eyes for a beat, and then said, 'Nothing. But guess what? Do you remember when I told you I wanted to work as a police officer?' Jake nodded. 'Well, the next best thing happened. New Scotland Yard offered me a position within the legal team. I just have to go for an interview and give my months' notice, and then I'll be all good to go. Soon you'll be seeing me around the office.'

'Oh, Lucy! That's fantastic news. I'm so pleased for you.'

Lucy leaned across Jake and embraced him as Elizabeth re-entered the room. Lucy let go.

'Everything all right in here? I saw Mamadou leaving and thought you were alone,' Elizabeth said.

'I'm just saying goodbye,' Lucy said, jumping out of her chair and exiting the room. Before she left, she stopped and faced Jake, 'See you soon, yeah?'

'Yeah.' Jake waved goodbye.

Elizabeth shut the door behind her, walked over and sat on Jake's bed next to him. Grabbing hold of his hand, she asked, 'Wasn't interrupting anything, was I?'

Jake smiled. 'I'll explain it all to you later.'

'I trust you, don't worry.' She bent forward and kissed him. Her lips felt good against his, and he wanted the moment to last like her beauty. But she pulled away from him, and said, 'Although, I fucking hope there is nothing going on with you and her, because I've got news for you.'

'What is it?' Jake asked.

'I'm pregnant, Jake.'

Jake was gobsmacked. He didn't know what to say. He was struck with excitement and euphoria. 'But how?' he asked, hugging her tightly. Doctors had assured them they wouldn't be able to have any more children after Ellie — and even then, her birth was a medical phenomenon. They had once told Jake and Elizabeth that, thanks to complications in both their bodies, they couldn't have any children at all, and that they had better look for alternatives. Since then they had had two, and a third was on the way.

'Another little miracle, I guess.' She kissed him again.

They hugged for the next few minutes and as Elizabeth rested her head in Jake's neck, her eyes found the envelope on his lap. She grabbed it.

'What's this?'

'Nothing. I'll open it later. It's not important. Right now, I want to spend time with you and the girls.'

Elizabeth called both Ellie and Maisie, and almost instantly, they burst through the doors. As they joined Jake and Elizabeth's side, Jake whispered something to Elizabeth and she nodded. They broke the news of the pregnancy to their girls. In that moment, Jake forgot all about his day and was focused on the one thing he cared for most in his life: his family.

And that night, when he was released from the hospital, he slept contently, thinking about his unborn child.

There were such things as miracles in the world.

He just hoped there was one that could bring Tyler back.

Next in the DC Jake Tanner Terrorism Thriller Series

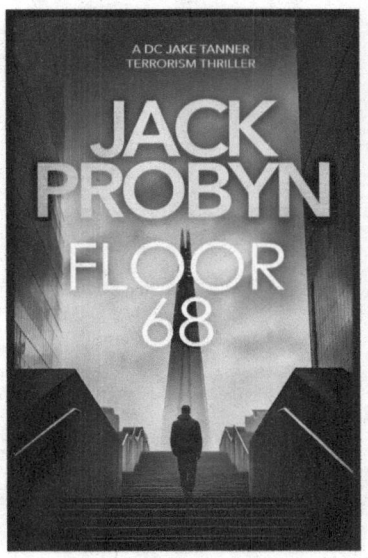

vinci-books.com/floor68

Detective Jake Tanner must confront his darkest fears to prevent a devastating attack and save billions of lives…

When a biological terrorist targets London's tallest building, Detective Jake Tanner must confront his own demons to stop a devastating attack. Trapped with his family and countless hostages, Jake becomes locked in a deadly game with a twisted mastermind. As he battles his PTSD, the detective realizes he may be the only one who can prevent a lethal airborne pathogen from decimating the world's population.

Turn the page for a free preview…

Floor 68: Prologue

A FRIEND FROM THE PAST

August 1, 2017, 22:17

Charlie Paxman was going to change the face of humanity. Forever. It was dying, and he was the cure. He had been for a long time. He just needed a little longer.

The smell of chemicals smacked him in the face as he entered his small, nondescript one-bedroom flat in Greenwich. The stench clung to his nostrils and the inside of his throat and lingered there. He coughed and convulsed. Chucking his bag on the sofa, he removed his hand from his mouth. It felt moist.

Blood.

Lined with something else Charlie had never seen before. An internal fluid he didn't know existed. *Strange.*

Creating the virus was beginning to have serious detrimental effects on his health. But soon it would all be over. His work would be complete, and it would be ready for release.

Charlie wiped the blood from his hand onto his trouser

leg. He moved around his flat, taking off his coat and placing it on the back of the chair in his office, before undressing to his boxers. Feeling his bladder press down hard on him, he went into the bathroom. The tension in his body relaxed as he pissed into the toilet, ignoring the splash back on his feet and legs. Leaving small droplets of urine on the seat, and with the stench of chemicals and poison rising through his nostrils, he decided it was time for his second shower of the day.

The first was in the morning. The second was when he got home from work, to remove the smell of greasy food and salt from his skin and hair. The third was just before bed, to rid himself of the outermost layer of chemicals in his pores.

Charlie stepped into the shower. The steaming water hugged his body and loosened the tense muscles in his back and shoulders. It had been another stressful shift. His manager had been on his case again, chastising him for serving food to the wrong table. It wasn't his fault he hated his job. It wasn't his fault he had been kicked out of a dream career he had yearned for since he was a child. It wasn't his fault the world's problems were taking immediate effect.

But it was his responsibility to fix them.

He switched off the shower, stepped over the lip of the bathtub and dried off, wiping the condensation away from the mirror so he could look at himself.

The man he saw was different to the one he had been a few months ago when this entire process began. The messy, unkempt blond hair receding at the temples. The high, hollow cheekbones that made him look malnourished. The lines on his forehead. The bushy blond eyebrows nestling above deep-set eyes, which held a haunted look that reflected the fluorescent bathroom light overhead. The five-day post-shave stubble that lined the sharp angles of his jawline. The thin frame, small shoulders, skinny waist and legs miraculously supporting the weight of his torso. The sinewy forearms, skeletal fingers and bony wrists.

It hadn't been long, and his body was already suffering. The coughing. The bleeding. The vomiting. The fatigue. His immense exposure to the virus had weakened his immune system beyond repair. And when the time came for it to be ready, he hoped he would be in a fit enough state to see it through — he hoped he'd be alive.

A lot had changed since he'd begun. And he had sacrificed even more. But it was necessary. The world needed to change. Humanity didn't know it yet, but it would thank him later. Even after his death, his name would live in infamy, forever written in the history books. Adored by many. Abhorred by more. But he didn't care; he believed that what he was doing was right, and he had the technological and scientific know-how to succeed.

Nothing was going to stand in his way.

Charlie dressed, shoved the towel in the wash bin, and returned to his desk. He started up his computer and played static noise to help him focus. To his right, quietly humming away, was a large metal cabinet with one glass vial inside, rotating. The glass was green, his favourite colour. He moved to the cabinet, pulled aside its small metal hatch, and peered in. The machine's harsh pool-blue light almost blinded him at first, but his eyes had long since adjusted.

Charlie inspected a timer at the top of the machine. Two more hours until today's incubation period was finished. The device had been running all day, silently building the world's most powerful virus. Fifty millilitres of clear, genetically engineered liquid. He felt proud. His life's mission in one small container.

Satisfied for the time being that everything was in order, Charlie slid across to his desk and opened the BBC News homepage. Breaking news articles about the worst terrorist attack London had ever seen littered the page. He read through them. Shook his head in disgust. What Adil and Moshat Hakim had done was nothing compared to what he could do. What he was *going* to do. The attack was minor, insignificant – the needle of destruction amongst the haystack of chaos.

His work was going to change the world.

Quickly bored with the images of burning train wreckages and an auto-playing interview with a police officer and victim – a man called Jake Tanner, whom the media and public adored – Charlie turned his attention to another article. It piqued his interest more than anything else.

He scanned the page. The story was about the World Health Organisation – the agency he had once been a part of and that had started this entire project. Their annual conference, usually held in Geneva, had been moved, and would now take place in The Shard, western Europe's tallest building, on December 2, seven months later than it was supposed to have been held.

A smile grew on his face, sending a strange tingling sensation coursing through his body. Charlie checked his calendar and noted the virus's completion date would be December 1. Four months away. The day before he would be reunited with old colleagues, old friends, and old enemies.

Time to get down to some serious work.

Pushing himself away from his desk once more, Charlie began his secondary preparations. Inside the wardrobe by the office door was an AK-47, an explosive vest, a saw and a handgun, surrounded by crumpled wads of aluminium foil, all wrapped up in some clothes and thin sheets of copper inside a duffel bag. The weapons, vest, and copper sheets were purchased earlier in the year through a contact he made by chance one night at the restaurant. Untraceable. Undeniable. Nothing would ever lead back to him, and by the time it did, he would be long gone.

Charlie placed one final item – a nine-millimetre handgun – in the bag and sealed the wardrobe shut with a padlock.

The countdown had begun, and he couldn't wait. He looked one last time at the article's featured image that filled the computer screen – a man and woman, side by side, waving to the camera, smiling, happy – and then began the rest of the work that needed completing.

Five metres away, hanging from the wall inside his flat, was another image of the same man. Except this time Charlie was with him, and they both held an award, grinning fervently.

The man was a friend from the past, soon to be seen in the future.

Floor 68: Chapter One

APPOINTMENT

November 28, 2017, 14:11

Adrenaline and endorphins surged through Jake Tanner's blood. The music in his ears blocked out the rest of the world while the gym's air conditioning set the hairs on the back of his neck and arms on end. The boxing gloves hugged his fists. He jabbed the bag again and again, feeling his body vent its anger on the big sack of sand. After releasing one final heavy right hook, he stopped to remove his gloves and wipe his forehead with the palm of his hand. A thin layer of sweat slicked off his skin, and he dried his hand on his shorts. He looked out of the windows as he grabbed a bottle of water. At the city of London. At the autumnal grey sky. At the pouring rain. At the droplets descending the windowpane. It was just after lunch, and the gym inside New Scotland Yard was empty. Nobody could afford to spare the time to come down here.

Except for him.

Over four thousand personnel hours had been logged

for everyone in SO15, the Metropolitan Police's counter terrorism department, since the attack on 01/08, and Jake's hours were less than ten per cent of that. The investigation had even stretched into other departments within the Met's Specialist Crime & Operations division. Jake had been allowed to come back to work on the proviso he shorten his shifts and carry out a reduced workload. Which meant the numbers would only increase for everyone else. And yet they were still no closer to finding Moshat Hakim, the terrorist responsible for the attack, or uncovering any affiliation he had with any terrorist organisation, either domestic or international. To make matters worse, investigations had been impeded by Adil Hakim, Moshat's brother. It had taken the cyber security team months to hack into Adil's seized computer hard drive, and when they were finally able to, it was blank. Adil had placed a fail-safe on it that wiped the contents after weeks of inactivity. Adil Hakim had won, and he was still fucking with them even though he was dead.

Just the thought of him annoyed Jake. Throwing his water bottle to the ground, he picked up a rope and began to skip. In recent weeks, he had been training hard, improving his physical fitness while allowing his mental health to fall by the wayside. Most of his time in the gym was spent working, preparing, and imagining the day he would reunite with Moshat Hakim. The day he would defeat him – sending him to prison for the rest of his worthless life. Or even better – and completely off the record – the day he would kill Moshat Hakim. It was a day Jake looked forward to.

'Supersonic' by Oasis played in his ears. The guitar riffs spurred him on. He breathed in and out rapidly through his mouth as he jumped to the beat.

The door at the end of the gym opened. DCS Mamadou Kuhoba, Jake's boss and one of his closest friends within the service, stepped through. He was a wide-set man with a large stomach, and his short, tightly curled hair was shocked silver. Jake stopped at once, dropped the rope to the floor next to his bottle, and removed his earphones.

'What's going on in here, then?' Mamadou asked, advancing towards Jake.

Jake looked around him. 'Petting animals at the zoo. What does it look like?'

Mamadou's face dropped. 'Funny. I was just wondering if you were all right.'

'Yeah.' Jake shrugged. 'Why wouldn't I be?'

'I've not seen much of you, that's all.'

'I've been busy.'

'So you keep telling everyone. I feel like I haven't spoken to you properly since that day. I'm glad you stuck with us in SO15 and didn't join MI5. I couldn't see you as a spook.'

'It would have been too much physical and mental strain. Elizabeth and I decided it was best I turn it down. Not just for me, but for the family, too.'

'I'm glad. Although I wouldn't want to be working there right now. Lot of backlash.'

'Why?' Jake frowned.

'While you were signed off, Director General Brockhurst declared that Moshat and Adil had been on their radars. They investigated but found nothing of any worth, so they stopped. It was his decision,' Mamadou said.

'Wouldn't be the first time they've let someone slip through the net, would it?' Jake said. He was referring to an attempted attack that had taken place in a shopping centre last Christmas that both he and Mamadou had thwarted.

Mamadou smiled, avoiding the comment. He reached into his back pocket and produced his phone. He stared at it a while, hesitating, as if afraid to speak about something on his mind. He cleared his throat. 'IT sent me the logs for your computer the other day.'

Jake froze.

'And?' he said, trying to act as nonchalant as possible.

'It made for interesting reading.' Mamadou looked to his left and gestured to the row of benches by the weight rack that ran along the wall. 'Shall we?'

Jake didn't respond. Instead, he found himself a seat and looked up at Mamadou as he sat opposite. The synthetic leather was uncomfortable, and he could feel himself sweating even more.

'We need to talk, Jake. Are you sure you're OK?'

Jake sighed. He hated being babied liked this. It had been constant ever since he'd returned from the hospital following the attack. Mamadou, Elizabeth, Frances, his mum – they all wanted to show him that they cared, that they were there for him. They acted like they knew how he felt. But they didn't. None of them did. How could they? How could he ever let anyone close to him know what he was feeling when he didn't understand it himself?

'What did you see on the log?' Jake asked. He found himself gripping the bench's edge until his knuckles whitened.

'Your internet searches, mate. PTSD. Symptoms, signs, treatments. Why didn't you tell me you were suffering from it?'

'I thought it would have been obvious,' Jake said, grinding his teeth. He chided himself for forgetting to delete his browser history. It was a rookie mistake, and now he was suffering the effects of it.

'Well, sure. It's assumed. But I'd not had any confirmation. That stuff is above even my pay grade.'

'How can it be? You're my supervisor.'

Mamadou leaned closer, resting his elbows on his knees. 'I thought you were having meetings about it.' He spoke softly, the quietest Jake had ever heard him. For a moment, there was no employer–employee divide between them. They were just two friends, having a chat.

'I was,' Jake said, looking to the floor. In the months succeeding the attack, Jake had had multiple counselling and therapy sessions with the in-house psychiatrists. But he was still no closer to finding peace, nor to finding the time, let alone approval, to chase Moshat himself. Jake had to live with the harsh reality that he had let the man go. That's what played through his mind every time he looked at Elizabeth, or lay next to her in bed. Every time he looked at his own wife, he was reminded of Martha, Elizabeth's mother, who had fallen victim to Moshat. Some nights he lay awake recounting the events of that day, reliving them, trying to think of what would have happened if he'd acted differently.

'Why did you stop going to the meetings, Jake?' Mamadou's face contorted as his concerns for Jake grew.

Jake fell silent.

'Come on, Jake. You can tell me. We've known each other a long time, and this is the first time you've shut me out. I can't help you if you don't let me. No one can.'

Jake opened his mouth to speak, but the words wouldn't come.

'I've been busy,' he said defiantly.

'With what? Don't tell me it's because you've been in here all this time.'

'Elizabeth. She needs me. I've had to reschedule most of

my meetings with the psychiatrist because she's worried about the baby. She's been dealing with a lot of stress. Her mum. Me . . .' Jake hesitated. He hated lying to his friend, but it was necessary. The simple explanation for it was that he didn't want to discuss his problems with anyone. Not even himself. Every time he searched on the internet for symptoms and signs of PTSD, he feared himself – worse, he hated himself – even more. The thought he could be susceptible to it, that he had let everyone down by suffering from it... It made him feel weak and vulnerable.

'When was the last time you saw someone?' Mamadou asked, touching Jake's leg, bringing him back to the present.

Jake searched his mind. 'September.'

'September? Bloody hell, Jake. That was over two months ago. A lot's happened since then. Has your PTSD been getting worse?'

Jake didn't respond, which was encouragement enough for Mamadou to continue.

'Why haven't you spoken about it with anyone else?'

'Because it's hard, all right? Admitting defeat like that.'

'Admitting defeat?' Mamadou rose. 'You can't be serious? Nothing about what happened on that day was normal. Nobody blames you for anything. Nobody went through even a tenth of what you did. Nobody.'

Jake looked up. Stared into Mamadou's deep, dark eyes. 'You did.'

'That's different. I've learnt how to deal with these things.'

'Have you been speaking with someone about your mum?' Jake asked.

Mamadou paused a beat, reached into his pocket and produced his mobile. 'Right, listen up. I'm not going to send you back to the shrink here; they'll get pissy about you lying to them and trying to get out of so many meetings for so long. I'll appease them for you. What I'm going to do instead is send you to the specialist I saw. She's an expert. Even if her methods are . . . unconventional. She helped me loads. Whatever she prescribes, I want you to consider trying. I did, and it went against everything I stand for, but I have to admit it helped. It's only a short-term solution. The moment it becomes long-term, you speak with me about it.'

Unconventional. Short-term. Long-term. What does he mean? Dozens of questions and concerns floated about Jake's brain.

Mamadou extended his hand. 'Give me your phone.'

After removing the earphones from the jack, Jake passed his mobile to Mamadou.

'I'm adding her details to your address book. Her name's Kim Olson. Just make sure Elizabeth doesn't see it. She'll start to think something's up,' Mamadou said. His eyebrow rose and the sides of his mouth flickered.

'That's the least of my worries,' Jake said, finding himself smiling. It was a long time since he'd done that. In the months following the attack, he had ostracised himself from the rest of the team, and it felt good to have a chat with someone he cared about, and to find something they could laugh about.

Mamadou returned his phone. Jake stared at the name and number on the screen.

'What are you waiting for?' his friend asked, clearing his throat. 'I'm not leaving until you book an appointment.'

Jake stared at Mamadou in disbelief. 'Come on, Mam. That's not necessary.'

'Yes, it is. I'm not having you flake out on me. You're making that call. And if you don't, I'll make it for you.'

Sighing, Jake stepped to the side and dialled the number, so that Mamadou was just out of earshot.

The person on the other end answered on the second ring.

'Dr Olson speaking.'

'Hi, Doctor. My name's Jake Tanner.'

Floor 68: Chapter Two

THERAPY

November 28, 2017, 15:06

Dr Kim Olson was an attractive woman in her mid thirties, with brown hair and even more vibrant earthy brown eyes – the colour of the leaves on the ground outside. Her high cheekbones and pursed lips made her look as if she were constantly posing in front of a camera. She had been born and raised in Norway. She was forced to study at a top university in Oslo, chosen by her parents. The only thing she had any control over was the subject she studied, and in the end, she'd settled for psychology. She had focused on the consequences of dealing with psychological trauma for members of the emergency services, and after two months of searching, had found counselling prospects in Norway slim, especially in the policing world. When she graduated several years later, she decided she would emigrate to England in search of a better career.

'And that's when I decided to consult freelance for high-profile cases – and individuals – in the UK.' Kim removed her glasses from her forehead and placed them on her nose. 'Enough about me. Let's talk about you. After all, that's why you're here.'

She was wearing a grey blazer with a white shirt underneath. The top two buttons were undone, revealing a small patch of skin just underneath her collarbones that still left everything to the imagination. She sat to the side of her desk, left leg folded over the right, with a small notebook resting on her knee.

'Thanks for meeting me on such short notice,' Jake said.

'This isn't how my clients usually arrive,' Kim said, nodding at his sodden top.

Jake looked at his chest and sniffed. His sweaty odour slapped him in the face. He hoped she couldn't smell it. 'Sorry,' he said. 'Blame Mamadou. He sort of sprung this on me.'

'How is Mamadou?' Kim asked.

'Shouldn't I be asking you that? Considering you're the one seeing him.'

'*Was* seeing,' she corrected. 'He cancelled our meetings a couple of days ago. He didn't tell me why, but I think he sorted everything he needed to. Although, in our meetings, he mostly seemed concerned about you.'

'What did he say?' Jake asked, his curiosity getting the better of him.

The sides of Kim's lips rose. 'Come on, Jake. You know that's confidential between myself and DCS Kuhoba. Much like this conversation between you and I.'

Jake stared at her. He didn't know what to say. He always hated these meetings, especially his ones with the resident shrink at the Yard. He was more suited to being the one on the other side of the chair, asking the questions, probing deeper into a suspect's life, diagnosing.

'From what I hear, Jake, you're something of a hero,' Kim began.

No, I'm not, Jake thought. He hated being called that. At first, he thought news tabloids printed that word for attention and sales. But the longer the investigation into the 01/08 attack, code named Operation Tightrope, continued, the more prolific and infamous Jake became. Journalists and members of the public would wait outside his house, stop him in the street, disturb him in a coffee shop or in his local Tesco, and ask him about his version of events. They all wanted to know the same thing: What really happened?

'I'm nothing of the sort,' Jake replied. 'I was just doing my job.'

'Don't be so modest. You saved thousands of lives. The death toll could have been far greater if it weren't for you.' Kim looked at him with open admiration; he returned her gaze with a scowl. He wanted to move the conversation forwards but didn't want to be rude about it.

'What else have you heard?' he asked.

'Mamadou tells me you're a psychology graduate.'

Jake prepared himself for a barrage of questions. 'How much more do you know?'

'Enough. So, I know how difficult this is for you. He also told me your previous psychiatrist prescribed medication for your PTSD. Is that right?'

Jake bowed his head.

'How long have you been on them for?'

'A few months.'

'Does your wife know?' Kim nodded at Jake's wedding ring.

'Nope.'

'Do you think she deserves to know?'

'I don't want to worry her.'

She scribbled something down on her pad. 'Why did you start the meds?'

Jake swallowed before responding. He was cautious about how much to tell her. How much was safe? How much was confidential, and how much would be relayed back to Mamadou at the end of it all?

'Night terrors.' A lump formed in his throat.

'Night terrors? Tell me about those.'

Jake looked at the ground, then at Kim, then back to the floor. Finally, deeming it a safe place to talk, he began. 'I'm still seeing him. Moshat. I'm still re-experiencing everything, again and again. That night. The explosion. The gun. The blood.'

'Has the medication helped in any way? Have the night terrors abated?'

Jake shrugged. 'It's not doing anything.'

Dr Olson nodded as she continued to write on the paper. 'And how frequent are these episodes?'

'Almost every night. The last one was today. I woke up in a puddle of sweat.'

'Is that a regular occurrence?'

Jake nodded.

'And what happened in this particular vision?'

'Moshat's face appeared. I was working at my desk, filing a report from years ago, and he was just there . . . at my desk, lingering in the background.'

'What case were you working on?'

'I can't remember.'

'Can't, or don't want to?'

'I don't know. It was something to do with Operation Tightrope.'

'But I thought you said it was a case from years ago?'

Kim asked, constantly making notes on her pad as she spoke.

'I did. It was. It seemed like years ago. But it was 01/08. I could see the images of my mother-in-law and Tyler on the documents, but it was dated 2012. I don't know why.'

'Is there anything that happened in 2012 that you might be repressing?'

He shook his head. 'Nothing that's even remotely related to this case.'

Kim fell silent as she made a final note on her paper. She pressed the pen to her lips and chewed the top. 'How much of this have you told your wife? Do you discuss with her the nature of your terrors?'

Jake hung his head low.

'You need to tell her, speak with her about it. The more you shut people out, especially your family, the more they'll separate from you. I can only do so much. I can only offer you a certain amount of help. The other fifty per cent you have to find yourself.' The hum of Kim's computer monitor seemed to reverberate around the room. 'If you can't confide in your wife, then there must be someone you can trust.'

'Tyler,' he said, surprised to hear himself say it. He hadn't referred to his friend by name for some time, and whenever Tyler came up in conversation with relatives or family friends or strangers, Jake always referred to him as just 'him'.

'There you go,' Kim said. 'Mamadou tells me you see him on the first day of every month. That's good. Your coping mechanisms are different to anyone else's. Completely different to Mamadou's. He doesn't visit his mother.'

'I thought that was confidential.' Jake's eyebrows rose.

'That bit isn't. So, tell me: What do you do when you see him?'

'I speak to him. That's it. Sometimes I make sure his grave is OK. Sometimes I leave it up to the staff − but they do a shitty job of maintaining it. He gave his life for me, and I'm not going to let the memory of him be ruined by some lazy people who aren't willing to do their job properly.'

Kim nodded as she made another, final note on the paper on her lap, underlining it.

'Here's what I want to happen. I'm going to prescribe you something, but before I do, I need you to tell me what Mamadou told you about me.'

'I'm not sure I understand.'

'When Mamadou referred you, what did he say? Anything about my methods?'

Jake hesitated as he considered, replayed the conversation in his mind. What was it he had said? 'That you were unconventional.'

Grab your copy…
vinci-books.com/floor68

About the Author

Jack Probyn is a British crime writer and the author of the Jake Tanner crime thriller series, set in London.

He currently lives in Surrey with his partner and cat, and is working on a new murder mystery series set in his hometown of Essex.

About the Author